BARRY SADLER

Barry Sadler was a legend among fighting men everywhere. A Special Forces and Vietnam combat veteran, he rose to fame with his hit song, "The Ballad of the Green Berets," and his phenomenally successful adventure series, *Casca*. He is also the author of numerous military thrillers, including *Razor* and *Rescue*. In addition to his careers in the armed forces, the recording business, and writing, Mr. Sadler fought in various armed conflicts as a mercenary.

His sudden tragic death in 1989 shocked the world. But the legend of Barry Sadler will live forever through his dramatic and authentic novels . . .

CASCA
The Eternal Mercenary

The unforgettable saga of a soldier cursed by Christ and doomed to fight forever, the *Casca* series is Barry Sadler's most exciting creation. In his never-ending adventures, Casca is plunged into battles across the world . . . and across time. The Vietnam War, the Middle East, the Mongol Rebellion, the Spanish conquest of the Aztecs, World War I, World War II—these are just a few of the wars Casca must fight . . . for all eternity!

Over two million Casca books in print!

CASCA

THE LIBERATOR

Paul Dengelegi

JOVE BOOKS, NEW YORK

CASCA: THE LIBERATOR

A Jove Book / published by arrangement with
the author

PRINTING HISTORY
Jove edition / November 1999

For information address: The Berkley Publishing Group,
a division of Penguin Putnam Inc.,
375 Hudson Street, New York, New York 10014.

The Penguin Putnam Inc. World Wide Web site address is
http://www.penguinputnam.com

ISBN: 0-515-12689-6

A JOVE BOOK®
Jove Books are published by The Berkley Publishing Group,
a division of Penguin Putnam Inc.,
375 Hudson Street, New York, New York 10014.
JOVE and the "J" design
are trademarks belonging to Penguin Putnam Inc.

PRINTED IN THE UNITED STATES OF AMERICA

10 9 8 7 6 5 4 3 2 1

ONE

The mass of drunken humanity stirred in the corner. Days had been foul and his drink dangerous. Scratching and belching, he dragged himself onto his feet. His thick hands and knuckles racked against his eyes and face. While his fingers traced the long and jagged scar from his left eye to his lip, he fell through the doorway into the warm African sun.

Squinting from the light, he tried to get his bearings. His feet kicked up red dirt from the dusty trail. Shielding his clouded gray-blue eyes from the scorching sun with his callused, greasy hands, he dragged himself on. The poison from the drinking he had done dulled his senses. He wondered what hurt more, his eyes or his head. Did not matter much. He was used to pain. Both at giving it and taking it. Mostly at giving it. All pain meant was that he was alive. Nothing new about that.

Two pathetic looking four-legged creatures, with limbs barely thick enough to make shadows, ran toward him begging for food. The man had nothing to give. He kicked at them. Understanding, they moved on. The red dusty trail was hot. Where was it going? It did not matter. All trails lead somewhere.

The man searched through his pockets and was quite

surprised to find one last gold piece. Tempted to return to where he had spent the last few days, or perhaps weeks, he slowly turned his aching head. Seeing that it would take a few minutes to walk back to the drinking hole, the man moved on. Two young girls, with sun-baked water pots on their heads, looked on toward the stranger. They wondered if the man had more scars than skin. The giant scar moved on.

He knew not quite where the trail was leading him. He followed the riverbank, which at least seemed to have a direction. That in itself helped. Didn't matter much. One place was the same as another. "Life is where you are." He recalled words of a friend long forgotten: Perhaps the world that he was nearing was an improvement. Nothing could be as bad as where he had come from. At least he was moving away from the water. Distancing himself was a good idea. The thought of not seeing the endless ocean for some time was a pleasing one.

He could still taste the saltwater with every fiber of his body. His greenish gray, leathery skin still burned from the sea. The man could barely hear as both of his ears were still filled with water, sand and God knows what other foul thing. Hearing nothing but the echo of the waves into eternity was a curse enough unto itself. His eyes and nostrils still pained him from having been in Poseidon's realm.

Casca had been on a merchant ship for three months. That and what had followed had given him an aversion to water, to say the least.

Kicking up red dust, the four slowly followed as he moved on.

TWO

As he had been hundreds of times before, Casca had been hired for his sword. It did not take a wise man to leave the mainland and look to find his sanity in the open sea. Having fought along and against the English and French during their endless conflicts, raided side by side with proud and wild Norsemen and then seen most of them die from the Black Death, was more than enough for Casca to desire to find an escape. Perhaps returning to the sea would take him away from all of that.

The dark destroyer had spread over the land killing all that it encountered. Every time it seemed it was finally gone, only a nightmarish memory, it returned with a vengeance. Just another thing men of the cloth blamed on the Jews. If not so, then God was merely thinning out the heard of evildoers, others thought. However that was not the case either.

Hundreds Casca had known who coughed and bled themselves to death from the hellish disease. God had little to do with it. Casca had seen men die of it everywhere his path had taken him, from the fjords of the north to the deserts in the land of Chin. The plague took all without prejudice. Distancing himself from it all, even if only briefly, was quite desirable.

He had found himself on an old, but apparently well-maintained merchant ship called the *Kuta,* "The Swift One," as it was referred to. It looked broad and cumbersome and Casca wondered how it had gotten its name, and more important, how it would take to the sea. Casca could just see it wallowing at the mercy of the sea under the winds of the angry Atlantic. Even with that in mind, the idea of being on board for a few weeks, going from port to port, had seemed an easy decision. Drifting on the open waters was not unlike on land, as he had no destination there either.

Talem, the bearded captain of the *Kuta* walked around on deck, grunting out orders. Like most captains, he seemed a man obsessed with the discipline of his crew. He yelled, spat and sometimes even kicked at them. Ending one of their lives to make a point was not much beyond him.

"A good crew should never get too comfortable," recalled Casca from voices of years past. Casca had been hired for his sword, which eliminated the need to do the filthy and exhausting grunt work that broke the strongest backs and wills. Having toiled at the oar for decades in the belly of slave ships likened this to a pleasure trip.

He had found it unusual to see this ship relying solely on the winds and the ocean currents, not needing the efficiency and maneuverability of oars. Casca had traveled the great ocean, streaming along the rapid currents. Not much steering had been done on those sturdy balsa-wood rafts; they had allowed the ocean to guide their craft, but perhaps they had been lucky.

Once on board, Casca had found himself drowned in a mass of humanity. Most were racing on and off carrying large leather bags and wooden boxes. He didn't care what they contained and was not about to ask. Casca had been hired for his sword and not to be someone to chat with.

Casca was surprised to see about three dozen men, armed to the teeth, loitering around starboard bow. All they appeared to be doing is shuffling about and making the merchants nervous. The workers scurried around, trying not to make eye contact with the beastly mass. They seemed to be as diverse as the clothes they wore and the languages they spoke. Looking toward them, Casca noted how unique the group was. Nearly half of them were missing eyes, ears, noses and probably some other unmentionable body parts. A poor excuse for henchmen, or men for that matter. For now it had to do.

"Your sword will find itself at home hanging by my side." The words awakened Casca from his long consideration of this motley group.

Casca slowly turned to face two filthy looking lowlifes, one more depraved looking than the other. The two stood side by side with sword and shield in hand, looking at each other, without words, trying to decide who was about to acquire Casca's sword. Casca yawned with gusto at them. Clenching their teeth like starved animals, the two rattled their weapons against each other, angered by Casca's reaction.

Sighing with contempt as he inhaled the ocean air, his eyes moistening from their breath, which distance refused to quench. He turned away, allowing the two a few more moments of not bleeding.

"Do not run, scarred one, make it easy on yourself. I am sure there is a broomstick somewhere that needs handling." The taller of the two laughed heartily.

Casca raised an eyebrow in surprise, wondering why these two men were so brave to challenge someone like him, why they could not see their own end while looking into his eyes. "The deck is clean. I doubt you wish to displease the captain with the stain of your blood," he answered, flexing his arms and rolling his shoulders.

"Come, you filthy dog, we were going to give you a chance to surrender your sword; now we will take it from your lifeless body. My brother and I will enjoy having you beg for mercy on your knees," Obad, the older and larger of the two, threatened, grinning with his hideous black hole. "Maybe on your knees is where you are used to looking at men from," he added, while looking at his brother with a filthy grin.

Except for making a complete sentence, there was nothing out of the ordinary about these two men in Casca's mind. They were the waste of what the bowels of humanity offered, thieving their way through life, causing misery as they bounced from place to place, probably even giving filthy dogs a bad name with their actions.

How could they be so blind to challenge someone like him? Bringing the cleanliness of dogs into the conversation also seemed unreasonable as these two likely held an aversion toward water. With a quizzical look on his face Casca watched the two.

A small circle of men formed around the three of them, giving little room to use any weapons. Foolish men wagered, believing Casca was overmatched, figuring he would be overwhelmed by the size of the two and the close quarters they enclosed the three of them into. The stink of something horrible clung to the two thieves like shadows. Twisting his nose in disgust, Casca eyed the larger of the two men that had challenged him.

The two were dressed in the scraps of some unfortunate scourge survivor, only a few well-placed straps and the stickiness of the clothes themselves holding the scraps of cloth together, unflatteringly covering their hairy bodies. Looking at their grotesque forms, Casca figured any kind of covering was welcome for the moment. It was likely not the first time they had accosted someone in this manner or offended them with their sight and smell.

"Let's end this quickly," remarked Obad, the larger of the two. "My belly grows loud, it has been too long. Perhaps this fool's portion will satisfy me," he laughed, while pointing at Casca with his blackened and stubby left hand.

Casca listened to this creature, trying to reason why out of all the men on this ship he was the one they had selected. His sword was clearly outstanding in its craftsmanship; however it was doubtful the two knew enough to appreciate the quality. Then again, possibly they were not the lowest filth the world had to offer. Patting each other on the back, soiling each other with god knows what unmentionable scum of their hands, the two enjoyed their last few moments of painlessness.

Sighing with effort, Casca stared at the two men. It was going to be quite a distasteful fight. Obad, the larger and braver of the two, towering almost half a foot above Casca, breathed heavily, nearly snorting into his rancid beard and mustache. Casca watched with disgust a foul liquid drain from the man's oversized nostrils, settling into his already boggy, greenish mustache. With every breath, his hairy nostrils drained, pooling onto his hairy lip, bringing the thoughts of decaying bodies into Casca's mind. How was he going to handle this beast without dirtying himself? Casca wondered. Somehow, splattering himself with blood or entrails did not seem as obscene as having to deal with this man.

Licking his upper lip, dabbing at it constantly with his tongue whenever a word's delivery became a hindrance, the man continued. "Come on, little one, this will only hurt a smidgen," the beast offered, attempting to taunt Casca with a playful voice. Bored by the incessant posturing, Casca removed his robe and pulled the sword from its sheath in one smooth motion.

A deathly silence allowed the two men to weigh their questionable decision for a few seconds longer. Flicking their swords in the air, they stood within a few feet of each other, trying to come at Casca from different sides. Only the clattering of chain mail broke the silence as Casca flexed his chest, the interlaced wire dancing over his taught muscles.

"Make it quick and clean," bellowed the captain from above. "I have no time for this foolishness."

Flailing away with all their power, the two men clashed swords with Casca's shield and sword. Backhanding the lighter of the two with his small round shield Casca knocked the man on his back, nearly pushing him through the deck, thereby allowing himself a few extra seconds to deal with the other one. Moving ponderously, the giant slashed at Casca's neck and chest, hoping the weight of his attack would drive Casca back toward the rail. Half a dozen men scurried out of the way, not wanting to catch the blade with their faces or be trampled by the monstrosity's fevered rush.

Taking one small step to his left, Casca allowed his adversary time to turn before striking with precision. Like lightning Casca's blade came down, separating Obad's right arm at the root of his shoulder. Obad swung his own shield, swiping at Casca's head with it, not yet realizing what had happened.

Blood sprayed the deck, scattering all that had been overly anxious to see the fight, making many of them cry like cowards. With horror in his eyes, Obad clutched at his right side, unbelieving of what had happened. Casca reached down toward the bloodied deck and recovered the still moving arm. Grabbing it by the wrist, he held the crooked appendage over his head.

In one motion he swung the newly found weapon, crushing Obad's nose and face with the splintered bone that had pushed through the disjoined end, splattering blood and the foul green filth that had been caked on his ugly face. Watching Obad crash like a felled tree, Casca tossed his weapon in the air. His mesmerized audience watched the severed arm spin and fall into Casca's hand, where he held it by the exposed bone. Obad's accomplice did not fare better upon rising to his feet, as he was knocked unconscious by his friend's own knuckles, wielded by Casca's arm.

The two would-be thieves lay in a bloody pile, their eyes transfixed on the still twitching arm that had felled them. Gasping for breath, Obad attempted to stop his shoulder from bleeding, knowing that each passing moment drained him of his lifeblood. Pleased with himself, Casca wiped his bloody sword on the smaller man's left shoulder, happy that he did not really have to get his hands dirty.

Obad whimpered quietly, calling to a god Casca had never heard of, and one that was not likely going to answer his prayers. Casca did not envy him. There was no place to tie his body and stop the bleeding. Salt and hot tar would be the only remedy for such a wound.

"Help my brother please," came the words from swollen and bleeding lips, "help him." Sympathy he would not get on this ship; perhaps his life would be spared, not much else. After all, the captain could not lose too many of his men so early on their journey.

Casca watched Captain Talem's eyes, their glances meeting for a moment. It was concern yet a look of satisfaction. A ship profited from men like Casca. One never knew when someone like him could be of use.

It was not the last drop of blood to be drained onto this deck. Looking back at the dozens that had held witness, it appeared, Obad and his missing arm would fit in quite handily.

Casca and about ten others were led toward their quarters. Keeping an eye on him, they followed carefully, some of them likely wondering why they were unfortunate enough to be sharing sleeping quarters with this creature that mocked his victims while disarming and overwhelming them. A few grunted with amusement, appreciating an argument well settled.

THREE

The cabin was small, dark and it stank. The *Kuta* was no thing of beauty. One could not swing a dead fish without hitting a few ugly faces. Casca moved toward the back of the enclosure and leaned himself against the dark, musty wood of the cabin. Unsheathing his sword, he sat down. Placing his long, curved Turkish sword across his folded legs, Casca scanned the mass of filthy men.

The sour smell of lion piss was unmistakable. The cabin must have been used in the past to transport lions as pets, or perverted death toys, for some rich and [illegible] nobleman. From old Carthage or Ptolemy's Alex[illegible]veled the hills of Rome, the water route had oft[illegible] bringing such beasts. The ancient R[illegible] famous for using lions for entertain[illegible] had taken part in such savage [illegible] seemed to have brought the Ro[illegible]zies and ecstatic shudders [illegible]inst man, beast against man [illegible] seem to make any difference. [illegible]mans loved it.

[illegible]ed the room. A tall, dark one stood [illegible]t in front of him. His eyes seemed to [illegible] that could have been in the cabin. He had one hand on a short sword while the other held a lance that nearly touched the damp wood ceiling.

At least a head taller than Casca and nearly twice as wide, he darkened the room with his stature, casting a shadow across most of it. The giant man reminded Casca of the gladiators that he had seen in Rome. The tall one was powerfully built, with thick shoulders and arms, and legs that looked like the stone pillars of the old coliseums of the Caesars or ancient Byzantium.

Looking down, Casca noted that the man was missing both big toes. It must had been quite a peculiar accident or battle wound, Casca thought for a moment. Most likely the man had been a slave sometime in his past and his master had decided to cut off his toes to prevent him from running away. Anyway, from running fast.

Casca looked on. Two skinny, furry creatures crouched in a corner mumbling in a very low tone. Their grunts were barely human as they gesticulated frantically, waving their knotted fingers into each other's hairy faces. Huddling in their joint putrid stench, it seemed that grooming was the order of the day, as Casca could make out thumb-sized lice grazing on their woolly stumps. They looked more like two vultures hovering over a week-old carcass rather than beings that walked upright. Casca was well versed in many barbaric languages but he could not pick out a word, and wondered if there were any worth picking out. Most likely nothing of importance. Probably bragging and comparing member sizes.

A fat, [illegible] beast sat with its legs folded, sucking on a greasy, [illegible]aw, goat leg. His name was Pug, as Casca later learned. Another name and face to eventually disappear into the [illegible] Casca's memories. With sticky yellow hair co[illegible] good eye, the mass seemed to be in a world [illegible]

Its pointy, black[illegible]ed at the sinewy and greasy bone. From th[illegible]ered from the pain of its diseased teeth or [illegible] greasy goat leg. It was difficult to tell [illegible] the beast grinned a hideous smile, [illegible]ied and noisy feeding.

Casca shifted his gaze. H[illegible]

much eye contact. One never knew when a wrong stare would lead to a conflict and loss of more body parts.

Four robed men huddled near the door. Their long stained robes swept against the filthy floor. One of them mumbled continuously as the other three leaned in. Casca was just able to pick out a few Arabic words. Nothing of significance or that seemed to make sense. Casca did not care much. He was not about to join in. Their bald leader seemed to stop for a moment, look around and continue. Casca noted his scarred lips, face and neck. A scar brother, Casca thought.

Amused by his own thoughts, Casca looked away and scanned the rest of the cabin. His eyes moved on, but his ears still picked up the scarred, guttural rumblings of the bald one. Just a few words, here and there, nothing intelligible.

Two young ones stood on the far side of the cabin, talking quietly and from time to time grunting in agreement. Mere children. No hair on their faces and probably no brains between their ears. Amateurs, Casca thought. Out for gold and glory. More likely plank walkers and shark food.

The last one in the cabin stood alone and appeared to let out a soft, steady hum. No words, just a tone. The crimson red hood covered all but his dark, angular eyes. He was very short, barely tall enough to hit his head on the door handle. The man was short, but Casca figured he was probably tougher than most men twice his size. Casca had met his kind before.

His feet were clean and bare. Casca noted a chain around his left ankle. Appeared to be of gold. Casca raised one eyebrow in mild surprise. Why would one wear such a tempting ornament in the company of these thieves and murderers? he wondered. The man's dark and deep-set eyes met Casca's. Casca thought of the great sage, Shiu Lao Tze, his friend and teacher. The deep-set eyes squinted lightly and then closed. The humming continued.

For now it appeared no one was about to engage Casca with words or action. With a hand on his sword, Casca closed his own eyes and rested.

FOUR

Surprisingly, there were no incidents of note for weeks to come. The coastal trader moved on south passing the Pillars of Hercules as it paralleled the shore. The crew tended to the ship while the merchants stayed out of everyone's way, making every attempt to stay clear of the armed men. Mostly all stuck to their own business, having seen how quickly trouble could be upon them.

Casca did not know of the destination. Neither did he care. For him one place was the same as any other. Life played itself out with different pieces in different lands. Time and faces may have changed but the rest stayed constant.

Most on board who were hired help did not seem to care much either and figured to stay out of trouble. The cargo was unknown and well locked away as it usually would be on most such runs. The hired help was there to do just that, help and stay out of the captain's path. Casca spent most of his days keeping to himself, walking around on deck, making minimal and trivial conversation.

The nights were stifling hot and Casca tried to spend most of them on deck where the eastern breeze kept him cool. All help was expected to sleep in their quarters, but Casca had never been one to be part of the herd. At night he would sneak out, try to make minimal noise while walking up the creaky wooden stairs, and walk around on deck undetected. If seen, he figured to threaten, fight or talk his way out of it. Casca was pleased, as no one seemed to care much. Most nights on the *Kuta* were the same. The sameness was to end soon.

Casca was not the only one staying up late at night. On a few occasions he heard whispers in the darkness. The wind would bring the sounds to his ears. Most of it was just idle chatter between men, however that was about to change also. On some nights Casca heard the scarred sounds of the bald one, Halim. On other nights he heard the low humming tone of the hooded Chen-Yo. Sometimes the midnight wind brought sweet aromas to Casca's barbarian nose. The sea had a way of playing with one's senses.

Most days were quite uneventful. The crew of the *Kuta* seemed to go about doing their jobs without much fuss or effort, as there was not much to do. Once in a while a fight broke out, to be quickly settled by the captain who had no desire to lose any more arms.

The cook, a man whose origins were impossible to determine, seemed to come up with concoctions that Casca with all his knowledge of exotic foods could not identify. The man had a wooden left leg from the knee down, which ended with a blunted knob, and a blackened and knotted stump for a left arm. He often grinned while serving the daily belly convulsor, showing with pathetic enthusiasm the obscene, turgid shape of his damaged appendage. Unfortunately, even that was not sufficient to take the crew's mind off of the foul gruel that substituted for food.

"Enjoy today's masterpiece, honored gentlemen," he often chided, pushing the same filthy bowl under everyone's nose, splattering another serving of near excrement into an awaiting stained receptacle. "I trust your bellies are not too delicate today," he laughed every time someone ran, spurned by his evil brew. "It would be so unfortunate if you could not hold down my specialty of the day, and upset our good captain."

For some unknown reason he made certain he offended all that he served. His life was safe. No matter how much he was hated, no one wished to trade places and end up serving food to these misfits. This crippled creature had made it his last mission in life to hold the wand of misery over everyone he met. His task did not go unfulfilled.

Whoever had hired this man to work with food must have been a sadist or had shoe leather for a tongue. Casca figured that the unique flavoring of the food was probably due to the cook mixing the chunky gruel with his wooden leg or stumpy arm. They were probably better off not knowing. Most food was served in stew form, tasting as if it had been cooked in the rat-soaked daily bilge water. The only way the lumpy gruel seemed to vary was in thickness and color. It filled the belly. For this crew that was all that mattered.

During daytime Casca stayed inside his cabin or on deck in the shade of the mainmast and ever-entangled rigging. With all its effort this crew never could or would get all the lines straightened out all at once throughout the ship. For all his attention to detail, the captain somehow never insisted in its perfection.

Watching this strange group of people on deck was sometimes entertaining. The tall dark one, Buta, would always stand as if at detention with his back to the rail, which barely came up to above his knees, sharpening his lance with his short sword. It seemed that he spent hours on end going through the same short repetitive motions. Casca wondered if at this rate the lance would likely not last more than two or three months. The tall one never spoke. The one time Casca had made eye contact, all he got was a blank stare, as if of someone who was blind or dead for three days. Casca had no special interest in making eye contact.

The two young boys never seemed to stop talking and grunting in agreement.

''He did, I am sure,'' sometimes Casca would overhear.

''Yes he did,'' the words were sure to come.

''No doubt, you are right,'' more words of agreement.

''I am glad you agree, I knew you would,'' endless flattery was certain to follow.

''After all, why would I doubt you?'' incessant rhetoric refusing to disagree.

"Thank you for agreeing," more thanks.

"I could not but agree . . ."

"I never doubted that you would . . ."

"Anything else would not be fair . . ."

"I would never be unfair . . ."

"I know you would never be . . ." The nauseating words of agreement, of nonconfrontation and flattery refused to end, no matter when Casca overheard them, forcing pain to anyone's ears who understood their droll peasant French affirmations.

Mercoux, the taller of the two, always spoke while holding his left hand in front of his mouth. The other, Lefont, grinned and giggled as a young girl would who had not yet had a man. "You are so right," he would often say.

One day the two of them stared at the tall dark man as if hypnotized. Casca noted that they were looking at his toeless feet. He wondered if they would ever get to be old enough to grow beards. Not likely.

The bald one, Halim, was quite active. No one ever spoke to him. He was always the one who spoke. His three cronies would just listen or, if on their own, remain silent and look down, nailing their eyes to the wooden deck. Halim walked around speaking to three others who also seemed to listen and not much else. Six sheep and one herder . . . , Casca thought. Not much that the seven of them could do, even if organized.

Casca watched the brothers, victims of previous days' greed, slowly walking side by side, breathing in the fresh morning air. Obad's eyes were hollow, his face looking closer to death than before. The last few days had not been kind to him, at times shaking uncontrollably, at other times retching over the sides of the boat, unable to hold food or water. Black tar covered his right shoulder and chest, for the moment having saved him from bleeding to death.

"The rot will take your brother's life soon unless . . . ," Casca offered

"Unless what, unless what? What do I need to do? Help me, please," rambled the younger of the two, surprised that Casca had addressed them. "How do I stop the rot? What do I do?"

Seeing his exasperated look, Casca pitied the two, knowing the pain that would come whether he was allowed to die or survived the cleansing of his wound. "Stopping the bleeding was only half of it. The black tar needs to be removed and his shoulder singed with a burning blade. If he is lucky, he will live with the pain; otherwise he will just die of it."

Obad, nearly delirious, his eyes fallen into deep dark sockets, stumbled as he walked, not appearing to even hear Casca's words, while his brother shook, knowing he was the one who needed to complete the task. The two turned away, heading toward the stern of the ship, whispering into each other's ear. For now they appeared pleased with Casca's words, yet Casca could clearly see revenge in their eyes. Perhaps Captain Talem's deck would not stay clean for long.

One night a storm had hit. The high winds ripped at the sails until the captain ordered them down. There appeared to be no immediate concern for the cargo. This puzzled Casca. The crates and large sacks that had been moved on board did not appear very sturdy, or even remotely waterproof.

The ship creaked as the soft eastern winds had been replaced by violent western storms. The high mast wavered back and forth under the breath of the gods. Casca had been in more storms than he could remember. One more did not matter much to him. He took his usual walk up the creaky stairs.

The wind was howling and ripping the navigational sails that the crew had forgotten or ignored. The storm was whipping up the angry sea, slamming it unmercifully against the wooden box. The hull groaned under the pressure of the storm. Holding on to the rail, Casca walked himself toward starboard. The salty wind ripped against his scarred face. Casca laughed at the angry sea.

Toward west the sea boiled in a mad fury as the waves pounded against the boat. Casca hoped that "The Swift One" was also "The Sturdy One." Lightning broke through, splintering the night sky. It looked like daylight. An angry daylight. The high mast struggled under the shrieking wind. Casca did not make it to starboard. Again, he heard the scarred voice of the bald one, Halim. The lightning had given away their position.

Huddled in a clumped mass, the six robed men focused on their leader. Crouching down, Casca listened, trying to make sense of the situation, but could not make out a word. One of them turned and walked away. Casca wondered if he had been seen. No matter. He was not about to let a bunch of filthy desert thieves get the better of him. It was not the first time he had had to deal with one. The man continued walking toward Casca. The wind howled in the night. Lightning broke the night sky again. Casca stood as he made eye contact with his next victim.

The man casually unsheathed his sword and faced Casca, acting as if he were just about to butcher some poultry for dinner. Casca smiled at the ignorant fool. The man raised his sword at an angle, ready to make halves of Casca.

"How dare you interfere with us? Allah will punish you," he bellowed, spraying Casca with his words, holding the blade up at an angle. "Your hell awaits you," the man concluded, as if completing a sermon, giving final warning before taking action. Obviously he had been paying too much attention to the incessant rambling of his leader and had not realized his adversary. In a smooth motion he swung his sword toward Casca.

Fiery blood raced through Casca's body and pounded in his temples. He had not killed in some time. Countless lives Casca had taken. From the ancient arenas of a decadent and bloody Rome to the golden mountains of the New World to, finally, the apocalyptic battlefields of the Christian Crusades. Another one was not going to make any difference, or set him over his limit. The ship's hull creaked in the grasp of the dark waters. Lightning broke through the night sky. The man was not about to die in darkness.

As the sword lowered toward Casca, fear filled the man's eyes, as he likely regretted his own words and foolish actions. "Help me, Allah," he gasped. He realized that this mass of knotted muscles and scars would be his executioner. Casca moved as the curved sword slashed harmlessly through wet air. The man's throat was in an iron vise. He slumped against the rail as Casca's fingers squeezed the lifeblood out of him.

His eyes met Casca's. For a moment Casca felt merciful. He was not going to torture this fool. With a swift motion he snapped the pulsating neck. Casca smiled again as darkness overtook his mind. It had been a long time. The man slumped to the deck. Lifeless.

The bald one continued. The storm had made him and his small herd of blind followers unaware of what had happened to their brother. Halim pointed west as he continued. The five nodded and looked into the black nothingness. The group hung on to one another and the rail as the sea crashed against the boat. Lightning and thunder broke through the night sky again. The robed men whimpered as blazing fire struck the boiling sea and lightning splintered the crashing waves. Halim continued unabated.

Lightning neared the boat. The five began milling around as Halim tried to control them. Thunder broke through the air, sending the bitter mist into their eyes and noses, burning their senses. For an instant Casca could hear nothing but his own thoughts as a cold, flowing vibration spread through his head and neck. Lightning struck again. The remaining sails were gone as the foremast burst into flames and the men scattered. Another one met his death.

He found himself facing a fiery-eyed Casca. As the man reached for his short curved sword, Casca grabbed at his waist. The struggle was short and deadly. Casca flexed his knotted muscles and the man found himself dangling upside down and catapulted overboard. The other ones were gone, quite oblivious to what had happened. As Casca turned toward the fire, three crew members reached the deck with axes in hand.

Casca watched as two chopped away at the burning mast while the third seemed to coordinate the task at hand. It did not take long. They appeared to be quite experienced, as leveling of the sails was used as a last resort during deadly storms that threatened to overturn a ship. They hacked from different angles and pushed the burning mast over the rail. The three assessed the damage, and moments later they were gone. The storm moved on slowly. Lightning was less frequent and more distant. Casca wondered what the new day would bring. No matter, he knew something was up.

• • •

The captain walked around in a rage. Sheepishly, the crew, apparently never having seen the captain quite so incensed, stayed away. Casca walked on deck and eyed the captain, trying to read his immediate thoughts.

The high mast was still intact along with the sail, but not much else. Blackened and crushed, the rail was nearly gone where the burning foremast had been knocked overboard. The ship was tilted slightly toward the bow, probably more storm damage. Clearing toward the horizon, the fog was dissipating as another hot and humid day was in the starting.

Casca quietly walked toward starboard and placed his back against the rail. No one spoke loudly. Whispers and grunts were the only things heard. Buta, the dark giant, stood by the rail, apparently oblivious of the situation. Casca walked past him.

The two young boys, Mercoux and Lefont, whispered to each other with fear and despair in their eyes. Chen-Yo just stood with his arms crossed, looking toward the western horizon. He did not appear concerned. He knew the situation was grave, but definitely not hopeless.

The *Kuta* slowly rocked east to west. Halim stood by his remaining men, with his index fingers by his temples, rubbing them in a circular manner. He had a just barely discernible smirk upon his sun-dried and cracked lips. The man had lost two of his compatriots, Casca thought, but did not seem the least bit perturbed. He had not cared much for the two, that was for certain. Just two pawns in his scheme. Halim stood facing west, with his hands shielding his eyes, scanning the horizon. Casca looked in the direction but saw nothing.

The ship was damaged but not incapacitated. The high sail was ordered up. Without navigational sails the ship could be maneuvered, but quite awkwardly and inefficiently. Casca was in no hurry. Another day, week or year was not going to make any great difference to him. Time mattered not. The only concern Casca had was with the bald one. Halim did not seem very threatening with his few remaining men, but Casca still knew something was about to happen. Casca had met and dealt with his kind before and had learned many painful lessons.

"Never try to out-argue an Arab or shortchange a whore," Casca remembered advice from the past. He touched his left shoulder and arm, pulling at his taught skin, remembering the horrible pain of having been burned at the stake. Nothing could have been worse.

The ship moved very slowly and haphazardly. The mainsail needed to be constantly adjusted—lowered or raised—just to keep the direction, as all other sails, including the jib, were gone. A dozen oars and a few strong backs would have been welcome at this time, Casca thought. The next two days were calmer as all went without any incident. Everyone appeared to be more at ease as the ship moved on slowly but steadily.

FIVE

One night, just as Casca was ready to walk up the stairs leading to the deck, he heard the voices of two or three men, whispering and scurrying on deck. *"Yala, yala,"*—"Move it, move it"—came the words from above. Casca hurried his steps. Suddenly, he heard axes biting into wood. Reaching the deck, Casca saw three shadowy figures chopping away at the high mast. The noise had awakened many others. Casca reached the deck at the same time as the captain and the first mate.

Talem called out for help at the top of his lungs, sending the first mate scurrying, nearly falling backwards. The three continued their sabotage undaunted. In seconds the mainmast was teetering. The three knew what they were doing. Casca hurried toward them, but it was too late. Their mission was over.

The high mast crashed against a cabin, broke through the rail and tumbled into the ocean, dragging with it the sails, shrouds, stays and all the rigging. Two of the three faced each other and completed their mission.

Raising their double-edged axes high into the night sky, they crashed them into each other's skull. Their heads exploded as the forged steel split them down to their waists, spilling their foul innards and flooding the deck as their lives ended.

They were not about to be taken prisoners. The third threw his axe toward the captain and hurled himself overboard. The captain crashed against the deck as he ducked the axe at the last possible instant. The man never reached the water.

His fate was not going to be that easy. He found himself face-to-face with a death much more horrible than drowning. Casca had him. He struggled to set himself free from the vise that had engulfed his neck. Casca lowered him to the deck and searched his eyes. The man knew that he was dead but would have probably preferred his own method of dying had he known his executioners.

The deck was full of people. Most of them were carrying goat-oil lanterns, trying to see what was happening. The captain raised himself from the deck and slowly approached Casca. Talem had the look of death in his eyes. His beard glistened in the glimmering light as the smoke from the lanterns darkened the deck. His piercing eyes cornered and penetrated the saboteur's eyes.

Pulling a short jagged knife from his belt, he put a knotted hand around the man's trembling neck. Casca let go. The man's eyes shifted back and forth between Casca, the captain and the rest of the men on deck. He knew he was dead. He just wondered what manner it would take.

The captain placed his knife back in his belt and held the man by the neck and collar. Talem studied his prisoner. The man was short, with black hair and thick, dark eyebrows. His oily, olive-colored neck slithered in the captain's grasp.

He spit at the captain. The captain did not blink or try to wipe off the bloody projectile as it oozed down his cheek. The man was bleeding from his mouth and nostrils, probably thanks to Casca's iron grip.

"My name is Kasim, and that is all you will know," the man offered, speaking in broken Arabic, brutalizing every word in his delivery. He further continued, "I may be dead but so will you be, soon after I meet Allah." The captain did not care. All the words he did not understand, but he had enough knowledge of the man's language to understand sufficiently. He knew that the man had just completed a suicide mission, and the worst was to follow. No doubt the man was about to die—whether Allah would receive him or not was another matter.

Dawn was breaking through on the horizon as Casca walked around on the deck. The day was going to be hot and deadly. It would bring Casca's worst nightmare. The captain had tied the saboteur to the rail overnight and placed two guards to watch him. He was going to let the prisoner think about death before dying.

The soft eastern winds rocked the boat. Without sails to maneuver with, the captain had decided to drop anchor overnight and make a decision about the future during daylight. The coast had been out of sight for days now and he did not want to take the chance of drifting farther into the ocean. The *Kuta* was no longer "The Swift One."

The deck creaked under Casca's steps as he made his way toward the rail. Casca eyed the prisoner. The man had a look of disdain about him. He knew he was about to die, but did not seem to care much. All that he appeared to care about was the method of his execution. His deep set, piglike eyes tried to penetrate Casca's. He did not like what he saw. Casca saw simplicity and single-mindedness in the saboteur's eyes.

The captain reached the deck as his men swarmed around him, trying to read his thoughts. Talem was boiling in fury. Here he was, in the middle of nowhere, with a crippled ship, with saboteurs on board and God knows what in the future. He approached the prisoner.

The prisoner smiled and spat at him. Having been tied up half the night must have weakened his aim. His bloody dribble only reached the deck at the captain's feet. He was not helping his own cause. Obviously, he did not care much.

Talem studied his prisoner. Everyone was up on deck. For the first time the two young boys were silent. Even they understood the graveness of the situation. The giant black man stood in the background, forever sharpening his lance while staring nowhere. Halim stood with his arms crossed, watching the prisoner. Their eyes met for an instant, then drifted away.

Casca sensed communication between the two. Turning his head away the bald one scanned the western horizon. And there it was. Following the direction, Casca noted two just barely discernible dots. He had been right all along. Everything had been planned. The dots grew larger by the moment. It was going to be a long day.

The captain approached the prisoner. "Bring this filthy thing to me," he ordered. Reaching out with his dried-out and rope-burned hand, he held Kasim by his greasy hair. Looking into his eyes, the captain tried to read the man's thoughts. All he got back was a blank, empty, unintelligent follower's stare.

"I will not disappoint your death wish," Talem reassured the prisoner with measured words of doom. "All of your brothers will die by my hands, one at a time, that you can be certain of." There was not much to hide, even if Kasim had wanted to, and since there wasn't, his leader had little to fear, as Kasim was barely a bit player. The man closed his eyes and started humming in a low tone. A quick last prayer before dying, most likely.

The captain let go and turned toward the west. He saw the two ships approaching and understood also. Looking back toward the prisoner, the captain shook him. The man smiled and laughed. Taking out his short knife, the captain released the prisoner with a quick flick of his wrist. With the two guards holding the man, the captain sliced his chest, not enough to kill him, but enough to bleed him to death. Slowly.

The first mate obliged with a smile as the captain called for rope. With thick, long rope, the first mate tied the prisoner's ankles together. A queasy feeling filled Casca's stomach. He had thought the two young boys would be the first to become shark food. He had been wrong. The captain was going fishing.

"Allah will punish you," the prisoner screamed, damning the captain to hell as his mind refused to understand what was about to happen. "He will not allow me to die, I have served him well . . ." he shrieked unintelligibly on and on, at times praying to his god, at other times cursing at him. The captain and his mates went about their task at hand, preparing for his end.

"I will tell you anything you want," Kasim finally offered. His eyes shifted from face to face, trying to find safe haven or understanding in someone's eyes. There was none to be found.

Unemotionally, with a low, steady voice, the captain silenced him. "There is nothing that you can give me." Looking around, the saboteur finally understood, as his lungs let out a soundless scream. Casca noted smiles among the crew members and looks of confusion, horror and disgust from the merchants and hired hands. There was nothing unclear about what was to happen to the man.

The two dots grew larger at the horizon. They were moving slowly but with a definite direction and purpose. It would be quite some time before they would reach the ship. Casca was on a dead boat and everyone knew it. Without the ability to move or even maneuver, they were a floating target.

The two ships were approaching very slowly. It was going to be many hours before they would clash. The captain looked around, trying to weigh the situation. Obviously everything had been planned. With the help of the storm, the saboteurs had completely crippled the ship. If they were to fight, they would be slaughtered, while if they were to surrender, they would still be slaughtered, but perhaps more mercifully.

Many of the crew would surrender, probably to be enslaved. The captain was not about to be taken prisoner, and if any of his crew were to surrender, he was going to scramble their brains with his bare hands. The thought of death filled his mind.

Shielding his eyes from the sun, Casca looked toward the horizon but could see no land. He was not about to be taken prisoner easily. These thieves of the seas would pay dearly to capture him. Being stranded on this crippled ship, Casca saw no way out other than fighting. However, there was more to this than met the eye.

Looking around, Talem tried to weigh the situation. Figuring it would take about four hours before the ships would reach them, he prepared to make his stand. But first there was the matter of Kasim, the saboteur.

Grabbing the prisoner by the waist, the captain threw him overboard. The man screamed as he plunged backwards into the tranquil sea. "Save me, Allah"—his shriek diminished as he fell into the water. Having had his feet tied together, the man was just barely able to stay afloat. Pitiful cries reached the laughing mates. Waving and splashing around he could just keep his head above water, inhaling mouthfuls of it every time he went under. The man probably figured he would drown soon, but his fate was not going to be that easy.

The mates cheered the captain on as he pulled the man out of the water, only to simply let him plunge back in. The crew members had seen this game many times before. The rest of the men on board of the *Kuta* had a look of disgust and confusion about them. Casca figured there was nothing to be confused about.

By pulling the man up and then letting him fall back in, the captain was creating maximum amount of splashing. This was not the first time Casca had seen someone fish for sharks; it just happened to be the first time that he had seen a man used as bait. All the splashing about was working.

Two sets of triangular dorsal fins appeared fairly close to the crippled ship. Sounds of understanding and horror filled the deck. Seeing the sharks, the captain pulled on the rope, lifting the man out of the water just enough to give the saboteur the full view. The man screamed as he turned his head toward the approaching beasts. Allah was not with him this time.

Another set of fins approached the ship from the west, joining the first two, churning the water under the dangling shark food. The captain's morbid laughter pierced the air as he bobbed the man in and out of the water, not unlike a child getting his first catch. The water boiled as the frenzied sharks tried to reach the now fainted man. Looking at the captain, Casca wondered how long this game of death would continue. These three sharks could have ripped the man apart in seconds had they been given the opportunity.

The captain was not quite happy with the game. Apparently the man had passed out from the shock, and this seemed to take all the amusement out of it. The two young boys huddled together, holding on to each other, trembling at the sight of this deadly sport. Casca overheard them whispering to each other, hoping that the man would meet a swift death. That was not about to happen if the captain could help it.

With fire in his eyes and saliva oozing from his ugly lips, Talem pulled the bait almost up to the deck. A sigh of relief filled the deck. Two of the crew members even crossed themselves, believing that Kasim, although a heathen follower of Mohammed, might be given a repricve. A mistaken sigh of relief—as the captain let go of the rope and the man crashed back into the water below.

With the captain quickly pulling the rope up, the sharks were unable to end the man's life. All the plunge did was to revive him. Finally satisfied, the captain lowered the rope so the man's dangling arms would just splash against the living sea. The water turned crimson as the man met a disappointed Allah. He screamed in agony as his left arm and shoulder were ripped from his body.

The rope was pulled up, raising the bleeding mass to temporary safety. His blood left his body as it sprayed the water below, feeding the frenzied demons of the sea. Bobbing the limp body in and out of the water, the captain finally appeared satisfied. Suddenly, in a scream of death, the man regained consciousness.

It was not to be for long, as he was finally allowed to die. In a matter of seconds the rope was empty, just hanging from the captain's hands. The sharks were gone as fast as they had come. With the grunts of pleasure of a man spent, the captain dropped the bloody rope to the deck and turned away from the sea.

Slowly, the ships were approaching. The captain looked around, trying to grasp the situation. Casca turned toward the two approaching ships as his right hand clenched around his curved sword, the calluses of his palm finding their way around the hilt. It was going to be a fight to the death. The weak would die or surrender, while the strong would just die. Casca was different.

He knew he would not die, but he also did not know

what the day would bring. The captain cupped his hands around his eyes, blocking out the piercing sun rays and the glare that bounced of the water, trying to see the approaching ships. He was not expecting to see anything in particular. Death was on its way. One ship was sailing straight toward them, while the other seemed to be taking an arcing southern route. No matter, the end would still be the same.

SIX

The burning sun was dissipating the morning mist. The slaughter to follow was going to have a clear arena. The captain, apparently having been in similar situations previously, gave orders. He knew well the orders were hollow, as this time all was lost. However, he was still the captain, and if this was his destiny, than so may it be.

The ship's mates were instructed to secure the cargo and then arm themselves. Casca found it curious that only two of them went down the stairs toward the storage area. The rest raced toward their cabins and returned within minutes armed to the teeth. The two checking the cargo were nowhere to be found.

The hired swords were all fully armed, as they all slept, ate and did everything else for that matter with sword within reach. Had they washed, perhaps they might have taken their weapons off, but with this group any experiences with cleanliness were highly doubtful.

Casca's eyes scanned the deck while his mind raced trying to recall a situation in the hundreds of confrontations in which he had taken part that would help him out. He had warred with slaves and kings, battled with beasts of land and sea, and there was not much that he had not seen. His eyes saw a doomed ship. All but he would perish.

Obviously all this had been planned to cripple the ship and allow for its easy capture and destruction. The storm had just aided the saboteurs. Casca wondered what the cargo was. Gold, most likely. He had seen men on four continents blinded by the yellow metal. Fathers had given their sons, while brothers had killed brothers to acquire what fathers had held. He had seen learned and foolish men give years, then eventually their lives, trying to learn the secrets of alchemy, to be eventually disappointed. At this point that mattered not.

Looking around, Casca saw swords, shields, a few spiked maces and more swords. Nothing of real use. Had he had any, Casca would have given all of his gold for a good Mongolian long bow and a couple dozen arrows. Years ago he had seen the garrisons of Kublai Khan take a man off his horse, at full gallop in a middle of a dust storm or at the earliest of dawns, with a well-placed arrow. Men and horses had looked as if lightning had knocked them off in mid-gallop.

How could there be no such weapons here? Casca's mind raged. They could do nothing but wait until the two ships reached and engaged them. Casca would have wagered his left testicle that the approaching ships had dozens of quivers bursting at the seams with well-sharpened and polished arrows.

The mates huddled around the captain, looking for leadership that would give them perhaps a glimmer of hope. Most had a look of despair and doom in their eyes. A few were accepting the next few hours to be their last. The captain barked out orders, but other than sounding the part, he could give them no leadership of any value.

The hired swords had no unity or organization of any sort, as they had hoped that their presence was enough, and had truly not expected to be needed out on the open seas. Casca saw Halim giving nonverbal orders to his few remaining men. He wondered how long Halim and his cohorts would continue breathing as he saw the captain turn and face them.

Halim knew that his mission and life were about to end soon. Pushing his way through his men, he reached the wooden rail. Laughing mockingly, he threw himself overboard and disappeared beneath the calm waters of the Atlantic. Before the captain could issue orders, his men ripped apart with their bare hands Halim's remaining accomplices. In moments, the deck was covered by a pool of torn flesh, arms, legs and organs. The sharks had nothing on these men of the seas, when it came to efficiency, speed or bloodthirsty lust.

The captain was not concerned about Halim, or his men, not having been captured. Their interrogation, torture and execution were not about to provide him with any great revelation, or pleasure for that matter. The captain, like most of his kind, was a simple man. Finding out why he was about to die was not that important. Trying to stay alive, perhaps save his ship, or just being able to take out as many of his enemies as possible was more reason for concern.

The ships grew larger by the moment. Both were large and appeared ponderous, but swiftly cut down the distance to their destination. The breeze was soft, but the sails were full and tight and Casca could feel his blood starting to boil. Eyeing the approaching ships, he slowly drew his breath as his right hand clenched around his sword.

The salty air of the seas expanded his chest as his lungs filled up. His heart rate quickened and breathing grew short and rapid as the immediacy of the battle to be fought awakened his being. Casca's mind focused on the approaching ships.

His eyes narrowed and muscles tightened as his mind raced through history and battles he had fought. He could smell the waters, the bitter blood that was about to be spilled, the putrid, rancid mass of sweaty worried bodies, but also a sweet aroma. He could not locate it, but it stirred something inside him. He had smelled it earlier, a few days before, when he had walked the decks late at night. The captain barked out orders.

One ship attacked from the northeast, with the sun behind it, while the other slowly approached from the west. The ships flew no flags. It mattered not. They were pirate ships on their way to a slaughter. Their tight sails rippled under the wind while the sun's rays danced upon the waters, intensifying the glare of the morning lights. Squinting his eyes, Casca studied his adversaries.

They were professionals. With the piercing rays of the sun behind them, they were about to take every advantage and minimize their own losses in this slaughter. The ship approaching from the northeast appeared smaller and faster. In minutes it was within arrow distance. Casca could see his own ship's captain clenching his jaws and pounding his fists in fury. Not even one blasted arrow to use from this distance, the captain thought.

They would have to fight it out hand to hand and hope the impending incoming salvo of arrows did not shred them into premature fish food. A small boat was lowered with eight men in it. All had bare chests, with just a sheet of gray cloth wrapped around their privates. Confusion set in around Casca. The larger, slower boat approached from the west, with its sails down, allowing momentum to bring it to its destination.

Casca looked around and saw nothing but fear, panic and confusion. The crew knew that if attacked, they would be butchered at their enemies' convenience. The whole crew and hired hands were at the ready with swords and shields in hand, standing in a defensive posture. Adding to their confusion was the approaching rowboat with eight half-dressed men. They appeared to serve no purpose.

They were carrying no bows, no weapons at all for that matter, no flags of identification or a leader that would serve as a courier. Squinting his eyes, Casca searched the rowboat. He saw nothing but short, hairy, ugly men carrying small pointy metal objects. Turning west, Casca noted three or four dozen archers lined up by the rail of the approaching ship.

Without warning, seven of the eight dove from the rowboat and started swimming vigorously toward Casca's boat. Casca considered the boat his, since he expected to be the only survivor. Puzzlement continued around Casca as no one could figure the strategy being employed. They did not have to wait long. The seven swimmers moved as if they were the death spawn of sharks. They all swam while holding sharp metal picks between their teeth. The ship's sinking was going to be accelerated.

Just as the divers reached the ship, a high-pitched shriek broke the calm air. Turning west, Casca saw a fiery sky as the air lit up with the blaze of flaming incendiary arrows. The breath of an angry God would have been calmer and more welcomed than the wall of incoming fire that torched the ship. Screaming, pathetic creatures ran and fell with bloody, bubbling flaming bodies, as chaos overtook the *Kuta*. A man fell at Casca's feet as his makeshift silver gorget failed him. He tried reaching for the shaft, but his hands quickly fell by his sides as his lifeblood left him.

The metal rain was relentless. Many died as their legs refused to obey, making them easy targets. Casca ducked as two arrows nearly blazed through his scarred face. From the west fire, while from the east water, would be the death bringer.

"Kill them, kill them," roared the captain, once again cursing himself and the hired help for not having any arrows to possibly save his boat. How could they have been such fools? he thought.

The seven divers attacked the ship's hull just underneath where a small rowboat was attached to the side of the ship, protecting them, as no one could get at them with their weapons. Some of Talem's men threw their spears and even their swords, hoping that perhaps they could prevent the sinking of their ship. Just as skilled carpenters, the divers wedged at the hull of the burning ship. Forcing their metal spikes between the boards, they quickly broke through the hull under the water line. Water rushed in mercilessly as the ship rocked from east to west. Nothing was about to stop the waters from bringing them down.

"Cut it off, cut it!" the captain's voice rang out again as he tried to get his men to remove the small rowboat from the side of his ship. It was too late. The hull had been breached and there was nothing that was going to prevent the ship from going down in minutes. It was the end.

Casca and the men around him had been given a death sentence without an explanation, a chance for a dishonorable surrender or at least for an honorable chance to fight to the death. The salvos of incoming flaming arrows continued and even seemed to increase in frequency. Casca could not understand the urgency of the kill. The sun-dried deck and hull burned as if it had been soaked in goat oil. Dark, deadly smoke engulfed the deck as panicked men squirmed in horror awaiting their deaths.

With his eyes lacrimating from the smoke and lungs that were coughing up blood, Casca waited in a crouch for the chance to fight. There appeared to be no reason for the two pirate ships to burn down and sink a merchant ship without at least plundering it or taking slaves. Casca's nose burned from the putrid stench of the scorched bodies. The smell of burning flesh usually aroused Casca, but the intensity of it all sickened his senses. Ducking another flaming arrow, he turned east. His nostrils picked up another scent.

There it was again, the sweet aroma, the one he thought he had imagined. There was no doubt about it this time. His nostrils flared and searched as his mind tried to filter out and identify the sweet scent. He had smelled it before, many years ago, perhaps a thousand. His mind raced as Casca remembered his long gone friend and teacher Shiu Lao Tze.

Lao Tze had sometimes carried the aroma. He had spoken of the fragrance worn by men and women alike, one that appeared different on anyone who used it. It was an oil that came from the leaves of the patchouli plant. Its aroma had been imprinted into Casca's mind. Lao Tze had said that the plant grew in a land even more to the east than the land of Chin. Casca wondered what this all meant. The aroma was the same but sweeter. Lao Tze had said that the aroma was different on everyone, but this was too sweet. Something was different. Very different. This was a woman's scent.

Casca could see nothing but smoke, men dying and more smoke. The two young boys, Mercoux and Lefont, had been the first ones to meet their maker. The first salvo of flaming arrows had pinned them against the deck cabin walls. They died together, their first venture into the cruel world becoming their last.

Casca's mind burned in intensity as his eyes scanned the slaughter. Men all around were pinned by arrows like pieces of goat meat at a conqueror's victorious feast. The soon-to-be-dead ran around aimlessly, grasping at their torn bodies, crashing against the rail and falling overboard.

Casca stayed low, crouching near the rail, avoiding the line of fire. Water was rushing in at an alarming rate.

The gimpy cook had found his way to the deck, to be quickly cut down by a rain of arrows. At least no one else would ever have to suffer from the man's cruel concoctions, Casca quickly thought to himself. The boat was rocking and gurgling as the inrushing water filled the lower compartments, crushing the weaker walls, chasing an army of diseased rats onto the deck.

The water would win over the fire, as the *Kuta* was sinking faster than it was being torched. With swords unsheathed, the survivors of the *Kuta* tended their wounds while anxiously awaiting a chance to fight and die an honorable death, rather then perish as weaklings. Looking east Casca saw a glimmer of hope in the eyes of the men around him. The *Kuta* was about to be boarded.

The incoming fire ceased momentarily from the west. The ship approaching from the east launched four grappling hooks to hold the *Kuta*. Within moments the two ships were side by side. Screaming madmen jumped on board the *Kuta*, swinging curved Turkish swords. Their long, bleached white robes glistened in the sun. Dark, deadly eyes led them as the madness of the kill overtook their being. Casca grinned, knowing this was his time to kill.

With two flashes of his sword he sent two men to hell. The men screamed in horror as their blood flooded the deck and drained into the smoldering wooden cracks. Swinging his sword around, Casca searched for more victims. Looking east, he watched as the pirate ship captain gave out orders.

The man wore a long black robe that dusted the deck and flapped in the wind as he moved. With swift and angular hand movements, he directed the massacre. Behind him stood a thin, coal black man hooded in a golden red robe, with a black braided rope tied around his waist and a short, straight sword that paralleled his belt line.

He had a happy and pleased smile on his fleshy lips as he watched the slaughter, while holding his left hand by his mouth, resting his middle knuckles on the point of his chin while holding his little finger at the corner of his mouth, between his lips. Within all the chaos their eyes crossed paths. The next moment took but an instant as it burned itself into Casca's mind.

The deck buckled under his feet. It happened suddenly but appeared to take place very slowly. Casca's body went numb as all his remaining senses came to life. The sweet aroma was like lightning as it shocked Casca's manhood. Over the smell of dying bodies and deadly black smoke the sweet scent permeated Casca's mind. The hull of the *Kuta* belched as it sucked Casca into itself.

Two men appeared on deck, emerging from the lower levels. Between them, a slight slender figure was being dragged and handled toward the pirate ship. The small creature barely came up to the shoulders of the two men whom Casca recognized as the ones who had disappeared earlier to check on the cargo. The cargo was not gold or precious stones.

It was in the form of a tiny person being hauled toward the railing adjacent to the pirate ship. Casca was falling toward the heart of the ship as his eyes caught the last glimpses of the world above.

The slaughter was ending, as the pirates had overwhelmed the crew and protectors of the *Kuta.* Talem, the brave captain, had been tied down to the railing, forced to watch the butchering of his men and the destruction of his ship. His death would not be torture enough for these madmen.

Obad, the poor fool that had challenged Casca days ago, did not live to seek revenge. Fighting desperately, using his left hand to swing a spiked mace, he was able to at least die the only way he wanted to, battling to his last breath side to side with his brother. In moments they too were gone.

The rest did not fare better. Chen-Yo had been cornered and impaled by numerous flaming arrows. He hung, slumped over the railing facing west, as his crimson red hood turned even redder with the blood that flowed from his veins. Buta, the giant dark-skinned one, fought on valiantly, but with no hope as six white-robed pirates surrounded and slashed at him with their curved swords. His life ended soon, as his soul merged with his ancestors. One last image burned itself into Casca's mind.

The slight figure being hauled away was wearing an immaculate silk robe. It must have been made by skilled craftsmen over a period of long hours. Its quality was unmistakable. As the figure was being lifted over the railing, Casca's eyes picked up the reflection of precious metal. The eastern breeze whispered to Casca as the silken robe fluttered in the wind and revealed the prize.

Again Casca's senses picked up the scent that he had not smelled in ages, also a lock of long yellow hair and a thin golden leg. The girl must have been no more than ten, but important enough to warrant the death of many. A brilliant leg ornament rattled around her shapely ankle. As Casca was sucked down into the bowels of the sinking ship, he took one last breath, bringing to the merciless depth of the ocean one last reminder of the world that he never again expected to be a part of.

The dark waters of the Atlantic closed in over Casca as the hull of the *Kuta* collapsed around him, dragging him to the ocean floor. The surface of the water rushed away as he was pulled downward. He watched while the hull was crushed like an old sun-dried ostrich shell and found himself being pushed down toward the rocky bottom of the ocean. Air bubbles escaped from his nose and mouth as they rose, distancing themselves from his drowning body. His last breath was ripped from him with the increasing pressure of the depth bursting his lungs and filling them with bitter saltwater.

Casca's body strained under the weight of the water and debris that was pushing him downward. The burning saltwater scorched his lungs, causing him to vomit blood, while his eardrums burst from the pressure, bleeding him mercilessly. The pain was almost unbearable, but somehow Casca maintained consciousness.

The crushed and mangled debris that used to be the hull of the *Kuta* twisted and rolled, but cruelly held Casca, forcing him to face the surface of the cold sea, and witness the end of the slaughter that he had been ripped away from. With glazed and clouded eyes Casca watched the remains of the *Kuta* drift away, along with dead and dying bodies, while he found himself being pushed down farther and farther.

SEVEN

Suddenly, Casca's eyes opened. He tried to breathe, but it appeared that he *was* breathing, or at least something alike to it, as his chest muscles heaved. His lungs were not taking in the salty air above the ocean but the bitterly painful salty waters of the depths. Every part of him ached except for his left arm that seemed to hover aimlessly over his crushed body. Casca looked around and tried to force his mind to understand the situation.

He could barely move. He hurt all over, except for his legs and left arm. Casca wondered why his legs did not ache, but quickly realized that blood was no longer flowing to his legs, as the weight of the twisted debris resting on his hips did not allow it to. He tried wiggling his toes but could not tell if they were moving. The water turned dark red over his face as his mouth let out a silent scream and his nostrils bled incessantly. Casca could just focus his clouded eyes on the bubbles that sped upward toward the surface. The air bubbles expanded as they rushed away from his mouth and disappeared in the yellow light of the reflected sun rays.

He tried focusing his eyes but the pounding in his head did not allow him a clear mind or control over his senses. A sudden cold overtook him as his whole body started shaking uncontrollably. For an instant Casca was happy as the thought of death filled his mind.

For certain Christ had not had this in mind when he cursed Casca all those centuries ago on Golgotha. Casca had been condemned to outlive the ages and wander the globe a constant soldier, forever fighting, paining and surviving, but that could not have applied to this. He was hundreds of years old but he was still a man, even if he had survived dozens of mortal wounds, he was just a man and could not breathe water.

Casca welcomed the darkness that started enveloping him, dulling his senses and gently warming him. A pleasant feeling of serenity eased his mind, and for a moment he thought he could smell freshly baked bread. His eyes no longer burned and his body seemed to stop aching. Casca closed his eyes and joyously welcomed death. It was long overdue.

He was definitely not dead. With his eyes tightly held shut, Casca gritted his teeth, while his whole body shivered and ached. He had hoped that death would finally take him. The fleeting moment of serenity disappeared and was overtaken by something very old and familiar: the sensation of pain and of being alive.

"As you are, so you shall remain," the voice of a thousand years past echoed in his ears. The curse of the crucified Jew would not be broken, as Casca would have to suffer longer waiting for final judgment and His return.

The waters were calm. The battle had been fought above on the sometime angry surface of the Atlantic, but the victims of the slaughter were laid to rest in a watery grave hidden forever from the upper world. Casca slowly raised his head as his eyes scanned the wreck of the *Kuta.* Parts of the once proud "Swift One" were scattered over the ocean floor, while most of it had probably floated and drifted away.

Casca shook his head and tried to free himself. He could not even shake, as his whole body felt as if it had been nailed down by thousands of metal spikes. Casca found himself thinking about that day, the day the Romans had tortured Christ and then crucified him. Was this the way Christ had felt? Powerless and betrayed? Christ had suffered and lived for a few days, then died and been taken down, and finally allowed to rest. Casca would be given no such reprise. He would suffer forever. Again, he shook his head trying to break his thoughts from the curse and nightmare that would never end.

The ocean floor was covered by naked and mangled skeletons. All the corpses had been picked shiny clean by buzzards of the depths that Casca was glad had not gotten to him. He wondered how long it had been since the sinking of the *Kuta*. Had it been hours or days, maybe months or even years?

Casca looked at his left arm. It was as wrinkled as the backside of an old hag and just as unattractive. The hair on his arm was moving with the undulation of the waters, but it was covered by a strange bluish green fuzz. Casca touched his face and realized that he had grown a beard, a long and wavy beard that moved with the motion of the waters.

He tried prying himself out from under the wreckage of the *Kuta* but could not even get his hand under the mass that was holding him down. It felt as if he had been buried up to the neck in quicksand or solid rock. Looking left, craning his neck as far as it would allow, he could see the remains of a man roped to what must have been the rail of the *Kuta*. It was the brave captain, Talem, who had been tied down and forced to watch the death of his ship and the bloody butchering of his crew.

Toward the right the bluish emptiness seemed to go on forever. Above him was nothing but water and the golden lantern that would settle into the waters ahead of Casca day after day. The sand was covered with the weapons of war—swords, lances, shields and arrows—left to mark the field of battle forever. The weight of his tomb and the waters above no longer hurt. Casca had become part of the ocean floor.

Even if not able to move, Casca had learned to hunt for food. His long and wavy beard moved with the currents of the ocean and seemed to attract creatures of all kinds. Some were quite tasty, Casca learned, as he would strike out and capture unsuspecting inhabitants of the depths. The nails on his left hand had grown long and curled up onto themselves, looking like the sharpened claws of an eagle. Casca had adapted to his new home.

For the longest time the nights were almost unbearable. The cold and darkness would overtake Casca and torture his senses. He tried to escape by sleeping through them, but reason and control of one's life were no longer a luxury that he could enjoy.

On moonless nights darkness was almost complete and Casca's own senses were his torturers as the movement of the waters and beasts within would punish him. Being bumped, slithered or crawled over in total darkness was not something Casca thought he could ever get used to. He looked forward to nights when the moon would hang like an anchor in the sky and keep him company.

Time went on, or at least it seemed to. Nights came and went. There was no way of telling and it mattered not. Forever was forever and it was unimportant if time passed quickly or slowly.

From time to time the sands shifted, covering or uncovering parts of the ocean floor, but Casca was always the same. As if by design. He had hoped that the salty waters and movement of the sand would eat away or dislodge him from his grave, but there was going to be no rescue or escape for him.

During a violent storm Casca had seen three or four galleys pass overhead struggling under the weight of the angry winds. He wondered if the crews above could ever imagine the grave they were passing over. Probably not, and it would not matter, as Casca knew his sentence would never end.

Upon awakening the next day, Casca was surprised to find himself in very different surroundings. The storm had greatly shifted the sands below. Casca wondered if he could perhaps move but quickly realized he was held down as well as ever, perhaps even better. Moving his left arm, Casca suddenly held something solid and cold.

Quickly turning his head, or at least as fast as the weight of the waters would allow, Casca found himself holding the grip of a straight double-edged sword. It appeared quite new and sharpened, with no sign of rust or wear, as if it had been dropped straight down from a galley that had passed overhead, into his waiting hand. Casca turned the blade over and smiled as the sun's rays reflected off its sharpened edge. It had been long since he had held such a handsome and delicious weapon.

With its sharpened double edge it resembled the Gladius Iberius that he had used and taken many lives with hundreds of years ago as a gladiator in Rome, but this had a blade almost twice as long and one and a half as wide. It looked well made, possibly English or French, perhaps a German sword, not useful except for a man of great strength who could wield it with power and speed. Its fine edge could have separated a desert merchant's beard from sand dust or the balls of a tick from the balls of the same.

Casca was surprised to see such a weapon, as the people of these lands preferred the curved swords such as the scimitar, or an old Thracian type blade. Perhaps the crews that had been in the storm the previous night had not survived the sea. The ocean floor was probably littered with dead bodies that fed the beasts below. They were lucky. Casca had survived but would have gladly exchanged places.

Time passed with few interruptions other than day and night. During daytime Casca would feed and then drift into a hazy and sometime painful slumber, while at night the motion of the waters would allow him a peaceful escape, a loss of consciousness. Hunting and surviving had always come natural to man, although Casca doubted this was what God had intended for the ones made in His own image.

The sword that had come into his possession had kept Casca's sanity. It held as new, refusing to rust. Obviously of no real use, it still reminded Casca of mankind, a symbol of civilization as he knew it, of his very existence. The eternal soldier.

The landscape shifted often, except for Casca, who remained the same, and the long sword that he always gripped. All remains of the sunken ships had drifted or rotted away, leaving no signs of humanity but for Casca, who was held as a prize on the ocean floor. The great Chinese sage, Shiu Lao Tze, had said over a thousand years ago that a man's life was like an hourglass; when the sand ran out, life had gone full circle for the last time and the man would die. But not for Casca. His hourglass would just turn again, with an endless supply of sand and turns. Time passed, but the cruel sea would not allow Casca a reference to its swiftness.

It must have been midday as Casca arose from his watery slumber. The morning kill had filled his stomach, although the meat had been quite difficult to chew and swallow. Casca had strangled his prey one-handed while he was battered quite handily by the endless appendages of the creature. It's beak, not unlike a parrot's, had pecked and scratched away at Casca, trying to smother him, but with no luck. He had tasted better even when there was nothing to eat but fly-swarmed three-day-old camel haunches dipped in cold goat fat. Nevertheless it had served its purpose.

Casca's eyes suddenly focused and his mind cleared as the instincts of the trapped soldier brought him to attention. A series of dark, oblong objects had appeared at the edge of his senses. He was not certain that they were really there, since he could not quite see them, but his instincts told him something was different. Something was definitely nearing him.

They were long, wooden rowboats spread out in a slightly curved pattern heading toward Casca. As the shape and number of the boats became more clear, a mystery awakened Casca's mind and quickened his pulse. Rowboats of this size would never venture more than a few hours away from the shore.

Casca was closer to land than he had ever dared to imagine. A large school of silvery blue fish rushed toward him and disappeared over his head. Next, two large ferocious sharks, with wide gray stripes on their backs, headed in the same direction at a rapid pace. The six boats were approaching but were impossible to see clearly. Casca's eyes narrowed as his upper lid strained and quivered, trying to allow the mind to focus in on the puzzle.

The boats were quite clear, with five oars on one side of each and an extended wooden counterbalance, much like an outrigger, on the other. The counterbalance allowed the rowing to be done from one side and also prevented the boat from tipping over. Casca could see no oarsmen, as his vantage point would not allow for it.

Between them there appeared to be a dark gray, shadowy mist that absorbed the light and changed the color of the water. Casca's eyes strained further trying to decipher the riddle. Another school of tiny fish swam overhead as the mystery of the boats became clear. Casca was watching an efficient and structured fishing expedition.

The wide and deep netting would sweep all that it encountered, allowing a single catch to feed hundreds. Metal balls had been added as ballast to straighten out the net and allow for maximum efficiency. Casca had observed the detailed technique of this method employed by many, as it had been used for thousands of years, even before the ancient Romans.

He had seen murals of these fishing expeditions on the ancient ruins of old Troy, along the western coast of Byzantium, at the entrance of the Dardanelles Strait. Such fishing appeared crude, but was quite productive. The net did not discriminate, as the selection of the catch would be made from a sea of slithering and flopping bodies that would be dragged onto the shore.

The curtain of interlocked netting swept toward Casca as the cape of an overlord or the dress of a rich woman ready to wed. The boats became more and more distinct as they approached Casca and his sandy grave. The nets had found their prey, as thousands of assorted creatures had already been entangled along the path of the boats. Looking straight ahead and down, Casca suddenly cried out. The nets were sweeping the ocean floor.

Was this meant to be or was it more torture for Casca to endure? His left arm trembled in anticipation as his head shook violently from side to side. He let out a silent scream as the saltwater rushed in and out of his lungs. For the first time since the beginning of this watery grave, Casca's insides burned and his body ached while his water-filled lungs hungered for air. The boats passed overhead as the net swept over his waiting arm.

Casca was never going to let go of the net. The rugged hand-woven netting ripped through the meat of his fingers, skinning him alive, tearing into the joints of his fingers, dislocating the bones, as he let out a scream of pain. Casca clenched his grip around the braided threads that would return him to his world. The great weight and momentum of the net tore Casca out from underneath the wreckage of the *Kuta,* creating a cloud of sand while entangling him within a mass of captured sea creatures, making him part of the catch.

EIGHT

The men scattered. There stood only one, who smiled. The lump of slithering, twisting bodies looked the same as the catch of any day, except this was different. Creatures of all shapes and sizes flopped around, aimlessly enjoying their last few moments of life or, more likely the last few seconds of an agonizing death dance. Their fragile insides collapsed as they could not bear the pressure difference of the outside world—except for one creature.

It was covered with algae, barnacles like the bottom of boats left in the water too long, and a peculiar red coral that seemed to be growing out of its neck and shoulder. Its flattened body was covered with intertwined bluish green hair and skin that looked like the belly of a hundred-year-old tortoise. It did not look like anything that these fishermen had ever seen.

Casca stared at the terrified faces and paralyzed eyes that seemed to focus on him. The eight men stood in a semicircle around the dying sea creatures, among which Casca had been unceremoniously dumped. The tallest of the men had not moved but stood quietly and patiently while all the time smiling at Casca. He reached out his hand toward Casca's left arm and shook it gently.

''Okhao Olokun, okhao Olokun,'' the man offered.

Casca tried speaking but all he could get out was a lungful of bitter and greenish water. He was in a new pool of liquid as his lungs battled for air while spewing out the poison of the ocean.

His lungs searched for sweet air as his chest and stomach muscles shook in spasms and rib-cracking convulsions, as he tried to accustom himself to his new surroundings.

"*Okhao Olokun,*" the man repeated.

Casca tried to talk, and attempt to communicate, but all he could get out of his mouth was more greenish ooze and the sounds of a man choking on his own guts.

The man who had spoken continued smiling, while still holding Casca's left hand. He was tall and muscular, without a drop of unwanted weight on his coal black frame. His eyes were blacker than black, so deep and without end that Casca found himself falling into them.

The man wore a simple red sash that his torso held up with a golden yellow braided rope that encircled his waist three times before ending in a large knot on his left hip. In his left hand he held a long rattle-staff surmounted by an elephant head with large and floppy ears, ears typical of African elephants. The staff appeared exquisitely worked and adorned, perhaps overly so.

Casca finally stopped coughing. He had nothing more to bring up. As he tried to rise from the yellow sands, Casca forced himself to inhale the ocean air. The shock of it burned his lungs as he lost consciousness.

Casca opened his eyes in complete darkness. He was warm and felt content for the moment. He could not feel his legs, torso or right arm, but felt comfortable. Reaching down with his left arm, Casca touched his sleeping body.

It was like touching someone else or a long dead body, cold and clammy and with no sensation. Raising his head, he tried focusing, but darkness was complete and unyielding. Suddenly he was blinded, as light was allowed to enter his resting place.

"*Okhao Olokun, ise Olokun . . . .*" Casca heard again.

His eyes quickly focused in on a young boy bringing a plate of yellow and red fruit. The boy never raised his eyes or head as he peeled the yellow fruit and fed it to Casca piece by piece. Its taste was not unpleasant, nor was its consistency, and it certainly pleased the stomach. The boy pealed one more. And another. The yellow fruit was to be followed by the sweet taste of coconut milk that helped buffer the bitter salty poison that Casca still had in his whole body. No sooner had the boy left, gently darkening the room, than Casca was asleep.

Casca awakened in agony. His whole body was on fire. Once again he was being tortured by his cursed sentence. Blood was returning to his limbs, slowly washing out the poisoned blood that had stagnated in his veins for the longest time. His muscles, bones and every fiber of his body were being awakened by nerves that felt as if they were on fire. Casca was aware of even the most minute fragment of his body, as his nerve endings were torturing him from his neck down to the hairs on his toes; even his nails hurt.

He shivered and shook trying to survive the pain of thousands of nails being driven into every fiber of his body. Trembling from the burning and despair, Casca pounded his body with his left fist, hoping to quicken the torture that he expected would eventually end. The torment, however, would continue for some time, as his strong body, hardened by hundreds of years of warring and surviving, would not allow him the escape of unconsciousness.

Apparently the pain had caused his loss of consciousness, as Casca found himself awakening and squinting from the yellow sunlight that watered his eyes. His eyes and lungs burned bitterly, while his ears ached from the pressure change. Casca moved his left hand, then his right arm, then his legs. They were all there and there was no pain, no burning and no numbness. He could barely move his legs, but they did not hurt. Reaching down, he touched his chest, waist and legs. From the neck down he was as thin, flat and emaciated as a bottom-feeder flat fish, but he could feel the blood racing through his veins. He body was slowly returning to life.

The hut entrance was open. Around the entrance, in a semicircle, sat twenty men with their legs folded under themselves, hands clenched in fists by their sides, resting on the sand, and heads bowing down, almost touching the sand in front of them. Only one stood. The one that had earlier greeted Casca. The man continued smiling, and slowly approached once he saw Casca open and focus his eyes.

"Okhao Olokun, ise." The words were familiar but still meant nothing. Perhaps a greeting of some local sort.

Casca tried getting up but his muscles failed him, only allowing him to halfway tumble-crawl off his makeshift bed. The tall one sounded the rattle with one quick and sudden jerk of his wrist, and two men rushed to Casca's aid. Gently holding him by the shoulders and back, they attempted to stand him up and steady him.

The walls started spinning as the hut collapsed onto itself, while the dusty red floor dropped underneath Casca's shrunken feet. The room bounced around uncontrollably in a frenzied, drunken dance, while the perception of up and down lost all meaning. The mud floor slammed against the sky as the straw ceiling ricocheted off Casca's eyes, bringing the salty depth of the ocean again into his bitter mouth.

His head shook, rattling his brain against his skull like the pebbles in a child's hand toy. The yellow sun rays burned Casca's eyes, but its warmth felt pleasant. Eventually the hut stopped its hallucinatory dance, as the grip of the two men steadied the sky and the ground, and Casca found himself outside the straw-covered hut.

"Okhao Olokun, ise."

Casca wondered which, if any one, of the words meant "hello." *"Okhao"* or *"Olokun,"* maybe *"ise."* The word *"ise"* he had only heard since he had awakened in the hut. Perhaps they called him *"Ise."* Perhaps *"Okhao"* was a greeting, or maybe *"Okhao Olokun"* was. Did not matter much as Casca had no response.

Steadied by the two men Casca stood barefoot in the golden sand, squinting slightly from the sunlight, focusing his eyes on the men around him. Looking down, he saw a skeleton barely covered by skin and sinew. His once muscular legs were gone, replaced by pegs fit for an old hag. He was surprised to find himself standing, wavering in the ocean breeze but remaining erect, once the two men let go of him.

The twenty men would not look up or even raise their heads off the sand. Their leader started toward Casca, smiling and approaching slowly. Reaching Casca, he carefully and curiously looked into his eyes. He was tall with straight, broad shoulders that glistened in the sun and arms that looked like coiled snakes.

"*Okhao Olokun.*" He tried again.

Casca's dried-out and shrunken throat struggled to form the words, while all at the same time trying to hold the man's eyes. "My name is Casca, and . . ."

The pain of his words ripped at his vocal cords as their lack of use tortured him. Had Casca anticipated the pain, he would have likely bowed his head and neck in acknowledgment of the greeting. The bitter juices of his stomach flowed into the back of his throat, punishing him for trying to continue.

The two continued looking into each other's eyes for a while. They could both sense intelligence, purpose and maybe even greatness. Communication seemed important but was proving impossible.

Casca could not recognize the language, the inflection or even the intonation used in the attempted communication. It appeared to be non-hostile, perhaps even friendly, but its meaning was impossible to determine. Looking up, Casca realized he must have collapsed again, sprawling uncontrollably in the sand, as his legs had apparently failed him once more.

The tall black man again sounded the long rattle-staff and Casca was immediately raised, gently returned to his hut and placed in bed. One of the men brought a wooden bowl filled with sweet coconut milk that Casca quickly made disappear. A cloudiness overtook his mind while he again drifted off to sleep.

Casca opened his eyes with a smile on his face. It had been long, definitely too long, since he had awakened such. Reaching down toward his waist, Casca again felt like a whole man awakening from a long night's sleep. Flexing his arms, he could hear his muscles and sinew rake against his bones, pulling on his tendons, his cartilage cracking his ancient rusty joints against each other and the warm blood coarse throughout his awakening body.

Shielding his eyes from midday's overhead sun, Casca exited the hut and turned toward the first tree that he saw. Lifting his head skyward with his eyes held tightly shut, rolling his head side to side Casca relieved himself noisily against the shell-like bark of a thin palm tree. His jaws crackled, popping in their joints, as his whole body shivered slightly from head to toe. It had been virtually forever since he had done such. Strange how simple pleasures were, Casca thought.

"Okhao Olokun, asama Ewuare, ise."

Casca turned around, not quite finished, and met the gaze of the tall black leader. About two dozen men kneeled, with their heads down, their eyelashes dusting the sand, not daring even to make eye contact. Amused by the situation, Casca turned and smiled toward the one apparently called Ewuare, and approached him, after shaking off the last of himself.

He saw amazement in the eyes of the one called Ewuare, and even in the eyes of the men kneeling, who would not dare look up into his eyes. It had only been a few days, but Casca was returning to his own ancient self. His transformation from the slithering sea creature found entangled in the netting to the beast that appeared before their eyes now must have looked miraculous.

Casca's body was repairing itself at an astonishing rate. His left hand, shredded by the rough fibers of the fishing net, ripped ligaments and torn cartilage, was completely healed, having only added a few thin white scars to his collection. His once flattened torso and legs appeared almost to have been expanded, having recovered their round features, as if air had been blown in from an ironworker's bellows. His muscles were thin by any comparison, but they were there.

His feet and toes were still flat, as if they had been pounded by some giant stonemason's hammer, and his nails were gone, but at least the greenish blue stumps were not hurting. The few days' rest and the endless supply of coconut milk and assorted fruits had once again repaired his tortured body.

His once muscular and indefatigable right arm was quite thin and bluish gray, just dangling from his crushed shoulder, but Casca knew that it would soon return to its muscular self, after a few more days of rest and perhaps some swordplay. Casca's left arm was huge in comparison, as it was the only appendage he had used for an undetermined length of time. Looking toward his chest, he saw it covered down to his belt line by a greenish blue raspy beard.

Within its fibers were a few fragments of red coral that Casca reached for with his left hand and untangled from his beard. He threw them to the sand toward his left. The previously always smiling leader suddenly shuddered and fell to his knees, and with meticulous care sifted through the sand with his long knotted fingers and carefully picked up every tiny piece of red coral that Casca had thrown down.

Casca had considered the pieces of coral a nuisance and was quite puzzled at the leader's sudden and almost panicked move. The men kneeling in the sand were virtually hysterical, breathing heavily, sweating profusely, and one of them had even keeled over, rolling about in the sand and clutching his knees like an infant.

Their leader, Ewuare, held the coral cupped in his two hands and offered them to Casca. Understanding that the coral must have some religious or ceremonial significance, Casca accepted the gift, and then, suddenly holding the leader's right hand open, returned the coral.

Ewuare fell to one knee and bowed his head toward Casca's feet. His men, apparently having never seen him such, started moving about on their knees, whimpering like frightened children, letting out cries of terror, drawing blood from their knees. Never having been one to be pleased by superstition, and perhaps not even by too much groveling, Casca decided to end the matter quickly.

Reaching down toward Ewuare with his only strong arm, Casca forcibly helped the black leader to his feet. Within moments Ewuare regained his composure and again started smiling at a very confused Casca.

All the activities and the blazing hot overhead sun had weakened Casca, so he decided to return to the shade of the hut and rest. Understanding this, Ewuare stepped away, enabling him to return unobstructed. Casca entered the straw hut, enjoying the relative coolness of the enclosure, and laid himself down on his makeshift bed.

The young boy very discretely and quietly brought a tray with coconut milk, some more fruit and a bowl of cool water. He had always groveled and kneeled without making any eye contact, but this time he appeared even more frightened. The boy struggled to keep his eyes from Casca, hoping he would not have to look into Casca's eyes. Casca accepted the food, quickly finished it, and then attempted to rest and try to make sense of this new situation.

He awakened the next day feeling much better. He flexed his muscles and stretched his neck, still feeling quite weak and stiff, but his strength was slowly returning. The bitter salty taste of the sea would not leave his mouth and throat, and his ears were still partially clogged, but generally he felt better.

Ewuare entered the hut and sat himself down, crossing his legs underneath him. Gently smiling, showing ivory white teeth that would have made a leopard proud, he looked into Casca's eyes just as he was sitting up in his bed.

"Okhao Olokun, ise."

"Okhao Ewuare, ise." Having heard the same greeting repeatedly the last few days, Casca took a chance and answered the best way he could estimate. He did not know why he was called *"Olokun,"* but that in itself did not matter, as he had been known by many names over the centuries.

Ewuare returned a soft smile as he cautiously looked deep into Casca's eyes. Taking a leather pouch from his belt he unfastened the red leather string around it, opened it, and showed its contents to Casca. The pouch held about a dozen pieces or red coral, probably the ones Casca had removed from his beard the previous day.

Ewuare took the pouch and its contents, placed them against his temples, and then, holding them with both his hands cupped, he placed them against the left side of his chest. Casca could clearly hear the pounding of the man's heart and the quickening of his breath. Extending his right arm, Casca reached out and touched the pouch containing the red coral and then touched Ewuare's forehead.

A smile of elation spread over Ewuare's thick lips. Bowing his head down, Ewuare stood, and then suddenly left the hut. Cries of joy and celebration were heard from outside Casca's hut. That was to be followed almost immediately by singing, whistling and more cries. Casca wondered what had happened, or even more precisely, what he had done. What was the significance of the red coral and of their brief, but apparently important meeting?

Casca spent the next few days resting, eating virtually nonstop—a habit that was easy for him to remember—and spending more time outside his hut. The people of this small fishing village appeared quite happy and pleasant but with all that Casca could not read them. They would bow gracefully, perhaps more frightened than anything else, unwilling to make eye contact, appearing to be quite pleased to be in his presence, but Casca felt they were expecting something in return.

The small village was located at the mouth of a noisy river, the Ovia, as Casca later learned. The Ovia spilled into the ocean while making a small delta inhabited by creatures, most of which Casca could not recognize. The village was situated on a small elevation just south of the delta, near the shore. Turning west Casca moved slowly toward the water.

The breeze shifted, turning in from the sea, bringing a salty taste in the wind, something that quickly made Casca turn away and grit his teeth with disgust. Hanging his head low, he reached for his knees, steadying himself, trying to break free from the nausea that weakened his legs. It was going to take some time before Casca would willfully return to the sea.

There were about forty huts arranged in a circular pattern, carefully constructed and very neatly maintained. They appeared virtually identical in size except the one that was likely Ewuare's. It was nearly three times the size of all others, overly adorned with wooden, ivory and brass shield carvings, depicting faces in all extremes of facial expression. The rest of the huts were quite plain, just single entranced, basic wooden skeletons, covered by dry grass, palm leaves and animal hides.

Leading to the sea was a narrow path, just wide enough for two or three men. The path was not long, barely a short sandy trail, but it allowed the village to be outside the reach of even the longest or deepest tides. Casca again walked toward the ocean, but did not reach the water. Contact with water was more than sufficient if it only involved drinking and perhaps washing. Just thinking about being ankle deep in the salty water would have probably been too much.

The small scalloped bay received the ocean waves smoothly, with likely breakers farther in, allowing the long and narrow boats to coast in gently, in water that was no more than a man's height in depth. Farther north, where the Ovia entered the ocean, the water was more turbulent, almost appearing to boil in certain areas, as the river brought the inland sediments to the ocean.

The wave-beaten shore was like gold dust. Had one found such golden sand anywhere else it would have fooled many. Casca kicked up the sand with his bare feet, staying clear of any long waves that the tide brought in, as his squinting eyes scanned the clear horizon. Once more he turned away from the ocean as the salty air assaulted his nose and throat.

There was nothing to see and he expected to see nothing. Casca was here, but that could have been anywhere or nowhere. Life for Casca was where he was. One place was the same as any other. He knew that he would eventually move on, and was not about to die here, or anyplace else for that matter, as the curse of the crucified Jew would follow him everywhere. There was no reason for concern, as this was just another flip of the hourglass.

The people of this place were more of a concern, as they were acting quite peculiarly, regarding and treating Casca as royalty, perhaps more likely as a god, or a messenger of one. It was not the first time such had happened to Casca. Hundreds of years ago he had had his heart cut out of his chest by people that thought him to be a god. Being thought divine was not as great as one would think, and was definitely not to Casca's liking.

• • •

The days to follow were pleasant. Each day he would awaken to find the young servant waiting, kneeling by the entrance to his hut, carrying fresh fruit, coconut milk and water. The boy would immediately jump and attempt to please, much more than one would who was following orders, or even one who was a slave, but like a man who had the fear of instant death or purgatory followed by interminable suffering. Casca had his own concerns.

It was days before he was able to finally hold the young servant's eyes with his own. It was by no chance that this young man had been selected by Ewuare to take care of Casca. Once their eyes met, it became clear. He was more than a water carrier or banana peeler. Casca had seen young men like him before, boys who were to become leaders of men.

"My name is Casca. Sit with me."

The young man could clearly not understand a word, but was also not about to flee. Whatever was about to happen he needed to stay. *"Asama Yrag, ise,"* he responded.

"Asama Casca, ise." Casca attempted using the language of these people. Looking at the one who called himself Yrag, he tried to communicate. He sat the young boy down and looked deep into his eyes. For some unknown reason, which probably the boy could not even figure himself, he became less frightened. The two had made contact.

For days they spent time together, as Casca tried to decipher the riddle of Yrag's words. For the longest time all the words sounded the same, with no beginning, middle or end, just a series of tones that rose and fell, wavering at the tip of Yrag's tongue until falling one way or another, yet still seeming to have no purpose.

At times the sounds came out of nowhere, as if Yrag were trying to throw his voice for amusement, or as if his lips did not need to move to make the sounds. Even when the sounds appeared to became words and sentences, they still held no meaning. It was a language unlike any Casca had ever encountered. Eventually that changed too. Slowly the sounds became individual words and the words gained significance.

• • •

It had been a few days since Casca had seen the one called Ewuare. All the while he had spent regaining his strength and learning the language of these people. Finally one morning Ewuare entered the hut after Casca had finished his first meal of the day, and sat down cross-legged, as he always did.

Shaking his elephant-surmounted rattle-staff twice, Ewuare created immediate silence. No one would break the silence; it was almost as if nature itself would comply, as if even birds and other creatures were seldom heard following his actions.

''Okhao Olokun, ise.''

''Okhao Ewuare, ise.''

The usual pleasantries were simple and brief, which Casca found to his taste as he had never been one to enjoy endless ceremonial rituals.

''I am very pleased that you have chosen my shores,'' started Ewuare, ''as we have long prayed and waited.

''Once you accustom yourself to dry land, unlike the heavy depth of the sea, your people will be ready to be led by the first one.'' Ewuare did not seem disturbed by Casca's lack of response, as the man apparently had his own timing and plan. He had to be certainly confident of himself while he continued his story, which he thought Casca was well aware of. Casca knew quite well that one could learn more by listening than by talking, as hundreds of years of positioning himself with friend and foe had taught him. Ewuare's words were still unclear, yet the intensity of his will and attempt at communicating enabled Casca to understand more than he had expected.

''The first one'' did not appear to suggest anyone that Casca could identify. Was Casca the first one? . . . or was it some supposed god that Ewuare was talking about? . . . or was it Ewuare himself?

The answer came soon, as Casca learned of this land and its people. Apparently Ewuare was in exile. He was the rightful ruler of many, but he had been banished by his younger brother, who had overtaken the throne of Benin and the Edo people. Oba Awanoshe, the king of Benin, ruled with fear and death, and with the power of superstition he had been able to achieve total control over his subjects. Ewuare, being the older brother, believed himself, as was the belief and custom of most peoples, to be next in line to the throne, but apparently this was not the case.

Casca was unconcerned about the plight of these people or who was the rightful ruler of this land, but for some reason, yet not understandable to him, he felt an affinity toward Ewuare. Perhaps he had seen something in Ewuare's eyes, something he had not seen since a young man named Temujin had clung to Casca, learning all there was to be learned about the art of leadership and war, to eventually become the Khan of all Mongols.

Ewuare believed Casca to be divine, sent by the sea, to help right what had been wronged by Oba Awanoshe. In his mind Casca had been sent, or had come on his own, as the legends had spoken of the bearded one from the sea, carrying red coral as the sign of power and earthly wealth, who would reclaim the throne to the rightful ruler. Ewuare was a man of few words, never having had to say much, as his wielding of the rattle-staff had usually been enough.

The decision came easily. The proximity to the water in itself was unwelcome, as was the thought of following the shore to eventually find a port that could only provide an ocean passage, and the further imprisonment of open water. Living on land, keeping as much distance as possible between himself and the open sea, was a much more appealing thought at this time. Life with these people had been pleasant, but the strange feeling that Casca had toward Ewuare he could not understand. Nevertheless it had affected his judgment.

Ewuare may or may not have been a king, but the mystery would not be solved here. Uncertain of his future and his calling, Casca decided to enter the dark continent. The last few days of rest had healed him, virtually brought him back to life, and even if life was not something he cherished, it was better than life eternally caged.

Casca was very surprised at himself. He had never experienced the feeling of indebtedness, quite a peculiar emotion it was, but if anything could have been, it felt right. If nothing else, he would go through the motions, perhaps finding other sources of pleasure along the way, while overcoming something he never thought he would feel again: a conscience.

NINE

Casca continued down the dusty trail. The four men followed him from a distance, altogether anxious and concerned, but well aware of their duties. Walking in unison, while holding on to the large wooden crate, they attempted to match speed with their hungover, delirious and perhaps mad leader. Casca walked on, staggering left and right, stumbling as he put weight on his stiff and decrepit legs, as an overburdened camel would on rocky or on soggy ground.

The crate contained nine wooden coffers of two different sizes, all covered with brass shielding. The shielding was quite highly worked, depicting men hunting, celebrating and performing certain ceremonial activities that even Casca considered unusual, and even beyond his barbarian tastes. The nine coffers contained an assortment of objects hardly to be considered more than overly ornate trinkets. Oba Awanoshe was to receive these gifts as the quarterly tribute.

Some contained brass cups or shields carefully crafted and adorned, but not something one would consider worthy of a king or divine ruler. One of the coffers held nine daggers with ivory handles, some that Casca actually found of interest. There were more carved ivory figurines, small wooden statues, brass bracelets with round and square links, more brass cups and a few brass plates that held highly polished green stones within their rolled circular rims.

There appeared to be nothing of great value contained within the coffers, except perhaps in the largest of the nine, the one whose contents were not known to any except for Ewuare, who had closed and sealed it. Its size was larger that the other eight, but other than its mystery, it likely held nothing but more of the same.

Neither the large crate nor the nine coffers had locks. The four carried no weapons, except for the small semilunar ceremonial daggers that they kept within leather scabbards trimmed with brass fittings. Ewuare had sent Yrag along to help deliver the tribute, knowing the other three would have been unable to carry out the task without the ability to properly communicate with Casca. The words they might have had, but sometimes that was not enough. Quickly Yrag had proven himself to Casca and Ewuare alike.

Casca found it strange that the quarterly tribute was being transported unlocked and unescorted. Had these men not heard of road thieves? Would the loss of tribute not anger Oba Awanoshe? Was this a land where opportunity did not create an instant thief or murderer? Casca knew he was about to learn much about these people and this strange land.

The road was flat and dusty. It followed the river's every turn, even if it would have made more sense to cut a straight path. Casca turned to see the four follow his steps with their heads bowed, moving in perfect unison, as if they were gliding along the road. Their barren and callused feet kicked up the red dust, creating a cloud impenetrable to the eye, to above knee level, giving the impression of a floating crate with four men attached to it. Beads of perspiration rolled down their sweaty, straining bodies, intermixing with the red dust, painting their legs a scarlet red.

The dust cloud moved down the trail. Casca stretched his drink-stiffened joints, trying to get his ancient blood moving in an attempt to cleanse his poisoned body of the overly copious flasks of palm wine that he had made vanish. *Days had been foul and the drink dangerous,* Casca laughed to himself, recalling the words of past drunken fools.

The mass of female flesh that he had pounded himself against had been quite generous with the drink, hoping to lessen his animal frenzy by dulling his senses and hastening sleep. Most of the men they dealt with would not get their money's worth, because if the drinking did not incapacitate or kill them, their pestilence would. This beast had been different. It reaped fleshly pleasure with the appetite of a thousand impious monks.

Casca gritted his teeth, spitting out dust, sand and the bitter salty taste of the ocean that had been trapped within every fiber of his body and had refused to leave. Covering his eyes from the painful sun with his quivering left hand, Casca moved on toward the heart of the empire.

It would take six days to reach Benin City, the capital of the empire and the sacred city of the Edo people. The first three days he would follow the river basin of the Ovia, the blue river that brought life and death to the ones who believed in it, and worshiped it. The fourth day, once they reached Udo, the city of ivory and the ivory masters' guild, they would turn east and head toward Use, from where they would take the road of Siluko to the walls of the sacred city of Benin.

The days were uneventful. Numerous times Casca questioned his sanity and cursed himself out loud, frightening the four, for having taken this journey to a land where he would be considered divine by some or perhaps to be feared as an evil god, and bringer of death by others. If the four that had sheepishly followed Casca were any indication, these people had been broken into fear and terrified by their leaders and ancestors over many years and perhaps generations.

As the days passed, Casca's strength slowly returned. He would test his power by wielding his long and flat blade, but a heaving chest and burning lungs and arms would soon remind him of his presently decrepit state. His skin was still wrinkled, like salty wet leather left out in the sun too long or the dried-out back of an old elephant, but its greenish hue was slowly wearing away as the penetrating sun's rays quickly bronzed his skin.

As time passed and he distanced himself from the ocean, Casca started feeling better and better. He could still taste the bitter salt, as a constant reminder of his underwater imprisonment, but the thoughts of his new surroundings and unknown future started overtaking his every waking moment, at least for the time being pushing the memories of horror away from his thoughts.

Casca was dressed in a red sash covering him from the waist down, looking more like a wrapped skirt, held up by a belt with leaf-shaped ends tied at his left hip, which also held his long and wide fighting blade. The sword hung in a vertical position, dangling by his sides as he walked, unlike the swords the men of these areas preferred, which were worn horizontally, paralleling their belt lines. The horizontally worn swords, looking more like European daggers, were quite short, not any wider than the width of a man from hip to hip. When death came, it would be close and personal.

The Gladius-like sword that he wore had long been admired by Ewuare and his men. They wondered how a man could effectively wield such a large and heavy weapon with sufficient quickness to defend oneself. Casca had held such swords before, and had taken many lives with its kind, but carrying it was all his muscles would allow for now. His monstrously huge friend Glam, of perhaps a thousand years ago, would have grinned while toying with this broad sword, twirling it as if it were an after meal food pick.

The weight and size of the blade could be to great advantage. Casca had crushed countless skulls, spines and even whole suits of armor with such a weapon. The receiver would not suffer long. If the blade did not kill instantly, the inward collapse of body armor caused sufficient blood loss to terminate any foe. The horror of watching chain mail or breast plate rip through tissue, gushing blood and entrails spewing grotesquely down to their feet was enough to frighten any but the closest of allies.

When needed, he had deflected his opponents' swords with carefully controlled blows, opening up their defenses, making them vulnerable. Chain mails had exploded under its crushing blows, spraying shards of sharp metal around, splinters ripping through the bard of horses, sending frightened men to cover as rearing horses overturned chariots of war. Visions of Rome's arenas rushed through Casca's mind as he tightened the grip on the oversized hilt. For now the proportions of the blade were enough to bring awe and fear to anyone who saw it.

Their journey was not hurried, although they did walk from dawn to dusk, except for a period at midday, when the sun was at its highest and hottest; then they would eat and rest, preferably in the shade of palm trees. The meals were quite satisfying. They would start and end with an assortment of colorful fruits. In between, all foods were washed down with the milk of coconuts, which were plentiful. Meals consisted of dried fish, large bulbous rootlike plants that were baked or boiled, and a delicacy that Casca soon came to favor—roasted or fried lizard.

The four enjoyed the everywhere-to-be-found lizards just slightly roasted, as the lizard's juices would overflow their anxious hands and allow them the extended pleasure of individually licking and savoring every finger. Having resorted to lizards only as last resort, as a source of sustenance, Casca preferred to basically burn them to a cinder and enjoy their singed and crunchy flesh, preferably without having to identify any private internal or external organs, or having to savor their sticky inner juices.

Casca watched the four of them impale the squirmy little creatures on straight or two-pronged sticks and roast them just long enough for the flames to singe their skin and end their lives. From there on they would devour their barely deceased meals with nails that would skin the beasts within seconds and teeth that worked like hundreds of tiny swords.

"This is the best part." Yrag smilingly offered the fleshy inner thighs of the lizards to Casca. "There is no doubt about it." Grinning, with a mouthful of the foul, slithering beast hanging from his teeth, Yrag offered a juicy piece to Casca.

"Must it move while being eaten?" Casca asked with a certain edge of sarcasm in his voice.

Not understanding his intent, Yrag answered between noisy gulps, ". . . It is the only way to truly enjoy their power . . . They give us their fearlessness and cunning . . ." The rest of his words were lost to Casca as Yrag returned to his noisy feeding.

What could he mean by their power? Casca wondered, apprehensive of the answer he was certain to get. He knew it was never wise to inquire when the response was uncertain. His fears were confirmed by Yrag's words.

"The power of the lizard only flows to us when its life has not quite left it. It has provided us with strength for generations."

Not quite understanding Yrag's words, Casca still suspected what the answer had been. "Wouldn't one get more power perhaps from eating a more fierce animal?" he questioned.

Surprised and maybe confused, Yrag continued eating, unsure of what Casca had meant. Rethinking his words, Casca figured how much more difficult it would be to eat the still alive flesh of a more powerful, but also much larger and fiercer, creature. Unfair as it might have been, somehow no people had ever chosen a highly palatable animal as a giver of strength and courage. It always had to be some unsavory beast. Suddenly Casca looked forward to ending the meal and allowing the sweet palm wine, which most of these people, thankfully, also cherished, to wash down the nauseating thoughts and aftertaste.

The five of them reached Udo the afternoon of the fourth day. The village was situated along the banks of the river, with the majority of the settlement on the west side, opposite from where Casca was. Udo was a relatively large community, having over two hundred wood-and-clay houses, as compared to the other smaller villages that Casca had passed along the Ovia. The dwellings were small and circular shaped, with mud floors, thatched roofs and single entrances that were covered with dried animal hides.

There was nothing outstanding about this village, other than perhaps the fear that each man, woman and child seemed to be carrying around in their pained eyes. Their demeanor was of people not knowing if their hearts would still beat when the sun came up the next day.

TEN

On the sixth day, Casca and the four men reached the outskirts of the capital. He was quite surprised and impressed by the grand size and appearance of the approach. The previously narrow road that allowed perhaps six men to walk abreast gradually widened as it reached toward the formal gate that appeared to be the primary, or likely the official entrance to outsiders. The four followed him closely while they made their way through the entrance onto a broad, straight avenue.

"Welcome men of the Uda Territory, welcome to you all," offered a short and robust man as he bowed, leaning over from the waist, becoming eye level with Casca's scarred knees. Tilting his head ever so slightly, Casca met the man's overwrought eyes. The short one appeared slightly nervous and confused as he acted out his role of receiver.

"You have walked many hot days and dusty roads. Welcome to the sacred city and the kingdom of the almighty and powerful son of God, Oba Awanoshe," continued the short one.

Son of God? Casca wondered. Sounded very familiar and quite unwelcome. *Disturbing* was more the emotion that quickly found its way back into Casca's mind; places and people might have been different, but the belief was not. God must surely have had many sons, as most kings and tyrants justified their right to rule with the same rationalization.

"We have traveled long and are pleased to be here," answered Casca simply in his broken, but the best diplomatic tongue that he could muster.

"I am Akheno, second to the great and noble Tajah-Nor, head of the Ibiwe, chief of the *eghaevbo* Nogbe. Your respite awaits you, if you will follow."

A simple name would have been sufficient, as the rest meant nothing to Casca at this time. Likely a flowery embellishment of the man's existence, to make him feel and appear important. He was a doorman, at best, a gatekeeper.

The city had been designed on a grand scale. Rome would have been impressed. The avenues were wide enough to allow ten chariots to race, meeting intersecting walkways with smooth corners, yielding to a complete panorama of the city from every location. It appeared as a large skeleton around which a city was waiting to be built.

The design had been made such by men of idealistic and utopian vision, allowing for privacy of dwelling, territory for ornamentation and expansion around oneself, but not by tacticians or by men of strategy. With its wide-open spaces and broad inlets, without any strategic ambush funnels or channels, invasion and occupation would have made marauders' mouths water. Perhaps this was a land that held no such concerns.

For all its width, most of the city had been built low to the ground on the outskirts. Most houses appeared the same, squarish or circular, with thatched straw roofs and single entrances that Casca had seen before. Farther inside the city, as Casca encountered dwellings of higher importance, the huts grew wider and taller, into houses and eventually into palaces.

The size and complexity increased, with many square galleries, apparent audience halls, formal gates and immaculately maintained courtyards and gardens. The shrubs and flower beds were meticulously maintained, as if they were paintings awaiting frames. Some of the larger palaces held tall turrets that surmounted their gates with highly ornamented brass-work carvings and enormous cast brass birds and snakes. It was a place as anywhere else, princes, chiefs and officials enjoying the best. The rich always did.

People's appearance was as diverse as one's mind could read, if one observed carefully. They all seemed to go about their business, barely noticing Casca and his men led down the walkway by the slightly limping Akheno. Coughing lightly into his left hand, Akheno guided them toward their dwellings. Casca watched the faces of the people, trying to read their fears and daemons. Looking into their quickly shifting and avoiding eyes, he was reminded of the brass and ivory faces on the shields on Ewuare's large hut. Within all their calmness and lack of emotion were faces screaming out.

Akheno lead Casca and his men to their quarters, providing Casca with private dwellings, while the four were directed to a moderate-sized palm leaf-covered hut. The large crate containing the quarterly tribute within the nine coffers was marked and placed into storage next to Casca's sleeping area. The place was clean and appeared comfortable, but it was definitely more than most would ever enjoy.

No sooner had Casca entered his sleeping quarters than he was surprised by the appearance of two young girls, one of them bringing two gold-streamed blue-and-white towels and a large bowl of steaming hot water, while the other held a cloth-covered tray with an assortment of foods. Without saying a word, they eased Casca to sit on a narrow wooden bench and placed his dirty, dust- and grime-covered feet into the hot water. The tingling and warmth of the water felt pleasant as Casca slouched and allowed his still flattened toes to unclench and relax.

The tray of food was placed within arms' reach, and Casca quickly proceeded to devour the steaming fried lizard and baked, sweet, orange-colored roots. Wiping the juices off his face with his hairy left forearm, Casca continued his noisy feeding with his right hand.

Looking down, he watched the two girls professionally and meticulously scrub and wash his still flattened, road-weary feet with a porous rough black stone and a washrag. Once the girls removed his feet from the bowl and started toweling him off from the knee down, his eyes observed curiously the black stone float around the bowl, bounce off its edges as it would hit the rim and spin around.

The girls kneeled by his feet, heads bowed down, with their eyes holding the floor, each using a towel to gently rub and dry his calves then his feet with even, methodical circular movements. After being dried off, he was led to an adjacent room where his clothes were removed and he was helped into a large wooden tub. He was amused watching the two young girls bite their lips and grit their teeth trying not to react to the sight of his unclad body.

The two were quite attractive and looked older than their few years in the world. Probably not much experienced, but that could change quickly. Both had clear and bright eyes, high cheekbones and immaculately kept hair. Most likely sisters, perhaps a year apart, Casca figured.

They both wore yellow wraparound skirts and long bright red-colored cloth tops, reminiscent of kangas, which draped tightly about their chests, accentuating their charms, and were flung over their left shoulders. Their feet were bare and shapely, while their toes were covered with red die, likely some local plant concoction that the girls used to attract young boys and probably drive men crazy. Casca tried making eye contact, but unsuccessfully as the two constantly looked down or shifted their gaze.

The girls continued their duties, without missing a beat even while washing his privates, as if they were some roots they had ripped out of the ground and were washing off or preparing for the evening meal. Still, the feeling was pleasant and Casca was not going to fight it; even if the girls' hearts did not appear to be in it, the reception was quite agreeable and looked promising. Casca's friend and former teacher, the great sage Shiu Lao Tze, had said that bathing induced vapors that were conducive to meditation, but Casca believed different. His thoughts were not so spiritual or contemplative.

Casca had never realized that so much time could be taken to remove a few water droplets from a person's body with a piece of cloth, but again, there was no reason to be impatient, as being pampered was not something one would quickly tire of. It had been too long since anyone had labored so intensively.

He was given a new, long red tunic with golden strands, similar to the caftan that men of northern Africa he had seen wear, with a sash belt into which he was urged to place his long double-edged straight sword. The weight of the great blade stretched and sagged his robe as its tip swung by his feet, barely missing the floor. He was then led to a third room, lit by four oval candles, that bounced light off the ceiling and threw shadows on a long and wide bed that appeared quite inviting to Casca. Laying the long sword down by his side Casca rested.

It was the day before the spring planting ceremony of Ishana. A day for celebration of life and well-wishing for the spirit of the people and the crops that sustained them. The day would start and end with festivities honoring the Oba and his right to rule.

Casca awakened with the first light of day and was pleasantly surprised to find the two young girls, the ones from the day before, standing at his doorway holding a large ivory cup containing some strange-looking concoction and a wooden tray covered with a variety of fruits.

Bowing from the waist, with their eyes nailed to the dirt floor, the two approached and placed the food at the foot of the bed. Taking short, shuffling backward steps, they moved away from Casca until the opposing wall bumped their cushions and held them up.

"*Asama. Asama ise,*" whispered one of the girls.

A greeting, a simple greeting, but without any reference to a name, Casca thought. It was the first time he had not been called Olokun. "*Asama ise,*" the other one also dared, her voice barely louder than the rustling of leaves. The two just stood by the wall, cringing with their eyes, hoping not to be rejected.

Perhaps they just feared his peculiar appearance and his importance in being the leader of the tribute deliverers and knew no more of him. He did appear quite different from all around, Casca knew quite well, in physical appearance and definitely in color, and likely he was the first non-black-skinned man that they had ever seen. His smiling at them with his eyes eased their nerves, allowing them to approach. For some unknown reason the two of them were more uneasy this day than on days past.

At least the silence had been broken, which was welcome in itself, giving Casca the opportunity to attempt to communicate in the language he had just started to learn. His vulgarian tongue would have to twist and contort into shapes that would utter the local savage sounds. Hundreds of barbarian languages he had known over the ages, and it was time to master this one.

Stuffing his mouth to capacity, and only slowing his hurried feeding to breathe, did not help his broken speech. His grunts were no more than those of a drowning or choking man. The girls had underestimated him, as he cleared the plate of food and washed it down with the bittersweet squeezings of some green fruit even before they were able to loosen up their tongues.

The older of the two, Anah, not having thought things out clearly, rushed out, likely to bring more food, without realizing that she was leaving a scared little girl alone with this beast that looked like nothing that anyone had ever seen, except perhaps in their dreams or nightmares.

Approaching her, with a barely perceptible smile, Casca neared the wall, closing in on the slowly shrinking and cowering girl. Raising her gently, with a wrinkled finger under her chin, Casca delicately stroked her forehead and trembling cheek, causing her to close her eyes, while he took in her childish but quite promising beauty. Her golden brown skin glistened from perspiration intermixed with a scented oil that covered her thin arms and legs. Casca breathed in deeply, enjoying the girl's sweet aroma, something that had always aroused him.

Closing his eyes, he felt his chest swell up, trying to take it all in, as his nostrils flared and his eyelids shuddered. The girl's chest rose and fell quickly, under the tightly covered sash outlining her round nipples, as Casca watched a droplet of water run down between her quivering breasts. He wondered who had enjoyed the moment more as he licked a bead of sweat off his upper lip.

The older girl returned to find Casca sitting calmly on his bed, scratching his chin with his thick callused fingers, while the other girl stood by the wall, leaning with her trembling right arm toward the doorway, trying to keep the room vertical. Casca continued his breakfast.

Casca spent the rest of the day enjoying the hospitality thrust upon him, worthy of a king or god. Amused by the bottomless pit that took the shape of a large knotted mass of muscle, Anah and her sister Okuse attempted to test the depth of his insides by offering an endless assortment of fruits, different roasted and fried meats, and sweets that made Casca's teeth hurt just from looking at them. Only the inevitable approach of midday and a change of schedule prevented them from approaching his limits.

Although he was about as clean as he had been in perhaps hundreds of years, he was bathed and washed vigorously three times during the day. He wondered whose benefit this was for, as the two girls seemed to be wearing less clothing while working harder and longer.

"Is there anything we have forgotten, anything you may desire?" Okuse, the younger of the two, inquired. "Anything?" she asked again, her words being brave yet her eyes and face still too fearful to show her intent.

"I did not realize there was more," Casca answered, awaiting her reaction. Anah, the older sister, her eyes unable to blink and her breath frozen in fear, waited. Had her sister lost her mind? she wondered. How dare she be so foolish and brazen.

Realizing what she had said, Okuse tried to escape her words. "Do you desire any more food or drink to please you?" Shaking, she stood pulling at her fingers, hoping that even if her words had been too forward, he would forgive her. "It will do for now. Thank you, Okuse," Casca returned, allowing the girls to breathe and gather themselves.

Nearly delirious, Okuse forced a smile and stood up. How had he even known her name? she wondered. She had never expected a god to speak her name. Realizing her impudence, she reached for her sister, thankful that she had not angered or disappointed Casca. Steadied by Anah, the two bowed for an instant and left his room.

It was not long before they returned, aware of their duties. Anah entered first, carrying thick towels draped over her left arm and holding her sister's hand with the other. Okuse did not seem to be needing any help as she entered the room with a bounce in her step. Raising her eyes, she met Casca's, allowing a soft smile to come onto her lips. Without words they led him toward a warm bath.

Emerging from this most recent bath, Casca stood in front of a large brass mirror watching himself, as he was being dried off. He was not the same man that the ocean had effortlessly swallowed possibly decades ago, to unceremoniously regurgitate due to a chance fishing run, but he was still fierce looking and would have made most warriors wary.

His body, crisscrossed by thousands of faint scars, was not the same huge knot of muscle and sinew that he had been accustomed to. His watery prison had robbed him of much of his strength and size, but had still left him with a ferocious look, and foreboding appearance that most would have been intimidated by. Casca's scraggly hair and recently shaved beard gave him an older look, if that were possible, and he almost thought he could see a few gray hairs.

Was it possible that he had actually aged? Was his interminable life weakened and shortened? He did feel less powerful and different. Lao Tze had said nothing is ever destroyed, only changed. What had he meant by that? Did that apply to all, or only Casca? Had his watery prison finally broken his curse? His questions would not remain unanswered for long.

Casca lost his concentration as the two girls turned him away from the mirror and dressed him in a new yellow tunic. Sitting him down, the older of the two, Anah, stood behind him while combing his hair with a tool reminiscent of a trident, a weapon that many ancient gladiators of Rome had used.

Crouching down, the girl pressed her breasts tightly against the back of his neck and shoulders, rocking in a circular motion, while continuing her work. It was definitely not a chance occurrence, Casca figured, as he could feel the full outline, every contour and detail of her charms. Anah was not to be outdone by her younger sister. Without words, Anah spoke to Casca. The comb's ivory teeth bristled and raked against his scalp as Casca closed his eyes and allowed the moment to pleasure him.

The feeling of pleasure was soon stolen as his mind raced through time, flip-flopping events, empires rising and falling, men and horses running, bodies being ripped and impaled, screaming and dying as the smell of death filled his thoughts. The instincts of the eternal soldier were alive, as the curse would continue. The day to follow would return Casca to the world he knew. The wheel would turn once more.

ELEVEN

It was the day of Ishana. Casca had been dressed as royalty. However, so did everyone else seem to be. Everyone appeared to have just stepped out of a bath, smelling like spring flowers, groomed to perfection, with immaculate hair and ceremonial royal garb. Except of course for the unimportant ones. A strange world it might have been, but was still the same as any.

Casca was reunited with the four who had carried the large crate containing the nine coffers, with all looking well rested and trying to appear unemotional, but with obvious fear and reservation in their eyes, and just a glint of panic. They showed Casca a sign of recognition from a corner of their eyes, but still refused to look at him squarely, except the youngest of the four, Yrag, who smiled and at times seemed to want to communicate with him.

Casca blended into the flowing crowd the best he could by walking between two groups of men carrying crates, while at the same time staying completely hooded except for his eyes, as many others did, and slouched over to hide his size. Walking slowly, matching pace with the bustling crowd, Casca pulled his hands within the sleeves of his robe, trying to hide his distinctly colored hands. Of no consequence, as most around him appeared to be oblivious of his particularity.

Casca scanned the approach to the palace, the wide but still overflowing avenue that sloped upward toward the brass gates that opened into the heart of the palace and the royal court. Hundreds upon hundreds of men, women and children streamed along the road without as much as even one distinct voice being heard through. Like a herd led to a distant river, they quietly advanced.

The royal court was orchestrated chaos. Hundreds, perhaps thousands, stood in groups facing the large doorways, all aligned at an angle to the core of the throughway, appearing as thousands had stood at the ancient amphitheaters of the Roman orators, rhetoricians and entertainers. Without an incline of the land, the mass struggled to stretch to their fullest, bobbing their heads, shifting from side to side, trying to get a clear view of the entrance to the palace. Within all their effort for an unobstructed look, Casca could unquestionably sense their worried and fearful anticipation.

A low murmur dominated the courtyard. About forty pockets of small groups clung to their individual leaders, staying within arm's reach of their loads, but eyeing the contents of the ones around them. All were dressed in long and flowing gold or red cloth, raised just far enough off the ground to avoid dragging and soiling. Most wore sandals woven out of smooth and thin red fiber, while a few walked barefoot, trying to keep their dress from touching their dusty feet. The morning was not yet warm and the western breeze was blowing briskly through from the coast, but Casca noted thin beads of perspiration forming and running down from behind their ears and necks.

A thousand men stood in a semicircle facing the palace entrance, waiting for the opening greeting ceremony, the Ottue, and the appearance of the almighty Oba. Around them, perhaps twice as many armed men stood with their feet slightly apart, holding rectangular brass shields with their left arms, and spears, taller then themselves, raised, with the butt of the shafts against the ground. Their number was much more than a ceremonial formation seemed to need, and their positioning also appeared to indicate more of a guarding or restraining force. Casca stepped toward the front of the crate, leaned slightly against it and watched the day's events unfold.

"This is the way you remember it, is it not?" inquired Yrag. They had not spoken in days, Casca keeping to himself, and Yrag apparently feeling more apprehensive as time passed and they neared the capital and their meeting with the Oba. Likely the discussion of a few days past had been all his nerves had allowed.

Casca was also surprised to be addressed, as virtually no one had spoken to him in days. All they had spoken of was food, staying clear of anything involving destiny or Oba Awanoshe. As for the matter of remembering, he had nothing to remember since he had never been here, except perhaps in the legends and folklore of these people. Looking toward the young one, Casca could see out of the corner of his eye the other three standing at a distance, trembling while at the same time trying to keep an eye on him. Yrag raised his head, while biting his lip, and again spoke.

"Have things changed much since your last visit? You are still pleased, are you not?" asked the very nervous and trembling boy. "I have waited sixteen planting seasons to come and see the son of God," continued a now much braver Yrag.

The son of God? Casca thought to himself. Here he was in a world so distant and foreign, but the cursed words still followed him. Just words, as the son of God could not have been the same.

Yrag's next question or comment was drowned out by the ear-piercing sound of a hundred trumpets. The ivory side-blown trumpets, the *akohen,* were held by the right hands of a hundred proud young men, with their left hands placed firmly on their left hips and their elevated chins angled toward the sky. Their joint sound froze the humanity of the courtyard as the attention of everyone focused on the palace gates.

The broad gates opened slowly, perhaps to add drama to the already tense day, as fifty armed men, wearing loud brass bracelets and holding short swords, came through. They opened a path toward the courtyard, creating a funnel-shaped wedge from the palace gates to the heart of the opening. The fifty were part of the Ifiento, the closest and most faithful of the Oba's soldiers, who cleared the path for him during festivals and ceremonies and unquestioningly defended him to their last breath, if the situation required. Members of the Ifiento remained the same for years, unless the Oba slaughtered them randomly, needing to demonstrate their blind and unwavering loyalty. Loyalty was easily procured by fear in this land.

Facing the crowd, with weapons in hand, they outlined an area into which came seven men, the Uzama, with highly decorated and ornate red flowing regalia. Their chests were covered by intricately worked and decorated sheet-brass cutouts that presumably, but most unlikely, followed the contour of their own physiques. The seven were dressed to the hilt, as apparently the effort had been made to leave no patch of skin or clothing unadorned.

There was no sound. Casca could hear nothing and no one except for his own thoughts, and only the beating of his own heart assured him that time had not stood still, as all around him became motionless.

On a copper-studded leather throne entered the Oba. Four obscenely large men carried the pedestal upon which the *ekete,* the royal leather throne, was moved just outside the palace gates, to the mouth of the wedge the armed men created. Huge masses of sweating flesh shook and reverberated in concert as the four men took their slow and calculated steps toward the enclosure, moving the *ekete* forward. Their clenched fists and straining eyes worked as one, preventing the *ekete* from even the slightest wobble or imperfection in its delivery, as any failing would lead them to a fate that would have made death appear pleasant.

The throne was supported by eight carved ivory legs, made from the long tusks of elephants from the land of Owo, and shielded on three sides by brass facings. Above it, held by four bifurcated, blunted prongs, was a bleached leather canopy that protected the Oba from the sun's rays. The Oba was shielded by darkness and could not be seen.

Tied to the *ekete* by a short, knotted and braided black leash stood a frightfully vicious-looking leopard. Sitting back on its hind legs, with its rear claws grabbing at the dirt, it let out a half-roar half-yawn, exposing its long and pointy teeth, making all around take a quick step backward, hopefully outside the leash's reach.

Then, suddenly, all were on their knees. Never having kneeled to anyone, even in chains, Casca slouched slightly, hoping that his unyielding would go unnoticed within the mass of groveling and whimpering royal subjects. The instant that it took all of them to genuflect went unnoticed by Casca, as time itself appeared to run unevenly and his perception of the events became unclear. The moment seemed to last forever, as the Oba was likely enjoying his power.

With the strident sound of a long *ukhurke,* the royal ivory rattle-staff, the wallowing ceased for the moment as all present regained their feet. The Oba used the rattle-staff, the symbol of authority transmitted through the father from all previous kings, as a magic wand to direct his people. Its sound was unmistakable, but its message varied, as its commands could mean death or unimaginable pleasure.

Casca was unable to see the *ukhurke,* but its sound was quite familiar as he had seen Ewuare use it numerous times with instantaneous results. Its symbolism and authority was limitless, as its power through fear and mysticism ruled the people of this land.

The trumpets sounded again as the throne was placed on the ground. The seven lavishly dressed chiefs, with studded ceremonial eben swords thrust in their scabbards, approached the throne one by one. Although staying clear and keeping one eye on the leopard, they kneeled on their left knees, offering their homage to the Oba, the son of God. Oba Awanoshe, still unseen, could be heard accepting their loyalties and interminable words of fidelity and eternal faithfulness.

In return, the chiefs received gifts of kola nuts placed into ekpoki boxes, and bladders filled with sweet and intoxicating palm wine, which demonstrated their devotion and their acceptance of the Oba's divine superiority and their own place in the court's hierarchy. As the last of them completed their homage to the Oba, the trumpets sounded again, indicating the end of the greeting ceremony of Otue.

One of them, a giant of a man, clearly possessing superior physical powers to the other six, caught Casca's eye, as he seemed to just be going through the motions of the ceremony, bowing less and not allowing his knee to touch the ground while he genuflected. His stone-like face exhibited the same subjugated, pious look as the rest of them, except for his dark eyes, which showed intelligence and insight beyond the ones around him. His symbolic lack of loyalty was subtle, but Casca's eyes immediately picked up the inconsistency.

"Ugie Erha Oba, Ugie Erha Oba," sounded out the voice of five men in unison. They stood like marble statues, with their heads held high, looking toward the sky, with their hands clenched into a fist aiming at the ground, while standing shoulder to shoulder on the inner perimeter surrounding the royal assembly. Their eyes appeared hollow and without life, not unlike those of one drunk on potion or spiritless from self-hypnosis.

A wave of shock and fear spread through the courtyard. Men started milling around, like sheep aware of the butcher's knife before a feast, unable to keep their place and their quiet, but unwilling to yell out.

Ten armed members of the Ifiento calmly and unceremoniously walked over to the five that had yelled out and escorted them to within ten paces of Oba Awanoshe's throne. The five complied without resistance, like cattle led to greener pastures.

"Ugie Erha Oba is no more, only Oba Awanoshe, the only son of God," bellowed an unseen voice as five bleeding heads left their bodies, spraying the crowd with their red death, rolling to the feet of the throne.

There were no screams or cries from the crowd. They had expected no different. The blood of the five flooded the immediate area around the throne, creating a sticky, blackened red mud as their life juices seeped into the dirt. The bodies were casually dragged away with the brass-tipped hooks of wooden staffs, leaving curved, snail-like, bloody trails, while the heads were allowed to remain and stare with lifeless hollow eyes into the crowd.

The palace ceremony continued. Within moments it was as if they had all forgotten, or the bloodletting had never happened, almost as if it had been planned and rehearsed. The five had been fools or fanatics. More likely, a simple demonstration of Oba Awanoshe's control and power, as he appeared to rule with fear and death.

The more things changed the more they stayed the same, as to rule by fear was, to rule completely, Casca thought. Many times past he had witnessed and taken part in such. This was a place not unlike others. The rattle-staff sounded again, initiating the tribute presentation.

A parade of men and animals crossed the path of the throne. Boxes filled with precious stones, brass and ivory carvings, bracelets and neck ornaments enriched by rare stones, daggers large and small, ornate and plain, bowls and plates, were presented to the Oba while men kneeled and groveled on their bellies, eating dust and sharing the dirt with bodiless heads, smearing their own bodies with the blood that had been spilled earlier, until allowed to rise.

Quite a distasteful sight, but Casca had expected no different. The smell of an ancient and decadent Rome filled his nostrils and awakened memories.

The *eghaevbo-nore,* administrators of the kingdom territories, had walked many days to bring their respects to the king, while trying to earn his acceptance and permission to live, as tolerance was all they had prayed for, or at least admitted to. Man and beast alike had come from all corners of the kingdom, as town chiefs had traveled themselves or sent their most trusted representatives to carry the quarterly tribute.

The territories had offered and sent their best. People of Hausa-Fulani, Ibo, Efik, Ibibio, Idoma, Ijo, Itsekiri, Kanuri, Tiv, Uhobo, and Uda had worked hard to please and placate Oba Awanoshe, as his wrath and minuscule patience were well known. The improper delivery or presentation of tribute had at times in the past led to death, or worse, as Oba Awanoshe had a way with pain. Adjacent kingdoms of Yoruba, Igbo and Igal had escaped his fury due to their distance and refusal of loyalty, something Casca later learned had greatly infuriated the Oba over the years.

"What refuse have you brought this year, Omobo? You are not planning to insult our Oba again, are you?" Chief

Edolo, one of the six Uzama, laughingly demanded. "Even your life must be worth something."

Omobo-Oro, the *eghaevbo-nore* of the Kanuri, brought his men and four beasts of burden to a stop. Shaking visibly, he motioned for his men to remove a large box from the back of one of the animals. Omobo coughed, clearly trying to gather himself and be able to deliver his short speech without his parched throat hindering him.

"I have brought wonderful things . . . It has taken us months to forge these special weapons. They are stronger than anything we have ever made before . . ." Omobo quieted down, cutting his delivery short as one of the Oba's men approached his tribute.

"Open the coffer, let us see!" Chief Edolo demanded.

Casca watched as ten long swords along with ten short, curved daggers were removed from the cloth-covered box. "They look no different than what you brought last year, and you well know what happened to those," Chief Edolo angrily demanded.

"The sword broke in one of the Uzama's hands," Yrag whispered into Casca's ear. "The man lost his eye and left arm, it is a well-known fact. He died after days of fever and misery," Yrag continued. "His loss was not forgiven by the Oba. All the couriers, other than Omobo, were executed," Yrag added as Chief Edolo approached Omobo and his swords.

"I am sure you remember what happened, Omobo?"

"That will never happen again. I am placing my life in your hands." Standing tall, he raised his chin confidently and addressed Chief Edolo and the rest of the Uzama. "We used the winds of the west to feed the flames of our forge. The fire was hotter than ever before. The metal was turned a hundred more times as my men tempered the steel. This steel will not fail you," Omobo insisted, breathing heavily, showing enthusiasm and certainty in his words.

"The winds of the west?" Chief Edolo inquired.

"Yes," Omobo enthusiastically continued, "we have learned how to harness the winds with special chambers. This allows the bellows to blow harder and longer, softening the metal, allowing us to control it. These will not fail you," he repeated his assertion.

Chief Edolo picked up one of the long swords and quickly smashed it against the thick brass shield one of his guards carried. Stunned by this, the guard fell back while still holding his buckled and ripped shield.

The sound shattered the silence, with all eyes riveted on Omobo. Would his head join the ones staining the dirt below? Confidently Omobo watched Chief Edolo survey the new sword.

Chief Edolo held the sword up into the sun with his left hand, while his right thumb passed over the fine edge of the blade. He knew steel was stronger than brass, but he had still expected to see at least some mark on the new sword. There was none to be found.

"These swords are not unacceptable." Chief Edolo nodded. "You will get to see your fat wife again," he laughed, "until next time that is."

"I thank you" was all Omobo was able to say, as he quickly backed away, allowing the day to continue.

The procession of men, animals and gifts continued until the sun bore down and burned from overhead. At times the *eghaevbo-nore* were put to the test, needing to demonstrate their loyalty and affection for the Oba, at other times having their tribute scrutinized and proven worthwhile. Not all were as fortunate as Omobo.

The pathetic ceremonial groveling and whimpering continued, only interrupted, quite infrequently, by Oba Awanoshe's grunts of acknowledgement and the growls of the half-asleep leopard, which licked its lips and pointy eyeteeth while it watched the crowd. It seemed as if every *eghaevbo-nore* brought or at least tried to present his tribute as being better or more appropriate and fitting for the Oba. Casca's distaste grew over the seemingly endless morning hours.

Most of the tribute was more of the same, differently presented or exhibited, but without any substance. The weapons appeared quite small, other than the ones Omobo had presented, and useless in battle, while the rest could not have sold for more than a gold coin, on a good day to a blind and brainless fool.

It seemed unreasonable that the tribute presentation had any other purpose than allowing the Oba to enjoy his power and control over his subjects. Casca wondered if the swords brought by Omobo would get the attention they deserved. He had seen what power such forged weapons held.

Some robes made of fine cloth attracted the Uzama's attention, along with intricately worked jewelry that the Uhobo presented. The Efik couriers brought four bull elephants, huge monsters that could help the Edo builders move trees and boulders. A few carts offered by the Itsekiri appeared sturdy, with well-designed harnesses that could carry man and materials alike. Other than that there was nothing of note.

The men of the Uda territory were next to present their quarterly tribute. Casca led the four men as they cautiously lifted and carried the large crate toward the center of the enclosure. Casca had kept himself covered up, and his foreign and frightening appearance had gone unnoticed by all.

The crate was lowered and allowed to rest gently on the sticky ground, within ten paces of the royal throne. The ceremony would continue, as Casca would be the one to receive the shock of the unexpected.

The large crate was quickly opened and its contents displayed to the Oba and the crowd. One by one the coffers were opened by the four men and walked to the foot of the *ekete,* from where the still unseen Oba could appraise and scrutinize them. Casca observed the complete lack of interest of all involved, from the men who had carried the royal throne to the seven ridiculously overdressed men of the high council.

Anaken, the *Ezomo* of the High Council, the one who had shied from genuflecting, and the now standing leopard were the only ones to show any signs of interest or acknowledgment. Further, behind the sea of the Oba's men, Casca noted a tall, overgenerously endowed woman push her way through the guards, trying to get a better look at the developing situation.

Through all that was unfolding Casca still noted her deep, almond-shaped brown eyes, radiant face and obvious charms, something that Casca had always had a weakness for. The amount of gold he had spent on such women over the centuries would have paid for a king's ransom.

The leopard started growling as it clawed the air and

exposed its long and shiny yellow teeth. No one appeared to be concerned for their safety, but its reaction stirred the crowd and brought a low murmur to those around it.

The last and largest of the coffers was removed from the crate by Yrag. With his sweaty, trembling hands holding the bottom edges of the box, the boy carefully placed it within arms' reach of the throne. Quickly, Yrag back-tracked, with his head down while leaning over from the hips, leaving the sealed coffer unattended.

"What surprises do you bring to us, young Yrag?" Chief Edolo questioned. "I suppose Ewuare was too busy to grace us with his presence," he continued showing clear contempt for Ewuare. Casca himself wondered, realizing what could become of them because Ewuare, the *eghaevbo-nore* of the Uda territory, had sent a boy to deliver the tribute.

"Such a small box, even if filled with gold it could not grace our Oba . . ." Chief Edolo quieted down from the sudden sound of the rattle-staff.

Concern and near apprehension seized Casca's mind as he also wondered what importance the box held, and what reaction he would witness. The rattling sound of the Oba's wand of power quieted the immediate crowd as all eyes were fixed on the mysterious box. Another sounding of the rattle-staff quickly produced its contents, as one of the high officials, Tajah-Nor, head of the Ibiwe, approached and broke through the seal.

The slender and frail-looking man kneeled down by the box, quickly dispensing of the burned red clay seal, and removed a small brass vessel, an *iru,* and a long, orna-mented rattle-staff topped by a large elephant head embed-ded with small pieces of red coral for its eyes. For an instant his hands quivered, struggling to hold the two objects, while his coal black face and neck actually appeared to flush and turn pale.

He struggled drawing his breath, trying to allow air into his lungs through a closed-up and gurgling throat, like a man choking on a lump of food or a well-placed fist. Casca's squinting eyes probed him, as an unreasonable and baseless familiarity with the man puzzled him for a fleeting moment.

Slowly raising himself, Tajah-Nor took the few steps that brought him underneath the overhead canopy and to the Oba's side. The seconds of silence felt like an eternity for most around, allowing Casca to take in and observe the situation and those involved.

Tajah-Nor stood by the throne, with his arms and legs visibly shaking, bowing to the Oba while presenting the two items. For the moment he looked like a man more concerned with his own existence and circumstance, shaken beyond reason, trying to cloak his own gasping for air with a quivering left hand.

In the shadow of the breeze-fluttered canopy sat a figure hidden from Casca's eyes. A silence spread over the courtyard as the throne creaked and the Oba raised himself. Casca had seen enough for a thousand lifetimes, but his eyes and mind were not prepared for this. This was a man whose equal he had never seen. In front of the throne stood Oba Awanoshe.

TWELVE

Casca looked toward the Oba's eyes, but he could not find them. They were there, but Casca could not comprehend what he was seeing or even focus on them. The eyes were a whitish pink held in an invisible pool of light. Drawing his head back slightly, Casca attempted to size up the beast.

The Oba stood tall and slender, with his red *ododo* ceremonial robe streamed with golden fibers rippling in the wind, creating a whitish yellow haze that in itself prevented a clear view under the canopy. "Come to me!" Voices seized Casca's senses.

Like the hot winds of the desert that shifted the sands and brought death to many, the fluttering created a mirage that the mind's eye struggled to decipher. The creature was paler than anyone or anything Casca had ever seen. In an ocean of dark bodies and faces stood the feared leader, so unlike all the rest.

The crowd was quiet, not at all surprised by the appearance of the Oba, more likely fearful of his untimely and unpredicted actions. The divine Oba would never rise during a ceremony; as it had been for hundreds of years.

The royal throne, the *ekete,* served to transport the Oba, and if he needed to get a better view of the surroundings, the surroundings would be moved or the *ekete* raised and turned. The Oba never stood or moved, as his subjects were not worthy of observing or scrutinizing him, unless he was displayed on a pedestal.

Casca was not aware of all this, or even concerned, as the unexpected appearance of the Oba ruled his senses. This was a creature unlike any. A low murmur and a nervous shifting about broke the silence as Oba Awanoshe slowly turned his gaze toward Casca.

"Welcome, Olokun, I have been awaiting you, as you well know. The words of the ancients from Ife have come true. Your arrival has already enhanced my power and strengthened my empire."

Pulling himself to his full stature, Casca discarded his robe, revealing to the crowd a contorted form, perhaps even more strange and unexpected than Oba Awanoshe's. The men around Casca shrunk back, astonished by the sight of this huge mass of scars and muscles, anchored on legs that looked like the sun-dried roots of a giant olma tree.

This creature could not have been of earthly origin, the fearful crowd thought, as its skin would have long darkened over the years, or it would have died from all the wounds it appeared to have suffered, unless it too was a God, sent by Osanobua, the Supreme One.

The blank stare of the dead eyes caught Casca's as the head of the Oba turned. Their eyes held each other as thoughts of strength, fear and uncertainty reverberated between their minds. Casca struggled to hold his own, as this strange creature seemed to possessed a hypnotic glare. "Come to me!" The words entered his mind once more. For an instant Casca felt overwhelmed, as the piercing hollow eyes created a trance that reached deep into his soul, searching his every inner thought.

Casca's heart slowed as a numbingly warm and stupefying wave spread through his veins, slowing his breathing and causing his fingertips to tingle. This was more than any drink could have done, as it quickly and mercilessly stifled his body. It was as if his mind were slowly being raped.

"You have come home. The Brotherhood is pleased . . . Your soul may rest now." With the obscene words, memories of the Brotherhood of the Lamb and their evil doings, came back to haunt Casca.

A slowly darkening and veiled stupor surrounded and overtook Casca and his immediate surroundings, as all within his sights disappeared, except for the iron contact that his mind and soul had with Oba Awanoshe. Thoughts of the Brotherhood's desperate search for him entered his mind. Could they have found him in a world so distant and alien? Oba Awanoshe could not be part of them . . . the pain of years and memories past returned to torture Casca. The connection was too much, as time and space whirled around, spinning a drunken dance, ripping Casca away from the present, toward the darkest and most cursed times of his past.

Casca's thoughts flashed back to that cursed and fateful day on Golgotha, when he as a young and brash legionnaire had plunged his spear into the tortured and suffering chest of Christ. The taste of the salty blood that had sprayed upon his face all those centuries ago burned his lips again. The words of the bleeding and dying Christ appeared on his lips as Casca's mind raced through the next thousand years.

"Soldier, you are content with what you are . . ."

Suddenly awakening from his torturous nightmare, Casca wondered if this strange creature could conceivably read or know any of this. While trying to maintain his sanity, Casca tightened his gut and bit the inside corner of his lip, drawing blood, trying to shake himself, hoping that the pain would break him from the momentary trance.

An instant later Oba Awanoshe broke contact, just as Casca's instincts perceived a narrow wall of fear. Gasping for breath, Casca steadied himself.

Reaching with a thin, cadaverous arm, Oba Awanoshe removed the *odigba*, the coral-beaded head collar worn by the Oba during ceremonies, exposing his shoulder-length, raspy, chalk white mane. His ivory-colored hair hung bellow his shoulders, lying against his back, unlike the others, whose hair was short or was arranged tightly beneath their ornate head ware. His bony and haggard shoulders pushed through his robe, further accentuating his emaciated, deathlike appearance, but it was his eyes that engrossed Casca's mind.

It was a strange world. Casca had known many dark-skinned ones over the years, from his early days as a gladiator in Rome, where Jubala, the giant monstrosity from Numibia, had almost ripped off Casca's testicles and changed their place with his eyeballs, to his exploits in northern and eastern Africa. Friends he had had in the dark continent to be eventually taken away by time or war.

He had met, fought alongside and against many dark men, men whom he had known for decades or for the instant that a dagger flashes through one's heart and ends life—but this was different. This one was quite different. His physical strength would have likely made no one fear him, but the aura his eyes and presence created were beyond anyone or anything Casca had ever encountered.

"Approach me, Olokun," came the thin and frail words of the Oba. The words appeared to be spoken softly, but the message was engaging and penetrating. "We will conquer many, as our campaigns will be the source that songs for all future generations will feed from," he continued.

This was madness. These were not the words of a man. No sane man would dare speak such to one he considered a deity. Casca had met many who believed themselves predestined to conquer a people or a land, but Oba Awanoshe appeared to be beyond that in self-belief and self-righteousness.

The creature was not crazy. Perhaps insane, since he believed his words and appeared to envision his destiny. Was this leader any different from the others? . . . Perhaps his appearance and demeanor were, but he used that as his source of overpowering control and leadership . . . Was Oba Awanoshe truthful or was he hiding something? . . . His approach bordered on insanity, as no leader with any reason would want to anger his own God, Casca thought as he tried to regain full control of his senses.

The Oba's words and wants were quite similar to the words of most rulers Casca had met over the centuries. The circumstances may have been different, but the basic reality was still the same. Casca took two unwanted steps toward the *ekete* as the Oba continued.

"The signs have been right, Olokun, God of the sea and

bringer of wealth and earthly possessions.'' The Oba reached out toward Casca and then the sky as the sleeves of his robe fell back, revealing two thin, bleached-out spiderlike arms. His bony right arm shook, sounding the rattle-staff, again bringing a whimper, then quiet to the crowd.

''The tribute you have brought me will lead us to certain victory, as my army will prevail carrying the sign of Olokun for its flag, as all will yield. My forces will be invincible.'' The mass of bodies in the courtyard trembled as one, shaking in anticipation and fear of the Oba's words.

''The harvest ceremony will bring more than it ever has. Before one grain is gathered, I will have all. My kingdom will reach to the ends of the worlds we know, to the frontiers of lands we are yet to learn about and conquer. The dogs of Yoruba, Igbo and Igal will know the wrath of Oba Awanoshe.''

The dazed and bewildered masses raised their heads toward the sky, as if hypnotized, and started chanting Oba Awanoshe's name in unison. A dark shiver of realization and doom ran down Casca's spine, as the words and reaction he was witnessing were quite commonplace in the annals of his mind. The frightened multitude of wretched souls responded in fear as Oba Awanoshe mastered them like infants.

The words he had heard often over the years, perhaps differently phrased, but the message had been the same. The smell of war was in the air, as another madman was about to send thousands to their bloody deaths, trying to meet his fate while taking his turn in conquering the world.

Standing within a few feet of the Oba, scrutinized by thousands of fearful dark brown eyes, Casca laughed to himself, amused at how quickly and easily he had gotten himself into another predicament. The land or people did not matter, as Casca always seemed to manage to find a conflict, and become reluctantly the hero to commence or terminate such.

These words Oba Awanoshe had likely spoken many times before, but the circumstances, due to Casca's presence, had made them more plausible and prophetic. The words of the ancients from Ife were echoing in the minds of many. Perhaps Oba Awanoshe was truly the son of God, and Olokun had returned to lead them to unimaginable prosperity and glory, and to the fulfillment of the prophecies. The ocean of men quieted, awaiting Casca's words.

"I am pleased to be here," Casca answered starkly, as he tried to read the Oba's reaction to his simple response. Casca's response was brief and without any great meaning, as the nature of Oba Awanoshe's reaction to his presence was not clear.

Ewuare had sent Casca to bring fear and uncertainty to Oba Awanoshe's mind regarding his right to the throne, while Oba Awanoshe acted as if a prophecy had come true with the delivery of Olokun, God of the sea. Oba Awanoshe behaved as if Casca were nothing more than a simple talisman, delivered to him as a trinket and bringer of good luck for his own personal gain. Casca wondered if he were merely a pawn in the intricate posturing between two brothers, caught in a classic dispute over the throne, or, more likely, just within a few steps of a true madman.

The day continued, as Oba Awanoshe made no further eye or verbal contact with Casca. Following their dramatic, but unfinished, standoff, Oba Awanoshe paid Casca attention no more than officially accepting the tribute, and then continued with the ceremony. Casca was treated no differently than any of the tribute deliverers, which in itself appeared unreasonable, as Casca's unusual appearance was usually enough to create panic, or at least a nervous stir. The Oba's attempt at placing himself on a higher pedestal than a supposed god was fairly transparent to Casca, as he could see confusion and fear in the eyes and faces of the Uzama, the high council.

They appeared to be uncertain whether Oba Awanoshe had truly gone mad, or possibly they themselves were witness to something larger than they dared imagine. Anaken, the *ezomo* of the high council, seemed to be the only one to remain unperturbed by the situation, as he carefully eyed Casca while weighing the moment. As usual, he could see beyond the surface.

This had surely been a new experience, Casca mused, as he had never met a man so brazen to consider himself above a god. Even the maddest had always kept their insolence and defiance in check, as even they held hidden fears and doubts.

The ceremonial day of Ishana concluded uneventfully, as no more blood was spilled, other than during the ceremonial sacrifices held by the *eghaevbo* Nogbe, the palace chiefs, during the bloody ritual of Igue. The bloodletting commenced without much warning, as a sheep, a goat, a large dark predatory bird, four rams and a hideous crocodile were quickly put under the knife.

Their lifeblood flowed into a large bowl and was quickly stirred with a flat and elongated ivory hand piece. As the blood of the creatures intermixed, warm with the cold, and thin with the thick, a long camel's hair brush was introduced into the bowl. Ooton, the old master of wandering souls, he who allowed life and death to flow without direction, having cheated death itself according to legend, made his presence known.

The thin and frail-looking man, possibly anywhere between forty and a hundred years of age, approached the putrid concoction. With a surprisingly steady and deliberate right hand, he stirred the brew once more with the brush and then approached the Oba's feet.

His withered features were death itself, as he would easily have been mistaken for a week-old sun-dried corpse, had he not moved. His wicked cough echoed of many years spent on a black pipe, as he sputtered a blackened bloody spray. The old one's vacant eyes and sunken orbits gave chills to all around, and even the Oba's gaze shifted, clearly disgusted by the sight.

With quick and short strokes Ooton produced two symbols upon the Oba's emaciated white shins. Casca noted nothing more than tolerance in the Oba's dead eyes as he tried not to make direct contact. The ceremony was so powerfully symbolic that the Oba would not do without it, no matter how much distaste he held for it.

"Forever may you live, Oba Awanoshe, the only son of God," Ooton hissed from his toothless mouth. "Water and land will receive their master now," he continued. "The signs have been correct, mighty one . . . Olokun is here to serve."

Oba Awanoshe stood in front of the *ekete,* emotionless,

almost like a man frozen in the icy wind, his face having kept the same look of distaste throughout the ceremony. Casca watched this obscenity unfold, nearly stunned by the mesmerized faces of the thousands who stood, praying to their icon, Oba Awanoshe.

The symbols were of water and land, something Oba Awanoshe claimed to be the overseer of. Oba Awanoshe had always found the ceremony to be quite repugnant, but it allowed him to renew his mystical powers and mastery over the elements. This would reaffirm his unlimited power over his subjects, as all would bow to the one that ruled creatures of water and land. Thousand stood like sheep led to a slaughter—conscious, yet unwilling to question. This bloodletting was nothing compared to the carnage that was to follow.

THIRTEEN

Days and weeks that followed were uncertain discomfort and overwhelming ecstasy. The frightened Edo people waddled in constant groveling and interminable genuflection at the mere sight of the scarred stranger, while Oba Awanoshe acted as if Casca were a simple good luck charm, a timely located rabbit's foot, to aid his cause and his empire.

The people of this land appeared to be strong willed and clear minded, except when it came to the belief in their gods, something that Oba Awanoshe seemed to take clear advantage of. The Edo knew the true legend of Olokun, the bringer of wealth and earthly possessions, but their fear of Oba Awanoshe controlled their minds even in their most private dreams, not allowing the words of the ancients to uncloud their thoughts.

Casca's life was pleasant and undemanding. His every whim and desire was cared for instantaneously to a degree that he had not seen since over a millennia ago when he had traveled to the New World. The people of this land, as most loyal and frightened subjects would, were pleased beyond reason to serve. Fear of the unknown was a powerful initiator. Many would spend hours or days watching his dwellings, hoping to catch even a fleeting glimpse.

When in public, Casca often sensed a deep and private pain in these people. His time and schedule were under no demands, other than selective ceremonies, when his appearance would bring happiness or fear to the Oba's subjects, depending on the Oba's desire.

Any and all earthly pleasures were within a blink of an eye, or the most subtle turn of his head or motion of his hands. Most likely he would never spend more than an instant feeling even the remotest hunger pang. His two loyal caretakers, Anah and Okuse, made certain of that. Food was always available and perfectly prepared. It was of the right temperature, size, consistency and always overly abundant.

There was not much need for anything more than for Casca to point, open his mouth, chew a few strokes, then swallow. A thin hand holding a mouth wipe would soon follow every morsel of food. Sweet palm wine would not be far behind.

"I trust we have forgotten nothing," Okuse often added, making certain there was no chance of any misunderstanding. "It would be unforgivable if we did," she would insist flashing a devilish grin. Anah no longer asked, and when alone with Casca, she made certain to leave a memorable impression.

Life was nearly perfect. His belly was never less than full, and any other desires he might have had were almost miraculously fulfilled. At such times Casca wondered if there really was anything more that he could possibly have wanted. The two young girls were eager to serve in all ways. Not wanting to disappoint them, he gladly obliged.

Within a few days his clothes no longer fit, as Casca watched his waistline expand, giving him the appearance of a bloated water hog. Looking at his reflection in a wall-mounted shield, Casca could no longer see the narrowing of his waist from the chest down, as his distended belly started overflowing. Every angular or robust feature had been replaced by sagging and rounded flesh. Any visible bulges were not of the muscular type.

The feasting pleased him, but the sight nauseated him more. Resisting pleasure was something that Casca, or any man for that matter, would struggle to master. He wondered if he could make up for the hundreds of combined years when fate had been unkind to him. Perhaps so, but Casca also realized that by then he would be unable to leave the walls of his dwellings.

Free time, which was overly abundant, allowed Casca to observe and learn about these people. He often watched men and even the youngest of boys handle spears, shields and copper-studded maces, flailing away endlessly, jabbing, thrusting and blocking, trying to master the weapons and themselves. All men had to be able to handle the weapons of war and be at the ready at a moment's notice. The sounds of metal on metal could be heard from dusk till dawn. War was never far away in this land.

Swordplay was always available, as any and all males old enough to handle a weapon were ecstatic to provide a challenge at a moment's notice. God or no god, they could not resist. Casca's heavy sword was unmatched, as his ever quickening and accurate blows had undressed the best that so far had been offered. The weight of his sword would easily parry opposing blades or crush shields as if they were eggshells. His make-believe adversaries would offer all their skill, to be quickly thwarted with minimal effort.

"I am ready to best your arm" were Yrag's words every time he challenged Casca's sword. "I have rested and eaten well. My arm is swift and powerful."

The words did not change much, becoming almost a way of greeting when swordplay was to be had. Casca had taken even more of a liking to the boy in recent days, realizing it was by no random chance Yrag had been sent along.

"This may just be your day," Casca often answered, "the night has been short and without sleep." His nights had been brief, yet rewarding, definitely not enough to weaken his arm. Contrary to what most believed, the sleepless nights only strengthened Casca.

A strong feeling of understanding, almost of friendship, developed quickly between them, allowing Casca to feel more and more at ease, often allowing himself an escape from what the people of this land perceived him to be. Yrag rarely even questioned Casca's existence with his eyes. Perhaps clouded by youth or faith, he essentially believed this was the prophecy of the ancients playing itself out. If swordplay was what Olokun, god of the sea, wanted, then swordplay he would get.

Casca and Yrag often crossed swords for hours, challenging the midday sun that mercilessly burned from overhead. Anah and Okuse watched them with concern, cheering them on, hoping no injury would come to Yrag. Eventually Yrag's wild, uncontrolled rushes were slowly replaced by strategic, well-thought-out plans of attack. He feverishly labored, hoping that perhaps for once his heaviest blows could disarm Casca's arm and make him vulnerable to a counterstrike.

"Your sword is too heavy," he often complained, every time Casca knocked his sword or shield out of his hand with a flick of the wrist. Grinning while gathering his strength, he would retrieve his sword and regroup, hoping that perhaps the next time would be the time when Casca's defense failed him.

Exhausted by the draining sun, Yrag rested on his sword, the tip digging into the dirt, holding his wrenched body. Sweat poured down his arm, flowing over his clenched fist, running down the length of the long sword. Gasping for breath, he tried gathering his words.

"Are you not pleased to be called Olokun?" Yrag startled Casca with a query. "Are you known by another name perhaps?"

Smiling at the nearly delirious boy, Casca approached him. "I have been known by many names." Casca remembered having been known by a dozen names, by friend and foe over the years, names that he could not recall and names that he did not want to remember.

"Casca Rufio Longinus is what I was first called."

"That is too many names—" Yrag caught himself too late, slapping his mouth with his left hand, aware that he had just challenged a god.

Casca smiled realizing Yrag was probably right, his smile eased the boy's momentary panic. It was too many names after all. "Casca will do."

"Ufio? That means 'bravest one.' That is what my people need."

Casca thought back to nearly the beginning of time, when his uncle had used to call him "Ufio," teasing him anytime he had showed weakness in front of strangers. To Yrag names did not matter; Casca was here as the ancients had prophesized. To what end? That would have to wait for now. The passage of time tore at Casca, once again punishing him more than even the slash of a blade. A melancholy feeling overtook him as he realized he had not thought of his family for hundreds of years.

Swordplay continued for hours each day, strengthening Casca's arm and soul. Without a long reprieve, the soldier in him was returning. Surprisingly, this was the first time that Casca actually felt Yrag and the people of this land appear comfortable facing him. This was something they could relate to, while all else that Casca represented was frightening and a mystery to them. Questions he had would have to hold for now, as the puzzle would eventually unfold. And then there was Ary.

Ary took good care of him. No one could ever question her reason for being. It was as if the perfect being had been created with him in mind. A flaw would not have found its way beside her. Not unlike Iriena of centuries ago, she who had found the sleeping warrior at the top of a mountain, Ary never questioned his reason for existing.

Iriena had listened to the legends of the frozen warrior who one day would come alive and save her and her people from the marauding savages who always seemed to find their way into her home village. She had waited long and listened to many tales of her savior who would come when needed to liberate her people.

Iriena had never questioned or hastened Casca's actions. Casca had saved her and her village when all seemed to be lost, taking her away and even giving her a child. Unknown to her, their child, Demos, was not of his seed. Casca had been cursed to live forever, but no one would keep him company over the centuries. His curse would not allow it. No one would be born of him.

Ary did not question either. She knew her place was with him, beside him, to support yet not to query his actions. When Casca would watch her, trying to find the thoughts behind her penetrating brown almond eyes, he found nothing but acceptance of what was to be. Her only answer would ever be ". . . The time has not yet come . . ."

Casca would spend long hours watching her, scrutinizing every patch of skin, strand of hair or curve of her body, trying to find an imperfection. She likely had none, or as most women, hid them well.

His appearance and presence did not appear to surprise or disconcert her in any way either. She did not seem to be following orders; however she was ever present at the right time, overly anxious to please and serve, without the slightest hint of questioning his existence. To her, his place was here for now. Casca remembered with great pleasure when he had set eyes on her on that festive day of Ishana, pushing her way through the crowd, finding a path between the shoulders of the Ifiento to catch a glimpse. Among the thousands, their eyes had reached out and met, as if predestined. It was as if she had expected him. Not unlike Iriena.

FOURTEEN

The summer winds brought the stench of war back to the Edo. Oba Awanoshe would once again sacrifice his people in search of his dark and twisted destiny. Undesirables would not be tolerated; neither would they be allowed to live. Thousands would die or, worse yet, meet the Oba's unmerciful hands. The wheel would turn once more as Casca would come face-to-face with death and despair, truth and deceit and the unforgiven path of his soul. His cursed destiny would again force him to decide the fate of many. The words of The Lamb echoed in the dark corners of his subconscious.

Anaken had summoned Casca to the war room. Four ridiculously overdressed couriers had nervously brought the word to Casca's dwellings. Yrag anxiously watched as they approached, making certain he went undetected. Casca had taken a liking to the young boy, who, although still apprehensive, had learned to deal with his fears and appeared to regard Casca as someone unique and worthy of respect, but not as a deity. Evidently it was not by chance that Ewuare had sent him along with Casca. The young one showed great promise as a future leader of men.

Yrag quickly slipped out of sight as the couriers made their way toward the house. Their yellow-and-red garb flowed in the breeze and raised dust behind their sandal-covered feet as they neared. Sideways shifting eyes betrayed their fear as they made certain neither one of them got more than a step farther ahead of the other. Apprehension was evident even in their nervous, quick-stepped approach.

Moving with a lack of unity, two of them grumbled under their breath, nearly letting out painful moans at times. Eight guards, guarding no one in particular, followed from a distance, but remained clear of Casca's dwellings. The four attempted to act as royal messengers, unconcerned and calm; however their own fears and reservations were obvious.

Informing Casca of the situation was clearly an unnecessary move, as his soldier's instincts had never failed him. He had expected it. Warring and bloodshed were his ever present companion. The news was of no surprise to him, nor were the frightened, poorly camouflaged faces of the four. Their distaste for what the war would bring was clearly apparent from their eyes.

Casca had been sharpening his oversized broadsword on a shiny black whetstone, taking slow and deliberate strokes, lining up the fine blade with his left hand while at the same time pulling steadily with his right, making certain the razor's edge would go unbroken from hilt to tip. He wiped the blade with his left hand, then rolled the slippery paste between his fingertips, feeling the fine grit left by the whetstone. Flicking the grimy paste off the meat of his thumb with the nail of his middle finger, Casca continued the slow and deliberate exercise.

From time to time he raised the edge to eye level, then returned to the whetstone, repeating until the fine metal blade's cut was undiscernible to the eye. The sun's rays would be incapable of finding the finely honed edge. It would then be ready. The flight of the sword would float as the extension of his arm, gliding unimpeded while encountering air, shield or flesh.

"Anaken awaits you," sounded the unnecessary words of the lead courier. Raising his head slightly, Casca acknowledged. It was time.

• • •

The noisy war room was filled with sweating bodies, nerves hardened by years of death, and the thick smell of future blood. The foulness of the air was not be remedied by the frantic fanning of the Ocsa women or the ladles filled with *ukhurhe-oho* extract. Nothing could cure the stench that burrowed itself into men's hearts. Anaken lightly flared his unevenly shaped nostrils, searching the air, reaching out to anticipate his men's fears and discern their weaknesses.

Casca neared the broad entrance to the war room, with his right hand on the hilt of his sword, while his left hand wrapped itself around the hot metal surface of a brass goblet that had been thrust at him by a sleek young girl. His callused hand rounded the cup, allowing its heat to gently singe the webbing at the base of the fingers. Squeezing tightly, he forced the heat to dissipate and relieve the tender sensation. The young girl quickly exited, all the while holding her breath, trying unsuccessfully to seem unfazed. The room quieted slightly.

Turning his head slightly, Casca noted her catch her breath once within safe distance. Rapid side to side movements of her shapely hips took her out of the area. Her girlish excitement had betrayed her. This moment she would likely treasure and retell countless times. Possibly a dozen girls had lost out, trying to be the one to carry the goblet. As she disappeared behind a curved corner, Casca's attention returned to the matter at hand. Women had no place in the war room. Men's concentration would only be broken by their presence.

Peering over the rounded brass rim, Casca noted the swirling, frothy juice of kola nut extract. The steam rose from the oversized goblet, sending wisps of biting vapor toward his face, clouding his gray blue eyes. His lips pursed and puckered while his upper teeth racked against the tip of his tongue in anticipation of the bitter concoction.

The pungent hot aroma found its way through his nostrils, swirling inside the hollow bones of his nose and cheeks, until finally arousing his brain. It was a taste he had grown to enjoy, perhaps more for its effects than for its flavorful qualities. One could never use enough honey or fermented sugar beet, extract squeezed to sweeten its acrid bite. Not unlike the day, this cup held neither.

Casca took his *agha*, the rectangular stool reserved for only the highest officials and ministers, quietly next to Anaken, the *ezomo* of the high council: Drawing his feet under the seat Casca placed his knobby elbows on his knees and rested his chin on his clasped fingers.

Anaken's quiet demeanor brought strength and reassurance to Casca, as he had always felt the man's righteousness. His stillness and air of quiet authority had a calming effect on his subordinates without bringing overconfidence or insolence.

As usual, no one wanted to admit to Casca's presence, or even come remotely close to looking him in the eye, since no one had yet learned how to deal with it. Other than Anaken, Ary and her daughters, Anah and Okuse, and his faithful Yrag, none had dared to make clear eye contact. Some had made feeble attempts while turning their heads, but none were more than bids to test their own courage. Acknowledging his existence was difficult enough even when their eyes reassured them.

The uncertainty of his being, the reality of his existence frightened them all. They had all been witness to his amazing physical feats and sharpness of mind, and were well aware of his peculiar distinctiveness, however believing that God or God's messenger would freely associate with them was difficult to accept.

Hoping that they would be unharmed, or perhaps that Olokun, god of the sea, would look at them in a favorable manner, was all they dared wish for. Casca took another painful gulp from his goblet while watching Anaken's quiet and motionless evaluation of his men.

"The dogs of Igbo have once again stained our land with their kind." Anaken broke through. The men quieted. "They will be punished," concluded Anaken.

"Ise Ezomo, Ise," answered all. "So may it be our leader, so may it be."

A very short speech, hardly a speech at all, clearly less than all had expected. Then again, there was little to discuss other than strategy. A loud and deliberate answer it was, but clearly halfhearted, Casca thought. These men waged war at the whim of their king with fear of question and, as Casca would find out later, afraid of their own dreams.

When night would come and they could not control their thoughts, the fear remained. A negative thought that may betray could mean death, or worse. Oba Awanoshe was Oba. He could see into their dreams and souls.

The how and why of war was no stranger to them. Oba Awanoshe had spoken and Anaken had delivered the message. Why not the Igbo? Casca wondered. Nations clashed with neighbors. If that was not available or timely, nations clashed within themselves, as conflict had never been difficult for man to create and self-righteously try and conquer foolish or evil opposition. Dispute rarely arose between people separated by another's land.

Proximity was more than sufficient to justify years or generations of bloodshed, often the initial cause of deep hatred having been long forgotten. Greed and mere lust for neighbors' riches or greener pastures had led many into war, more times than Casca could remember. People lived, warred and died. Except for Casca, who would forever hold witness to man's sins.

The following days brought nothing but death and destruction to the Igbo. Oba Awanoshe's motives had been different. The carnage that Casca came to witness was unlike anything he had seen in many years.

"Their kind will not soil our land," echoed the words of Oba Awanoshe in Casca's mind. Oba Awanoshe had carried a hatred for the people of Igbo beyond anything the Edo could understand. Their ways, language, customs and mere appearance were beyond tolerance to the Oba. Casca was no stranger to men like Oba Awanoshe, men that Casca had had the displeasure to meet over the years.

Anaken's men had been prepared to destroy and conquer, not to defend or survive. The most sadistic executioners that Casca's mind could recall would have been shocked by the brutality. Oba Awanoshe would have it no other way, as there would be no mercy.

Thousands of finely trained Edo marched east toward Igbo-Ukwu, the capital. This was clearly not a force acting in surprise to an invasion by the evil Igbo. As Anaken's troops approached the water, Casca could see that dozens of rafts had been prepared to cross the Igala, just north of where it met the Great River, which separated the two kingdoms.

"Move along, in groups as prepared, move along," the voice of Ijebu one of their sub-commanders herded the Edo warriors, driving them in tightly ordered formations.

The procession of warriors was loaded in groups of forty onto these rafts in less than two hours. Sitting cross-legged, they placed all weapons and gear by their feet, staying low to prevent the wind from displacing the rafts. "All of you stay seated until told to rise," the steady voice of Ijebu continued.

Using minimal steering, a makeshift rudder was employed to navigate downstream, diagonally crossing to a clearly preset landing area. The riverbank was smooth, with fine gravel and yellow sand reaching up toward the shore and farther inland into the sparse forest.

Farther in, the thickness of the forest blocked the light that had penetrated the branches from the east. An ominous darkness presented the invaders with a foreboding appearance. It was as if the lack of light itself, not the forest, served as the border between the kingdoms.

"Stay sharp. Oba Awanoshe is watching over you," Ijebu continued, wielding the Oba's name not unlike a whip. "He is here with you."

The rafts drifted in from the shallow water until they embedded themselves in the rocks and sand, allowing Anaken's men to debark without even getting their feet wet.

"Move it, you lazy dogs, no more sitting until we set up camp." Ijebu's voice spurred them along. None of the men needed to hear Ijebu's commands more than once. Likely none of them ever did. The ones to do so paid dearly.

Looking southwest around the bend of the river, farther downstream, they saw a clearing along the shoreline where the rafts were going to stop upon returning. Not much appeared to have been left to chance. Casca turned his head, marveling at the order and attention to detail of the Edo command. The transport continued all morning, until the sun burned from above.

Casca traveled with Anaken and twenty members of his most loyal personal aides and guards. The men carried weapons and provisions that only a few, along with Anaken and Casca, would enjoy. Soldiers would be the same here as anyplace else, with the lowest ranks being given the barest of essentials.

As the overnight camp was set up on the east side of the river, it became more and more obvious who the invaders were. The "Dogs of Igbo" were nowhere to be found. There was no invasion threatening Oba Awanoshe's land or people.

It was more likely that the Igbo were not even aware of what awaited them at dawn. North of the camp, along the river, a nearly vertical slope reached up from the breakers to a good-sized horizontal plateau, which overlooked the area.

Inaccessible from the river, it appeared as a perfect sentinel post or defensive position. Casca was surprised to see no lookout posts there, or anyplace nearby along the river, where the elevation provided by the curving banks could have provided great range for the eye to oversee or for a well-armed unit to defend from. The lack of lookout posts was going to cost the Igbo dearly. Night approached as the camp settled in.

Slowly licking his greasy left hand, Casca finished his portion of cold lizard. Even cold, and pressed under the weight of all the gear he had insisted on carrying, it held a certain quality that he reluctantly relished. The female carried on even when old and unheated. The heaviness of its slightly bitter aftertaste, probably its crushed and smeared eggs, was soon remedied as Casca approached the end of the meal.

Not unlike the kola-nut brew, the lizard's unpleasant qualities were also part of its attraction. Eating anything that squirmed in and out of wet holes, calling a swamp or bog its home, would have been clearly repugnant for Casca; however recently these strange creatures had become an overwhelming favorite.

When in "the hold," he had survived by ripping apart living creatures with his own clawlike hands and fingernails, and devouring them while a pulse still traveled in their opened veins. At least these had seen fire and had stopped moving before being eaten.

A feeble consolation. Casca laughed at his own thoughts. But one worth considering, since he often pondered of a more favorable fate.

He must be able to breathe through his ears. Casca remembered words from the past, times at which he had astounded people with his endless appetite, having made all that did not move or have wheels disappear within his belly.

I doubt if he even does breathe when he eats, returned the amused words of Niccolo Polo, recounting a two-day feast in Khanbalic, a celebration in honor of Kublai Khan's nephew. *He would never cease eating if a sword or wench did not call upon him.* The booming voice of a friend long forgotten echoed in his ears.

Casca wondered if there were any kind of living creature that he had not yet tasted. What could be stranger than the round black eggs of fish from the land of northern Chin, or slabs of warm blubber taken from creatures that still moved around on deck while one fed?

He was never certain whether to swallow the black eggs whole, or snap them between his teeth and allow the strange juices to spatter against the roof of his mouth, darkening his palate. *Spray them against your throat, don't fear them Old one.* The voice of Fedyor of the northern seas brought back bitter memories.

Surely this was a barbaric custom that he could never truly enjoy. Why the effort to pursue such when the fish that provided the strange seeds was always more palatable? Sweet butter and bread would quench its taste, but then why suffer the bitterness? Perhaps the bitterness would sweeten the taste of the bread and butter to come? he sometimes speculated. For certain it was a peculiar palate that could enjoy such.

The warm slabs of blubber he had eaten while whaling in the northern seas, cutting large portions while the creatures squirmed on a bloody deck at his feet, were a ritual not much saner. His friend Fedyor never could get enough of the nauseating warm blubber. Laughing at such thoughts, Casca continued eating. He had after all survived the putrid concoctions aboard the *Kuta,* where the dead-rat-floating bilge water had often improved the intended flavor.

Eventually some even more obscene creature would find

itself on his dinner plate, to nauseate him further, although after having eaten everything that lived on the ocean floor, Casca found that difficult to imagine. Sweet palm wine followed, saving Casca from further unpleasant thoughts until his distended belly finally urged him to stop.

There was no urgency for a clear mind, as the enemy was not to be encountered until the following afternoon at the earliest, and unlike most sweet wines this one did not punish the next day. Belching wet and loud, Casca leaned back against his gear and faced the sky.

"Pass the flask over, move it . . . now!" The voice of Ijebu was unmistakable in the night, the man ordering palm wine with the same vigor and authority as he had used leading the crossing of the river. His voice was the only one breaking the silence, until, finally satisfied or properly medicated, the man quieted down.

The stars were no different here and now from the last time Casca had rested prior to killing. For that matter, the stars had not changed much over the last thousand years or so, while he had roamed the earth. The dark curtain would roll over and over, showing different angles during the course of the seasons; however it would always appear to be the same when each season returned.

When he had traveled far south, he had seen the familiar stars cling closer to the northern horizon, perhaps to make room for other stars, but other than that they appeared virtually unchanged. No matter where, the thousands of twinkling eyes forever held witness to man and his crimes.

Some religious sorts considered it blasphemy to even question the unchanging eternal order of the starry carpet. God would not have created anything that allowed disorder or imperfection, and anyone who thought different would need their beliefs corrected. Some required more terminal persuasion. If death were necessary, so it was provided. Casca thought different, as he pondered the heavens.

A pale and hazy moon hung overhead just as it had done seemingly forever as he had rested at the bottom of the ocean. How long had he been kept prisoner of the depths? The salt of the ocean reentered his well-medicated thoughts as the memory of pain returned as companion.

A star blinked at the edge of the horizon, south of the

camp. It looked familiar to Casca. He knew he had seen it many times before, sometimes looking more fiery red, other times holding a yellow glow when clouds passed over it. The ancient Greeks, so many years past that not even Casca had been born, had named it after the god of war. How appropriate that was now and always.

No matter where Casca had traveled and warred with man and beast, it had kept him company. A thousand years past, when his heart was being ripped out of his chest, the red wandering star had watched from above. This time would be no different; it would again watch from high above as men died below.

The wandering star still ascended at dawn or dusk to make its low, arched path over the horizon and hold witness. Lights that had kept him company over the years were still the same.

"You hold no fear toward our Oba . . ." Casca turned his head in mid gulp, spilling the sweet wine over his chest, watching Anaken's calm face maintain its inquisitive look. Certainly the palm wine had dulled his senses, but he was not even sure if that had been a question or a statement of fact. "You certainly do not make your thoughts easy," continued Anaken.

Casca was in no hurry to respond. Slowly swallowing, he allowed Anaken to further position himself and attempt to gain some physical comfort before the expected answer.

The always calm Anaken twisted in unease as he continued, unable to maintain his customary near royal demeanor. "How can you so easily be among us, without expecting, demanding or wanting . . . I am at times uncertain what I believe in myself as I . . ."

Anaken stopped suddenly, becoming aware that he had given away too much and had spoken without even allowing for a chance at an answer. Looking into Casca's eyes, he smiled.

"All but children know to allow time for a response, not to suffocate the conversation, or to speak in haste . . . I had not made the error in years." Anaken leaned forward and extended a new flask of palm wine to Casca as he finished his words.

Reaching with his left hand, Casca received the flask. "It

would be unwise to hold no fear,'' offered Casca as the swig of wine allowed his words a temporary respite.

''I do not know if you are Olokun, or even the chosen one sent to lead us, but I can also not believe my Oba,'' declared Anaken anxiously. ''These words may bring me death, I well know, but I must speak.'' Finishing his thoughts quickly, he hungered for a response.

''You are right'' whispered Casca to a shocked Anaken. ''About your Oba, that is; your intuition has led you well.''

''You come from the great water, do you not?''

''In a manner of speaking yes, but that is not what you mean.''

Breathing slow and shallow, Anaken attempted to gather his thoughts at once. Repositioning himself, he leaned in toward Casca. ''You must know the effort it took to challenge my Oba, as I . . . ,'' added Anaken uneasily. The veins in his forehead traveled like streams, pulsating with every beat of his heart as the man tried to regain his composure. The pressure in his heart rose, pounding in his forehead until with both hands against his face Anaken tried to control himself. Reaching toward Casca, he received the flask and took a small sip. With every muscle of his body he tried to calm and restrain himself.

''You do not consider him to be your true Oba,'' broke through Casca unexpectedly.

''That is true,'' declared a now suddenly more calm and nearly comfortable Anaken. ''It is true.''

It had taken Anaken long to finally speak. He had rehearsed his thoughts over and over, trying to find a proper way. Still they came out disorganized and hurried. He had hoped the situation would arise that allowed for such control, but in his heart he knew it would not likely happen.

''How does one prepare to speak to a god?'' mumbled Anaken softly, more to himself than as a question.

Amused by the thought, Casca recalled the past years and the thousands who had thought him divine, or the devil himself, and had been eager to serve or anxious not to disappoint and bring an early demise.

Anaken had led thousands of men, had decided the fate of more in an instant, as he had been born to do, but nothing had ever prepared him to speak to a god.

After weeks and weeks of uncomfortable posturing, attempting to read the man's thoughts and fears, Casca knew the time had come. His own reluctant curiosity would be satisfied all at once as Anaken finally opened up. Breathing heavily, exhausted by the effort, Anaken leaned back against a fallen tree trunk that he had been using as a back rest.

Thirty or so feet away, in the darkness of the night, one of Anaken's most trusted lieutenants, Ikan, had gathered the rest of the private guard, making certain Anaken and Casca would be undisturbed. Ikan had been one of Anaken's top men for years; having battled tirelessly side by side, at times saving each other's lives. Once more they would fight together to do the Oba's bidding. Ikan knew well that Anaken had long prepared for this night to speak to Casca, a time when their futures could hang in the balance.

"The people of this land, my people, have suffered too long," Anaken finally commenced. "It was many years ago when it all began, at a time when I was barely old enough to truly understand how my world was about to change. My father was an old man, and in the last years of his life he tried to teach me about the darkness in men's hearts. Those would be lessons of great value, as the years to come came to prove." Anaken's eyes darkened as he continued.

"I was not even ten of age, but the memory is as clear as if just a day old. The feast of the harvest ceremony was just beginning as the greatest of Obas, the true father of the Edo people, Oba Uwaifiokun and his queen were enjoying the celebration of Igue, the ritual of divine kingship." Anaken took a long swallow of wine as the words, although still painful, now freely flowed, easing his mind.

"The crops had been abundant for the last five seasons and the land had not known of war for years, as the kingdoms of Igbo and Yoruba were at war with each other and their neighboring states. We knew of nothing but peace and prosperity. Oba Uwaifiokun was particularly pleased with himself for having been able to circumvent any hostilities, while at the same time watching his most hated of enemies fight amongst themselves, clearly weakening their own position in the area."

"His firstborn, while only six years old, was already showing himself to be a quite promising little prince and future heir to the throne. The young prince showed maturity and insight beyond his years. While many young ones would play loudly and uncontrollably, he would sit quietly observing and pondering the reasons for their actions and reactions. A great leader was in the making.

"The queen was expecting her second child to be born within a few weeks. Men of wisdom had foretold of another son, just as the Oba had hoped for. Our land had known peace for nearly ten years, a time during which Oba Uwaifiokun had gained the love and admiration of his people, and even the respect of his enemies. Just as peace was all that I knew at that time, the tides of fortune quickly turned without us even realizing it for years to come." Anaken's dark eyes glistened and almost appeared to give off a reddish glow as his words slowed, as each thought further weighted down at his heart.

"It was a day as no other. The skies had been quiet, without even the slightest of breezes coming in from the great waters, or the scent of the forest coming from inland. Now that I speak of it, I realize how suddenly it all happened." Casca watched as Anaken was reliving a distant, yet overwhelmingly powerful memory. A memory that even all these years later brought pain and distress into his eyes.

"As our Oba and the royal court were enjoying the ceremony of Igue," continued Anaken, "it became apparent to all present that the skies had darkened slightly, although without even the faintest of clouds present in the sky.

"A breeze had picked up from the direction of the great waters, bringing an unpleasant taste of brine with it. Most of us became agitated, as there appeared to be no reasonable explanation for the darkness that had fallen upon us, or the winds that had never been known to bring the salty taste of the great waters so far inland.

"Our Oba stood up, and arm in arm with his queen, he walked up the ceremonial pedestal to where everyone could see them clearly. Standing in front of the royal *ekete,* the same one that had been in the family for hundreds of years, with both hands raised, as if putting them on everyone's shoulders, he tried to ease the moment. His queen stood by, raising her head with a pleased look of admiration and love toward her king. Thousands milled about nervously, yet confident that all was well.''

Anaken slowly closed his eyes as the bitter memory drained his thoughts. Regaining his strength, he resumed his painful words.

''Within moments it was if night had come and a storm was imminent. The disoriented crowd stirred in uncertainty and fear . . . The wind smelled odd, . . . almost burning our throats and eyes. . . . The moment had taken a sudden chill with the cutting winds, as a frightening midday darkness fell upon us.''

Casca found himself shifting about in uncertain discomfort, as the words of a shaken Anaken stirred something distant, yet quite familiar in the recesses of his mind. ''Until we meet again . . . ,'' Casca mumbled to himself, reliving demons of the past.

''An unseen thunder bellowed in the distance as the wind picked up, whipping the red dust against our faces. Struggling, the sun was unable to break through the invisible layer of darkness, as if magical hands were stifling it. The heavens broke open with the thunder of a thousand dying souls, as a reddish blue light descended upon our Oba and his queen. A surge of flickering lights danced across their bodies, twisting and lashing about, like the giant fireflies that bring the rains. Hazy and smoldering light ran over their faces, torturing them with the power of the dancing blue lights.

''Shrills that thundered like screaming thoughts came upon us, words we could not understand, yet frightening and foreboding. Just as suddenly as they had appeared, the blue lights sped through the stunned mass of people, disappearing toward the unseen great waters. Within moments it was as if it had never happened. The skies were bright and clear, without a cloud to evidence the vanished storm. Nothing had changed except for our Oba and his queen. They both lay motionless, slumped on the podium, staring with vacant eyes toward the sky.''

Casca lay still, with the last of Anaken's words refusing to leave his mind or the echo to leave his ears. The moment had overwhelmed him. Turning his eyes toward Anaken, he sensed the man's pain. The seconds of silence had awakened Anaken from his momentary daze, and he continued.

"We would not know for years, but those few moments changed our world more than we could have ever imagined. Our king and queen were dead. He with his hands still reaching for the skies, and she with the life of the unborn still kicking within her belly. Few of us can remember clearly the moments that followed. A child entered our world, the darkest day of our history, as two royal souls left us."

Anaken's head slumped toward his chest as his shallow breathing slowed even further. The words to follow were not easy.

"Our kingdom fell into chaos. It had come without warning. Not even the ancients from Ife had foretold of this. The child born of that blue light is our Oba Awanoshe. Death and misery followed."

They sat motionless, without a word exchanged between them for nearly an hour. The noises of the forest were their only companion. Gentle winds rustled the leaves nearby, adding to the eeriness of the moment. Anaken sat and rocked side to side with vacant eyes staring off into the dark night, while Casca waited patiently, knowing not to hasten the man's pain. The palm-wine haze that had crept over Casca's mind had now clearly dissipated from the telling of the dark tale.

"The years to follow, almost imperceptibly at first, brought great change to our land," continued Anaken. "Following our Oba's death, because it had happened so unexpectedly, our leaders did not know which way to turn. No Oba had died so suddenly in generations. Even on his deathbed, the last words of a dying Oba would have led us. This was not to bc the case. Should the young prince, Ewuare, barely six years of age, take over as Oba or should the council take power until the age of consent was reached by the young one? We had no answers that we could trust." Leaning back, Anaken rested as the painful memories of years past raced across his mind.

"The moments of that day will forever be burned into my mind and soul," continued Anaken reluctantly. "The young prince born of that blue light did not come into our world easily. His mother was dead, but it was unclear if that was also his fate. The royal guards had spent their whole lives training to defend the Oba, eager, and many anxious, to exchange their lives for his. However they had no response to this. They stood paralyzed.

"The only one who acted was the old man, Ooton, he who challenged light and dark with his wicked ways, who quickly rushed to their side. He knew of a way to save the unborn. He had done it countless times on wounded wild beasts, but never on a woman. Considering such would have likely ended his life in the past, but now, not trying might have possibly meant the same.

"What followed was no way to come into this world. The old man sliced her belly open vertically, just from beneath her belly button down toward the middle suture of her hip, then in one swift motion he pulled out the child. We all stood horrified at the sight, not certain which obscenity was more overwhelming, the sudden death of our beloved Oba or the barbaric actions of Ooton.

"Only the scattering of pearls torn from her *ododo,* her red royal dress, broke the deathly silence of the moment. Her body, so savaged by the swift movements of his blade, refused to bleed. Not unlike opening an old sack that had carried sweet roots, he hacked away at her, cutting through skin, sinew, muscle and then finally the sack that held the unborn, until it yielded the child. Her skin was like old leather, singed by fire and aged by the desert winds, distant from when it had held flesh and bone. The blue light that had overtaken her just moments before had obliterated any semblance of life from her body. It just lay there as an open and discarded shell."

Casca and Anaken sat in silence. Time passed as the blanket of stars moved across the sky on its journey toward daylight. The red wandering star had disappeared beneath the horizon over the trees as the tale had been told, while the constellation of Orion awoke in the northeast. Casca watched the cloudy star beneath Orion's belt drift in and out under the dark wisps of the night sky.

Sleep was not to come easily this night, as fatigue from the long day had been replaced by deeper emotions. Casca watched Anaken sit quietly with his eyes closed, resting, allowing the darkness of his memories to distance itself from his thoughts. Anaken's lips moved slightly, perhaps a comforting prayer to ease his pain. They sat, each hoping not to have to make the first words. There was not much more that needed to be said for now, and Anaken knew it.

FIFTEEN

The coming of dawn brought the beginning of the end for the Igbo. Anaken's forces, rested and anxious, proceeded southeast toward Igbo-Ukwu. Casca and Anaken had awakened from a short slumber just before daylight, without speaking a word. There was not much more Anaken would share with Casca for a while. The rest would have to wait. "The time has not yet come" is all that Anaken would whisper, echoing words Casca had heard from Ewuare. Foreboding yet meaningful words. Prophetic words that would haunt Casca.

As thousands marched, Casca brought his steps up to speed, once again a soldier ready for battle. A distasteful and obscene war it would be, not much more than an execution. The more things changed the more they stayed the same in this world. Once more the hourglass would turn, as Casca would witness a slaughter of undesirables.

Anaken's men had spread out, marching in an elongated crescent moon formation, outlining one-third of a circle. Casca had taken part in many such campaigns, where a simple forward movement of troops suddenly surrounded opposing armies, catching the enemy in a crossfire, bringing swift surrender. Not unlike military formations of the past that had brought death and destruction, the Edo wave of death brought the end to the Igbo. Many were driven by the frenzy of the kill and lust for blood and booty, while most only fearfully obeyed orders. Orders of death that soldiers of thousands of years past had feared not to follow. To the Igbo it did not matter much, as their blood would flow just the same.

Youthful blindness and the blood fever of the kill drove many along the front lines, so chosen for their lust for destruction. With ear-piercing screams they rushed through the thinning forest, eager to reach the clearings that housed many of the smaller villages. They ran with a blind rage, swords, shields and spears flailing, eager to meet the unsuspecting enemy. The wall of madmen burst through unprotected dwellings, annihilating all that lived and offered resistance.

"Die, you filthy monsters." The sounds of blind hatred rang out from time to time as some of Oba Awanoshe's most loyal, nearly mindless followers screamed as they did the Oba's bidding. Fire and steel cut down the Igbo as lightning would the sun-scorched tall grass. Bloody maces broke through huts and stables, leveling all that stood, splattering the life of man and beast alike. Blood flooded the land, hastening the killing frenzy as the dead were hacked beyond recognition and their limbs and bodies scattered.

The wave of death continued undaunted through the morning hours, perhaps even accelerating, driven by a morbid hunger for the kill. The earth thundered and shook under the pounding feet of thousands as they made their way east, toward the heart of the Igbo empire.

At the edges of the advancing crescent, men were ten to fifteen deep, while halfway through, the semicircle would be nearly sixty men front to back. Water, weapons and supplies were brought along the rear of the formation and handed up as needed, not allowing the charge of the wave to be hindered. When the front lines tired or were thinned out by death or injury, reinforcements moved up, not allowing the Igbo a moment's reprieve.

Seriously wounded or dead were left behind, to be collected later. They would not be allowed to slow or in any way impede the attack. A perfectly trained and orchestrated charge rained brisk and uncompromising terror. The end would be swift and merciless.

All that stood in their way was destroyed by a relentless rain of steel. The few that resisted died quickly. Swift ones who attempted to work their way around the advancing lines were trapped and butchered around the edges of the formation. The only ones that survived were deserters that ran for their lives and the ones allowed to live as slaves.

"Kill them all, as they will poison us with their kind . . . None of them can be left alive," thundered the voice of Nevaad, one of Oba Awanoshe's subcommanders. The man had been nothing but a lowly private guard just weeks previous, yet he had suddenly found himself in charge of a hundred men. He drove his men into the kill blinded by insane loyalty and his own twisted desire to rid the world of the Igbo. "Let none get away," he continued screaming. Spurned by his words, his mindless underlings intensified their attack.

Anaken and Casca, along with a few of Anaken's most loyal men, fell behind, refusing to take part in the slaughter. They were not needed and were happy not to take part. Their somber and resigned faces, unlike those hypnotized by the kill, slowly followed the wave of death, not joining in, yet unwilling to stop the carnage. Casca watched the pain in Anaken's eyes as they walked side by side, the last words they had exchanged echoing in his ear: *The time has not yet come . . .*

Midday brought the army of Oba Awanoshe to the outskirts of Igbo-Ukwu. As the last of the trees thinned out, a wide open plain opened up, revealing the sacred city of the Igbo. The ground trembled as thousands fled eastward, running for their lives, seeking refuge, hoping and praying that they would be saved by the armies of Igbo-Ukwu. That was not to be.

Defensive forces had been completely overwhelmed, as lack of organization and panic had clearly overmatched them by the fury and sheer number of the invaders. As they ran for haven, they were cut down from behind, men, women and children alike, anyone not fast enough to escape from the marching Edo warriors. The ones fleet of foot would gain little, false hope and perhaps a few more seconds of life, moments of horror, as they would carry the memory of brutal death a while longer.

Farther north of the city, herding cattle and sheep, a few dozen young men and women attempted to flee, abandoning their families and their city. It was not much longer until their end came, as the northern arc of the slowly enclosing Edo army overtook and trapped them. The circle of death was slowly closing, tightening the vise, as the people and city of Igbo-Ukwu were suffocated. In the end they would die just like the rest. Oba Awanoshe would have it no other way.

The city was not unlike Benin City in size and grandeur. Its approach was a flattened and dusty open field, slowly elevating to the outskirts of the city. Farther east, on a small plateau, sat the inner city, Igbo-Ukwu itself, home of the royal family, city administrators and ones fortunate enough to be allowed into the protected areas. Better fortified than those of the Edo capital, its enclosure walls, twenty feet in height, dominated the approach.

The esplanade, the flat open area immediately in front of the primary walls, would have normally provided a clear stretch where the defenders, strategically placed along the rampart, protected by the parapet or the enclosure of turrets, could rain arrows or lances on the attacking forces.

This was not to be, as thousands ran for shelter, making such defense impossible, madly pushing their way through barricades and the fortified gatehouse as their pursuers rushed them like beasts driven to slaughter. The ones slower of foot were overrun by their own, as cattle stampede over the fallen, or were impaled to the ground by the onrushing invaders.

Not unlike a bowl submerged under water or grain, the area between the enclosure and the inner wall filled in rapidly. Screaming and crying men, women and children huddled in fear, trying to find shelter or protect one another. "Have mercy, allow . . ." an old woman pleaded, trying to cover her two children with her body. She did not live long enough to finish her sentence.

The rest did not fare better. Panic overtook them as the usually open space provided by the outer bailey could not contain them, as more and more desperate souls poured into the now overcrowded square. The ones not crushed by their own panic were cut down.

The sheer weight of their numbers, overwhelmed by hysteria and fear, started a wave that brought utter chaos while buckling the inner gateway and attached wall. Within moments the inner wall that had stood nearly thirty feet tall collapsed from the pressure of thousands, crushing all without prejudice, exposing the royal palace and adjoining buildings.

Sight of the slaughter that followed would have nauseated any, as thousands were quickly put to the sword. The conquering forces never gave any of them a chance to plead for mercy or foolishly stand defiant. ''Don't kill our babies,'' two women cried, trying to shield their children.

''Certainly not,'' Ajobe, one of Nevaad's underlings, mockingly promised. ''Not as long as you ask.'' Backhanding them out of the way, he allowed two of his men to put the women to the sword, impaling them against the blood-soaked dirt. Ripping two boys out of their arms, Ajobe made certain to end their lives while the women could still watch in their last seconds of consciousness.

Ajobe quickly followed with ''I think I will let your girls please me for a while,'' trying to make sure the horror of their own deaths was not enough punishment for the two mothers. ''They will do for a while,'' he added, pulling the two hysterical girls by the hair with his left hand, while he slashed their clothes off with his short sword.

Laughing while he watched the two girls cower in fear, he pushed them toward his men. ''Remind me to spend some sweet time with the young saplings later,'' he added, instructing one of his men. ''Their fine young bodies will need some time to be broken in.'' He grinned at his men. Ajobe's men returned the ugly leer, snickering to themselves, almost drooling at the sight of the frightened unclad girls.

Casca bitterly watched from a distance, knowing this was not the time to act, also vowing to end Ajobe's life in short time. Perhaps the two girls would not live, but neither would Ajobe get to defile them. The onslaught continued.

Hypnotized, the Edo executioners followed through with

Oba Awanoshe's foul orders. Men of all ages—the old, sick and decrepit were the first to die in the mass execution, flooding the land with their blood. Of no fault other than being born Igbo. Crops would grow richer and taller on these grounds where the red water fed the land. It was always so.

All women other than the young and the ones able to carry the seed of men were quick to follow in death. Oba Awanoshe had no use for the old, diseased or the crippled. No one else escaped the bloodletting, other than a few hundred able-bodied young men, who were spared, and the royal family.

Oba Awanoshe's orders would be followed to perfection. Casca had learned from Anaken about Oba Awanoshe's insane and unyielding hatred of the Igbo, ''and their kind'' as he referred to them. Their physical appearance, perhaps shorter of stature, with higher foreheads and flatter cheekbones, was something that Oba Awanoshe despised and thought obscene. He had always spoken of their clearly inferior intelligence, foul ways and foul gods.

Not unlike most madmen, Oba Awanoshe did not need much fodder to crave death. All he could see was that the Igbo had proven proud and stubborn, refusing to yield to his will. For that they would pay dearly. Casca watched in agony as a people were slowly erased from history.

The palaces were looted then destroyed by fire. Anything of value was seized, placed in bundles, crates or baskets and prepared to be taken on the long trek back to Benin City. The three hundred or so young men who had been allowed to live watched in horror the destruction of their homes and the death of their families, then were forced to carry all the spoils of war, plundering from their own homes, leaving nothing but death and destruction behind.

Being allowed to live would not be sweet for them. Their home was left in ruins, burned to the ground, nothing but a mound of smoldering ashes to mark where a once great city stood, the winds of war carrying the smoky remains of a once proud people and land, scattering it to the four corners of the world.

Before turning back east, Casca took one more look over

his shoulder, watching the doings of another madman of the world, following a warped and insane destiny. The Igbo would be no more.

The journey back to Benin City was uneventful, as the caravan of enslaved men, women and loot snaked its way back toward the river. Not much was heard, other than the rattling of ankle chains and groans of suffering. The prisoners' resigned faces, no longer twisting in agony, told the tale.

Every step farther, as the distance grew from their home, settled more of the end for them and their people. Carrying the pilfered goods, the young men held on to the last vestiges of what once was their land and heritage. An obscene thing it was, carrying the spoils of victors. Their world had ended, even if life still flickered in their bodies. Igbo-Ukwu was dead.

Anaken's men walked quietly, drained of energy and enthusiasm. The darkness of the previous days had settled a daze upon their minds and souls. The fury of the kill had overtaken them, the lust for blood and loot had led them, yet now, as hours and days passed, their soul searching could and would not be stifled, no matter how much their fear of Oba Awanoshe and his power terrified them.

More and more, moments of clarity and reason wedged back into their consciousness, dissipating the clouds of the blood fever. Slowly, they dragged on, quietly, each and every one hoping that an uninterrupted quiet would veil the dark truth.

Others continued their celebration, noisily retelling the moments of the kill, adding myth as their steps brought them closer to home. Even a soft chanting of Oba Awanoshe's name could be heard from a small group as they reveled among themselves. Herding the group of young girls and women, they whistled and patted one another on the back, pointing and wagering over the terrified female bounty.

Victoriously, a small group of men cheered on, hailing their commander Nevaad in his actions. Walking with a loathsome look on his round face, he devoured a piece of roasted meat he held in his right hand, from time to time grinning at his men. Spurned by them, he sang an old victory song, his toneless voice only interrupted by gulps of wine that he poured down his throat. Their mindless celebration would go on for days.

Ajobe staggered drunkenly, spewing the palm wine from his bloated belly faster than he could inhale it.

"Have no fear, little girls . . . I will not disappoint you," he belched, prodding with the butt of his spear the bare backsides of the two girls he had taken as his own bounty. "The two of you will keep me warm for a while."

Casca watched from a distance, overhearing every foul word that left Ajobe's squalid mouth. It would not be long before Ajobe would feed the worms. That there was no question about.

Casca returned with the rest, flanking the main troops, keeping mostly to himself, pondering the nightmare he had witnessed. It was useless for him to try even momentarily to rid himself of the dark thoughts he held for Nevaad, Ajobe and the rest of them. These were not men. They were the refuse of humanity that had found their way to positions of leadership, and in doing so served the darkest of human deeds.

Casca had taken his share of lives, countless more than any man alive probably had, yet this was not the same. No beast kills just for the killing! . . . Attila the Hun had thirsted for blood and glory, but had never systematically destroyed a people . . . Genghis Khan had created empires larger and more powerful than the world had ever seen by assimilating and absorbing people, not by wiping them out. War is war but this was something beyond that. What could possibly have been Oba Awanoshe's plans? wondered Casca. Even with half of the kill, the Igbo nation would never rise again.

He had taken part in many wars, raids and even acts of vengeance, but this was clearly beyond that. Walking along, with his head down, slowly shaking from side to side, nearly mumbling to himself, Casca pondered man's evil ways.

It did not take long for news to travel. Not halfway back to the banks of the Igala, Oba Awanoshe's messengers met and greeted the victorious return of Anaken. Songs retelling the tale of his newly legendary triumphs were not far behind, Casca thought, hearing the overwhelming words of congratulations. Perhaps too great words of praise, Casca figured. Praise with signs of concern and even fear beneath them.

Had Oba Awanoshe so clearly underestimated the resistance the Igbo would offer, or was Anaken such a supreme military leader? Perhaps false words of praise, as no sitting ruler has ever joyfully greeted a returning army with a seemingly invincible military commander at the helm. The Igala was no Rubicon, but Casca could nearly feel the ghost of Julius Caesar in the winds.

SIXTEEN

This was no glorious return. It certainly did not feel like one. Casca sat in his oversized bath, eyes closed, head leaning back against a pillow-covered plank, trying to allow the pleasures of the senses to separate his thoughts from the previous days. It was not easy. Nearly impossible.

The steam swirled from the fresh buckets of hot water Anah and Okuse, Ary's two girls, were dumping into his bath, clouding his eyesight, but not allowing his mind to drift. Not unlike the caldarium he had at times enjoyed, alone or preferably with female company, years ago in old Rome, the hot water bath area that he had been provided with was quite pleasing.

The baked clay bath was deep toward one end, where one could almost stand, and shallow enough at the other, just deep enough to allow one to lie down and have water cover them. Its smooth and rounded edges allowed comfort and support, outlining Casca's tired body while the adjustable headrest cradled him. Adjacent to the shallower area were two rest seats where washers could sit with comfort and easily handle their work.

Anah and Okuse were eager to do so, but this day Ary only allowed them to tend to the water and the aromatic candles that lit the room and swirled the smoke as it mixed with the water's hot vapors. Okuse furrowed her brow and sharpened her eyes, as she had hoped to please Casca and ease his pain, but a quick glance from Ary discouraged her from protesting too much.

Just a young girl, Okuse could not understand his torment, and just tried her best, in her childlike way, to please him. Anah quickly completed her tasks and disappeared quietly, knowing not to challenge her mother at this time. Oblivious of this, Casca attempted to allow the warmth of the bath to comfort him. The escape of sleep would not protect him, as thoughts of the slaughter stabbed at his mind. Not even Ary could help for now.

She softly ran her hands over his forehead, slowly stroking the sides of his head, rubbing his temples gently, trying to hasten his sleep, or perhaps allow a temporary distraction. It would not be easy, she knew well, even from the short time she had known Casca, as her heart could feel his pain and tortured soul. Looking up, with a tired smile, Casca nodded slowly. She was a wondrous woman, Casca knew well.

His thoughts drifted back once again to times long past, to his love Lida of Helsford and to Iriena, yes, magnificent and beautiful Iriena, she who had found him high atop a mountain, eternally watching as a guard, a sentinel, there to oversee and protect her village.

Iriena had prayed and believed that the frozen warrior would rise and save them when the most desperate of times would be upon them. Patiently she would wait, as the legend had foretold of the man who stood watch until needed. He would wake and free her people and land . . . when the right time would come . . . Casca's eyes snapped open, startling Ary, who had thought he had just drifted off to sleep. Ary's words . . . *the time has not yet come* . . . were eerily familiar, from a thousand years past, the whisper of Iriena once again come back to haunt him. The wheel would turn once more. Ary continued, her gentle touch easing Casca toward a light slumber.

Their return had been celebrated with days of song and wine. The intensity of the feast nearly allowed people to forget what they were so overjoyed over. Oba Awanoshe was no fool. He knew well how sometimes pleasure can ease pain and weaken memories. For now he would allow his people a brief escape.

The three hundred young men were not to be so lucky, as, they were immediately slaughtered following their delivery of the bounty. Soon they would be forgotten. They bled and died like sheep that had given their last bucketful of milk and now were set to be drawn onto a spit, primed to be roasted. Their usefulness had run out.

The women and girls, possibly thousands of them, awaited a more horrible fate. They would be allowed to live and carry the seed of their new masters, the Edo, in their unwilling bellies. The Igbo race would slowly be erased, as new generations of Edo were to be in the making.

"I am ready to best your arm," came the nervous words of Yrag. Casca sat and smiled at the boy, watching him go through his sword exercises. "I have rested and eaten well," he continued, thrusting forcefully with ever quickening blows while greeting Casca in the same manner he had done often before Casca had left for war.

"This may just be your day," Casca answered, the way Yrag had anticipated he would. Yrag knew Casca had no desire to spar, yet he had hoped it could serve as an easy distraction. By the look on Casca's face Yrag quickly realized that this was not to be the day.

Yrag sat cross-legged on the ground, looking up at Casca's heavy eyes. Casca smiled at him, wondering how much the boy understood of what his world was about. He gritted his teeth thinking back to the days past. It had not been near long enough to deal with the horror of what Oba Awanoshe had brought upon the Igbo. Only the wind kept them company on this morning as they sat quietly behind Casca's dwellings.

"I have heard tales of what monsters the Igbo were," Yrag finally broke the silence after minutes of deathly quiet. "They are vile and deceitful, I have been told. I am glad you have escaped unharmed. They were hideous to look at, weren't they?"

Casca wondered what to say. How simple it was to cloud

the minds of the young, he thought. Yrag had apparently fallen easily.

"I do not believe they were monsters," Yrag continued, startling Casca with his quick turnabout. "They could not be so much unlike us, could they?"

"Their blood ran red while they died," Casca responded. Yrag sat, nodding his head, watching Casca's eyes.

"The night has been short and without sleep. Stand your ground or prepare to be taken prisoner." Casca quickly jumped to his feet, grabbing his long sword, offering a challenge on this day of contemplation.

"This may just be my day," Yrag was quick to respond as he leapt to his feet, standing with readied sword, eager to once again challenge Casca's heavy blade. He smiled, elated that Casca would take his challenge as he had done dozens of times in the past.

Circling each other, they swung at the air, their eyes understanding the truth about what the war with the Igbo had brought. It was no secret, everyone understood it. Casca nodded in acknowledgment, pleased that Yrag had not had his mind clouded by Oba Awanoshe and his lies.

The following days brought uncertain comfort to Casca's life. It was difficult to believe people could get used to a god, but it seemed they had accepted his place in their lives for now. Hundreds of years ago, when he had visited the New World it had not been much different. After a while people of Teotha had accepted him as the messenger of Quetza, perhaps the Quetza himself, there to relay the words of their almighty.

Shuddering at the thoughts, Casca remembered the agony of the day when the high priest Tezmec had removed his still beating heart. With a flash of light the shining blade of golden flint had raped his chest, striking hard and deep, separating his heart from the vessels that fed his body.

Casca had wondered if that was going to end his life, and the curse of the Jew be lifted. It was not to be. The curse was to continue, as rising from the stone altar Casca snatched his now empty heart from the priest and placed it back into his chest. The curse did not break, allowing him a final exit from this world. Tezmec had ripped out his heart, for all of his people to see the messenger of Tectli Quetza who had come and *failed* to fulfill the legends of his people.

The agony of those distant times sent a shudder of cold darkness through Casca, ripping him from the horror of the flashback. It was certainly not a memory to relive. The idea of liberating these people became even more disconcerting.

How could and would Casca know how to fulfill the prophecies of the Edo forefathers? And why should he? All anyone would say was "the time has not yet come." The more he heard it the more it sounded like scripture being quoted by a religious sort, something he was not quite fond of. As members of the Brotherhood had hunted him over the centuries, he himself had become part of scripture, inadvertently inspiring words to be chanted at spiritual and sacrificial ceremonies. Being woven into a people's legend or religious prophecy was not something to desire.

The time had not come, and Casca had no idea what anyone expected of him to do when the right time did arrive. *You are here for a reason. The Edo people will live on because of you.* The words of Anaken sometimes revisited Casca's thoughts. Ewuare had spoken of being the rightful ruler, of banishment and of ancient legend and prophecy. Who was Casca to decide right and wrong for these people and how their history should unfold? Would anyone one hundred years from now know or care of the past? Did this tiny portion of the world really matter to anyone other than these people? Casca held great affection for Ary especially, along with Ewuare, and recently had come to respect and admire Anaken, but was that enough to challenge a madman and perhaps alter the history of these people?

And what if he was to fail, as he had apparently failed the people of Teotha all those years ago? What obscene punishment and torture could Oba Awanoshe unleash upon him? Having his heart ripped out once a millennia was more than enough, even if he was immortal. Casca wondered about his warped and perverted sense of amusement. Something clearly only centuries of interchanging pain and pleasure could have brought.

Once again how easily he had gotten himself into such

a situation, pondered Casca. Perhaps it was a chance for redemption. From what? And to what end? Clearly a puzzlement. Casca found himself mouthing the words of his questions and unsatisfying answers. He knew it was not far before he would lose an argument to himself. Definitely not something he desired, as sanity was certainly a precious commodity in his world. It was time to think of else.

Concern for the days to come overtook Casca's thoughts as he pondered his place in these people's lives and their expectations.

Ary and her daughters were wonderful in all ways possible. They spent every waking moment creating a world of paradise, allowing Casca an escape. Every mentionable or unmentionable worldly pleasure was there for the taking. After hundreds of years he did not imagine there were unexplored or untested experiences and pleasures.

But somehow, as if by blind fortune, or perhaps design, these women ventured beyond anything Casca had ever imagined. He had considered feeling guilt or discomfort from spending time with both mother and daughter, but that he had gotten over hundreds of years ago. There were much greater evils in this world that men freely reveled in. It was not as if he could receive a curse more evil than what his life was. Except for brief moments as such, it had been a world of hell.

Ary did not seem to mind sharing Casca with Anah and Okuse; on the contrary, she appeared to be honored, hopeful of it. Perhaps if not her, one of them could carry the child of Olokun. After all, Casca was the prophet, messiah, deliverer and all that was hope wrapped up in one. An assignment that carried great weight, but not the first time Casca had been given the role.

The girls treated it practically as if it was a competition between each other and their mother, each trying to outdo the others in all imaginable ways. The younger of the two, Okuse, seeking to show her sophistication and knowledge of men, had at times tried to act shy and submissive, believing this would entice him.

She had come a long way from the first time they had met, when Casca's mesmerizing eyes had made her shudder with nervous excitement and had driven her to her knees, allowing him to slowly take in her childish beauty. It did not take much to have Casca crave her beautiful and young body, then or now. Okuse had become quite brave as she foolishly attempted to wear out Casca with her youthful energy. It was long before that was to happen.

Anah was more of the seductress, using her body and hypnotic eyes, playing games, trying to tease Casca and make him eager with anticipation. Gliding like a gazelle, with loose veils and brightly colored kente, or unfitting oversized kanga that many of the brave young girls seemed to wear when trying to make an impression, Casca would get a feast for the eyes before she would *allow* him to get his prize.

The multilayered strips of kente, slowly falling away, added to the hypnotic dances that Anah playfully used. Beneath, her young warm body, heaving from exhaustion and covered with beads of sweat, joyfully greeted his broad shoulders and scar-crossed chest. She would then be ready for the taking. Casca would not disappoint.

Embarrassing or challenging their mother was not much beyond them. At times they would team up, sending their mother on make-believe errands or attempting to misinform her on his whereabouts. Ary knew better and sometimes did not mind playing along, as she had played the same games on her own mother many years before. Who was Casca to interfere with such family tradition and rivalry? He had long ago given up trying to understand women, more so trying to understand mothers and daughters.

"I thought I was going to die," Anah whispered softly to Okuse one morning as the two stood alone in the garden, not realizing that Casca could overhear them. He stood at the entrance to his dwellings, looking outside into the morning sky, amused at how their voices carried to his ears by the eastern breeze.

"I could not but plead. All the air had left my body last night. My mind was clouding up as everything had turned dark," Anah continued. Okuse listened with a look of concern in her eyes, not knowing what her sister was talking about.

''What happened,'' she begged worryingly, afraid for her sister's life.

''It was horrible. For what felt like forever I could not get my breath. I thought I would never breathe again. It was horrible,'' she repeated her frightful words.

Okuse grabbed at her sister's shoulders, trying to get her to tell what had happened. ''I thought everything was great. It was too good to be true.'' Okuse paused momentarily, then continued. ''You must tell our mother. She must know we are all in grave danger.''

Casca stood by the doorway biting his lip, enjoying the moment, knowing well Anah could not hold up much longer with her ruse. Turning slowly, he caught them in the corner of his eye, Anah attempting to look somber and frightened, while Okuse grasped for a solution. ''I will never allow it to happen to me. He will never have me alone, never. It is horrible. I do not care who he is. I cannot believe I have let him touch me!'' Okuse stomped her foot, angered by what Anah had relayed to her, yet thankful she had not lost her sister.

''How did you get away?'' Okuse inquired. ''Did you beg for your life? What finally happened?''

''I thought it would never end,'' Anah confided to her. ''He had me in his grasp. I could not even scream for him to let me go . . .''

Casca turned away, nearly laughing out loud listening to Anah, wanting to leave the two of them alone, yet needing to hear when and if she would let Okuse off the hook.

Whispering, Anah continued. ''He had me on my belly . . . he was on top of me . . . I thought I was going to die . . . I could just not breathe . . . He just would not stop.'' Anah stopped telling her tale, trying to torture Okuse a few moments longer with her story.

With her eyes tearing up, Okuse begged for Anah to continue. ''Did he threaten to kill you, kill us? We must get away now!''

''Oh no, not at all,'' Anah finally concluded. ''It was the best night of lovemaking ever. The intensity of it just took my breath away. I was merely begging for him to stop so I could gather myself. He mentioned something about reaching a new level, or something like that. It was the greatest ever . . ."

Anah could not complete her story as Okuse nearly knocked her off her feet with a jolt of both hands, realizing that all along she had been duped, set up for her sister's enjoyment. Anah's lack of breathing had had nothing to do with having her life nearly extinguished.

Laughing out loud, Anah called for her sister to return, as Okuse ran through the garden, not even noticing Casca and her mother approaching. Eventually she would return. Perhaps Casca would need some tending to tonight.

It was not long before Casca saw Anah and Okuse talking again, Okuse fiery eyed for having fallen so easily and completely for her sister's story, and Anah feeling guilty for having so upset her sister. It was not the last time the two would play tricks on each other, something they were both well aware of. For a while Anah knew she was at Okuse's mercy.

Casca enjoyed their company for many nights to come. His bed was never empty; Anah and Okuse made certain of that. Unless he wanted it so. It was not an undesirable existence. Hours and sometimes even days would pass, days during which Casca was able to forget his cursed existence, past and present.

"It is my turn," Casca once heard them argue. "You are wrong, and anyway he prefers me."

"Enough of you two. You are lucky I have been patient with all this foolishness," Ary sharply had to interrupt. "Enough already. Do you think anyone will want either of you when you argue like this? Are both of you crazy? How dare you jeopardize everything! This is not a man . . . this is our savior, this is Olokun! Behave yourselves or neither one of you will ever be allowed to see him again!" Her words echoed in their ears from that moment on never challenging their mother again, realizing it could all end in an instant.

Casca knew well this was an insane situation anyway. He was not certain which was saner, being thought of as a messiah or the affinity he had with the three of them. He had spent such time with mothers and daughters, yet this was different. He cared for them deeply, all of them. Their affection for him might have been due initially to who he was, but now that had changed. He had not felt like this in longer than he could remember. Their emotions were pure. Right or wrong, they loved him.

Guilt was clearly a wasted emotion after all these years of pain and sorrow, Casca had come to realize. If life allowed for a respite, for whatever reason, so it would be. He had suffered enough over the centuries. Those allegedly of cleaner souls and without sin often held darker and more sinister secrets, and took part in more repulsive perversions.

The louder men of conscience and faith yelled and preached the more it seemed they harbored obscene thoughts and desires. He had known many such men over the years, at times joyfully managing to end their foul bloodlines, easing the world of such filth.

Casca's sins and weaknesses, if such they were, were few. Had he loved mother or daughter, it would inevitably end the same. Even the ultimate pleasure and gift of love would still always be taken from him, as time was not on his side. Time was a predator that would invariably leave him alone in the end. Casca laughed at himself, bitterly amused at how dark thoughts too often seemed to accompany and overtake his few moments of pleasure.

SEVENTEEN

Oba Awanoshe was not very demanding of Casca. Public appearances were few and he had not been asked to speak or even be spoken of at any events. He almost felt ignored, as if perhaps he had served his purpose, magically allowing for the Edo to overwhelm the Igbo, and now Oba Awanoshe felt he had outgrown his welcome. What way was this to deal with a god? Nearly pinching himself Casca realized his own foolish thoughts of his own existence.

At the least Casca had expected a triumphant gloating for the overwhelming victory, or a confirmation of Oba Awanoshe's previous contention that the Edo forces would be invincible with Casca as the leader, a symbolic bringer of good fortune and earthly wealth. He got neither. The Edo were happy that Oba Awanoshe was pleased with the outcome of the campaign and did not question their immediate good fortune. This level of comfort, however, did not last long.

Within days Oba Awanoshe's iron hand returned. A few executions took place, punishing people for an assortment of insignificant or nonexistent actions. Many of Anaken's commanders were reshuffled and given lowly posts, after years of service, fidelity and loyalty out of fear—yet still loyalty—while a few disappeared, making many wonder if they had been killed. No one dared question their circumstances, as Oba Awanoshe was well known for his infinitesimal patience and mercy.

Some that had never shown anything approaching leadership qualities were unreasonably promoted, given decision-making posts beyond their abilities. Panic, paranoia and fear came back to a people who were quickly returning to their suffering ways. Oba Awanoshe's royal guards, nearly tripled in their number, reverted to their old ways of cruelty, public beatings and harassment, plunging the lowly Edo people back into terror and uncertainty. Things had changed, yet they remained the same.

Anaken was not praised for his victory; his successful campaign was merely acknowledged. An obviously transparent action by Oba Awanoshe, Casca thought, as this clearly indicated the Oba's concern about Anaken's popularity and his potential threat to the Oba's reign. It would not have been the first time that a military commander overtook the throne. Oba Awanoshe had hoped for a successful campaign, but this had been too easy.

Slowly, days of misery returned. Celebrations, song and wine were long forgotten as the reality of the people's own existence set in. The spoils of war were not theirs to enjoy, only the dark memories of their actions. Once more they had been led and controlled by Oba Awanoshe. The Edo people soon came to realize that the last few days of festivity had been nothing more than a bitter mirage.

Unlike them, as time passed, Casca found himself lost in the pleasures that life offered. He had decided that for the time being he would not hold concerns, not beyond his daily life anyway. He knew well it would not last long, but why fight it for now? Perhaps he could make up for hundreds of years of suffering and pain. Ary and her daughters certainly tried to make it so.

Anah and Okuse did not allow days to become repetitious or even remotely mundane. Food they provided always managed to surprise Casca in its variety, exquisite preparation and taste. The nights were no different. Without being prompted, one of them always found an exotic way to entertain him. Not wanting to disappoint, or be disappointed, he happily obliged.

Many nights he spent in Ary's arms, allowing himself to be lost in her world. As she slept, he often enjoyed the still of the night, feeling her warmth by his side, nearly allowing him to escape the reality that would inevitably return.

Strange noises off in the distance sometimes brought concern to Casca's sleeping mind. A soldier he had been, a soldier he would remain. His instincts, even while sleeping, were on guard. The sounds were mostly the muffled bellows of elephant calves or other animals. At times Casca could hear Anah and Okuse, giggling like the young girls they were, keeping each other from sleep with their embellished stories.

Long nights spent with Ary did not disappoint. Leaning back against the cool wall, while sitting on his bed, Casca searched Ary's eyes. His gaze swept across her face, at times shifting toward her neck, endlessly admiring her. Sighing softly, he smiled at her.

"I trust I do not displease you in any way," she whispered, breaking the silence. Knowing that was not nearly the case, she sat by him, holding his right hand and caressing his arm.

"I suppose not. There is nothing to be found . . ." Casca rambled on, almost oblivious of her words.

Realizing he had barely heard a word she had said, Ary intensified her efforts, making certain he would be unable to ignore her. Nearly catlike, she slipped across the bed, sitting across Casca's legs, facing him, locking her ankles around his back. Looking up at her, Casca realized he had not paid attention.

"There is nothing anyone could find . . . ," he whispered once more, running his hand across her face and neck, then slowly moving down, his fingers tracing the smooth skin between her breasts. Caressing her, Casca gently shook his head side to side, then nodded with a smile. Her raised eyebrows made him acknowledge that she did not know what he was speaking of.

"You are perfection, there is nothing that anyone could find that was not so . . ." Pulling her closer, he kissed her deeply, Ary now understanding what he had been speaking of while staring at her.

"Will you give me a son?" she whispered, nearly out of breath from his words and lips. Frightened by her own words, surprised that she had dared, Ary looked deep into Casca's eyes. "Will you?"

"I cannot . . . No one can be born of me . . . That is my destiny," Casca's response stabbed at him, as he remembered the curse that assured his loneliness across the centuries. "I wish it could be different."

Sitting back, Casca held her face with both hands while lost in her eyes. "I wish it could be." Casca flipped Ary's hair over her shoulders and continued caressing her neck and arms. Ary closed her eyes, sighing deeply, and arched her back. She did not question anymore. Casca's lips were once more upon her.

Warm nights, aided by the pleasant eastern breezes, were intoxicating, allowing for the mind and soul to rest. At times when he would wake, the stillness of the night wrapped him in contentment. He would look with great pleasure at Ary, watching her gently breathe, a smile almost finding its way onto her beautiful lips.

It had been weeks since the fall of Igbo Ukwu. Time had passed uneventfully, days and nights melding into each other, bringing nothing but comfort and pleasure. Casca awoke suddenly, stirred by something unseen. Looking over his left shoulder, he saw that Anah slept by his side, almost purring, like a content lion cub. "I need to breathe . . . ," she mumbled in her sleep, ". . . please . . ."

Okuse had left sometime after he had drifted off to sleep, and had likely returned to the room that she usually shared with her older sister. Casca was not the only thing they tried to share alike.

Raising himself onto his elbows, Casca tried to find what had awakened him. There was no sound that came to his ears, and it was likely not what had broken his sleep. Reaching toward his right temple, Casca's fingers could feel a bead of perspiration trickle along the artery that extended beneath his ear. Something deep inside his sleep had been working all along, disturbing his subconscious, enough to make him perspire and to wake him. The air was still, as it had been for the last few days, yet something was different, different enough to have roused him. He could recall nothing from his dreams that might have caused him to stir.

Sitting up, Casca swung his feet over Anah's slight body, trying not to wake her. Without sound, her lips moved, at times appearing to plead. His toes grabbed at the floor as he shifted over to the left, eyeing the window. A slight wind had picked up from the south, fluttering the short, streaming yellow valence hanging from the pelmet by the foot of his bed. The midnight stars cast light and shadow upon his window, unsettling his vision.

Breathing in deep, Casca filled his lungs with the night air, closing his eyes, quietly trying to find what had awakened him, seeking to pick up a scent or feel the slightest vibrations or sound. The wind gently whispered, puzzling his nose for a moment, but there was nothing there. Perhaps it was nothing. Just unsettled nerves, nerves always at the ready, not unlike a sleeping beast's, always ready to pick up and run, or fight, even in the deepest of sleep.

Lying back down, Casca eased onto his side as Anah gently nuzzled her way in against his chest, pressing her body as close as it would allow. "I want more," she again mumbled in her sleep. "I need, I need." Her beautiful face rubbed into his neck, wetting him with her full lips, letting out a near whimper in mid sleep. Breathing deeply, he stroked her head gently, pulling the thin red cover over her tiny naked body. For now, he would let her sleep.

The following morning once again brought the winds of war back into Casca's life.

"It is morning." Okuse's soft voice roused him from deep sleep. He awoke as she brought in a silver tray with fresh juice and freshly baked grain bread displayed on it. Casca watched as she held a small copper bowl filled with warm and sweet honey and generously dripped its contents onto steaming bread.

"It smells delicious." He tried to compliment her through a yawn, as he attempted to awaken.

Wiping the sleep out of his eyes with a warm, moist

towel in her right hand, Okuse handed Casca the oversized cup of fresh juice, trying not to spill a drop while continuing her early towel bath.

Her way was gentle, yet he clearly sensed Okuse's concern, as he would once again leave them, in their minds perhaps never to return. Crinkling her eyebrows, she instantly changed her demeanor as she turned toward her sister.

"Move it, you lazy heifer. The morning sun should be burning your eyes by now."

Kicking her still sleeping sister with her right foot, she tried to steady herself while continuing with the warm towel, and attempting to feed Casca all the while. Gulping down the bittersweet juice that followed the honeyed bread, Casca smiled at her, amused by her balancing act. Casca had never seen Okuse so upset, yet he knew her reasons. This might have been the end.

Anah awoke groggily, as the kicking had rapidly turned painful. She was ready to snap at her sister, but quickly stopped, as she realized that she had clearly overslept.

"Stop it please, please," she pleaded as the weight of Okuse's kicks were almost keeping her down. Backing out of the bed, she disappeared hastily though the doorway. Casca smiled, nearly embarrassed for having been caught, warranting Okuse's upset look, as he had unashamedly followed Anah's exit through the doorway with his eyes.

"How dare she." Okuse attempted to sound motherly. "I might just need to speak to her. Our mother will be quite displeased with her laziness. Is there anything else that would please you?" Okuse asked, realizing that suddenly she was alone again with Casca. "Anything?"

"My reveille has been without fault," Casca responded, pleased by the food she had brought, and embarrassed by his staring at Anah while she had departed. "Thank you," he added, his words and smile disarming Okuse's recently upset eyes.

Casca stood in front of the polished copper mirror, naked but for the cup he held in his left hand and the remaining bread morsel his right hand still palmed. Ary had entered the room and joined in with giving him a warm towel bath.

The warmth of the towels, along with the firm and constant pressure, invigorated him instantly.

Finishing the last of the bread, he wiped his mouth on his left forearm, to have it quickly sponged off by Okuse, who gave him a half-smile half-frown. She knew he was set to go and was not about to displease him in any manner. He needed to have a clear mind, not one clouded by insignificant dribble. Attention had always been great, yet today he was getting an overly meticulous going over.

With a sad but hopeful look Ary quietly whispered into his ear, ''Your time is near.'' Looking down into her beautiful brown eyes, Casca smiled, understanding her words.

This day they spent together, enjoying each other's company, trying to get out of each moment everything it could provide. Anah and Okuse, reluctant as they were, understood and stayed clear of their mother and Casca unless summoned. She had been overly generous and indulgent with them in regard to Casca; perhaps she had hoped all their charms might even work on a god, and possibly convince him to stay and protect. It would not have been the first time a god had been tempted.

To avoid any chance of losing precious time, they stayed inside his dwellings, away from the onlookers, well-wishers and religious sorts who hounded Casca, attempting to read the future from every one of his deliberate or inadvertent actions. ''Speak to us, let us know what to do''—the words did not change much. ''Have we failed you? Help us.'' The words did not deviate, no matter where Casca had been, and who the god of the day might have been. People could be week and pathetic in any land.

Casca had had it with them—no matter where he had been, veiled men, speaking in tongues, waving their hands and rolling their fear-filled eyes, overreacting from even the slightest happenings. All those people ever brought was fear and confusion, often leading men to blind sacrifice or death.

With Ary's dwellings adjacent to his, Anah and Okuse were able to dart in and out, bringing all they were asked for without the slightest of resistance or procrastination. Unfair as it might have seemed, Ary was still their mother, and Casca had shared himself more than even they had hoped for. This was not the time to question her.

Few words were spoken between them. As always she could nearly read his mind, and even when not perfectly so, the results were more than most could have asked for in life. This day they spent walking in the garden, enjoying the peace and quiet the solitude could provide.

The following days would bring none of the beauty this day provided. War was at hand, with all its obscene death and likely execution of another people. History repeated itself regardless of century or location.

The baked clay bath was filled with hot water as Casca was undressed. The sisters had finished their tasks and quickly exited the area, leaving behind gold-streamed towels and Casca's sandals. Okuse had attempted to ask Casca if she could stay, pouting her lips and dropping her eyes, but a quick glance from her mother made her regret her moment of weakness. Ary had no patience for such foolishness at this time.

Gingerly stepping into the steaming bath, Casca closed his eyes, waiting a moment until his body acclimated to the heat. Warm vapors enveloped him, beads of perspiration running down from his temples to his neck. Opening his eyes quickly, he smiled as Ary's arms anxiously awaited him. Dressed in nothing more than the bow in her hair, she took him with eager anticipation, her hot-oil-covered skin undulating against his body, gliding in a warm embrace.

This was no cleansing bath. Leaning down on the shallow inclined rest, Casca allowed his arms to fall by his sides as Ary lay upon him. He joyfully exhausted every bit of pleasure from this moment. Perhaps it would be long before next time.

Casca slept until darkness fell upon his room. When he opened his eyes, Anah's beautiful smile greeted him.

"I knew it would be my good fortune to sit here when you awoke," she giggled in her playful manner. "Okuse has left just a few moments ago," continued the young girl as she rubbed the sleep out of his eyes with her girlish charm. "What is your pleasure?" she whispered while leaning in, loosening the veil around her bosom just a hair's distance from his face. "My sister won't be back for nearly an hour," she indicated with the most obvious of intentions.

"I see you are awake at last. I had feared morning would come." Obviously exaggerating her words, Ary came into the room, bringing a tray of food. She knew well Casca would not sleep through the night. There was more time to be spent together. Stomping her foot with displeasure, Anah exited quickly, making every attempt not to make eye contact with her mother. Smiling at both of them, Casca sat up and took the cup of hot kola-nut brew Ary had handed him.

Sitting down in front of Casca, Ary took his hands.

"I cannot imagine where my girls ever got all that brazenness and enthusiasm," kidded Ary in a low whisper.

Gently rubbing his hands, massaging every joint between her delicate hands, tugging at them slightly with her soft fingertips, she looked up into his clear gray blue eyes. Seeing concern in her poorly camouflaged expression, Casca pulled her up toward him.

"You know I will return," he whispered to her.

"I do not fear for your life, for all I know you really are Olokun and are immortal, but I fear losing you . . . I know eventually time will separate us. I had lived all these years alone, just with my daughters, but now I cannot imagine life without you."

Biting his inner lip, trying to hide his anger and frustration, Casca cursed at his predicament. Damned he had been. To love and be punished, forever losing anyone he had ever cared for.

"I am sorry for my words. I know I have no right to complain or feel sorry for myself. No one could have been more fortunate than I, to share this time, knowing it will eventually end . . ."

Drowning her words out with his lips, Casca pulled Ary toward him. Hungrily he kissed her, not allowing her time to think. Perhaps foolishly, he tried to ease her suffering, yet he knew of nothing else to do. What a remarkable woman she was. So carefree, yet so insightful and passionate. Separating their lips softly, Casca smiled at her.

"I will return to you," he tried to ensure her. "I regret I can promise no more."

"I knew you would come to us. My daughters and I had

known about the legend of Olokun for years. As the last years had been punishing us, we knew the time was near. All my people did.''

''You must know I am not Olokun of your people . . . ?''

''It is not important if you are the god of our prophecies. Our time together has been more precious than any god could have provided. However, I do know that you will deliver us.''

Sitting back, Casca smiled and admired Ary. He thought of being angry at her for expecting so much. But that was not about to happen. It was nearly impossible to hold anger toward her, that he had learned over the last few months. Had she known what a strange life he had had and what even stranger circumstances had brought him to their shores, she would not have been so confident of her savior. For a moment, loves of times past clouded in his distant memories. He could remember no one else for an instant. How great it would have been to remain with her. God or no god, his time here, with her, had eased many past years of suffering.

Unfortunately, Ary insisted he had a higher calling. Damned be it. Is this where redemption awaited him? The crucified Jew was not likely to make his return here. Casca raged at his curse, shaking his head and exhaling deeply.

Looking up, he could not help but smile. Her beautiful, bewitching eyes disarmed him.

''Forgive me,'' she whispered softly. ''I can feel your thoughts paining you.'' Reaching out, she held and caressed Casca's head, bringing him closer, attempting to comfort him with a deep kiss.

Once again the night brought pleasure and pain. The pleasure of this wonderful woman and the pain of her words, the pain that she and her people had endured over the years. Not unlike Anaken, she shared the history of her people with Casca. From back as far as when she had been a mere child, she remembered the death of the Oba and his queen who died in the blue lights, the birth of ''the second one,'' he who was to become Oba Awanoshe, and the many years of pain and suffering at his cruel hands. Perhaps not unlike the history and plight of many other peoples, but this Casca could not ignore. Her words burned at his soul.

"When you look at me like that, it makes me believe that you are truly not Olokun."

"Tell me more of your people," responded Casca, not wanting to completely disillusion Ary, and perhaps also wanting to give her a glimmer of hope.

Looking at Casca with uncertainty, yet understanding, Ary continued her tale. "It was not long before knowledge of Oba Awanoshe spread through the land. We had heard tales of men born as him, ripped from their dying mothers, but not of ones who looked so much unlike us. Even men who had traveled through the northern deserts to find their way to our lands, or come from the great waters on wooden ships, had looked more like us than Oba Awanoshe.

"The initial fear of his appearance soon dissipated, but his actions and demeanor quickly brought misery and pain. The council of the elders had taken to leading us since the true crown prince, Ewuare, was not yet of age."

Casca remembered with pleasure the many days spent with Ewuare, the man who had found him along the shores of the great ocean, looking more like a creature of the depths than a man. His fondness for Ewuare, perhaps more than just affinity toward the true crown prince, a certain feeling of righteousness, had been sufficient to lead him on this mad journey into this land of mystery and pain.

"We had hoped," continued Ary, "that in a few years Ewuare could take the royal throne, as expected of the first-born male. That would not be. The elders foretold of plagues and death, reading the old prophecies. They believed that the death of our Oba and his queen had been destiny and that the young prince, even though he was the second born, should rule. Many had wondered if he would be able to rule, but we were afraid to question his existence. No one, however expected him to be so unlike us. By the time we understood the scourge and anguish he was about to bring upon us, it was too late."

Ary's words of anger, sadness and even desperation ripped at Casca's heart. Caressing her face, he wiped a tear out of her eye and brought it to his lips. Looking up, she smiled at him and continued reluctantly.

"Before he even reached ten years of age, Oba Awanoshe had assumed complete control. We had been blinded by fear. Most of us, but not all. Fear of the old prophecies and, as time passed, even greater fear of Oba Awanoshe and his powers. Soon he had mastered us like children.

"No one dared question him. The old man, Ooton, that evil spawn of hell itself, had found his way into the heart and confidences of Oba Awanoshe. No one remembers Ooton as being anything but an incarnation of evil; his magical ways had always challenged life and death. Many of our elders remember Ooton as an old man even when they were children. Some consider that black pipe of his, with its never-ending smoke, as his lifeline to the beginning of time. No one had ever seen him without that foul thing hanging from his lips. With Ooton's help and mystical ways, Oba Awanoshe has been able to always hold fear over us.

"By the time he had reached twelve years of age, he had grown into what you see now. His patience and understanding were minute, while his tolerance was even less than that. He randomly executed officials, even members of the clergy, and reshuffled most of the military commanders. A few had come into his favor, only to be quickly banished, killed or worse. Oba Awanoshe has a way with pain, as you must know by now. The uncertainty of life for the present is and has been torture. I and my daughters have been allowed to live and have been harassed little. Anah and Okuse know of the horrors of life outside our home. I could not, and would not want to, completely shelter them from the horrors that haunt our people. For reasons unknown to me, we have survived."

Quieting for a moment, Ary raised her head and looked deep into Casca's eyes. "Perhaps there has already been divine intervention. We were allowed to live to receive and serve you. The ancients must have known of your eventual arrival."

"Perhaps I have been the fortunate one," offered Casca. Embracing her, he watched Ary with sadness and admiration. In a man's world such as this, this brave woman had never lost her strength and clarity of thought, even if clouded by legend and prophecy. As a mother she had cared for her children and survived in such a world of mysticism and misery, doing as needed to survive. If believing in him had given her strength, so be it.

"In recent years," Ary resumed her story, "Oba Awanoshe and Tajah-Nor formed a strange alliance. No doubt not trusting each other in the least, but an obscene relationship that strengthened both of them. His henchmen, interrogator and executioner, Tajah-Nor has done all of the Oba's evil bidding."

Casca searched his mind, trying to recollect the reason for his familiarity with Tajah-Nor. He had met the man the first day of Ishana, the day Oba Awanoshe had received the quarterly tribute from all the territories. Tajah-Nor, following Oba Awanoshe's orders, had opened the largest of the nine coffers, the one that contained the small brass vessel, the *iru,* and the rattle-staff topped by the elephant head. These Casca and the other four had brought from the territory of Uda, as instructed by Ewuare. Ewuare the first-born.

Casca shook his head, trying to rid himself of whatever was stifling his mind, preventing him from thinking clearly. The sight of the frail-looking Tajah-Nor, trembling while handing over the *iru* and the rattle-staff, replayed in Casca's mind. Tajah-Nor had later stood by the royal throne, eyes shifting, with his left hand by his mouth, trying to weigh the situation and his possibly questionable future.

"In his early years, Tajah-Nor, a man no less evil than Ooton, had in his own ways ascended to the high post of chief of the *eghaevbo nore,* the head of the Ibiwe, the highest of our councils. Treason and murder had been his loyal companion, allowing him into lofty positions. His attempts at pleasing the Oba had always been clear and obvious. Your arrival has given him cause for concern, but apparently not enough to act on it, as far as I have been told.

"Fear him, he is as evil as the Oba himself," Ary suddenly gasped. "He has no mercy and will take any action to preserve himself, at no matter what cost."

Clutching at Casca, she held him, almost caressing him, trying to protect him, as if he was a child.

"I will not let him harm me . . . or you, that I promise,"

responded Casca, nearly overwhelmed at the sight of this brave woman trying to protect him.

"Tajah-Nor has never made it a secret, his loyalty to the Oba and his never-ending attempts at pleasing him. Times past he tried to persuade Oba Awanoshe to take a queen, or so I have been told, but the Oba has always refused. Many of us wondered why he did so. It is almost as if at times he has shown disgust for his people, and their appearance. Neighboring kingdoms have offered their daughters, in an attempt to form an alliance and keep peace, but he has always rejected them.

"Young or old, princess or not, he has never shown any interest. Some have speculated that he has no interest in women, no matter how young and beautiful. Men always prefer their women young, younger than most admit to, but even the youngest he has rejected. We have had no answer, Tajah-Nor has tried, but never successfully to please him in this regard. The council of the elders has shown concern that the royal bloodline, going back two dozen generations, foul as it has become, will be interrupted."

Even a bloodline that has become such, still must go on . . . they often mumbled to themselves. "Any mention of the first born, prince Ewuare, was not heard. The level of paranoia, the fear of being found out, extinguished any attempts of bravery. Trusting your words to anyone but the voice in your own mind was foolish and a possible invitation for death. Oba Awanoshe's ears were everywhere."

Casca did not want to hear anymore. How much more could there have been? Every century has its monster, a cruel beast that enslaves and destroys its own. Perhaps Oba Awanoshe would be remembered as such over the centuries, as many others have. Casca's concerns were once again elsewhere.

Pulling Ary up close against his chest, he kissed her, his lips gently indicating that he did not want to hear anymore. Watching her tell her tale had been painful. Perhaps he could take her away with him. But where, and to what end? But what about the words that were ringing in his ears not long after Ewuare had found him along the seashore? *The time has not yet come.* Possibly this was the right time, and

Oba Awanoshe needed to die before he butchered another people. The frustration of Casca's predicament ate at his cursed soul.

Anah and Okuse broke the deathly silence, bringing in trays of food and drink and placing them on a knee-high rectangular table. "There is lots more," Anah reported, trying not to disturb them. "We have prepared all of it ourselves," she offered, unsuccessfully trying to make conversation. Sheepishly smiling, with just a hint of bitterness in their upturned lips, they made their exit, leaving Casca and Ary alone for possibly their last night together.

"We hope it pleases you" were the last words to be heard from the sisters. The aroma of a dozen delicacies swirled, intermixing, creating an overpowering blend Casca was glad he did not have to resist. The girls had done well. Casca and Ary sat on the floor, feet drawn underneath them, all the while holding hands.

Breaking her hold, Ary reached and handed Casca a large cup of his favorite kola-nut brew. Smiling, Casca accepted it, knowing this evening was not going to need any further stimulation than the woman at hand. Closing his eyes, breathing in the honey-sweetened vapors, he took a few sips, enjoying the irritation his taste buds still encountered, no matter how much honey the cup held.

The setting was a feast for the senses. Delicacies he had enjoyed previously crowded the table, along with dishes he could not identify but was anxious to taste. Anah and Okuse even with jealousy in their hearts, had still been quite generous with the feast. Not unlikely Ary had had to adjust their attitudes for this evening. One taste of each was going to easily overload his usually receptive belly.

Parting his lips, Casca attempted to remark on the perfection of the presentation, but Ary had other plans. With a gentle turn of her hands, she covered his mouth. There was no more that needed to be said tonight. Pulling her hand back, Ary felt a warm moist area where Casca's lips and tongue had left their mark. Shuddering, letting out a soft cry, she faced her man. Almost forgetting herself, she proceeded to further perfect the evening.

Standing up, Ary closed all the curtains and gently blew out all the candles that lit the room. Sitting back down, legs crossed underneath her, she lit a small candle just behind her, enough to barely light the immediate area behind her and a small portion of the table.

The night was still and near complete darkness. Even the slight breeze coming in from the ocean had died down, creating an eerily quiet moment. They sat facing each other, the small rectangular table between them. No sound was to be heard, and no ray of light irritated the eye, just the warm glow of a candle, sending undulating shadows from behind Ary. Her soft hands reached out and closed Casca's eyes with a downward movement of two fingers, allowing him a last glimpse of her beautiful smiling face before complete darkness overtook him.

In complete silence and darkness the indulgences of the evening continued. Past and future disappeared as Casca was overwhelmed by the moment and the uncertain anticipation of what was to come. Ary had her ways.

Warm and moist delicacies came to Casca's lips. He could hear nothing but his own thoughts and Ary's fluttering shallow breathing. At times palm wine followed to wash down the contents, at other times bitter fruit chased away the sweetness of what had been, leaving him guessing as to what was to come.

Expertly his tongue searched her fingers, as hard and sweet grapes were brought to his lips. Bread soaked in juices of fruit or honey found its way onto his palate. His teeth crushed the soft and sweet raisins the bread held. Following the edges of her fingers, his tongue reached toward the inner webbing between them, exploring her hands. Bursting a fresh date between his tongue and palate he hungered for more.

Cool palm wine washed the remains, quenching his thirst, yet exciting him for what was yet to come. The tantalizing sequence of tastes, their sensual and unseen delivery, exhilarated Casca beyond reason. Reaching out, he tried to hold her, only to be pushed back down to his seat, the feast to continue. It was not yet time.

The sensuous feast continued until possibly Ary herself was unable to resist the melding of their bodies. The temptress had had enough. Pulling him up, caressing his warm chest and shoulders, she guided him toward his bed. Easing him down, she stood back to first also give him a feast for the eyes. Gliding her hands across his face with a gentle stroke, she allowed him to open his eyes.

Breathing deeper, Casca pulled himself up to his elbows, anxiously ready to enjoy her beauty. Casca smiled, amused at how after all these centuries and countless women, the anticipation of watching a woman undress was still nearly as intense as the first time. Especially when it was a special woman like this.

Facing Casca, with her back to the solitary glimmering candle, she disrobed. Light danced across her shoulders, bathing the enclosure within a pool of light and shadows, hypnotizing Casca as her dress dropped over her shoulders, the turn of her hips rounding as the cloth was deflected in its descent. Slowly she opened the veil that had been draped around her neck and chest, allowing it to also fall to the ground. Casca watched it glide, moving as if hindered by the air itself, pausing momentarily as it caressed her breasts.

Sitting up, Casca reached out, holding her hands, pulling her warm primed body upon him. Their bodies melded into each other, touching and embracing, trying to please without limits. Ary held his eager right hand, caressing her face and bosom with it. Pulling back, Casca hesitated, concerned that his rough, scar-covered hand might hurt her. Ary smiled and intensified her actions, pulling his hand across herself, each raised scar and roughness of his hands further intensifying her reactions.

Putting his hand down by his side, Ary leaned over Casca, allowing her breasts to brush upon his chest, shuddering as each ancient battle scar and wound now brought exhilaration and passion to her as her body moved over his. Quickening her pace, placing her grip on his upper arms, she looked into Casca's eyes, holding his stare seemingly forever, refusing to blink, never letting up with her fevered, furious dance.

The bewitching continued until, unable to control himself, quieting her protestation with his lips, Casca pulled himself upon her. Their bodies became one, twisting and bending, unknowing where one's flesh began and the other's ended. Passionate and tireless, the still of the night kept them company.

EIGHTEEN

Oba Awanoshe's troops advanced toward the land of Yoruba. Anaken, along with two of the Oba's recently most trusted *edogun,* his war chiefs, were leading the assault. The strategic charge would be made by Anaken and his most experienced men, along with two new field generals, Conah and Nevaad, whom Oba Awanoshe had recently promoted from basically out of nowhere. Conah had been one of Tajah-Nor's underlings, never having shown anything but complete loyalty and allegiance to Tajah-Nor and Oba Awanoshe. His previous position had involved keeping security personnel loyal to the Oba. Basically an executioner and clearly not a man to lead thousands into battle.

Nevaad was a former member of the Oba's private guard, a man with endless weaknesses, more concerned with his belly in recent years, just another puppet the Oba could control. His only experience in battle had been taking part in the slaughter of the Igbo, a time when strategy and tactics had been unnecessary. At no time had he ever shown any leadership qualities. Conah and Nevaad's recent advancements had been some of the changes that had unexpectedly followed Anaken's return from Igbo-Ukwu.

Anaken's charge of one thousand men headed northwest

toward the borders of Yoruba. Not unlike the assault on the Igbo, Casca followed along with Anaken's private guard, loyal men who had been in his charge for as long as they had been soldiers. The taste of war—more of butchery than of war—was very recent in their minds, a foul taste that a few weeks of revelry and rest had not cleansed. Nevertheless, this was not a position one chose when one fancied; they were soldiers, while Oba Awanoshe was Oba.

Two days' hard march brought them to the outskirts of Udo. Anaken ordered camp to be set up on the eastern shore of the Ovia, just north of Udo. Casca remembered having passed the village of Udo on his way to the Edo capital. How ignorant he had been of this land and its pain just so recently, he mused.

Things looked the same, but Casca knew people here were well aware of all that the last few months had brought. The fall of Igbo did not bring them riches or pleasures. Oba Awanoshe did not share the plunder except with a select few. The village of Udo received tolerance, for now. And they knew it. Being subservient, sacrificing their young men in the never-ending campaigns, and their young women in the Oba's obscene plans, was something they had painfully learned to accept. They knew of the strange creature who had come from the sea, perhaps to be a savior as prophesied by the ancients from Ife. Some had given up on the legends of Olokun; others still held on to the only thing they had left—faith.

Once more war was at hand. *It is a man with foolish reason who campaigns more than once a season . . .* The melodic, nearly poetic words of Shiu Lao Tze echoed in Casca's memories. Casca knew quite well that an army driven so was often doomed to failure.

Where there are big rewards, there are valiant men. The words of Lao Tze resounded. Only an experienced leader who promoted and rewarded his men properly could receive allegiance and enthusiasm over time. *A great general,* the words of Lao Tze returned to his ears, *does not bring his men into war once more before the harvest. The body and soul must rest, even if the mind cannot forget.* Words of wisdom many generals had learned to live by, while others had died thinking otherwise.

The following day brought them through the land of Owo on their way to Yoruba. Yoruba was vast and its people spread out unevenly throughout the land. Anaken's troops were allowed to pass unhindered, the people of Owo tempting fate as Oba Awanoshe had apparently made a pact for safe passage through a narrow section of Owo that separated Edo and Yoruba.

Crossing supposedly neutral territory left Casca uneasy, as alliances were made and broken with great ease, as he had learned from lessons past. It appeared unreasonable to Casca that their passage through another's land would be so allowed. Allegiances lay where one's interests were.

Having passed just north of the capital city of Owo, Anaken's men set up camp and rested before the following day's assault. Plans appeared too simple and rehearsed, bringing further concern to Casca. Why had there not been any scouting reports, or even the smallest of skirmishes? Was there not a need for constant intelligence updates? After all, this was a vast land, where communication was difficult, needing runners or perhaps smoke signals. No Yoruba posts had been overrun, or noted as recently abandoned while they marched by. Were the Yoruba going to be overrun not unlike the Igbo, to become just another former people? Casca had more questions than answers.

Watching Casca sipping on his kola-nut brew, Anaken approached, sat down and leaned against a fallen tree trunk. A shallow yet wide stream rumbled noisily a few hundred feet south of the camp. Crossing it had been awkward and time consuming. The clay mud had stuck to everyone's footwear and any clothing that had dragged, slowing them down and unpleasantly caking between their toes, forcing them to set up camp prematurely. Quickly hardening, the brittle clay had to be scraped off immediately, as it entered every crack and crevice of their feet, causing misery to the ones that procrastinated.

Some of the supplies had been lost in the river by the inexperienced men, mere boys who had been dragged along to act as chattel. Definitely not a pleasant crossing, especially if one had to do it in a hurried retreat.

"Your time is nearing," offered Anaken, breaking the silence.

Uncertain how to react, Casca sat back, sipping on his drink, half-grunting half-nodding in response, forcing Anaken to eventually continue the conversation.

"You will be ready when the time comes, won't you?" Anaken further questioned.

Knowing this time he could not cough or grunt his way out of a response, Casca answered.

"The time is unquestionably approaching," stated Casca, elevating his voice, causing Anaken to be uncertain whether it had been a question or a statement of fact. The burden of not knowing ate at Casca.

Unsure how to respond or to further expect an answer, Anaken quickly changed his focus.

"We will advance two hours before sunrise. By dawn we will be in Yoruba territory. The forces of Conah and Nevaad have been coordinated accordingly, Conah coming from the northeast, Nevaad from the southwest. Any defending forces, no doubt caught by surprise, will be funneled and surrounded, forcing them to surrender or suffer catastrophic losses. Oba Awanoshe believes the Yoruba will concede to him without a fight—"

"You do not believe that truly," interrupted Casca.

"Not at all," answered a very calm and not the least bit surprised Anaken. Casca found himself further bewildered by his circumstances. What was on Anaken's mind? he wondered.

"Our strategy is to occupy and force a surrender, making it obvious that resistance is futile," continued Anaken.

"You well know that will not happen?"

"Clearly so. The Yoruba will be crushed. That is the Oba's will," answered Anaken very calmly, further settling Casca's suspicions.

"The plans are to slowly envelope any defending forces, causing a slow retreat toward Otto, the Yoruba capital, where Yoruba's religious leaders have their dwellings on the outskirts of the city. Oba Awanoshe knows the Yoruba army will not abandon their priests on their retreat and perhaps regroup elsewhere. They will have no choice but to eventually stand their ground. When they dig in for a fight, a fight they will have. Our superior forces will overwhelm their unprepared and disorganized army, crushing them easily. As it has been said, to the victor go the spoils,'' completed Anaken.

Quite simple and calculated, Casca thought. Also unreasonable. Overtaking a nation in such a manner was unpractical and not likely to happen. Whether the Yoruba surrendered or fought a losing battle, occupation would be short-lived. The land of Yoruba was huge, with endless supply of men and raw materials. So far from home, the Oba's forces would be unable to occupy indefinitely.

The Igbo had been a nation of few, where completely overtaking and destroying them had been possible. Igbo people and land had been raped and laid bare, to be replaced by Oba Awanoshe's twisted dream of his own men using the Igbo women to produce a new generation of Edo. Slowly all that was Igbo was to be erased, as new generations were to be born.

Yoruba, due to its size, location and number of people, was much different. Any type of long-term occupation was senseless. Oba Awanoshe would have to leave thousands of his men just to maintain control. Such forces would not have it easy so far from home. Harassed and ambushed, their number would be constantly cut down, making it impossible to keep order. As far as Casca knew, that had never been the Oba's method. A shattering defeat, followed by years of torture, was his way of domination and subjugation.

Systematically Yoruba would be drained of its resources. Anyone showing even the remotest sign of resistance would be killed, and possibly but very unlikely, over many years, the nation would submit and become a controlled territory. A people that yielded and begged for mercy was what Oba Awanoshe had in mind.

Casca knew that Anaken too was quite uneasy and disbelieving about the strategy employed.

Dawn did not come as planned. Casca had awakened a few hours after midnight, with his ears to the ground and the palm of his right hand holding the earth. Sitting up, he breathed in. Looking over to his left, he saw Anaken also sitting up. Their eyes meeting, a small nod of their heads was all that was needed. They were about to be overrun.

There was no time to get prepared. With the wind at their backs, sound had not traveled in their favor, forewarning them; neither had the breezes that bring the smell of men and animals over long range. All that traveled their way was too late in the warning, vibrations the ground carried of thousands of men and animals in a mad charge ready to swarm and overwhelm the foolish invaders.

Casca stood with sword in hand, his blood boiling and heart pounding. Looking up, the morning stars were still hours away. The night would hold witness to the massacre of a thousand of Anaken's men.

The first wave of Yoruba soldiers hit them hard. Bells and trumpets filled the air with their deafening roar, bursting eardrums and unbalancing clear thought. The sound of battle approached, sending shivers of oncoming death to Anaken's men. Many of them had been awake before the wave of thunder overtook them, having also felt the impending attack, and were at the ready. That, however, was not going to make any difference. It was obvious they were outnumbered by at least threefold.

Chaos ensued as the fleetest of Yoruba were upon them. The first charge broke apart any semblance of organization. Even the smallest pockets of Edo soldiers were quickly dispersed, to be slaughtered by the sheer weight and number of their executioners. Just as it seemed that Anaken's men might be able to hold up and slow down the charge, the second wave of Yoruba's toughest and fiercest warriors were upon them.

The quarter moon lit the battlefield. Flashes of steel upon steel splintered the night, the fireflies of death raining upon men. Screams of horror, of man and beast, traveled over the plains as the morning approached. A sea of blood and body parts littered the ground as hundreds died, many with their weapons still in their sheaths and the drunkenness of sleep in their eyes.

Back to back, Casca and Anaken fought. Many died at their feet, but a moment's respite was all they had as many others threw themselves blindly at them, hoping their sheer volume would overwhelm Anaken and his closest guards. Flailing away desperately, Anaken's men tried to stay alive and with their last breaths protect their leader.

The Yoruba charge, like the locusts of the ancient plagues, kept coming. Mounds of steaming meat, crushed and pierced by ugly yellow bone and spear alike, surrounded Casca. As he stood on the top of dead and dying flesh, Casca's sword, nearly with a life of its own, sent dozens to their deaths. Blood poured from endless wounds, running down his chest and shoulders, enveloping him in a crimson veil. The fever of the kill, having clearly overtaken him, took the lives of many.

Imperceptible at first but slowly accelerating, a small pocket of Anaken's men started moving out of the crushing vise of onrushing Yoruba men. They broke through the sea of death, where men already dead still stood as the crushing wave kept them erect. They fell to the soggy ground only when enough had died, piling into heaps that the coming day's buzzards would feast on.

Breaking away, about thirty of them with Casca holding up the back of the line shifted out of the large mass of the dead and soon to be dead. Fighting desperately, Anaken took a sorrowful look back, seeing the last of his men brought to their knees, to be slaughtered, as none of them were about to allow themselves to be enslaved. Oba Awanoshe was not the only one known for cruelty with his battle prizes.

Picking up speed, the remaining two dozen or so followed Anaken's charge, crossing the cursed shallow stream that had forced them to set up camp prematurely the previous day. Many fell, to be trampled to death before the thick yellow water could even fill their lungs with the foul, stifling silt. Their torn and bloated bodies would feed the crocodiles overnight.

Sending nearly two hundred men, one of the Yoruba leaders appeared determined not to let anyone survive this battle. Charging through the stream, they gave chase. Casca thought of just standing his ground and fighting until he was hacked to pieces or the weight of men crushed him to the ground. *I will return to you.* His words to Ary came back to haunt him. Not that there was time to think, but he could not remember anytime past when a promise to a woman had ever entered his mind while the heat of battle had him in its grasp. *The time has not yet come.* Once more Ary's words came back to torment and confuse him.

Twisting and turning, his men were driven backwards. Hacking away madly, Casca and Anaken, standing side by side, were making every attempt to thin out the Yoruba onrushes as long as their sword-wielding arms did not give up on them. Taking a look over his shoulder, as much as the moment allowed, Casca eyed their destination. Not unlike an ancient hunting charge, they were about to be forced and pushed over the side of a cliff into a ravine.

It did not look like a very steep or high drop, but more than enough to maim and crush their bodies. The first to fall most likely would die; perhaps the ones to follow would have a chance to survive, cushioned by the dead bodies of their mates. Looking left and right, Casca could see there was no way around this fall. They had not noticed during the fever of battle that they had been herded toward the fall, with many Yoruba already having placed themselves, ready to receive the soon to be plunging bounty.

How many beasts, Casca wondered, had ended up on a spit, roasting over long hours after such a fall? The thoughts nauseated him, bringing new energy and vigor, bringing life, back to his weakening arm. Three more met their demise, falling at his feet, to be walked over as others took their places, continuing with the charge. Another three died a brutal, bloody death from the weight of Casca's sword, the horrible screeching of splintered bone joining the rest of the obscene sounds of death.

The precipice was upon them as the weight of bodies pushed them over. Facing the fall, Casca braced himself. Five had already gone over, screaming, awaiting the hardness of the ground below, in death to finally end this night of horror. Focusing his eyes, Casca met Anaken's for an instant just as their feet left the side of the cliff.

Long pointed spears were awaiting them. Some held to the ground, with sharpened metal points facing upward, toward them; others hurled skyward to hasten their meeting with flesh.

Bodies flying over the cliff were met in mid-flight, to be impaled, falling to the ground like arrow-pierced birds. Two men landed on the rocks below, their heads and bodies exploding from the momentum of the fall, staining the ground with themselves.

Once more Casca's curse brought him pain and salvation to others. Falling out of control, he crashed to the ground below, clutching at the spear that had caught him in the middle of the chest, above his heart. Nearly crying out, he grabbed at the blood-covered wooden shaft, just as the ground had rushed up and met him. The force of the blow knocked the wind out of him, stifling his breath, breaking the wooden shaft just beneath the flesh of his back, splintering the wood beneath his ribs.

Rolling in maddened pain, twisting and turning in the agony of ruptured lungs and heart, Casca somehow found his way back onto his feet. Drawing all his strength in one gasp, he tried to force air into his blood-filled lungs. A horrific scream left his throat as air finally rushed in, splattering a bloody spray through his nostrils, and for a moment startling the Yoruba warriors who were already upon him. Anaken had fallen and miraculously rolled to be standing near Casca, ready to defend himself with his dying breath. Ten more of his men survived the immediate impact, six of them already on their feet ready to fight. The others, impaled or crushed, had found peace.

Completely surrounded, they fought on. Encircled and overwhelmed, standing back to back, swinging with all they had left, Anaken and his men were going to make certain to leave an impression in the minds of the Yoruba. Flailing away with his right hand and parrying the rain of blows with the shield on his left forearm, Anaken, out of the corner of his eye, watched in astonishment Casca still standing and fighting with the shaft of the wooden spear sticking out of his chest.

With blood rapidly draining out of him, Casca battled like a man possessed. As he swirled around, the wooden shaft became a weapon of its own, braining anyone that got close enough that Casca did not have a chance of impaling with his broad sword.

The pain of the spear burning a hole in his chest, exposing his fragile lungs to the dirt and air, maddened Casca beyond control. Refusing to give in to the pain or the extensive loss of blood, he cut down his adversaries like a man wielding a sickle during harvest.

Splattering and liquefying the brains of another, the spear finally broke right at its entrance to Casca's chest, sending splinters of wood into his heart, the whole length of wood locking within his chest, from the front of his ribcage to the back. Casca was beyond pain, his single-minded actions maintaining their rain of death upon the Yoruba.

More of Anaken's men died, leaving only half a dozen to contend with perhaps another hundred Yoruba warriors. The six of them formed a small circle preparing for the last rush, one that would finally overrun them, ending it all. However, that was not to be. A horn sounded off in the distance, and within moments the circle of six were left to stand in a pool of blood and spilled flesh. Turning toward Casca, they all watched this beast that had defied any sense or logic, who had fought on when he should have been dead.

A man pushed his way through the now standing Yoruba men. Clearly a man of rank and power. Holding his crushed left arm with a bleeding right hand, he eyed his men and the six remaining Edo warriors. Blood poured from his left cheekbone, exposing raw, mangled flesh. Looking at Casca, his eyes hesitated, while quickly searching this strange white creature that had refused to die.

Casca, with the first moments of stillness since possibly six hours previous, was finally hit with all the pain and agony of his numerous wounds. Had it not been for this moment of truth, he would have likely collapsed in pain and near exhaustion.

There was complete silence. The stillness of the moment was deafening. Not a cry of man or beast was heard in the distance or close by. Casca could hear nothing but the screeching of his lungs trying to push against the wooden spear and the clotting blood that was overtaking his chest cavity.

Walking up close, the Yoruba commander slowly took in the sight. Eyeing Anaken, he exchanged a few words Casca could not understand. Looking at this mass of bleeding men, he raised his newly deformed left hand and pointed southeast. Anaken did not need to hear any more. The six of them would be allowed to live.

A small path opened up between the stunned Yoruba warriors, some appearing to want to protest, others confused and exhausted. Holding on to one another, Anaken's remaining six guards passed through the mass of Yoruba warriors, following Anaken and Casca, who, leaning against each other, slowly worked their way out.

The return home was slow and excruciating. There was not much that needed to be said. Each of them tended to their own wounds, trying to stop the bleeding, wrapping bandages tight where the body allowed, trying to do enough to make it back home.

Unable or unwilling to help one another, they kept to themselves, at times muttering prayers or obscenities, mostly whimpering from the pain. The six of them followed the trail back south, heads down, trying to spend as little energy as possible, knowing that the long trek home would test their strength of mind and body.

Off in the distance a herd of antelopes kicked up dust, nearly darkening the sky itself as thousands of them thundered by. A few dozen giraffes, their long necks wavering above the rest of the herd, attempted to find one another and move as a group. Underneath a tree, lion cubs and their mother stretched out, their stomachs gorged with the day's kill. Peacefully they slept in the shade.

Nearby, hundreds of wildebeest drank from a drinking hole, oblivious of the rest of the world, enjoying the coolness of the rock ledge–shaded waters. None of their lives had been affected by man recently, as men had been too busy hunting one another.

At the end of his wits, nearing despair, Casca moved slowly but steadily, knowing each moment brought him a step closer to Benin City and Ary. Unable to deny it, he could feel each step growing more and more difficult, his body slowly giving up.

"Should we help him?" sometimes Casca overheard. "He is Olokun, he does not need our help," the response usually came. "He has survived that impossible wound. I am sure his body is slowly healing itself,'' the voice of Ikan, one of the survivors, reassured them.

They moved on, wondering if their wounds would get the best of them, end their lives so far from home.

Casca's curse was gradually crippling him. Each movement of his legs and arms sent shivers of cold and numbness to his legs. Feeling as if singed by fire or ice, his toes and feet were responding less to his commands, becoming just pieces of meat and bone attached to his legs.

The painful horror of the shaft in his chest was slowly settling, to be overtaken by a frightening numbness. Digging into his spine with each movement, compressing and tearing at his nerves, the memories of having been pinned down under the wreckage of the *Kuta,* paralyzed from the waist down, came back to haunt him.

Reaching toward his chest, not wanting to look, he felt the broken end of the spear sticking out of him. Previously he had tried to grab it and perhaps force it out of himself by pulling or pushing, knowing well the pain it would bring, but his wicked curse would not allow it. Just as he had feared, his flesh was growing back around the broken shaft, making it part of his chest. Casca could not feel the shaft coming out of his back, but knew the same healing was taking place.

That blasted piece of wood, his body was going to keep within it, sinew and muscles growing around it, trapping it more and more as time went on. As time passed, the regrowing flesh embedded it into his spine, further cutting off any messages his brain might have wanted to send. The feeling of death was steadily moving up along his legs toward his hips and stomach. Casca was slowly becoming paralyzed.

Anaken and his six remaining men were not in much better shape. Each with broken limbs or deep lacerations that tortured them as they moved. Seeing Casca, they wondered how it could be for this man to live. Perhaps he really was Olokun, or Olokun's messenger, but if that was so, why had he allowed this to happen to himself and all the Edo?

Watching him struggle, each step becoming more of a formidable task than the previous, they pondered if he was going to make it back home. Fearing and not knowing what to do, they kept to themselves. At times Anaken appeared as if he were going to try and help Casca, but for reasons unknown to him, he did not dare. Not much different from Casca, they had more questions than answers.

It took nearly a day to cross the thin strip of land the people of Owo had allowed them to traverse unopposed just a few days previous. Unhindered, they moved on, knowing the town of Udo and the Ovia River were not far ahead.

The high sun was unbearable. Wounds had become sores, tissues dying and sloughing off from the heat and lack of proper attention. The leg of one of Anaken's men had started to fester, turning yellowish green, bringing with it a foul, filthy stench.

Anaken's voice broke the silence. "Help Ikan, we must do it." He turned, facing Ikan with sadness and conviction. "We have to, my friend." Anaken tried to comfort him.

Ikan's fevered face shook, well knowing what helping him meant. He gasped for air, trying to find strength and bravery somewhere in his failing body. Biting his lip, he took two more steps then stopped. Easing himself down, he sat with his head held high. It was the last time he would ever take such steps.

"I am ready. I will make it home," he declared stout-heartedly, without showing the least bit of doubt.

With the help of the others holding him down, Anaken cut off Ikan's leg from above the knee, discarding the diseased limb. Ikan had proven strong beyond reason, only allowing a single tear to trickle down his worn and grime covered face as he watched Anaken's sword separate his leg from the rest of his body. Using a makeshift splint and a broken branch for a wooden leg, he was likely to make it back home. Holding his bloodied spear as a crutch, he struggled on.

Casca did not help and no one had expected it. They still could not understand why he was living. If not the initial injury itself, the extensive loss of blood or the fever that accompanied such trauma should have killed him days before. Deciding not to question something they probably could not understand, they moved on.

It took all of Casca's strength and determination to continue. He no longer hurt. It was more of an entranced state of being. Casca's legs moved and he walked, his will refusing to give up, but he could not feel anything from his mid-chest down. At times faint sensations made themselves present, but even that Casca could not be certain of. He was not about to question it for now. As long as he could move, it was a good thing.

Having reached the town of Use they knew Siluko Road was going to bring them home within a day. Almost no words had been spoken the last few days, with all energy spent just to keep moving.

Anaken had regained some of his strength, his mind finally able to concentrate on more than surviving the pain of his injuries and the constant effort of walking steadily. Ikan was probably going to make it back home, but it appeared the rotting disease that had taken his leg was also going to take his life.

The putrid smell had returned to his body, the fetid yellowish discharge traveling up his thigh to his hips. There was no place to cut him again. He seemed to know it, yet apparently was only concerned with returning to his home. Tears ran down his cheeks, rolling up into dusty blobs while they made their way into his beard, eventually even the stream of tears drying up, as his body slowly was extinguishing from life. Gritting his teeth he took slow, deliberate steps.

"I will be all right." His words of near self-hypnosis were all that was heard from him. Dying on the road, to feed the buzzards, was not acceptable.

Casca had been in a feverish daze for the last few days, having eaten almost nothing, only water keeping him from burning up. The rest of them were in fair enough shape, strong enough to walk and think of what had become of them. They quietly wondered if the same fate had completely destroyed the armies of Conah and Nevaad.

Were they the sole survivors? Had this, the worst and most crushing campaign imaginable, completely decimated the Edo army? Who would defend them if Yoruba or other opportunistic neighbors were to attack? The thought of their home and families undefended, at the mercy of incensed neighbors, frightened them. Is this what Oba Awanoshe's blind greed and evil desires had brought them to? The anxious thoughts, as if all of them felt at once, accelerated their excruciatingly slow pace.

The early evening hours brought them to the outskirts of the city. People watched in horror these wretched survivors, painfully struggling to return. Onlookers were just that, whispering to one another muddled broken words to be barely heard came to Anaken's ears.

Casca remembered just a few months previous, the moment he had entered Benin City. All the pleasure and pain he had enjoyed and endured. It felt like years had passed. Received by no one, they entered through the city gate, each going his own way, finally having made it back.

NINETEEN

Casca awoke to Ary's gentle voice. The well-lit room weighed upon him, smothering his vision, hurting his head like a dagger in between the eyes. Struggling to open his eyes, raising eyelids that felt like boulders, he reached for her. Holding his hand, she smiled and kissed it softly. Watching her eyes, Casca tried to read her thoughts. He saw joy, yet pain, in her beautiful face and big brown eyes. And something else. Concern. Concern for something greater than all of this.

Mouthing a few words, Casca realized how weak he was, his lips straining to make sounds. Holding his head, Ary brought a cup of cold water to his lips, wetting his mouth with her fingers.

It felt cool and refreshing. His dry lips anxiously absorbed the moisture, begging for more. Looking down, Casca could see the bump in his chest where the spear shaft was still lodged. It moved with every labored breath he took, almost like that foul thing had become part of him. Making the smallest attempts to move, he realized that once more his legs were not going to obey him. Lao Tze had said life moved in circles, Casca remembered. Shaking the somber thoughts away, he looked at Ary.

"I told you I would return to you," whispered Casca

softly, forcing a weak smile from his cracked lips.

Ary's eyes, filling up with tears, told of great pain for the man she loved. Hiding her face in his hands, she took a moment to regain her composure before looking up.

"I never doubted it," she answered with a sweet smile, wiping the last tear from her left cheek.

Raising his head, Casca could see Anah and Okuse peeking in from behind the curtained doorway. Impatiently they tugged at each other's arm, trying to get a better look and their mother's attention. Not far behind he could hear Yrag's anxious concerns. The two girls had pushed their way through, shoving him out of the way. Knowing no one would enter Casca's sleeping quarters until Ary said so, Yrag had let them fight their losing battle.

"Stop cowering and come in," demanded Casca with a feeble attempt at sounding nonchalant. "I will need your help, Yrag. Your strength and steady hands."

Furrowing her brows, Ary put her hand on Casca's chest, feeling the tip of the shaft pushing through his skin.

Entering the room, Yrag looked him up and down. There was no way he could help, Yrag figured. It would be impossible to pull the shaft out of his chest, even if he had dared to try, as there was nothing to grab. He had accompanied Casca all this time, doing his bidding, at times nearly being his friend, but now he was not about to try something insane like this.

Seeing misgiving in his eyes, Casca tried to show more determination. "It is the only way. You must do it!"

Standing by the side of the bed, Yrag put his trembling hand on Casca's chest. His hand rose and lowered with the movement of his shallow breath. Spastically coughing, Casca tried to force air into his collapsed and clot-filled lungs. Pulling his hand back, Yrag cried out seeing a drop of blood work its way through the skin, leaving a mark on his hand.

"I am unable to do this . . . my friend." It was the first time Yrag had addressed Casca in such manner. Shaking from head to toe, he stood back.

Casca smiled. Reaching out with his own unsteady hand, he demanded, "You must. You must do it!"

Yrag's face turned ashen and lifeless, as he finally realized what he was being asked to do. The wooden shaft could not be pulled out. Casca was asking for something much more brutal and violent.

The four of them stood by his bed, Anah and Okuse sobbing, Ary holding firm, trying to show strength, while Yrag attempted to find someplace in his heart and soul that would give him the bravery and strength the task ahead of him demanded.

There was no other way. That blasted thing, thrown by a Yoruba warrior, had found its mark perfectly, causing more pain than Casca could have ever imagined, but not bringing death. His shallow breathing quickened at the thought of the pain to come.

He could feel nothing now, his body was dead from the chest down, but he also knew that in an instant, lightning would strike, the agony to torture him once again. The curse of Christ to preserve and pain him all at the same time would continue once more. The wheel turned again.

The room was prepared. Casca was placed on a middle table, with one of equal size behind him and one the height of a foot table, no taller than a man's knees, in front of him. Stripped to the waist, he was laid on his back with his head raised, taking gulps of palm wine from Ary's helping hands. Curtains covering the windows had been removed, lighting the room with the morning rays.

With Ary's help, Casca shifted over the table, leaving his shoulders and head on one table with the rest of his body on the other. The gap between the tables held his chest where the spear had impaled him.

Yrag stood by with a fuller, a thick-handled blacksmith's hammer, in his powerful hands. He no longer trembled in fear and anticipation. He understood.

Casca watched Yrag raise the hammer high above his head while standing on the low table, ready to bring it down on a small wooden shaft that Ary was holding with her hands above the point of the spear sticking out of Casca's chest. Not knowing if he could ever draw a breath again on his own, Casca gasped for air.

He blinked an instant later to see, with time frozen in his eyes, Yrag bring the hammer down over his chest. Lightning struck his mind as thunder shook into his chest with the impact of the hammer. Hot and cold flowed from his spine, sending shivers of pain, with a thousand daggers, into every fiber of his body.

His body boiled in the agony of the moment that seemed to refuse to end, as the flames that traveled along his nerves reverberated between his brain and spine. The painful memory of having been burned at the stake by the blasted Persians returned to torture him.

Unable to breathe in at the moment of the impact, his eyes were overwhelmed by the brilliance of the white light that overtook his senses. In between the beats of his heart, that was just a flash in time, a last picture of the room was frozen into his mind.

Ary holding the wooden spike, ignoring all else . . . Anah and Okuse sobbing uncontrollably, each holding and wetting his hands with her tears . . . and Yrag following through with the blow of the hammer, arcing downward, teeth gritted in concentration . . . the hammer falling from him, as if yanked from his hands by an unseen power, hurling it against the wall of his dwellings . . . and Yrag falling and crying out in horror and fear as he brought his bloody hands to his mouth, agonizing at Casca's feet, the splattered blood burning him like boiling tar. The light disappeared from Casca's mind's eye as the room fell over him, the outside light extinguished momentarily, turning into darkness, smothering the room and his mind.

Awakening, Casca took in a deep breath. The inrushing air felt good. Slowly his senses coming alive, he opened his eyes.

"He is awake! . . . He is finally awake!" cried a young girl, startling Casca.

Shifting his gaze to where the sound had come from, Casca saw Anah fall over her stool while trying to find her way out of his room. Taking a moment to gather himself, he breathed in deeper and more forcefully. It definitely felt good. The pain and numbness were gone. Reaching toward his chest, Casca's hand encountered a soft cover and smooth skin. A small bump met his hand as he reached toward the middle of his chest.

Raising his head, Casca watched his toes wiggle freely and effortlessly. There was none of the cursed deadened numbness or even the uncomfortable and miserable needle-pricked tingling in his toes. Sitting up, he stretched then put his hands over his thighs. Yawning like a hyena, he smacked his dried tongue against his lips and palate, trying to get them loosened and wet. Stretching his arms, Casca grabbed at his muscles, squeezing them until they hurt. It was all there and it all felt good.

Sliding off the bed, Casca stood on weak but solid footing. Smiling to himself, he sat down and reached for a cup of water Anah had left on the table in her hasty exit. Drinking deeply, feeling rejuvenated, he stood up once more and looked around.

"Once again you have returned to me."

Casca turned toward the doorway, his eyes meeting a smiling and crying Ary. Reaching him, she put her head against his chest while her arms coiled around him passionately.

"How long was I gone?" inquired Casca.

"You have slept for nearly three days. At times you have stirred in your sleep, even sweetly mumbled at times . . ."

Amused by her reply, Casca laughed. "Sweetly mumbled?"

"I cannot remember for certain, but it is possible I heard my name a few times over the last three days while you slept," answered Ary coyly.

"Two nights ago you startled Anah by sitting up in your bed, eyes closed but with your head up, sniffing the air. Anah thought you were looking for her, that presumptuous little girl, and she offered her hands to you, but apparently, even in your sleep you were preoccupied. After a few minutes of tasting the air, still with your eyes closed, you lay back down. Yesterday," she continued, "you awakened briefly, and without you even opening your eyes, Okuse fed you five cups of cold water. She denies that two of them were palm wine, but I have my suspicions."

Okuse had entered the room, looking as innocent as possible, feigning surprise at her mother's words. Casca knew better. He had never hidden his weakness for some things.

Anah had also returned to his room, dragging a half-dressed Yrag with her.

Turning toward the window, Casca looked out into the morning sun. The air felt good and crisp. Breathing in deeper, he tested his chest by pounding on it, not unlike the giant apes he had seen in the jungle. Once again his curse had served him well. Seeing both Anah and Okuse giggle at the sight, he stopped. Another day was at hand to bring pleasure and pain.

"Anaken sent one of his men daily. At night he came on his own, to see the miracle. We did not know for certain if you would live, the sleep having overtaken you instantly following the moment when the wooden spear left your body. You lay there, lifeless except for your breathing, so shallow we could not even tell for sure. The first day was as if death was at our door, deciding to take you now, or perhaps let you linger in between here and the afterlife. Some thought you would sleep forever, or until the gods brought you back to them. I myself never doubted your return."

Smiling affectionately, looking up into his eyes, Ary continued. "Your time is approaching." Grasping at his arms, with trepidation in her voice, she whispered. "It had to come. Tomorrow is near."

Speaking abruptly, only broken words coming to her lips, not knowing how to control her deep set emotions, and unable to keep looking into his eyes, she laid her head against his chest once more.

The concern and pain he had seen in her eyes just moments ago returned to haunt him, making Casca once again question his place with these people. For now, if time allowed, Casca needed rest to regain his strength.

Yrag approached and uneasily put his left hand on Casca's chest. Without even realizing it, his right hand searched Casca's back, where the wooden shaft had been forced out so violently by the blow of his hammer. Shifting his head in front and behind Casca, he marveled at his handiwork and the miracle that had preserved Casca.

The skin was bruised slightly, nothing more than one would receive carrying firewood on a bare back. Soon that would fade away, leaving another scar to tell a story and decorate his already crisscrossed, illustrated back.

"Thank you, my friend," Casca offered, using Yrag's words from three days past, when he had reluctantly agreed to help him. "You were brave beyond your years."

Pulling his hands away, Yrag looked up at Casca and smiled. Life had certainly changed for him over the last few months. Helping carry the tribute-filled coffers without dropping them had been his only concern not that long ago.

"I might just have to be reminded to thank Ewuare for sending you along with me. He would certainly be proud of you."

Hearing the name of Ewuare made Yrag's eyes light up instantly. Proudly, he stood up to his full height. Pulling his shoulders back and throwing his chest out, he stepped back, allowing the "impatient sisters" as he had been calling them behind their backs, to get at Casca.

Casca welcomed Anah and Okuse's embrace, more of a nervous smothering of his body than a true embrace.

"Just like my mother, I never doubted that you would return to us," Okuse chirped, gently gliding her hands over his chest and shoulders, still amazed at his incredible recuperative powers. "I knew you wanted the palm wine when you awoke," she whispered into his ear, making certain no one else could hear.

"My sister and I will help you regain your strength," volunteered Anah, knowing Casca had never had any complaints with them and their personal attention. "I thought my warm embrace was what you desired when you woke up two nights ago from your healing slumber," she wetly whispered into his other ear, not knowing what Anah had said, but also not wanting to be outdone in any way by her sister.

Untangling himself from the overly anxious girls, Casca slowly walked out into the garden. As he sat down under a tree, the gentle winds rustled the leaves over his head, allowing the sunlight to break through, flickering at his eyes. Even the bright and piercing light felt good, invigorating him, bringing strength and exuberance for the day to come.

He knew further trouble was in the waiting, surprises that

this land refused to stop bringing, but his future was here for now. Ary's words and poorly camouflaged somber mood had easily given it away.

"Take this for now." Ary interrupted his contemplation. "The girls will bring food and drink to us soon. You must be hungry. Very hungry."

Taking a cup of honeyed coconut milk from her, Casca downed it in one quick gulp, the stream of milk barely touching his lips. Licking the rim of the cup for the last drops, he set it down by his feet.

"I trust they will be generous. I do have a week's worth to make up for," kidded Casca, knowing Anah and Okuse would never disappoint.

"You do not ask of the Yoruba, and our defeat?" inquired Ary softly.

"A thousand men died. There is not much else to be said about them," Casca almost growled through pained lips. Ary's eyes dropped from Casca's sudden answer.

"What of Oba Awanoshe? How many has he executed for their failure?" Casca's words turning somber yet angry did not surprise Ary.

"The Oba has not been heard from since your return. He is not one—"

"There is plenty more, you know," chimed Anah and Okuse in unity, placing a large tray of food at Casca's feet.

Leaning over, Ary handed Casca a plate of food and a cup of cold palm wine. Taking it from her, Casca's eyes followed a tear that quickly ran down her cheek, turning the corner of her delicate jaw. Slowly pushing the tray and cup down, he held her by the arms and pulled her to himself gently.

"You obviously have no way of knowing why I still cry," sobbed Ary. "I have been unfair about that. My sister's husband, a wonderful man I had known ever since I can remember, died along with most of Anaken's guard. He was a good man. My sister misses him terribly."

"I am sorry for you, and for her," offered Casca, knowing that even after hundreds of years he still never knew when and how to console someone. "I trust he died quickly and painlessly."

"He died in her arms. Decayed from the poison of war."

He looked at her suddenly. "In her arms?"

"I forget you did not know of him by name. He returned with you, Anaken and the others. His name was Ikan. Anaken had cut off his leg to prevent the rotting disease from taking him. He died in his own bed less than two hours after your return. My sister Zil, my baby sister, has been heartbroken."

Casca remembered, wearily, seeing the man crawling along the dusty road, using a stump as his leg and a crooked branch and his bloodied spear to hold him up, all the while his body melting away, festering incessantly, the foul smell and discharge moving up his withered form.

He had fought gallantly, overmatched like the rest of them, fighting a lost battle for a madman. In the end, the poor soul had found peace at last with the ones he loved. Whoever had said war was hell, was wrong. War took everyone, sinners or not.

"He fought on bravely," words to console Casca offered, "forsaking himself to defend Anaken and the ones around him, while others cowered, offering to be taken as prisoners, to foolishly try and preserve themselves. I did not know of him, but he fought side by side with me, asking no quarter. During our return, he showed incredible determination and strength, single-mindedly focused on returning home. Your sister Zil should know that."

Casca knew well it was much easier to lose faceless thousands than to watch even one close one suffer and die. He had done it more than any man. At times, the calluses that covered most of his body, easily washed away from his heart and soul. Over the centuries he had buried more allies and loved ones than he wanted to recall. When war did not take them, predatory time did.

Eased by his words, she smiled her bewitching smile, bringing Casca back from his ever returning dark thoughts. Ary knew Casca would have greater concerns when the new day came. In days, this was to be just a distant memory.

They sat quietly, enjoying the tranquility and healing moment of silence and of each other. Off in the distance, the wailing and crying of two or three elephant calves and the frustrated yells of children broke the quiet. Putting the calves through their paces was not easy. They were likely too young, as were the children trying to master them. In time the elephants would learn to yield.

Broken from the moments of peacefulness and serenity, Ary insisted Casca take some of the food and drink. She knew he was stubborn, but also that he had to regain his strength. It had been a miracle; now she was going to help it along. The plate and the whole tray was empty in moments as, not very reluctantly, he complied.

As he and Ary sat side by side, their knees nearly interlocked, Casca finished off the last of the morsels, thinking of the day to come. Anah and Okuse did not give him much chance to rest, bringing more, doing their part in the miracle that had restored him, also trying to see if for once they could find the depths of his appetite.

Finishing with their chores, the girls made their way out of the garden, knowing their mother had no time for foolishness now. Walking backward, Okuse smiled a devilish seductive grin, in no uncertain terms making sure Casca's eyes caught hers. Turning around, she slowed down, walking away with an ever accentuating sway of her body, flicking her hair at Ary in indignation for having hurried her off.

Again knowing better, Anah disappeared not to raise her mother's ire, having learned lessons past. She knew if opportunity arose, Casca would find her. Not unlike her, he had never disappointed before.

"Enhora, the harvest festival, is only ten days away," Ary broke the silence. "It has always been a great time for us, with days of celebration, even in the days with Oba Awanoshe. As cruel and evil as he is, he has allowed us to enjoy the fruits of our labor, moments to rejoice and celebrate. Food and palm wine flow freely while the youngsters play, enjoying sweet treats made by all the young girls. The *edion,* the village elders, retell tales of times past, legends of our people from before written time.

"Young boys compete with the sword and spear, each trying to outdo the other, in the meanwhile impressing the girls and, if fortunate, winning them over. I would not be surprised if Anah were to enter the competitions this year.

With Yrag's teachings, she could probably best many of the boys." Apparently still within ear shot, Anah returned, wearing a proud grin. Turning her head, she held Casca's eyes with her own while enjoying the moment. Then, with her head raised high, she slowly walked away again, making certain Casca could not but follow her with his eyes.

"As you did in the spring," she continued, while ignoring her daughter "all the territories will send their tribute. However, I do not believe there will be anything that will please the Oba this time. There will not be much to celebrate either. Even though he had not been heard from since the disastrous campaign against the Yoruba, most of us dread what he will probably bring upon us."

Sighing painfully, remembering dark times, she reluctantly continued. "At times in the past when the crops or the tribute were poor, Tajah-Nor attempted to please Oba Awanoshe with gifts. It always failed. Tajah-Nor has never been able to find a gift that pleased. Two years ago Tajah-Nor brought the twin sisters of Oba Otheby from the land of Isoko as brides for the Oba to placate his anger and pleasures. Oba Awanoshe had the girls returned with a message of disdain and contempt for Oba Otheby. The beautiful girls of Isoko were shamed and received with scorn upon their return, for having failed in making an alliance with Oba Awanoshe. No one knows what became of the young girls.

"It was not the only time he refused a bride. Many have been offered, with the same outcome. He has never shown any interest, no matter how young and beautiful or of what royal blood. Couriers have not fared better, many giving their lives for delivering an unsatisfying tribute. Their deaths have come often over the years. Many lost their lives one year ago, in ways no man should."

"What happened with the men of Conah and Nevaad? Were they also overwhelmed and butchered?" inquired Casca.

"No one knows for sure. As far as I know, none of them have returned. It is feared they met the same fate as Anaken's troops."

Casca sat back thinking of the thousands that had been sent to fight an unwinnable war, but no one could have predicted this. How could they have been so unprepared and foolish to believe the Yoruba were going to roll over without a fight?

Fifty feet away Casca watched Yrag patiently spar with Anah, blocking her awkward and sometimes obvious blows with a flick of his sword. For weeks now Yrag had expertly been teaching Anah, an eager and willing student, the basics of using a sword and shield. Okuse had never shown interest, insisting it was just foolishness on Anah's part.

The day was hot, with the sun beating down, weakening Anah's arm with each swing of the sword. Noticing that Casca was watching, she tried her best to impress, swinging the sword with increased vigor, trying not to over-swing and open herself to a counter blow. Yrag was not anxious to embarrass himself either, making it look effortless while picking up the pace, trying to deflect each blow and find an opening.

The sword on its own was heavy enough to hold and wield, further exhausting Anah. The shield was different. It was not like the huge pavis used by some of the foolish crusaders, large enough to cover the whole body but too cumbersome to thrust from behind, and too heavy to carry. Casca had seen men tipped over, falling under their oversized shields, their arms locked within the grips, helplessly crushed like snails by the spears of attackers or hooves of onrushing horses.

Memories of the huge Roman formations, holding up hundreds of shields, moving in unison, an impenetrable wall of metal rolling over the land, came back to Casca's mind.

The small bucklers, undersized round or four-sided shields, were of no great help either, too small for defense unless expertly used. If used such, a man could parry with one, and in one swift motion knock a man or horse down to the ground.

Casca had used shields of different shapes and sizes over the centuries. He had caught more arrows, swords and ugly faces with them than he could recall. One could not do without a shield, but unless one were expertly trained and strong, it could become more of a burden than an ally.

This shield was different. Yrag had made this one, further impressing Casca.

Instead of having layers of metal on top of one another, weighing it down, it only had a metal framework. Stretched over it, Yrag had arranged layer upon layer of sun-dried animal hide. In between the layers he had patiently placed a combination of wet red clay and black ash. He allowed each layer to dry before another hide, then more wet clay was placed, and the structure slowly became a light shield, easy to carry and wield.

The slightly oval shield became hard as metal, yet very light to carry, looking more like the discarded carapace of a tortoise. Perhaps not as strong as a metal shield, but more than strong enough to deflect swords and arrows. Anah had found it efficient and easy enough to use.

Giving ground, she backed away as Yrag moved in, accelerating his mock attack. "I will fight you to the death," Anah gasped, causing Casca to smile as he wondered how many hundred times he had heard those same words over the centuries. "Death would be too easy. You will be punished beyond," Yrag bellowed in a frightening manner, shaking Anah, causing her to retreat.

Ary and Casca sat back and watched their friendly, though now competitive, fight. Finally exhausted, Anah dropped her sword and shield to the ground, kneeling, offering her neck to Yrag in jest. "Have mercy, I will do as you please," she panted with the last bit of reserve.

Good-naturedly laughing, they embraced briefly. Casca smiled to himself, seeing the obvious desire in Yrag for Anah, knowing that he would never dare. Not unless Casca allowed it.

Casca had slept well. He was not certain who had made the decision, but they had allowed each other to fall asleep that night. Casca awoke after midnight, his stomach finally settling down after that obscene day of eating, when he had tried not to disappoint his eager servers.

He was not certain what had awakened him. It was unlikely that it was Ary's fearfully prophetic words of the day to come. Casca had been tempered well enough by hundreds of wars not to allow the apprehension of things to come to eat at him.

Sitting up in his bed, he listened for the sounds of the night. Next to him, Ary slept quietly, this time without the slight smile that he had gotten used to seeing during the night, a narrow frown almost finding its way onto her face. He watched her body rise and fall under the movements of her shallow breathing, her perfect form outlined under the thin cover.

Leaving the bed, trying not to disturb her, he took the few steps toward the curtained window. Pulling the curtain aside, he hitched it against a wooden clip by the window frame. A warm breeze fluttered the cloth as he fastened it, bringing the sweet night air to his nose. With the moon hanging high in the sky, and wisps of clouds passing over it, the days spent imprisoned under water, unable to not look up at the sky, came back to haunt Casca. Shaking his head to chase away the thoughts, he breathed in deep.

Looking out, he could see the nearly clear night sky, darkening for the moment as the moon disappeared behind a reddish cloud, a small rain of shooting stars sweeping across the west. He had heard of wishing upon one for good luck. Foolish thing it was, he thought; many did not recognize good fortune when it came upon them, others did not know how to use it to their advantage.

An old Roman centurion had told him about seizing the day as it came. Perhaps the following day his time was really going to come, as Ewuare, Anaken and Ary had always prophetically whispered. His place with these people would reveal itself. Then he would seize the day.

The childish giggling of Anah and Okuse could be heard nearby. Casca wondered when they ever slept. Their endless energy and enthusiasm had challenged him in many ways. Flaring his nostrils while turning his head, Casca tried to pick up the scent coming from the surroundings, perhaps from their dwelling.

It did not seem to come from that direction, but it was something definitely sweet and alluring. The night could play tricks, he figured. He could hear them talking, stepping on each other's words, laughing and fighting all at the same time. The night wind brought many things to his senses.

Casca smiled to himself, realizing that he could overhear most of their conversation. Not surprisingly they were talking about their mother and him.

"... he really prefers me, that should be obvious by now, I do look like her a lot, and I am much younger after all," insisted Anah, making her case.

"Well, I am younger than both of you. You have to be blind not to see how he looks at me and desires me," fought back Okuse. "You should worry abut Yrag, he has watched you with lust in his eyes ever since he arrived."

"Yrag, he is just a boy. What does he know about women?" snapped Anah. "And no, he has not been watching me."

"Denying it won't change the facts," returned Okuse. "Why do you think he teaches you to fight with the sword? You are no match for him anyway. A dangling coconut would be more of a challenge than you."

"What do you know! Maybe he likes to teach swordplay."

"Maybe he likes to teach swordplay, maybe he likes to teach swordplay," burred back Okuse. "He just wants an excuse to spend time with you and stare when you do not pay attention to him."

"Well, at least he notices me. Even if he is just a boy," yelled back Anah, laughing at the same time.

The two of them laughed and yelled, as two sisters would, trying to outdo each other, getting the last word in. Casca had obviously noticed Yrag, a blind man would have, no matter how much Anah denied it. One day perhaps they would be together. Casca would eventually depart.

Before long the discussion returned to Casca and his preferences.

"You know he does not want to think of our mother when he is with you. Unquestionably he prefers me," started Okuse again.

"You are too young, and do not know how to please a man," countered Anah. "He just does not want you to feel unwanted. Of course he prefers me."

"That is not true," sobbed Okuse. "You are wrong. From the first moment he had his eyes on me, and you know it. My body is perfect. Time hasn't pulled on it, like yours."

Their sisterly bickering continued, and was likely to continue through the night. Unlike their mother, the day to come did not concern them.

Casca did not mind being wanted and fought over. Decades of pleasure would have to pass to make up for the miseries of the past. He figured worse things could have happened than these three women in his life, even if eventually it would have to end. It always did.

Turning his head, his attention was again caught by something unseen. He had sensed the same uneasiness a few times over nights past. It had to be something. His senses had never failed him. Breathing in deep, with his eyes closed, he tasted the air, while his ears listened carefully, trying to pick up anything that broke the still of the night. Frustrated by his inability to detect anything that satisfied, Casca returned to his bed. Perhaps a good night's sleep would remedy, sharpening his senses.

Ary had turned in her sleep, the cover shifting down by her side. Casca looked back toward the window, realizing he had left the curtain still hitched. The moon had once again reappeared, lighting his dwellings. Turning his head toward the bed, Casca smiled, watching Ary sleep while the yellow lights danced across her body.

Returning to the bed, he sat and placed his hand on her shoulders, moving it along with the moonlight that caressed her. Sighing from the warmth of his hand, she awoke with a smile. He would not get a restful night's sleep after all.

Sleep had been brief, but not surprisingly Casca felt invigorated and refreshed. Still bothered by whatever had roused him the previous night, he sat eating and contemplating the day at hand.

Eating his morning meal of sweet bread, fruit and assorted juices, Casca stretched his muscles and again tested his body. Clenching his fist, his hand hungered for the broadsword. He put his left hand by his temples, feeling the juices pulsating and flowing in his veins, the soldier's blood awaiting battle. Pounding his chest beneath the heart, he could feel his chest anxiously rise and fall. All pain had disappeared from his chest and back, nothing more than a slight soreness remaining. The curse of the Jew had served him well.

Anah and Okuse scurried around without making a sound, no details left to chance, the morning meal being perfect as always. Casca watched them, thinking back, almost hearing the sisterly bickering of the night past. He wondered if he had shown favoritism after all. They were both lovely and unique in their own ways. Their enthusiasm and affectionate nature made them even more irresistible.

Peeking at him as they turned, the girls went about their chores, Okuse momentarily catching Casca's eyes and almost showing concern for the previous night's words, as if she had been found out. Sitting back, Ary smiled at the situation, surprising herself by not feeling awkward and unnatural about the whole affair. After all, he was Olokun, who had come to deliver them.

It was the day of *ogiso-oro*, "the quickening of the land," just a few days before the harvest festival of Enhora. On that day, once again the *eghaevbo-nore,* the administrators of the kingdom territories, would send their best to gain favor and placate the Oba, whose patience they did not want to challenge. Another year of not bringing his wrath was what most had hoped for. If by chance the Oba could be pleased, their lives might just be improved for a while, at least until his wrath returned. Times past, the administrators had lost their position or their lives by not satisfying the Oba.

Casca was dressed near royally, his red-and-yellow streamed outfit almost putting him on display with its grandeur. He felt uncomfortable, stifled by the dress, but Ary had insisted and the size of it allowed him to easily keep his broadsword hidden underneath. He had learned it was always good practice to bring weapons where they were not welcome.

TWENTY

Once again Casca walked down the broad avenue with Yrag at his side, following the slope of the road that ended at the giant brass gates, leading into the royal court. Four stiff-lipped escorts led them toward the palace gates, unsuccessfully trying to hide their misgivings for the day.

Unenthusiastically the escorts moved on, trying to act their role, clearly unhappy with their assignment, but also not foolish enough to disobey Tajah-Nor's orders. Exercising their roles, they herded away the few stragglers that had found their way in front of them, slowing down their pace.

The thoughts of a few months past returned to Casca, the day he, Yrag and another three had brought the tribute-filled coffers, walking this same path to the royal court. That incredible day when he had met Oba Awanoshe, and the madness that was him. Much had happened since, pain and pleasure, the curse of his life. This day promised the same.

Yrag nervously shifted about, constantly pulling at his clothes, trying to loosen them from around his neck and catch his breath. Covered with perspiration, beads of sweat joined and ran down his cheeks toward his neck. Wiping his forehead and face constantly with the sleeves of his robe, he tried to keep pace while not falling over his sandal-covered feet. Gathering himself, he stopped and breathed in deep, trying to master his trepidation. Amused, yet understanding his nervousness, Casca put a friendly hand on his shoulders.

"Your thoughts returning to the first time we did this?" inquired Casca, trying to ease Yrag's tension.

Stammering from discomfort, Yrag answered. "I am unable to help my nerves. Anah has told me of this day to dread. She told me she fears for my life."

"She cares for you. You might as well get used to that," Casca reassured him. "You may not know it yet but she has you trapped. The two of you will be good for each other," he offered, trying to steer Yrag's thoughts away.

Not knowing what Casca had meant, Yrag inquired, "She is not for me . . . What do you mean trapped? . . . She couldn't be. Her place is with Okuse and Ary, to be there for you. That has been predestined, as you well know. Is that not so? If that . . ."

Seeing Yrag so overwhelmed, Casca again tried to comfort him. "In time I will be gone, you must know that. If you believe in prophecy or not, you must know my time here is short. Someday you will be a grandfather telling of these days." Casca was surprised at his words, sounding as prophetic as others recently had, words coming without doubt, as if he himself knew it would all end soon.

Looking up at Casca, Yrag smiled halfheartedly, unable to think of anything past this day, trying to understand his place in this world and what the future would bring. Not knowing how to respond, he nodded his head.

Approaching the palace gates, the mass of people and beasts milled all about, men and women nervously pushing their way through the crowd, trying to find calmness while fighting their own demons. This was to be a day of celebration, with days of the same to come, but it was also a day of uncertainty if years past were any indication.

Carts of food and drink filled the alleyways, overburdening the space available, people with strained nerves leaning against one another, trying to find their way. Four female elephants were herded along, saddled beasts that swayed from side to side like overburdened camels, further crowding the alleyways. Two of them sounded off, sending people running along, hastening their steps and quickening their hearts.

Men and women, dressed in the best ceremonial garb their means allowed, crowded all around Casca in groups, some brave enough to try and get a momentary glimpse of his eyes while turning their heads, others to afraid to even try, most too concerned about Oba Awanoshe. The four escorts, striving to do their best, attempted to control the situation. Moving two of the beasts ahead, two young girls still decorated them as they moved along, while three men with hooked brass-tipped prongs tried to control them and herd the noisy creatures toward the courtyard.

Buckling on its hind legs, one of the elephants toppled its restrainers, throwing its unsteady rider clear off the howdah, to land in the middle of the crowd. The howdah, the canopied seat on the elephant's back, was quite plain and poorly made, unlike the ones Casca had seen used in Burma or India. He had ridden on sturdy, well-protected saddles hundreds of years past, while accompanying Marco Polo on his way to the land of Chin.

He recalled Marco marveling at these creatures, wild and destructive, able to level a village when out of control, while at other times able to perform the most meticulous of feats, moving and placing huge logs or boulders with perfection. Casca recalled an old battle-scarred bull falling over, crashing, seemingly out of control, nearly braking its own back, while trying to protect Marco during the fall. The table adjacent to Marco had been crushed, but the young explorer had escaped without a scratch.

These saddles barely supported two men, and provided minimal protection without even allowing for proper handling of the beasts, a clear need, as these giants could level an army of people or the walls of a city.

Stepping out of the beast's way, Casca watched many run for their lives as this mountain of armored flesh seemed to be out of control, probably ready to mash them under its tree-like legs. Regaining their feet, the two nearly overmatched restrainers hooked the out-of-control beast with their metal prongs, showering it with vile expletives, eventually calming it down. The insanity that was this day continued, with an ever flowing current of man and beast.

• • •

Separating from the mass of humanity, Casca and Yrag followed the four, who led them down an alleyway, heading toward the royal court. They quickly reached the Ogbe, the portion of the city that housed the royal palace. Turning up the last alleyway, the escort brought them to a side gate.

The brass gates were slowly opened, creaking as they moved, allowing enough room for the six of them to pass through as a group. Out of the corner of his eye Casca noted the now gimpy Akheno, the little weasel of a man who had received Casca months ago when Casca had made his first entrance into Benin City.

The previously robust Akheno, one of Tajah-Nor's underlings, stood awkwardly by the gateway, deathly coughing into his hands. His eyes met Casca's for an instant, the man not sure whether to act officious or allow for the glint of a smile. Casca wondered what had happened to the little man over the last few months that had destroyed his body so.

Akheno wiped his soiled hand on his already bloodied dress, looking more and more like a man who might not make next year's festivals. Casca had seen many taken by the brutal, wasting coughing sickness. Much farther north, where winters were long and unforgiving, Casca had seen his share of men and women alike suffer and die from the same plight. His great love, Lida of Helsford had been taken by the disease. How he had loved her . . .

Shaking the melancholy memories from his mind, Casca eyed Akheno almost with sympathy. Akheno would cough until his dry body would have nothing to give. Blindness could not be far behind. Eventually, just like the rest, he would fill a hole in the dirt.

"Would it be impossible for Olokun to remember me? . . . I was the one fortunate enough to greet—"

His words cut off, Akheno stood, appearing dumbfounded by Casca's response. "Certainly I do. You, Akheno, let me into this great city." Casca twisted his lips in a smile of acknowledgment, for a moment still feeling for this walking dead. Not knowing how to respond, Akheno bowed his twisted body, realizing he had nothing more to offer.

"I am honored great one, I . . ." Akheno appeared to want to continue, but fear and confusion restrained him.

He was still the same in other ways, a gatekeeper, perhaps with improved standing, as he now kept one of the palace gates. The sound of his voice resonated in Casca's ears, as if his words had been delivered with a different tone from the rest.

Moving on, Casca and Yrag's trek brought them into the crowded courtyard, this time adjacent to the large doorways. The first time Casca had been here, bringing the Uda territory's tribute, they had stood hundreds of feet away, lost in the crowd of thousands, facing the entrance to the palace. This time it seemed they would take part in the proceedings, adjacent to where the *ekete,* the royal throne, was to be brought in. Casca's eyes scanned the countless masses.

They had all been here in previous years to take part in a celebration of harvest; this time it was going to be different. The heavy aroma of thousands of nervous people permeated the palace yard. No wind blew this morning to dissipate the stench of the masses, the heavy, still air suffocating all. Flowers by the thousands adorned people and the surroundings, yet Casca could smell nothing but the tension of countless bodies.

Dozens had labored feverishly to perfectly decorate the courtyard with flowers of all colors, freshly cut early in the morning. Their work had been arranged in bunches all around, hanging from the gates and looped in strands between trees, attracting bees to the new man-made field.

Yellow and red garlands, tightly bunched and tied end to end, covered the heads of many young women and girls. Others wore colorful wreaths of flowers, suspended in loops, festooned in their head gear. For all their beauty, these adornments did nothing but veil the crowd's fearful faces.

The courtyard was filled to near capacity, except for the semicircular area extending in front of the palace gates. Two hundred royal guards and thirty members of the Ifiento entered the area, followed by one hundred young men, carrying the *akohen*, the ceremonial side-blown trumpets.

Eventually the other twenty Ifiento, the senior division

of the Oba's most loyal guards, would enter this space, along with the seven members of the Uzama. The remaining space would eventually fill in with ceremonial dancers, some of the Oba's personal assistants, Tajah-Nor, the Oba's right-hand man, and the Oba himself.

A slight breeze had picked up from the east, awakening Casca's senses lightly from the heaviness of the still air. Looking all around, he saw thousands anxiously facing the palace gates, shifting within the overcrowded spaces their bodies had found for themselves. Standing side by side, also within the semicircle, less than twenty feet from the still closed palace gates, Casca and Yrag watched the day unfold.

The sound of a hundred *akohen* froze the courtyard, quieting all within the instant the strident pitch reached their ears. All eyes were transfixed on the palace gates as ever so slowly they were opened. The broad gates creaked from the weight, both sides turning on their overburdened hinges, sweeping the dirt in front of them as they opened.

Four men strained under the burden of the task, all the while attempting to complete their work in an impressive royal manner, without upsetting their short-tempered superiors. The last twenty of the Ifiento, taking slow, deliberate steps, made their entrance into the enclosure, leading the way for the seven Uzama and eventually for the royal *ekete*.

The twenty Ifiento, men who had been trained since birth to protect and defend the Oba and the Oba's wishes, slowly made their way into the enclosure. Looking side to side, holding people at bay with their glare, they walked into the clearing, lining the small rectangular space just in front of the gates, ten on each side.

"Out of the way, move it," they ordered no one in particular. "Make room for the honored Uzama."

With shields in their left hands, they pretended to push the crowd back, the ones supposedly brave enough to move in, although Casca thought it unnecessary, as none seemed eager to approach. More of a ceremonial gesture than anything else. "Back away, back away," their threatening voices repeated, warning anyone who took even one step toward the opening.

The Ifiento, now joined by the thirty who had already entered the area, made certain they provided more than sufficient space for the seven Uzama and the pedestal that supported the royal throne. "Stay right where you are," the Ifiento insisted, showing much greater concern, almost a panic, acting more protective than Casca had ever seen them before.

Behind them, the gates continued opening gradually, allowing Casca to get a quick glimpse inside. Fifty feet behind the gates, the four huge men he had seen previously carry the throne stood by, holding the pedestal that supported the royal *ekete* on it, awaiting the final sounding of the *akohen,* signaling them to advance. Grasping tightly at the handles, with their primed arms covered with sweaty lather, they waited, preparing to move as one, to delivering the throne with perfection.

The seven members of the Uzama, led by Anaken, still taking the role of the *ezomo,* slowly made their entrance. Casca had wondered if Anaken's position within the Uzama had changed. For now all appeared the same. Puzzled by this, Casca contemplated the Oba's thoughts.

Could the Oba have been so forgiving to accept Anaken's completely failed campaign? After all, he had suffered the most crushing defeat imaginable, having lost nearly a thousand, returning with only six of his men.

The Uzama advanced, the western breeze picking up for the moment, streaming their flowing regalia, the moving air whistling against their sheet-brass cutouts, clattering their endless metal ornaments against one another. Their overly crowded medallions chimed from the wind, creating an unsettling, nearly hypnotic whistling that further quieted the crowd. With the sounding of the unseen *ukhurke,* the royal rattle-staff, all fell on their knees, aware of the Oba's imminent entrance.

The royal throne, carried by the four men, was brought through the palace gates. A deathly quiet overtook the courtyard, the instant the first of the four came into view. With the sound of the trumpets gone, the eerie feel of time standing still settled in upon Casca. Ever so slowly the four men rested the *ekete* against the red earth, even the dust kicked up by it rising slowly, finally settling down by the feet of the deliverers. For a time that seemed like eternity nothing could be heard.

The second sounding of the rattle-staff came, breaking the silence, signaling the beginning of the Otue. The tedious greeting ceremony seemed to last forever, as the seven Uzama approached the still hidden Oba and kneeled one at a time by the *ekete,* showing their devotion and acceptance of the Oba's divine superiority and their own place at the Oba's side. Some, in a symbolic gesture, pointed their short eben swords at their own hearts, demonstrating their loyalty and willingness to giving their lives at the Oba's beckoning.

Once more Casca watched as Anaken still defiantly refused to allow his knees to touch the ground while facing the Oba, only his dress brushing at the dirt in front of the *ekete.* Casca marveled at Anaken, remembering that first day when he had witnessed the same contempt on Anaken's part, his unwillingness to surrender in body and spirit to the Oba's will.

"He did it again, just as you have said," Yrag muttered under his breath, elbowing Casca lightly to get his attention. "Why will he not yield? Is he asking for death?" he inquired, bringing his head closer to Casca's.

Casca smiled to himself, almost nodding. "He is a man. If death comes, he will look it in the eye from his feet."

With the last of the Uzama taking their turn genuflecting by the throne, the trumpets sounded one last time, signaling the end of the interminable greeting ceremony of Otue. Casca watched the *ekete,* still shielding the Oba behind the three brass facings and the leather canopy that protected him from the morning sun.

With the main crowd on his left, the *ekete* in front of him and the palace gates on his immediate right, Casca could see opposite the throne, behind the wall of well-armed Ifiento and other palace officials, Ary and her sister Zil standing within the crowd of women. Ary's concerned eyes met Casca's for an instant, momentarily communicating her love for him. Casca smiled with his eyes, betraying his strength for a moment to Yrag, who watched the two of them speaking without words.

The rattle-staff sounded again. Frozen in time, they all stood awaiting the appearance of the Oba. Without moving stood paralyzed. In all his years the Oba had stood only once in their presence. The day of Ishana, during the spring planting ceremony, when the scarred stranger had made his appearance. Madness and death had followed that day closely. This day did not promise better.

Next to him, in full ceremonial garb, stood Tajah-Nor, looking down at the Uzama with contempt. Apparently the ceremony of Iron was about to take place. The mock, symbolic battle pitting the seven Uzama against the Oba's closest supporters was at hand. Ugie Erha Oba the principal ceremony honoring the Oba's father, the ruling Oba attempting to repay the debt he owed to his deceased father for providing him with the authority to rule had not been permitted in years. This powerfully symbolic gesture, that not surprisingly Oba Awanoshe did not allow, also included the ceremonial battle of Iron.

Casca had seen the Oba's complete lack of tolerance for anything that referred to divine kingship or the strengthening of the king's spiritual powers, other than for himself, during the spring planting celebration of Ishana. The five

Oba then had
owed to remain
ceremony of Otue
d mention the Oba's

the complete absence of
ngthened the Oba's position,
s authority to rule by the will of
e by side, the seven Uzama drew
om their scabbards and placed their
eremonial shields on their left forearms.
come to all that oppose Oba Awanoshe,''
ssed, spraying the sand with his filthy mouth.
all,'' he repeated, eyeing both Casca and An-

th a worried look, Yrag glanced up at Casca, trying
find something that would reassure him, even if just for
the moment.

The Oba's supporters, including Tajah-Nor and four of his men, faced the seven Uzama. The hundred *akohen* sounded off as the two groups of men eyed each other. Shifting and turning, attempting to get the best advantage before their mock battle ensued, the Uzama dug in, forming a convex semicircle. With the sudden quieting of the *akohen,* the ceremonial battle commenced.

It was not long before the Uzama in a hurried retreat were vanquished. A fairly pathetic showing from the Uzama, even if it was only for show, Casca thought. Without having made one forward step, the seven Uzama retreated until backed against the palace walls, throwing their weapons down, begging for a quick death.

Triumphantly, the Oba's supporters swung their swords over their heads, in a mock gesture decapitating the Uzama members. To the cheers of the whole courtyard, they returned to the Oba's side, foolishly grinning, congratulating one another on their bravery, enjoying their hollow and preposterous victory. Dusting themselves off, the seven Uzama quietly returned to their positions inside the perimeter, ready for the day to continue.

''The past shall be banished. It is time for a new beginning.'' The sudden words of the Oba instantly quieted the courtyard. With these words spoken, Oba Awanoshe stepped back beneath the canopied cover of his *ekete,* nearly out of sight to all, his figure within the shadow of the royal throne.

"Then so it shall be done," bellowed Tajah-Nor, bringing fear to all.

"Olokun, you too shall be banished. You are a false prophet, a failed messenger from our gods," erupted Tajah-Nor suddenly, glaring at Casca with prejudice. "You have failed us and yourself. Oba Awanoshe had received you in his graces, yet you have done nothing in return. You are nothing. Your recovery from the wounds of war have done nothing to improve your standing; it has helped no one but yourself. Any powers you may have serve no use to the Son of God. If the endless waters are generous, they will receive you. We will not have you. You have brought us neither wealth nor earthly possessions. Only death and loss. The *iru* you brought, along with the elephant-head rattle-staff, will also be buried and forgotten. They have become meaningless. False gods we do not need to perpetrate a mockery upon us. Return to the great waters."

Thousands stood, stunned at Tajah-Nor's words. They had not thought it possible for what had unfolded to ever happen. Oba Awanoshe, through the words of Tajah-Nor, had rejected Olokun and the prophetic mission that he had insisted Olokun was on.

"We will not allow your presence to poison our present and future," continued Tajah-Nor. "You will be returned to the sea once you witness the glorious new beginning of the people you have failed." Pausing momentarily, perhaps for effect, he allowed everyone to grasp the weight of his words. Looking back at Oba Awanoshe, then glaring down at the crowd, he continued. "Olokun is no longer amongst us."

Casca watched the madness of this day unfold. Tajah-Nor had turned away, in essence dismissing him and all that Oba Awanoshe had insisted he represented to these people. Breathing nervously, gasping for air, Yrag shifted about in pain, wondering if he too would pay for Olokun's failings.

Attempting to gather himself, Yrag stood his ground,

forcing a smile onto his lips as he turned toward Casca. Understanding, Casca nodded his head, proud of the young man who would stand with him, accepting death as his fate. For Casca it would not be so easy.

Searching with his eyes, without making any sudden movements, he found Ary behind hundreds of bewildered faces. She stood, nearly delirious, her eyes swelling up in tears, holding on to her sister Zil. They too wondered if they would become part of the past.

TWENTY-ONE

The cleansing of the past continued. They all watched in horror as five men were brought in, tied down onto inclined pedestals. The five were stripped to the waist, their hands, feet and hips tied with thick rope, the strands of which were threaded through the planks that supported their backs and heads. In a frenzied, irrational, drunken haze they stood, awaiting death.

Casca witnessed with repulsion and anger the sight of these five brave men, ready to be punished for someone else's alleged failure. More likely they were the chosen sacrificial lambs, taking their turn in a world where flesh was cheap. Over the last thousand years Casca had seen such men drench the earth with their blood.

They were the last remaining survivors of Anaken's failed campaign. Casca and Anaken, along with six men had returned following the brutal defeat at the hands of the Yoruba. Ikan had been the lucky one. He had suffered terribly, the wounds of war, traveling for days as his body decayed away, having to have his leg amputated and the flesh-eating disease that had consumed his body. At least he had made it home and died with his loved ones. These five would not be so lucky.

Casca wondered if Oba Awanoshe was mad enough to

have allowed thousands of his troops die to gain more power over his people. Nothing was beyond him, according to Anaken and Ary. The entire Yoruba campaign had been questionable, from the uncertain plans, lack of intelligence and logistical support, to every detail, including their strategic approach and deployment of troops.

Perhaps Oba Awanoshe had sacrificed thousands of his troops to gain complete control, by banishing a god, an act that would have been unimaginable by anyone. Who would dare cast out a god?

He had also accomplished the complete stripping of power and influence from Anaken, the *ezomo* of the high council. It was not impossible that Anaken's overwhelming victory over the Igbo had brought enough fear to Oba Awanoshe to actually consider such a drastic, obscene strategy.

Conceivably Nevaad and Conah never campaigned along with Anaken against the Yoruba. No one had heard of them ever since, good or bad. They likely never took to the field of battle, Casca thought.

Lost in his deliberation, Casca did not notice the appearance of Ooton, Oba Awanoshe's angel of death. The old one, looking closer to death and decay than a few months previous, approached the five men.

"It is the water of fire," exclaimed Yrag, with a hushed voice, yet nearly out of control, burying his nails into Casca's arm as they apprehensively stood side by side.

Ooton slowly made his way next to the first prisoner, the one closest to Casca and Yrag. Casca recognized the bound man, Esigie, one of Anaken's most trusted. He had fought bravely through overwhelming odds, defending his leader and friend Anaken with his every breath. Casca remembered his firm voice and powerful hands holding the legs of Ikan while Anaken cut off the man's diseased limb. Esigie had labored feverishly to bind the severed leg, for the time being stopping the surge of blood that left Ikan's body. Using his sword, Esigie had made two makeshift crutches, enabling Ikan to return home.

Looking closer, Casca noted that Esigie had also not escaped the battle uninjured; he too was missing part of his left hand, probably a remnant of a wound that had refused to heal. His mutilated arm now lay there with the unforgiving ropes digging into the meat of his hand.

Esigie turned his head side to side, trying to make eye contact with someone in the crowd. Casca noted a tall, thin woman standing within feet of Ary, holding her head in her hands, mourning perhaps more than all around her. Her eyes met Esigie's and embraced his in a last good-bye.

The silence was so devastating that Casca could hear Ooton's skin crack and wrinkle as the cadaver of a man walked. His meatless legs and arms were nearly pierced by the yellowish bone which threatened to push its way through his skin. Not a drop of moisture found its way to his body, which more and more looked like a corpse long dead and dried out by the desert. Creaking at the joints, yet almost gliding, ghostlike, over the reddish dirt, Ooton and one of his helpers approached the beaten down warrior, one on each side of him.

"It is the water of fire," whispered Yrag, this time just tugging at Casca's newly welted arm.

Casca had heard about this in passing, never having given it much thought or attention. In other places people had referred to strong drink as "water of fire" or other colorful terms. Genghis Khan had named a drink "widow maker" for its potency for killing foolhardy men directly or indirectly, by the fights it always seemed to instigate. This was drink of a different kind. Casca watched Yrag's fearful eyes and ever quickening breath follow every movement the old man made.

Ooton opened a vial that he had kept in a pouch by his waist, drawing everyone's attention to it. Pulling the stopper out, he signaled to his accessory. The brute of a man, approaching Esigie from behind, held his chin and face in an armlock while the other hand pinched his gasping nostrils. While he forced the man's mouth open, Ooton drained the contents of the vial down his throat. In one quick gulp it was all gone. They both let go, allowing the man to gather his breath.

There was nothing to see for a few moments. Casca had thought the foul liquid was a slow-acting poison, designed to torture the body and mind before killing. The poor man was not going to have it so easy.

In seconds his eyes cleared up, a smile almost finding its

way upon his face. Breathing comfortably, Esigie eyed Ooton, apparently unable to show contempt. As he held Ooton's eyes, his chest started to rise and his breath quickened. Still, he appeared to feel no pain, or even discomfort. The other four prisoners soon followed, the last of them taking the drink without a struggle.

Casca watched men and women all around him cringe in uneasiness watching this unfold. Some hid their eyes behind their hands or veils; others stood stone faced, preparing their minds to hide them from the sights to come. Yrag, wiping his sweaty brow continually with his now drenched left sleeve, craned his neck and rose to his toes trying to get a better look. Pushing down on Casca's left shoulder, he again whispered.

"The water of fire . . . I have heard of it before . . . The poor man, all of them."

It certainly did not seem to Casca that any of them was suffering up to this point, but it was also obvious it was just the beginning. He had seen potions destroy a man's body by ripping his innards and bowels apart, until he bled a horrible death, or maddening him with the pain they inflicted on the mind. Men had always found creative ways to deliver pain, by force or treachery.

Looking over the crowd, Casca tried to find Ary's eyes, but without success. Ary had buried her face in her sister Zil's shoulder and neck, the two of them trying to console and support each other. They too had seen the water of fire before.

Standing patiently Ooton and his helper watched the three men. The old man reached and held the left arm of Esigie and placed two of his fingers on the inside of his wrist. Casca had seen this before many times as healers of the past had tried to read how men's hearts beat. Some had suggested that a great healer could tell all there was to know about a man's health from the beating of his heart. It was doubtful Ooton's interests rested with the overall health of Esigie. Tajah-Nor stood by the throne, moving his eyes between Oba Awanoshe and Ooton.

"He is ready for his journey," coughed Ooton, all the while holding his fetid, rotted pipe with his festering, nearly toothless gums. Two putrid teeth hung from his foul mouth, one on each side, a yellow fang sticking out from the top and a filthy brown thing pointing up from his emaciated lower jaw. The repulsive sight reminded Casca of an old Arab curse: "May you have but two teeth that never meet." Casca hoped that only food, not a woman, would ever have to view his ugly black hole.

Taking out his mouthpiece with his left hand, spraying the ground with a dark bloody spray, heaving violently, like a man who was at death's door himself, he added, "He is strong, he will make a good showing."

Tajah-Nor nodded in agreement and faced the crowd. "We will bury the past with these five men. Failure will no longer exist among us. That is the will of Oba Awanoshe." Turning to Anaken, grabbing him with his cold stare, Tajah-Nor concluded. "You and your family will live. Live with the memory of what you have brought onto thousands and the lives of these five wretched failures. Do not beg for death. This is your punishment."

Casca watched Anaken's emotionless eyes quiver with pain. He struggled not to blink, or to show any response to his sentence. Right or wrong he would carry the memory of this day for the rest of his life, having to replay it in his mind's eye every time before sleep would come, possibly to be chastised by thousands, perhaps even having his children and children's children live with the memory of the day.

Ooton and his accomplice approached their first victim. Esigie cried out in pain, as without much warning or fanfare Ooton's hand came down and crushed his crippled hand with a heavy mallet. The sound of bone cracking and splintering brought a deathly silence. All anyone could hear was the voice of Esigie agonizing from the sudden blow.

Biting his lip, a trickle of blood overflowing, running down his chin and neck, Esigie tried to control himself, to avoid if possible providing pleasure to anyone who enjoyed his torture. The next three blows came quickly one after the other, each more devastating than the previous, pushing shards of bone into the wooden plank.

Without a moment's respite to gather himself from the shock, Esigie let out one long continuous howl. The pain was beyond anything he could master. Stepping back,

Ooton admired his handiwork and almost smiled at Esigie's mangled hand, offering a satisfied grin for a job well done. Handing the mallet over to his underling, he stood by Tajah-Nor.

Gasping for breath, Esigie watched his smashed and flattened hand refuse to bleed. The strength of the blows had apparently crushed his bone and tissues together, preventing his lifeblood from draining away. A sideways slash of the mallet quickly changed that, splattering the crowd. Esigie cried out once again, unable to withstand the pain. As a soldier and personal guard of Anaken, he had been trained his whole life to endure the pain and injury of battle, but this was beyond that.

Casca closed his eyes gently, awaiting the man's death as Esigie quickly bled from his lacerated stump of an arm. It would not be long now before the shock of the injuries and loss of blood would allow the man the escape to unconsciousness. Then death could take him peacefully and quietly.

Feeling Yrag's hand on his shoulder again, Casca refocused his eyes on Ooton. The old man quickly approached Esigie and angrily pushed his helper out of the way. Ooton pulled a pouch from his belt and poured a yellowish red powder from it into his cupped right hand. Pouring the grainy dust from his hand onto the bleeding arm, he slowly rubbed it into the torn, pulsating flesh.

Esigie cried out from the burning sensation and the pressure of Ooton's hand. Within moments the bleeding stopped, turning the clumping blood into a bubbling thick mass. Esigie watched in horror and amazement his left arm refusing to bleed any further. Death would not come that easily, not if Ooton could help it.

The battering continued. Ooton rained blows over Esigie's broken body, smashing every bone in his left arm one by one, each bone of his hand becoming a target of the unrelenting mallet, each finger nearly liquefied by the power of the blows. When there was nothing left, the right hand followed.

Once again Esigie cried out in pain, at times screaming uncontrollably, at other times sobbing, yet not begging for mercy. The other four men bound adjacent to Esigie shook violently from side to side, unsuccessfully attempting to free themselves, knowing their fate would not be any different. Watching Esigie suffer so, knowing what awaited, maddened them, caused them to shriek, piercing the hearts and souls of all who stood by watching. Some in the crowd quietly cried, joining Esigie in his pain, others whimpered helplessly. A few with their heads bowed down just prayed for a quick death.

Gathering his breath, Ooton relented in his assault momentarily, stepping back for all to see the results of his butchering. "Beg for mercy, beg for it." Casca heard Tajah-Nor's voice. "Do it and death will come swiftly."

Pained by the shock of his injuries, Esigie cried out, finally begging for mercy. Tajah-Nor smiled. Casca watched the horror of this day, knowing well he could do nothing for this man or for the other four who would be next. His hands gripped the broadsword, the blade hungering for the evildoers. Quivering, his knuckles white from the grasp that encircled the ridged hilt, Casca pushed the weapon back into its sheath. It would be of no use for now.

Esigie's broken body shook and agonized in pain, the effects of the battering still reverberating in his flesh. He coughed, gasping for breath, trying to bring air into his burning lungs. Ooton had been right, he was strong and would endure a lot of punishment before dying.

Recovering from his own effort, Ooton continued. The mallet came down again, shattering Esigie's right shoulder. Once again blood sprayed from his wounds, darkening Ooton's clothing. It was time. Esigie was ready to lose consciousness and die.

He had suffered terribly. Darkness would come slowly, blurring the nightmare that was into a softened reality, eventually giving place to complete darkness. Death was welcome. Casca allowed his eyelids to close slightly, awaiting for the last few seconds of misery to pass.

It was not to be so. "It is the water of fire," whispered Yrag. "It is working."

Casca's eyes snapped open, as he wondered what Yrag was talking about, for a moment having forgotten about the potion all five men had been forced to drink. He looked at Esigie's face, the white of his eyes flooded with blood, every vein in his face bulging, pounding, as blood flowed, ready to burst from the pressure of his beating heart. The reality of what was happening finally hit Casca. He remembered with horror that Anaken and Ary had spoken of it before. Oba Awanoshe did a have a way with pain, pain that made men wish for a swift death.

The hammer came down again and again, tearing Esigie's limbs to shreds, splattering his blood and flesh, further darkening the blood-soaked earth. He no longer resembled a man, his head and body the only thing remaining, his legs and arms having been transformed into flattened and torn tissue that no longer held on to his torso. Nothing fastened him down but the one strand of rope that encircled and held his waist. Esigie cried out continuously, the moments of agony feeling like an eternity, his maddened scream awaiting death to take him and end it all.

He was punished worse than any man could have been. The water of fire was working. The burning potion traveled through his veins, pushing the unforgiving fire along, awakening every cell, every strand of tissue, his nerve endings ablaze with the lightning that only the sky should bring. The water would not allow him the sweet escape to unconsciousness.

Ooton stood, gasping for breath, in complete exhaustion from the massacre, wheezing like a man spent with ecstasy. Coughing violently, oozing a dark offensive spittle from his trembling lips, he dropped the mallet at his feet, signaling for his aide to help him stand. Depleted of energy, but not of enthusiasm, he would continue. He was not yet satisfied. Esigie would have to pay longer.

"This you will all remember." Tajah-Nor sounded off again, bellowing louder than all the screams within the courtyard and Esigie's continuous cries of anguish. "Look at him, Anaken, look at him. It is your hand that is ending him. Do not doubt that," concluded Tajah-Nor.

Anaken stood as if frozen in time, his eyes no longer focused on anyone or anything. Around him everyone stood in shock, trying to find their own way of accepting the madness that was this day.

Recovering momentarily from the effort, Ooton once more applied the reddish powder to Esigie's bloody stumps.

He was not yet done. There was not much life left inside Esigie's body, but what there was burned from the evil one's potion. Once again the bleeding stopped, the bloody stumps having turned into blackened and singed clumps of tissue, momentarily extending Esigie's life, to suffer further.

Raising the mallet from the bloody earth, Ooton stood at the base of the inclined pedestal. Turning side to side for all to see, he made certain there was no doubt what he was about to do next. He held the weapon high in the midday sky, light glinting and shining into the crowd from where blood did not cover the bringer of pain. The hammer struck down in between where Esigie's legs had been. The horror of his screams thundered, displacing the sound of all that anyone had ever heard before.

Nevertheless not even the pain inflicted by this obscene blow could overcome the effects of the water of fire. His body and soul would have to suffer unmercifully from the curse of the potion. It fired every cell of his body, stirring every message that flowed through his mind, preserving him, preventing the veil of darkness from overtaking him.

In what felt like an eternity, the sound traveled throughout the courtyard, embedding itself into the memories and souls of all who were there. This they would carry for generations. Ooton stood with the bloody hammer over his head, the foul juices of life trickling down from the raised instrument of torture, running over his arm, finally dripping to the ground. His chest heaving from the pleasure, spent from his effort, he watched Esigie suffer. And then there was silence.

With one final blow Ooton crushed Esigie's forehead, embedding the hammer into the bloody plank. Ooton dropped his weary arm, the spiked hammer sticking out obscenely from Esigie's crushed and mangled body. Not even the water of fire could prevent this from giving Esigie peace.

For minutes there was complete silence. Even the remaining four men strapped to the wooden planks were quiet. There was nothing in their minds that could prepare them for what they would also have to endure. Perhaps madness could take them, numbing them from the torture to come. This day of pain would continue for a while longer.

For what seemed until the end of time, the four remaining men stood on the edge of death, giving their lives in the most loathsome of ways, paying for their failure in battle. The water of fire punished them until their last drop of blood drained, trickling to the ground. Then their nerves were finally allowed to rest, extinguishing the misery and ceasing to send messages of pain to their minds.

Exhausted by his efforts, Ooton ordered his helper to carry out the slaughter, making certain death would not come too easily. Ooton stood by Tajah-Nor and the royal *ekete,* watching the four men give their last breath, intermixing their cries of agony with those of the aghast spectators.

Deadened by what he had been forced to witness, Casca's mind curiously drifted. With clouded eyes he watched Tajah-Nor stand beside the *ekete,* a pleased smile dominating the man's face, allowing this moment to satisfy his obscene needs and fuel his dark scheme. Tajah-Nor looked toward the royal throne, then back at the thousands who stood with heavy and frightened hearts. His shifting eyes further betrayed him, additionally affirming Casca's concerns that he had plans beyond these savage executions.

Within all this madness Casca's senses pulled him away, pushing off all that was close and previously overwhelming, almost silencing the cries of agony. Once again his heart raced, remembering a few days past when he had awakened from sleep, searching out the night wind. Breathing in deeply, he sensed something from a long time past.

The hypnotic trance broke with the voice of Tajah-Nor awakening him.

"The past is gone. Long live Oba Awanoshe, the true son of God."

"Long live Oba Awanoshe, the true son of God," sounded out throughout courtyard, repeating over and over, at first quietly then with voices rising, the sound thundering higher and higher until Casca thought his eardrums would shatter.

"So it will then be done," came Tajah-Nor's voice, instantly quieting the crowd.

Rising from his royal throne, Oba Awanoshe once again made his appearance from beneath the canopy.

TWENTY-TWO

"These four are here to serve me." With these words Oba Awanoshe turned back toward Tajah-Nor, signaling with his left hand, then returned to the sun-covered *ekete.*

Casca's eyebrows raised with curiosity as no one had appeared, and no one had expected. All around him men wondered what else this day could bring. Yrag, momentarily relieved that apparently no more would be punished for having failed in some manner, breathed in deeply and almost leaned into Casca, trying to communicate his relief for now.

From behind the palace gates four men appeared, dressed unlike anyone in the courtyard. They walked two by two, quietly and with confidence. Coming into the enclosure, they faced Oba Awanoshe's royal subjects. Thousands stood watching these four men, scrutinizing their strange dress and even stranger appearance.

Casca had seen such men many times before. But not in this land. These men were far from home. Helmets covered their heads, with long rectangular nose pieces extending down, protecting them from potential slashes of swords or maces. A chain mail hood hung from the rim of the helmets, protecting their brows. Leather-lined body armor encircled their chests, while long, narrow swords hung freely from their belts, dangling by their feet.

The two in the front wore gray tabards, short tunics that covered their armor; however they bore no coat of arms. Not that it would have made any difference for these men. Casca knew well their allegiances most likely lay elsewhere.

They stood confidently, even in a place such as this, surrounded by thousands of wild-eyed, distraught people. The thinner of the two was slightly built, with an almost feminine quality to him, yet he stood strong and decisive, clearly a man of power and authority. His arrogance was veiled, but unmistakable.

Standing more hunched over, with wider and thicker shoulders, the other one appeared to force himself to shift his eyes as slowly as possible while taking in the crowd. He too showed confidence, with just the slightest hint of reservation. Their hands were thick and worn, unquestionably having wielded heavy swords over the years.

Behind them, two larger men wore plain dark surcoats, stained by time and wear. Casca noted these two men, standing behind the other two as if at detention, concealing small cone-shaped objects beneath their clothes on the left side, just above their belt line. Looking like standard hunter's flasks, it seemed unreasonable to Casca that they would be hidden.

Their right hands were large and rough, with ugly blisters and scarred splotches from burns that appeared to have been repeated many times over the years. The callused, blackened skin told of singed tissue that had never had the chance to heal properly.

The smaller of these two men, still at least six feet in height, sported a blackened reddish mark under and around his left eye, and some blistering still present from the burn he had obviously suffered recently. There were few ways these injuries could have occurred. The four stood with their heads held high, allowing themselves to be scrutinized while they themselves watched the crowd.

The four white men stood in silence. Casca had seen their kind before. It was unlikely they were here to help anyone but themselves.

"These men have also suffered at the hands of the Yoruba," offered Tajah-Nor. "They had been generous and trustworthy with the beasts of the north, only to be deceived. The goods they brought to barter with were taken and their couriers held for ransom. Many of them were killed by the treachery of the Yoruba dogs."

Casca did not care much what story Tajah-Nor planned to sell his people. Previously the Igbo had been the cursed "dogs." Having failed at a successful trade was a poor excuse for what Tajah-Nor suggested the Yoruba were guilty of. That in itself was hardly a crime in this world.

These four were no saints themselves and had likely deceived and misled the Yoruba at every turn. Casca had heard Tajah-Nor speak more than enough times to know that lies came when his lips moved. The truth about the success and fairness these four men and the Yoruba enjoyed did not matter much.

In some way Oba Awanoshe was going to use them to his advantage to control his people. It was very unlikely the four were here for any other reason than to pursue their trade by whatever means necessary.

Looking back through the royal gates, Casca's eyes searched off in the distance. A few servants scurried about, running in and out of the palace, preparing for the celebrations to come. Scantily clad concubines hurried up some stairs, preparing themselves for another sordid exercise. There was nothing unusual about either one of these groups, but something would not let Casca rest.

Something deep inside him ate away at his senses. He did not know what he expected to see, but he knew there was more to this day still to come. His instincts had rarely failed him and now they were warning. Nodding his head, Casca continued his desperate search. These men were not what had caused his concern or lack of sound sleep, but for now he returned his attention to Tajah-Nor.

"They do not ask for much," continued Tajah-Nor, "but they will be handsomely rewarded. Oba Awanoshe's generosity will see to that."

Casca wondered how seriously Tajah-Nor took his own words, or whether he thought anyone believed in them. Oba Awanoshe's people had never received but scraps of anything that anyone could consider reward or generosity.

"It is a new beginning. With their help we will defeat the Yoruba heathens and their false gods," indicated Tajah-Nor pointing to the four men. With these words Casca could almost sense Tajah-Nor looking at him out of the corner of his eye, assuring himself his words had sent a message.

"We will help each other," concluded Tajah-Nor. "Vengeance will be ours to take. The Yoruba will know death."

Casca grinned at Tajah-Nor's broken words and fragmented speech. He certainly did not sound very convincing. Then again, the four men could not understand his words and the Edo people did not need any convincing, as they knew better. Some probably wondered about Tajah-Nor's brazenness in rejecting Olokun of their legends. Just posturing, nothing else.

Eventually, his words ceasing for the moment, Tajah-Nor signaled one of his men. A large wooden crate, twice as large as a full-grown man, was wheeled in by two of his helpers. Six men strained to place it upon a small platform in front of the royal *ekete,* facing the courtyard for all to see. Buckling from its awkward shape and size, they trembled, fearful of an improper delivery. This was not a good day to invite Tajah-Nor's wrath.

The huge box was raised enough off the ground so the thousands crowding around could get a clear look. From it, a large covered wooden frame, nearly ten feet in height, was removed. It held the outline of a man standing erect, holding an object in his right hand.

Any sounds that were still heard quickly quieted down. This was part of no ceremony that anyone had ever seen. People craned their necks curiously, trying to get a better look, glancing at one another, shrugging with their eyes.

"This we give to honor our Oba. Long live Oba Awanoshe!"

Suddenly standing up, Oba Awanoshe stepped out from under the canopy and made his way adjacent to the hooded object. Standing erect, facing the crowd of thousands, he shook his royal rattle-staff, awakening everyone's voice.

Once again Oba Awanoshe's name reverberated in the courtyard, as thousands chanted in unison. The noise was deafening. With the voices echoing, the intensity of the sound itself stirred the air, nearly numbing people's bodies with the waves their voices created. Casca watched Yrag rub his hands, trying to shake the numbing, prickly feeling the sound had produced. The four so-called merchants took a backward step, startled by the booming voice of thousands, nearly overwhelmed by the sight of the Oba.

The long black cloth covering the object was set afire. It quickly burned, sending black smoke into the sky, the flames reaching farther and farther. The blaze hungrily devoured the cloth, exposing the figure it held. It was unmistakable. An eight-foot statue dominated everyone's attention, causing cries of admiration and fear from the ones close enough to clearly see it.

A near replica of Oba Awanoshe burned fiercely, sending sparks as the fire attempted to consume it. Oba Awanoshe stood by, his rattle-staff held by his side, mirroring the burning icon. Dwarfed by the fiery image, he stood defiantly, glaring out at the crowd.

Not a sound could be heard other than the crackle of the blazing statue. Time passed and the image burned. People watched in amazement as the fire raged, refusing to die. Nearly an hour went by, further astonishing all present in the courtyard. The four white merchants eyed one another, clearly unprepared for the sight they were witnessing.

Eerily the burning statue stood. It was a near replica of Oba Awanoshe, from his royal dress, to his thin elongated arms and legs, to his flowing white hair and cold deep set eyes. An oversized rattle-staff seemed to grow out of the statue's arm, not unlike the one the Oba held. The fiery inferno burned on, but the statue refused to be consumed, bringing awe and shock to all. Casca had seen this before.

"Why does it stand?" Voices from the crowd drifted to Casca's ears. "Why won't the fire devour it?"

The statue was made of long and short fibers of a white substance. The pieces had been carefully woven and arranged, creating a clear likeness of Oba Awanoshe. Some of the shorter strands had been compressed and molded forming his arms and legs, while the longer ones had been threaded tightly in cords, making up his body and neck.

Within the head, neck and body of the replica, straw and

cloth had been filled in tightly, giving the appearance of a solid object. These fueled and maintained the fire, with imbibed oil that blazed out from underneath, sending bluish red flames from within the head and body. The head was also made from pressed fibers that had been crushed and packed tightly. Around it, short fibers had been placed in bunches giving the outline to the ears, nose, mouth and eyes. Long strands hung from the nearly lifelike skull, eerily mimicking the Oba's hair.

The statue burned on and on, refusing to be depleted, staggering the minds of those who had dared to challenge their belief in Oba Awanoshe's deity. A bluish purple haze engulfed the burning image, the fiery air creating a cloud of uncertainty, distorting what the eye could see.

The glowing, pulsating light enveloped Oba Awanoshe and the rattle-staff he held, the two forms melding, mimicking the flaming statue, creating an overpowering image. Yet it was nothing more than a mirage. How devious Tajah-Nor had been with this masquerade. He had orchestrated this day and many others to perfection.

No doubt many could remember the death of Oba Awanoshe's father and mother, how they had been consumed by the blue fire that had come from the heavens. Anyone not old enough to have witnessed or remembered it had heard the tale countless times of the day the gods had taken away the royal family and brought them "the son of God." Casca had seen the reaction of the crowd watching the cursed blue flames shoot out and engulf the statue.

Dancing over and caressing the image, the blue lights mesmerized the crowd. The burning oil had been mixed with a blackish powder that created the blue flames and an aroma that also brought back the memories of a distant battlefield to Casca's mind. Now the same flames had been unable to consume the likeness of Oba Awanoshe, preserving him, clearly a message from the gods. How could anyone dare doubt what they had witnessed? Tajah-Nor had done it again, bringing fear and uncertainty to Oba Awanoshe's subjects.

Slowly the fire died down, leaving a bleached, ghostlike form, hypnotizing all who were there to see, overwhelming all who witnessed. The quiet was complete, for now not even the western breeze willing to break the silence. The image of Oba Awanoshe stood unchanged, the fires of heaven and earth unable or unwilling to destroy it.

Casca had seen the white strands burn before. There was nothing remarkable or godlike about it. In ancient Rome, possibly fifteen centuries past, the material had been used by the Caesars as cremation cloths during ceremonial burials or wicks for everyday use by the lowliest of citizens.

Many foolish men had attempted to breathe in its burning spirits, believing they would ward off the devil's hold. The lucky ones had been singed by the white glowing strands, turning them away; others, less fortunate, had their lungs destroyed by the vapors. Man's inventiveness knew no bounds when trying to bluff his way out of the netherworld.

Casca had witnessed the cloth used to stifle fires in thick layers, even preventing the blazing heat from penetrating. With a heavy heart Casca remembered how his friend, whom many had revered as a great man for the ages, had died trusting that the white cloth would save him.

Pliny had traveled to the roaring fires of Vesuvius, believing that the white threaded cloth he wore would spare him from the raging blaze and the heat it brought. He had died along other brave men, from the poisoned air while trying to save many in the villages below, the cloth failing him, leaving him among the ashes for all eternity.

Casca shook himself from the memories, once again pained by the hundreds who had died, leaving him to go on and suffer with the remembrance.

''Oba Awanoshe, the son of God, lives forever,'' boomed the voice of Tajah-Nor. Casca's heart raced and he started to sweat, not from Tajah-Nor's words, but from something else. There was no doubt about it this time. There was something nearby that awakened the nightmarish memories of the recent past. Casca coughed, spitting bitter and salty. His eyes started to burn and his ears ached from the pressure.

Shaking his head slightly, squeezing his eyes as tightly as he could for a moment, he tried to break the spell. Feeling his hands tremble, he grasped them together underneath his robe. Momentarily questioning his own sanity, Casca attempted to gather himself, trying to master his emotions.

Painfully, the bizarre ceremony continued, the crowd of thousands further and further losing their sanity to the magical world that Tajah-Nor was attempting to create. The frozen statue stood, looking much taller than it really was, etching into everyone's mind the memory of Oba Awanoshe's image, defying fire itself.

Casca watched Tajah-Nor's eyes holding the crowd . . . and then it happened.

"It is time," whispered Tajah-Nor, taking everyone by surprise, as all his previous words had been like thunder, embedding themselves into people's thoughts.

Shivers ran up and down Casca's body from Tajah-Nor's soft-spoken words, echoing Anaken and Ary's prophetic assertion of his mission with these people. How ironic it was, Casca thought, to have Tajah-Nor speak the words that would set Casca upon his path to his final destiny. Tajah-Nor had allowed to escape his lips the affirmation that would eventually be his undoing.

"Long live Oba Awanoshe. The son of God," continued Tajah-Nor in the same understated tone, forcing everyone to bear down and take in all of his fateful words. With this declaration he pulled himself up to his full height, standing within two feet of the royal *ekete*. He stood in all his twisted glory, straightening his ceremonial eben sword within the braided black sheath on his belt, his golden red robe fluttering in the breeze. Apparently pleased with himself, he signaled one more time with his left hand.

A small carriage pulled by a saddled elephant was led into the enclosure. It moved ponderously, its hooves thundering away, raising dust as it delivered the mystery. The rider hung on to the howdah, obviously anxious to complete his mission and make a quick exit. Two men quickly unsaddled the beast and led it away. They quietly disappeared behind the brass gates, allowing everyone the opportunity ponder the moment.

"This we give to you," offered Tajah-Nor, bending deeply at the waist, bowing toward the royal throne. With these words, he settled in, allowing the day to make history.

Casca's eyes scanned the courtyard and the mystery the carriage held. The four merchants had stepped back, shifting their eyes between Tajah-Nor, the royal *ekete* and Oba Awanoshe's prize. If they had thought the day was for them, they realized different now. Oba Awanoshe was Oba.

Once again Casca's senses came alive, further burning his eyes and nose. Reaching toward his face, he brought a reddened air bubble on his fingertips from his nose. Filling his lungs completely while closing his eyes, he tasted the air and the scent it brought. He heard movement within the carriage as if something were trying to get out.

With a slow, leveled sweep of Tajah-Nor's hands, the carriage doors magically opened, revealing the gift. Looking up, trying to focus his eyes, Casca's line of sight found the wooden carriage between himself and Tajah-Nor's contented eyes. Standing with a pleased look on his face, smiling with his fleshy lips, Tajah-Nor brought his left hand to his mouth, resting the middle knuckle on the point of his chin.

It all fell into place, the curse of his existence and the horror that the years past had brought upon him. For an instant all light disappeared from Casca's vision except for that which lit the wooden carriage and Tajah-Nor standing behind it. All else was gone from his thoughts for a moment, his mind refusing to accept what his eyes were witnessing. Casca stood frozen as the mystery revealed itself. Once again the eastern breeze whispered, bringing a sweet scent to Casca's nose, awakening memories of the unknown past.

It was her. And him. That day on the *Kuta,* years past when the deck had buckled underneath Casca's feet, plunging him into the watery grave, she had been there. Just as he had. The two brutes had brought her from beneath the decks, carrying her onto the pirate ship, moments before the ocean had swallowed the sabotaged *Kuta*.

The tall, thin girl emerged from the enclosure of the carriage for all to see. The bracelet was still there, rattling around her shapely ankle.

Yrag shook Casca's shoulder's vigorously, trying to get his attention, and perhaps an explanation for his reaction. "Tell me, tell me . . . what is it?" He once again shook Casca. Casca could feel and see nothing except for the girl and the cursed Tajah-Nor. It all made sense now. It was he all those years past who had masterminded and carried out the sinking of the *Kuta* and the death of all aboard. Everyone had been slaughtered horribly, except for Casca and the girl. She had been the reason for all this.

That bald creature, Halim, along with his robed cohorts, had sabotaged the *Kuta,* crippling it, allowing for its easy capture and destruction. It was years later now, Casca realized the horror of it looking at the girl. There was no doubting her existence. She was a woman now, perhaps six or even more years later, but it was definitely her. Casca wondered if he could really smell the patchouli plant in the air or if it was just a maddened memory that had reawakened.

And then there was Tajah-Nor. For months now Casca had searched the recesses of his mind, trying to understand the reason for his uneasiness, as if they had crossed paths before. That instant in time when all at once these images had left their mark in his tortured soul. His mind spinning, Casca's thoughts drifted into the past, recalling the weeks aboard the *Kuta,* the horror of his watery prison, which apparently had lasted years, the pain and torture it had brought upon him. All because of this girl.

She had been the prize that for years Tajah-Nor had searched for to please Oba Awanoshe. Who knows how many others he had sacrificed, how many had died in his selfish quest to be in the Oba's favor. It was doubtful Tajah-Nor had more noble reasons for his actions. Nothing else had ever pleased the Oba. Perhaps someone not unlike him would.

Tajah-Nor had been there, standing on the deck of the pirate ship, directing the massacre of the *Kuta*. The irony of it all nearly made Casca laugh out loud, exasperated by what this moment had brought. He along with her had fallen into this world, one to strengthen the other to possibly undo it all.

She slowly stepped out of the carriage for everyone to see. All eyes were transfixed on her and Oba Awanoshe. For years he had rejected all such offerings, however this time it possibly could be different. Oba Awanoshe approached her. She was beautiful, she was perfect.

Her sunned blond hair hung loosely by her sides, flowing

down by her waist, embracing her faultless form. Casca watched her blue-green eyes sparkle behind her endless eyelashes. Her delicious lips quivered, parting and closing, her tongue wetting them, protecting them from the caress of the breeze.

The perfection of her immaculate face became etched into Casca's mind, forever holding him captive. God's eyes must have lingered on his creation after she was brought into this world. Like a feather in the wind, the sun's rays bathed her golden locks in their warmth, shifting and undulating in the eastern breeze. Her silken robe did nothing but enhance her beauty, enveloping her in a mirage of innocence and perfection.

Standing by her, Oba Awanoshe, as expressionless as ever, waited with his eyes frozen in a lifeless stare. The sleeve of his royal *ododo* fell back as he took her left hand. As if in a trance, her eyes no longer clear, she reached out with her flaxen white arm, caressing his hand upon her.

"Go with him," Tajah-Nor whispered. "Your god awaits you," his filthy depraved words continued. Her eyes clearly unfocused, falling into nothingness, raised toward the Oba's face. The years of preparation served her well as she smiled at him. "He awaits you," once again Tajah-Nor whispered.

"Long live Oba Awanoshe and his queen." He repeated the words, at first very softly as fear still held everyone hostage, and then louder and louder. With emotionless eyes Oba Awanoshe looked down at this frail creature, pulling her closer to himself.

"Come to me," he ordered quietly, further hypnotizing her with his glare.

The obscenity of the moment rattled Casca, awakening him. What had become of this girl? The words repeated endlessly in his mind, nearly suffocating his thoughts. Casca thought of closing his eyes, to have to witness this most distasteful of sights.

His eyes searched her face, her familiarity awakening memories of the past. The thoughts ate at his mind. It was impossible that Casca could have known her. Most likely of noble blood herself, the girl had probably been snatched from her life of royal privilege, to be thrust into an alien world to serve a madman's plan. Weakly she stood by Oba Awanoshe, her head raised, but her eyes unfocused, looking beyond him, her smile having disappeared.

The stupor breaking momentarily, Casca noted a wide grin find its way upon Tajah-Nor's face. He had finally done it. The beast had succeeded. Oba Awanoshe would ultimately be satisfied with this prize. She looked unlike anything any of them had ever seen, more like the Oba himself than any that he had ever been offered. Perhaps she was a goddess that had been sent to complete him.

The totality of this day's events was overpowering. Casca's mind was spinning from all the day had brought, trying to take it all in. How would the Edo react to this day? he wondered. A day that deified an Oba who had brought nothing but fear, pain and death to them. How could anyone be brave enough to ever question one as him? If the fires of hell were powerless to take him, how would anyone ever dare oppose him? Casca's concern for these people intensified, bringing back the painful tales Anaken and Ary had shared with him about this land and its people.

TWENTY-THREE

Casca returned to his dwellings. He could not recall the steps or how the day's ceremony had ended, but had found himself walking in through the house gates with Yrag lagging a few feet behind him, talking to himself in voices. The whole day had been one big befuddlement; it had been too much. His mind raced from the need to end Tajah-Nor's life, to freeing the poor pathetic girl that had fallen into this nightmare, to concern about the four supposed merchants.

Suddenly Casca held great disquiet for this land and its people. What would happen to Ary? He had not felt like this for a woman for seemingly forever. He wondered who was more of concern, Tajah-Nor and his newly found favor with the Oba, the Oba himself, who had elevated himself among the gods with the actions of this day, or the four merchants who were "here to help." No matter, Tajah-Nor would need to die soon. Casca had met his kind before.

Casca sat in silence. No one dared break his solitude. From a distance Anah and Okuse whispered to each other, even they knowing not to interrupt his thoughts. Yrag rested in an adjacent room, backed against the wall with his chin on his knees, hugging his legs. His sword and light shield were by his side.

Rocking back and forth, he hummed an old battle song

about pride and freedom. It was something that would be soon revisited. Watching this day's lights slowly fade away, darkening his room, he feared what the new day would bring. He knew his time had also come. Ewuare had sent him for a reason.

"We will make our way to Anaken's house after nightfall," Ary suggested, breaking the silence. "He is expecting us."

Casca knew that was the case. The day's events had left no doubt his time was nearing. His thoughts kept returning to that fateful day on the *Kuta* when the two pirate ships had engaged them. The battle had been brief and bloody. He had often wondered why no one had been taken as prisoner. Strong backs and willing arms were always needed, even if they required some compelling to cooperate, even if only briefly utilized, to row in the belly of a ship until their backs broke and spirits died.

It all made sense now. These pirates had other orders. It had been a simple butchering, with one purpose in mind: the acquiring of that girl had been it, and nothing more. All who died had meant nothing. They were just more flesh that time would forget.

Awakening from his momentary daze, Casca looked up at Ary's smiling face. Raising his head, he caressed the soft hand that she had placed on his shoulder.

"Anaken awaits us," he simply responded.

Under the cover of darkness they made their way to Anaken's dwellings. There was no apparent reason to remain veiled, since Casca had been virtually dismissed and ignored by Tajah-Nor and Oba Awanoshe following the day's events. He had been told to return on the day of Enhora to witness the final glory of the empire. Then he would be allowed to return to the ocean. Casca found it nearly impossible to believe the turn of events; however this night held other concerns.

He arrived accompanied by Ary and Yrag. Ary had been quiet, somehow realizing that the following days would bring great change to her world. Yrag walked like a man, someone who had suddenly grown up, passed from being a boy to becoming a man.

Hugging the light shield with his left arm, he straightened

the sword by his waist as they moved in the night. He began to understand why he had been sent along, the responsibilities he would share, the tasks he would have to follow on through. Casca had known all along the young boy was more than a box carrier or pillow fluffer.

Anaken's dwellings were quite impressive. Perhaps not a palace, but not far from it. Nothing could compare to Oba Awanoshe's imperial palace, or would likely be allowed to challenge it in grandeur, size or adornments. Not unlike Casca, Anaken had been dismissed as a man of power, for now allowed to live and suffer from the loss and pain he had brought onto others with his failed campaign.

The entrance was simple and practical. Two guards kissed the ground as Casca and his limited entourage approached. It would be minutes before they would rise and make a halfhearted attempt at eye contact. Their loyalty and respect for Casca had not been diminished by the day's events. They were Anaken's loyal men.

Casca made a feeble motion toward them in an effort to raise them from the dusty ground. Fighting within themselves, they returned to their position adjacent to the doorway. Once inside, Casca was met by Anaken, still the *ezomo,* if only in title and not in actual power.

For most of his life he had controlled the military and the fate of thousands, but for now his fate hung in the balance, possibly at the mercy of Tajah-Nor. Casca had seen what the madness of power had brought in people.

Without a word spoken, the three of them followed Anaken's lead. The dome-like alcove, lit by a handful of goat-oil lamps, created a feeling of secrecy and strength. Bright sparkling amber glittered under a few glass-covered scones, bending the light, distorting what the eye revealed. Water droplets worked their way through the creases above, dropping from the stony topside, ringing eerily as they landed against the marble floors. Casca could hear Yrag's shallow yet rapid breathing following him as they made their way up a dozen stone slab steps.

"Make yourselves comfortable," offered Anaken, "even if only for a few moments." Sitting at the head of a large rectangular table, he placed both his hands on the cool dark wood, stroking its rounded edges with the palm of his right hand. Perspiration rolled off his battle-worn hands as he continued working his palms against the smooth rim of the table.

"I have made every important decision while sitting here. My grandfather made this table when he was just sixteen years of age. He was a great man. Only good things have come of it," he concluded, closing his eyes for a moment, perhaps reliving a personal remembrance.

"Do not feel awkward, or unnerved. We all have our superstitious demons," he added, seeing his guests unsure about the moment.

Sitting down, they took the refreshments offered by two of Anaken's daughters. The two girls, not much younger than Ary's daughters, stood with pride, obviously aware of their father's fortune, but also unyieldingly at his side. Wearily they looked at Casca, having seen him in public at ceremonies, but never up close. Unable to help themselves, they stared, following the many battle scars that crisscrossed his huge arms, neck and face. Taking a hot cup of kola nut-brew, Casca eyed Anaken.

Not unlike himself, Anaken had been quite disturbed by the day's events. There had been too much not left to chance. He had suffered terribly wondering if the whole campaign against the Yoruba had been a horrible ruse. What madman could fabricate such subterfuge?

Could Oba Awanoshe or Tajah-Nor have been so concerned about his popularity and rise in power to put together such an obscene plan? Having had to watch the last of his remaining men, men who had fought so valiantly to protect their leader, die such a horrible and demeaning death, had not been much easier. Men deserved to die as men not chattel. The water of fire had ravaged them mercilessly, draining pain from every nerve fiber until there was nothing to give.

Seeing Anaken's pained eyes, it was clear this world was about to change. With unspoken words they knew there was great concern. The time had come.

Anaken broke the heavy silence. "Oba Awanoshe is meeting with the four travelers tonight. We must know of their plans," he suggested.

"My sister Zil will help us out," offered Ary. "She owes

our Oba much.'' Bowing her head, Ary remembered Zil's husband, Ikan, gasping for breath as the flesh-rotting sickness was taking him. Not unlike most of them, Zil had a debt to pay.

TWENTY-FOUR

The four of them approached the royal palace before midnight. Tapping lightly on the servants quarters door, Ary quickly awakened her sister Zil.

"We need your help," Ary whispered through the crack of the door, pushing the thin reed-covered drape open, peeking in, cautiously looking side to side.

Before Ary could even finish her words, Zil moved them inside the curtained enclosure while rubbing the sleep out of her eyes with her free hand. All sleep left her body seeing Anaken and Casca follow Ary through the doorway. Nodding her head, she led them.

Following an intricate labyrinth of corridors, doorways and stairways, they made their way into the heart of the royal palace. Moving in near complete darkness Zil felt her way through until, whispering as quietly as she could, she brought them to a stop.

"I believe they are all here," she whispered in the lowest of tones. "I must go now," she added in a fearful voice.

Quickly disappearing, she pulled Ary along with her, leaving Casca, Anaken and Yrag at the edge of a corridor, nearing the entrance to a wooden balcony. The darkness was near complete, with just a glint of a yellow glow coming through the cloth of the drape covering the portal. As he edged his way toward the light, words he had not heard in many years came to Casca's ears. The clammy, sickly sweet sound of an old French dialect. Crawling toward the undersized doorway, Casca loosened the binding that covered the opening.

Two men sat at a table. Tajah-Nor leaned back on an *agba,* the rectangular stool the royal palace offered to its highest, holding his head down, preoccupied by a long object his hands held. Oba Awanoshe stood away from the oversized table, hidden by the darkness of the poorly lit room. He watched the other four from a distance, shifting his weight slowly from one foot to the other.

One of the two visitors Casca had seen during the day sat adjacent to Tajah-Nor, also handling a long dark object. The other man stood at the head of the table, with his head angled down, talking to a man nearly a foot shorter than him. Casca could not recognize the little man as he had his back to where Casca stood and spoke in a low monotone voice. Gasping for breath, he coughed violently. It was that little creature, Akheno. Apparently he was more valuable than for just holding gates ajar.

Engrossed in his own little world, Tajah-Nor sat in silence, ignoring all else. He sighed as he moved his hand up and down along the shaft of a weapon Casca had not expected to see in this land. It looked unlike the ones he had seen before, but its shape and function were unmistakable.

Holding it in his lap, the stock of the weapon paralleling his left thigh, Tajah-Nor moved his quivering right hand over it, enjoying the moment beyond reason. As he sat back farther, it moved upward, its tip reflecting the yellow light of the candles, awakening memories as the glint of metal entered Casca's eyes. Casca had seen and used its like before.

Pitched against the table there were four more of the same, bundled tightly in dark cloth. Leaning against them, nearly embracing the wrapped package, Tajah-Nor put his hand inside the cloth, while at the same time still holding the one he had handled before. A foul smile crossed his face as he returned to moving his right hand against the side of the one he held. His eyes searched the dozen or so pouches that had been piled randomly on top of the table. Turning his gaze toward Oba Awanoshe, he appeared barely able to contain his pleasure and excitement.

Pulling himself closer to the opening, Casca pushed slowly with his toes, dragging his head over the edge of the enclosure, just able to look down and observe the whole room from above. Slithering by his side, Anaken also pulled up, peering nervously over the brim of the wooden rafter.

The instruments of death were laid upon the table in the room below. It had been years since Casca had seen such. They were long and thin, the wooden stock elongated and carved of dark wood while the metal barrel, fastened to it by iron bands. The barrel appeared to be of forged iron, clearly not something that would have been made in this land, while the well-shaped wood stock ended in a round and slightly wider section, covered by a butt plate.

Casca remembered using something not unlike this, perhaps heavier and larger, of a more ancient design, years ago in the southern German states. A hand canon they had called it, the thunder frightening all around while the lightning it belched from the forged steel barrel made many of the locals cross themselves, believing it was the lightning from God's eyes. Casca had been hired by the town of Augsburg, along with another thirty men, to the contingent of the Swabian towns in their war against Holvarth the Great of the neighboring German state of Ulm.

Holvarth had been just huge and blubbery, without any greatness to him. His town was blown off the face of the hillside, while he drowned in his own blackened juices and entrails from the hand cannon that had blasted him against his own bed. He had been too slow and ponderous to even pull on a robe as the interlopers entered his home, and provoking his executioner with his foul sight and words did not extend his life or endear him to any.

Eventually the cold of winter pulled all the heat out of his body, sending vapors into the night sky as he came to resemble a harpooned whale, charred by the fires of hell. No one, including his people, mourned for long. Just another bloated tyrant to feed the worms.

Casca remembered standing by the pool of death, his ears

still shattered from the blast of the cannon. It was days before his ears stopped ringing and the burning smell of the blazed powder left his body. Casca shook from the memories, the unmistakable smell of the ablaze powder returning to singe his senses again.

The burning powder, which many had thought the devil himself had brought from hell to punish and conquer, was something Casca had seen many times past. Kublai Khan's magicians and entertainers had used it for their illusions, magically allowing objects or people to appear from thin air as the unsuspecting crowds were still blinking, trying to refocus their eyes.

Casca recalled Marco Polo's youthful voice cry out, frightened yet delighted by the moment. It was not long before Marco looked forward with anticipation to the magic of the land of Chin. There, during the celebration of the new year, the powder had been used to shoot colorful flames into the sky from bamboo-reinforced barrels, delighting young and old.

Today, however, there would not be much to celebrate. The burning powder was here to deliver the instrument of death.

"What are they saying?" Anaken whispered lightly.

Casca's mind returned to the place where Akheno's words came from. He had not expected to hear them in this land. Especially not what he was about to hear.

"One hundred will not be enough . . . not for what we are offering . . . what about . . ." His words stepped on, Akheno looking at Tajah-Nor for help, then coughing violently into his stained left sleeve.

"You are being unreasonable. Even half of that—" The merchant himself was unable to complete his words as Akheno quickly retorted.

"Monsieur Escarg, Tajah-Nor is a reasonable man. He respects your bartering skills. I believe he is willing to offer . . ."

"What are they saying?" Anaken queried once again, drowning out Akheno's last words. Even in this darkness, Anaken eyes could read the concern in Casca's face as they turned toward each other. Without a word spoken, they hoped they were both mistaken.

Clearly Anaken could understand nothing of what had been said. Akheno struggled but was able to communicate with Escarg and apparently the other one, in his fragmented, slowly delivered words. Casca could not imagine where the little devil of a man had learned the foul tongue. Yet he spoke it clearly and apparently was able to understand even when he was spoken to rapidly.

The other traveler was dressed differently and appeared to be of another stock. His origins became clear moments later as Escarg quickly turned to him, calling him Harper, as they continued to discuss their business venture in English. With a clear English accent, Harper delivered his monotone words, his lips barely parting under his rich mustache.

Escarg struggled with his words as his handle on English was quite limited. In his experience Casca had only seen the men of the two nations end each other's lives, but apparently for now they had joined up, creating a combination that further concerned Casca.

Turning back toward Akheno, Escarg continued in French, distorting his face as the words came out.

''We will help you use the *bâstons-a-feu.* Not before long you will master its use. It is the thunder and lightning of the heavens. The 'sticks of fire' will make you invincible.''

Casca had seen the bâstons-a-feu, aptly they were named ''sticks of fire'' as they belched smoke and fire on one end, while the other end delivered a metal slug, viciously smashing anything it encountered. The weapon could take out a man or horse, even going through a horse's chamfron, head armor, or the breastplate or chain mail of a soldier.

Many he had also seen deformed or killed by the faulty use of such a weapon. Storage outposts or palaces had been leveled to the ground by the cursed powder, the inferno brought to life by the spark of one ember, leaving nothing but charred remains, incinerated by the fire that burned under the cover of water.

When used improperly, Casca had seen the sticks of fire blaze through a man's face, disfiguring him as the burning powder would not be quenched easily. The smell of singed tissue burning relentlessly was something that clung to one's memories forever. He remembered that the other two men who had accompanied Harper and Escarg, wearing the burns and scars of the weapon's probable misfiring.

"Oba Awanoshe requires more and more of the powder that burns," Akheno insisted.

"Your bartering has been unfair, offering so little," Escarg protested. "You will easily be able to replenish your losses, and to conquer anyone that opposes you," he continued, insisting defiantly.

"Five hundred is all we will accept in exchange for . . ."

Once again Akheno's words were lost and Escarg's eventual response stepped on as Anaken anxiously interrupted, turning Casca's ear away from the words below. Twisting within their confined space, Casca and Anaken sweated profusely from the lack of air and their own uneasiness. Farther behind them Yrag had not even attempted to enter the small passageway and crawl along adjacent to Casca. He tensely waited, making every attempt to breathe quietly.

"Maybe we can agree on three hundred, but you will have to offer more, three thousand more," Escarg suggested, pursing his unsightly lips.

"Three thousand more . . . Oba Awanoshe will never agree to that, not unless . . ." unable to complete the offer, Akheno excused himself with a shallow bow and attempted to speak to Tajah-Nor. Appearing oblivious of all, Tajah-Nor still stroked the shaft of the weapon, as if waiting for it to come to life.

"They want five thousand. I believe they will trade three or four hundred sticks of fire for five thousand. It is a good trade, a very good one," Akheno insisted, breathing heavily while raising his voice, sounding pleased with his position in the bartering.

Breaking from his depraved self-indulgence, Tajah-Nor stood and sighed. Turning toward Akheno, darkening his eyes with anger, he insisted, "We need five hundred of the sticks of fire and twenty extra barrels of the powder that burns. Without the powder they are useless. Even if they refuse all five hundred, we must have the powder!" Tajah-Nor demanded trying to keep his voice low and demeanor unfazed, but clearly agitated with Akheno and the exchange at hand.

"What about the five thousand? Monsieur Escarg insists," Akheno asked timidly, not wanting to raise Tajah-Nor's ire.

"You are weak. And he knows it. Do not ask him . . . tell him," Tajah-Nor hissed between clenched teeth, pushing Akheno down with his eyes, scolding him with his stare. Their exchange, no matter how quiet, still agitated Tajah-Nor, who knew this was of great importance. There was little choice, since only Akheno could communicate with these men. For now he was indispensable. Tajah-Nor looked at Akheno as someone who would be out of his favor rapidly unless his performance improved. To Casca the two of them looked as if they had spent too much time together in private quarters.

"What about the Igbo?" Akheno suggested. Smiling and nodding, Tajah-Nor directed Akheno back toward the table and an awaiting Escarg.

Turning toward Escarg, Akheno tried to stand as tall as he could. Coughing at his side, he cleared his throat.

"Oba Awanoshe, the true son of God, and the great Tajah-Nor, head of the Ibiwe, chief of the *eghaevbo nogbe*, are ready to complete their offer."

Casca turned his head, trying to get his ear as close as possible, making certain no words would be lost to him. Anaken, realizing the moment of truth was near, bit his lower lip while breathing deeply, watching Casca's intent eyes.

"Oba Awanoshe will have the five hundred sticks of fire and an additional twenty barrels of the burning powder," Akheno stated in a firm voice, trying to hold back any cough that would weaken his delivery and diminish his assertiveness. "However, Oba Awanoshe can only offer four thousand of his warriors in the exchange, the other one thousand will have to be women, women of the former Igbo."

His words nearly stopped Casca's breath. He had known it all along, but had refused to believe it. Oba Awanoshe was going to commit the ultimate sin and sell thousands of his people into slavery. His depravity was beyond reproach. Escarg's response was nearly lost on him as the reality of the Oba's evil settled in, his destiny becoming clear.

"He will have them in four days," Escarg agreed, allowing a slight smile upon his ugly lips.

"At that time we will make the exchange, the *bâstons-a-feu,* but only ten barrels of the burning powder for the four thousand men. The one thousand women you offer is a disappointment. However, they will be welcome; after all, we do not want to completely deprive our newly purchased chattel of amusement. Perhaps even one of us might need a diversion on the long trek home. Some of them I am certain we will find not unattractive. Eventually they too will be of use." Laughing zealously, Escarg reached out with his right hand to complete the agreement.

Returning the sentiments with the evil tone that men like them had in their hearts, Akheno shook Escarg's hand heartily. Cackling like starving hyenas eyeing a fallen animal, the two enjoyed the moment thinking of their deal. "They should keep you entertained for a while," Akheno agreed, holding back a cough, not wanting to disturb this moment. "No doubt they will be of some use," he continued in broken French, enjoying his handling of the deal and opportunity to impress Tajah-Nor.

Having found a moment's silence, Anaken nudged at Casca's stiffened shoulder, trying to get a response out of him. Casca turned and caught Anaken's questioning eyes. There was no need for an explanation, as Anaken understood. The two of them lay there in silence and near darkness.

Tajah-Nor, Akheno and Oba Awanoshe would need to die soon. Casca's predestination and mission had become undeniable. The unbearable voice and words echoed in his ears, embedding into his soul, tearing at his heart. Escarg had shown his true self the moment the deal had been made. The life of these people meant nothing more than that of livestock to him.

Akheno's few steps brought him back toward the table. Grinning from ear to ear, the little man proudly relayed his last spoken words to Tajah-Nor. Feeling good about himself, he boasted of his bartering skill and the deal-saving suggestion regarding the one thousand Igbo women. After all, the women had been bounty themselves, he figured.

Also pleased with the outcome, Escarg turned toward Harper in his broken English,

"We have an agreement for four thousand of their men. I could not get the whole five. That would have been nearly half their present force. The other one thousand will be women and—"

Not allowing him to finish his words, Harper snapped back. "The loss of four thousand may not weaken them enough, we may be unsuccessful . . ."

Whispering, not wanting to show any sign of distress, Escarg placed his right hand on Harper's shoulder. "It will be enough," he hissed between barely parted lips, trying to force a smile onto his face. "We will still overrun them. Our three ships still have over six hundred trained men who have been anxious for weeks now. They are hungry for the kill and the bounty. The Edo will succumb to the surprise of it all. We will still have the weapons, and the few in their possession will be useless without the proper training and the powder."

Realizing Escarg was probably right, Harper smiled, making certain both Akheno and Tajah-Nor went unsuspecting. "We will need to coordinate properly," he whispered, while all the time smiling, showing cooperation to Tajah-Nor.

Casca was in no way surprised himself. He had never expected this to be a fair exchange, no matter what the agreement had been. A depleted Edo army would be slaughtered and easily conquered by the superior weapons of the slavers. The fear and apprehension from the sticks of fire would be more than enough to overwhelm such a superstitious people as the Edo.

TWENTY-FIVE

The three of them returned to Casca's dwellings. Casca and Anaken walked side by side, unwilling to break the silence, allowing each other the solitude to deal with the insanity of what they had just witnessed. Following behind, Yrag kept to himself, knowing it was best for now. He had seen death in Casca's eyes. Olokun was ready to deliver his people. Without a word exchanged between them, they walked in the dark.

It had come to this, Casca lamented. A world gone mad. It was certainly not the first time he had seen men sold into slavery. Unlike most have thought, *this* was the world's oldest profession. However, the ease with which Oba Awanoshe could dispense of his people was repugnant. With the use of five hundred such weapons, who knew how far he planned to conquer and destroy. How many nations would be wiped off the face of the land, to become nothing but stories of legend? And what of Ary, and the rest of them? The time was now.

Ary anxiously received the three of them, but refused to ask any questions once her eyes met Casca's. Even she knew. Sitting down at his table, Casca faced Yrag.

"You must go. It is time."

Smiling at him, Yrag responded. "My father Ewuare will be pleased to see me."

Casca had felt it all along. It was not by chance that Ewuare had sent Yrag along with him. Returning his smile, Casca nodded his head.

There was not much else to be said. Yrag knew all these months spent with Casca had likely served him well, preparing him for such a mission. Gathering his sword and light shield, Yrag made his exit after a quick glance of good-bye caught Anah's eyes.

It was a night that did not lend itself to much sleep. The madness of the previous day had been overwhelming. It had been too much. The obscene torture of the five men, the sudden arrival of the merchants, the staggering shock of seeing the girl given as an unwitting bride, and the realization of what Oba Awanoshe's dark plan was. The nightmare of Casca's underwater imprisonment, all those years spent suffering, had a sobering effect. It was too much for him to withstand. His time had come. Clearing his thoughts, he walked toward the doorway and looked into the darkness of the night.

The new day would bring great change to this land. Oba Awanoshe could not be permitted to follow through with his plans. He, along with Tajah-Nor, needed to die soon. Even if the slavers were to overwhelm Oba Awanoshe's forces, which they were likely to do with ease, all they would do was take thousands as slaves, but Oba Awanoshe would most likely remain in power to continue his evil reign, perhaps for decades.

Generations to come would live in a world of death and despair under Oba Awanoshe's tyrannical rule. Casca could not allow that. He was in too deep. Allowing either—Oba Awanoshe's reign to continue, or the slavers to overthrow his kingdom—was no solution.

Yrag had left under the cover of darkness. The plan had been set in motion. The news of the slavers spread like wildfire. By morning Escarg and Harper had left, heading back toward the shore to set up their trap. They had been unaware that their plan was found out.

Throughout the night Anaken's most trusted had gone

from house to house informing them of what was to come. Thousands had gathered by morning, encircling the royal palace, creating an impenetrable wall of armed men. The Oba's few hundred loyal followers, men who throughout their whole lives had been taught to defend and support the Oba, now stood as the only defense between the angry mob and their Oba.

The struggle was brief. The weight of the mob pushed its way through the gates, collapsing the iron bars, ripping the hinges out of the ground. Falling over one another, they advanced, stepping on and crushing anyone that got in their way. Their own madness led them.

The Oba's archers had tried to slow down the attack with relentless salvos of arrows, but that did not last long. Hiding behind their shields, the men stormed the courtyard, answering with their own arrows, cutting down any that opposed them, with swords and flattened spears, or crushing them with shields.

The thundering of their voices overtook the courtyard, drowning out any orders Tajah-Nor or one of his underlings might have attempted. Closing like a vise, thousands pressed against the Oba's diminishing forces. As minutes passed, the defenders weakened from the sheer weight of the mob, eventually being completely overrun. Most of them, the lucky ones, died swiftly.

Leading the charge, Anaken and Casca broke through the Oba's private quarters, pinning down the defenders, forcing many of them to surrender. The last fifteen members of his most loyal guard, the Ifiento, still stood defiantly, ready to bleed their last drop of blood protecting their Oba.

Casca had no desire to kill the last of them. He pitied their limited existence, yet he knew these were men without choices. Surrendering was not something their minds allowed. Within moments their lifelong duty was completed. They died with sword in hand, falling with their last breath. A wasted life it had been.

In a dark corner Oba Awanoshe stood defiantly. He held his left hand out by his side, palm up, trying to hold and control the invaders with his presence. His rattle-staff lay by his feet, useless and without any power. He had sounded it repeatedly, hoping that after years of nearly magical power it would now help spare his life. After all, he had been born by the will of the gods.

Tajah-Nor and his few remaining personal guards stood in a semicircle, apparently ready to defend, most of them hoping their lives would be spared, or ended quickly. It was clear in Casca's eyes that their loyalties were available to be changed if survival was a possibility. Only their fear of Tajah-Nor's wrath and his infinitesimal patience had kept them allegiant until now.

Cowering in a corner, Akheno coughed and cried in convulsions. He had sought refuge in the last place to be overtaken. Looking toward Tajah-Nor, he pathetically searched for help. Tajah-Nor had his own concerns.

"I was just—"

A flick of Anaken's spear instantly quieted the pleading Akheno, the butt of it catching his plump belly, ripping the breath from his body. Anaken, and no one else for that matter, had any interest in hearing that Akheno had just been following orders. Casca had heard those weak words too many times over the centuries.

"Quiet down, you fool," one of Anaken's lieutenants barked at Akheno. "You are dead, you just don't know it," he gritted, the foam leaving his angry mouth running down his lips.

Akheno gasped for air, trying to form words, wondering if there was anything that would lighten his sentence. No one wanted to hear his words, no matter how pathetic. He struggled, but nothing intelligible came from his empty throat. His eyes searched the men that would be his executioners.

There was nowhere else to flee and no one to give him sanctuary. The coughing sickness would not get the chance to take his life slowly and painfully. Death would accompany him soon, while purgatory would keep him forever for his sins.

Putting the sword in the sheath by his side, Casca approached Tajah-Nor. Breathing in deeply, he allowed his racing heart to settle down and his mind to focus on one man. Beside him a bloodied Anaken wiped his own sword on his left forearm, ignoring the shaft of the broken arrow protruding from his chest just underneath his left shoulder, ready to complete, and end, it all.

"Oba Awanoshe, the son of God, commands you to stop," Tajah-Nor declared obstinately. Trying to stand his ground, he bellowed once more. "It is the will of the gods that you stop. Oba Awanoshe commands you."

Oba Awanoshe commanded no one any longer.

He stood, glaring at the intruders, foolishly hoping that the fear he had always held over his people would serve him once more. His mind could not comprehend the insolence of his subjects. How dare they challenge him; after all, he was the son of God.

There was nothing to fear anymore. He was a creature perhaps at one time resembling a man, presently just a beast sent by hell, that now stood powerless and pathetic. An emaciated and shriveled monster that was to die and bleed when steel was to strike him. Hell would be burdened by his arrival.

Tajah-Nor watched with apprehension as Casca approached him. Standing two feet apart, they stared into each other's eyes. Still holding his short eben sword in his right hand, Tajah-Nor eyed a very calm, yet full-of-anger Casca looking deep into his soul. As they searched each other's thoughts Tajah-Nor himself attempted to find a hidden memory that had reawakened in his own mind. The two of them stood in complete silence for moments that seemed to last forever.

The rage of a thousand years entered Casca's body. His blood boiled in anticipation of the kill. Tajah-Nor needed to be punished with more than the fear of death or death itself. Casca's eyes radiated anger and doom as he peered into Tajah-Nor's dark heart.

The man whose actions had punished him all those years in his watery grave was going to pay dearly. Tajah-Nor using Oba Awanoshe's name as the will of God had brought too much misery and suffering to too many people.

Frightened by what he saw in Casca's eyes, Tajah-Nor's whole body trembled while he tried to stand his ground. Gathering a last burst of strength and courage, he struck.

Casca ducked down, allowing the sudden slash of the eben sword to pass harmlessly over his head, and an instant later he dug his clenched left fist at an upward angle into Tajah-Nor's exposed right side. The man's previously attached rib tumbled inward, shredding arteries, veins, nerves and any other tissue it encountered, bursting his lung, while splintering and tearing into his backbone, cutting all that stood in its way, finally the shard of bone embedding itself into his spine.

Tajah-Nor stiffened immediately, without even a breath leaving his mouth, and fell forward, his eyes paralyzed from the shock, crushing his face against the marble floor like the carcass of a creature herded off a cliff during a hunt. His sticky red blood flooded the white floor as it gushed form his voiceless mouth, draining away in the crevices left by the imperfection of the stones.

Casca calmly drew his left hand back, watching splinters of the man's crushed ribs stick out of his reddened knuckles. Flexing his left hand, straightening out his fingers, he discarded the ugly shards of bone.

Tajah-Nor lay on his back, his nearly vacant eyes looking into nothingness, falling from life, frozen in time. Gasping with all his might, he tried pulling air into his flooded lungs. Gathering his remaining strength, he attempted to move, yet his body would not cooperate. His arms flailed away as he tried to push himself, seeking to sit up and not drown in his blackened blood; however, his body would not comply.

Screaming from the horror of it all, he shook violently, begging to get his feet to cooperate. "Please, please," he pleaded. "Get me to my feet," he implored one of his lieutenants. Tajah-Nor's punishment was not unlike Casca's. He would lie there, unable to move, possibly to die soon, perhaps cursed to be at the mercy of others, yet never able to move on his own. Death was not to take him yet; life would be ever present to punish him.

Breathing deeply, Casca stepped back, fatigued by the last moments. An unseen darkness came over him as his eyes left Tajah-Nor. The day was at end. He had no quarry with Oba Awanoshe. His concerns lay elsewhere for now. Turning away from it all, he left Anaken and his men to complete the task at hand.

Walking through the smoldering palace, Casca made his

way toward the front entrance. Smoke and ashes fouled the air, tearing his eyes. Bodies littered the hallways, the courtyard and the wide avenue, the beautiful approach to the whole palace itself looking like the scorched fields of hell.

Many guards had died foolishly defending the Oba, perhaps unable to help themselves as decades of painful lessons had instilled their duty upon them. Others, with unclouded thoughts, had welcomed the revolt and been anxious and pleased to help.

Casca could hear nothing and see little. His vision had narrowed, allowing him to discern only enough to lead him toward Ary. As he walked through the courtyard, the fresh smell of death further numbed his senses. Hundreds or perhaps thousands had died, while freeing their minds and souls.

Out of the corner of his eye he noted a decrepit crushed body, one that had been mangled beyond recognition, obviously tortured extensively, disemboweled and left to rot in the sun. It lay there in an unnatural twisted position, with gaping wounds that had refused to bleed, as if the body had been without life itself.

Possibly it was Ooton, the Oba's evil messenger of death. Casca's senses could not tell for now and he did not care. It did not matter. Oba Awanoshe and his reign were in the past.

As he walked alone with his rambled thoughts seizing his mind, Casca's ears still picked up the sound of steel on steel, the cries of agony as steel met flesh, and the songs of victory. After a while all the noises melded into one another and Casca could discern nothing. Soon it would be quiet and his mind would be allowed to rest. Dawn would bring songs and cries of joy with the rebirth of the Edo people.

TWENTY-SIX

Ary's concerned yet smiling face received him. It had been a long and exhausting day. She knew no words needed to be spoken for now as she led him inside. Spent from emotion and revenge, Casca slept. Caressing and cleansing his wounded body, Ary stood by his bed, at times kneeling down, listening to his beating heart as she worked. Her warm touch soothed him, allowing for his sleep to continue.

''He will be all right, won't he? He has to be all right,'' Okuse whispered to her sister while holding her tiny hand in an iron grip. Standing behind Ary in the doorway, the two of them anxiously stretched their necks, trying to see over their mother's head.

''I do not know,'' replied Anah while laboring to free her hand, twisting her wrist desperately, attempting to free it from the painful hold, at the same time hugging and comforting her sister. ''He does not look badly wounded to me,'' she added. ''He is probably just exhausted.''

The two of them hovered over the foot of the bed once Ary allowed them to enter, trying to see as best as they could, and at the same time not wanting to anger their mother with their eagerness. Ary knew not to push them away, for she could see their teary-eyed and worried faces.

Casca slept with a serene look on his face. His rising and falling chest comforted them as they watched his scarred and embattled body move peacefully. Quietly and softly Ary ran a warm cloth over his face and neck, discarding the filth and smell of battle. The dark stains of death quickly disappeared, leaving his knotted muscular body to be admired. Ary's healing hands continued to bathe him as he slept. Sighing with relief, Okuse finally let go of her sister's bruised hand and smiled sorrowfully.

Casca was unhurt, nothing but superficial cuts that would be near gone by morning. Shifting side to side with the gentle movement of Ary's hands, he slept. Nothing was going to wake him for now. Standing up quietly, Ary herded out her overanxious daughters and pulled a red drape over the doorway, darkening the room.

Morning came with Ary's soft lips bringing Casca back from his long sleep. Smiling at her, he sat up, rubbing the long night from his eyes, allowing the morning to receive him. As he breathed deeply, the aroma of the fresh air and the early meal awakened and aroused him.

"The night was quiet," she offered, pushing a steaming bowl of sweetened kola-nut brew into his awaiting hands. Sitting on the bed by his side, she caressed his arms, running her fingers along the deep cut on his left arm. Marveling at his recuperative powers, she looked deep into his eyes.

Sitting up, Casca tasted the air. Even it felt better this morning, almost sweet. Peering into the frothy drink, he inhaled the invigorating aroma, allowing the quiet and peacefulness of the morning to momentarily veil him from the day to come. Looking into Ary's eyes, he took in her warmth and beauty. It was not unpleasant to wake to her. Seeing him, she smiled, while again bringing her lips to his, making certain he knew this was no mirage. Putting his drink down by his side, he allowed a long passionate kiss to awaken him for now.

"I thought you were going to sleep forever. It has been nearly twelve hours," Ary continued.

Looking down at his bare chest, Casca ran his fingers over the new scars. Half a dozen new cuts crisscrossed his chest and shoulders from the previous day's fight. A deep laceration nearly encircled his left arm, trailing off under his elbow. Looking down, he watched Ary kiss softly at his wounds, caressing his injured left arm. It too had closed up and appeared to be healing at a rapid pace.

He could not remember how in the heat of battle he had suffered these wounds, or who had caused them. Much of the previous day was still clouded in his mind and would take time to settle. The originators of these wounds would never get the chance to heal their own wounds—that was the most that he could recall.

His skin had healed leaving nothing but slightly raised red lines for now. In a day or two they would all be gone, blending in with the hundreds of other scars that told the story of his never-ending cursed life.

"I have never slept for so long, so peacefully," Casca exclaimed with surprise.

It had been a long time since his mind had permitted such restful sleep. The torture of things unknown had not allowed him the sweet escape of sleep for months now.

"Anaken sent one of his men hours ago," Ary continued, momentarily interrupting her gentle kissing. "He will soon be here himself."

Casca knew all along that the brief magic of this morning was to disappear soon. Oba Awanoshe and Tajah-Nor may have been gone, but his mission was not yet over. The reality of his existence quickly returned as Ary brought his sword and dressed him in a new tunic.

Giggling with delight, Anah and Okuse elbowed their mother out of the way as they helped with Casca's dressing. Ary was not going to deny them for now; she knew well that Casca was not to return to them anytime soon, or possibly ever.

Anaken stood between two of his subordinates outside Casca's dwellings. Patiently waiting, they allowed Casca a few moments before departing. They also knew it was likely he was never to return. Stepping slightly in front of his subordinates, turning west toward the ocean, Anaken leaned into the wind, hoping the morning breeze would invigorate him.

Gently rubbing his injured left side, Anaken gritted his teeth, holding back groans of pain. Standing alongside him, the two guards tried offering words of support and encouragement, though they had seen the same wound take the lives of many. With such wounds, if the bleeding did not kill them the fever that followed often did.

The arrow had been difficult to remove. Anaken had suffered terribly having the tip of the arrow pushed through the meat of his chest finally removing with a gush of blood that took hours to stop. Casca wondered how deep and serious the injury was, seeing Anaken cough blood at times, as if the arrow had pierced the tip of his lung.

The fluke of the projectile had been barbed with inverted hooks, causing great damage upon its removal. Pulling it backward would have been nearly impossible, but due to its design, even pushing it through the flesh had caused great injury. Only the Oba's closest guards possessed these ugly weapons that tore flesh from the bone in such an obscene manner. None of them would ever live the day to fire such a weapon again.

Anaken had been lucky. Had the arrow been anyplace lower, within his chest or belly, he would have not survived its extraction. He now stood with his left arm nearly useless, his elbow and forearm tied to his waist, his fingers nervously grabbing at his belt.

"You will need to teach me to heal faster," he jokingly addressed Casca. Laughing at his own words, he coughed, further irritating his injured shoulder and chest. "I have no time for these distractions," Anaken said, attempting to minimize the severity of his injuries. Holding his left arm and shoulder with his good right arm, he tried to steady them, preventing the jolting it caused to further torture him.

He had seen Casca injured much worse than the wounds of the previous day—these had been nothing but superficial slashes—however he could not but marvel at the amazing way that his body was protected and preserved. It looked as if Casca's injuries were already weeks old.

Casca had nearly forgotten about his own minor irritations and the speed at which he had recovered. Being cursed sometime had its benefits.

"Ewuare awaits us," he calmly stated. "By now I am

certain Yrag has properly delivered the message and prepared for battle."

Casca turned back toward the doorway, watching Ary and her daughters stand with a miserably melancholy look in their eyes. A single tear rolled down Ary's cheek, running toward the corner of her tightly pursed lips. Silently reaching for her, Casca wiped the tear from her face with his left hand and brought it to his lips. Pulling her right hand also to his mouth he kissed her fingers gently.

Anaken watched the two of them exchange quiet words while staring into each other's eyes. Casca held her tiny hand against his mouth, tightly pressing her delicate fingers against his lips. Standing by his side, with him she tried holding back her tears. Kissing her hand gently, he looked up, unwilling to let go with his eyes. There was not much that their eyes and faces did not tell. Spoken words were no longer needed.

Anah and Okuse stood close, trying to comfort each other, finally realizing that it had come to an end. What could he say to them? No words would soothe for now. Casca cursed himself as he held their hands, watching them. Ary, forcing a smile onto her face, proudly stood by, refusing to show any further signs of weakness. Casca needed his strength and confidence now; his mind needed to be clear and focused.

Meanwhile, Casca slowly shook his head side to side, cursing the passage of time. How many more times would he leave the ones he loved behind? Were they to become nothing but uncertain faces in the recesses of his mind? This was more torture than the wounds of battle themselves. These would never heal, festering for years, punishing him without reprieve. There were no words to describe his affection for all three, yet he knew that he could not stay with them. The wheel would turn once more as his cursed life led him away.

TWENTY-SEVEN

Thousands had gathered in the royal courtyard to offer their services to Anaken and Casca, anxious to follow them toward the coast. They knew a great and glorious battle was likely at hand, to truly free their world. The thought of dying along the way or in the heat of battle did not hinder their fervor.

Happiness and anger was obvious in their eyes, the joy of freedom and the loathing for their former Oba and his demonic plans. By the thousands they cheered and rattled their weapons, showing their support.

"Long live Anaken, long live Anaken," they chanted. "Death to the invaders, death to them."

With their unquestioning loyalty, Anaken and Casca had easily defeated Tajah-Nor and the Oba's remaining forces. Nearly a thousand men had remained faithful to the Oba, giving their lives, their deaths finally erasing the last of the evil reign. The Edo people had regained their world and hearts for now. For the moment they were free. Free until their land was to be invaded by a new and possibly more evil threat.

A thousand men followed them out of the courtyard. Proudly they cheered and continued exalting Anaken and

Casca's names, singing of the legend of Olokun, the one who came from the sea to free his people.

As he walked by the palace gates, Casca's eyes caught the sight of an obscene mass of flesh. All fallen warriors had been moved, to be buried with honor the following day, yet this one had been left behind. Even the Oba's men were to receive such treatment and be allowed to rest in the afterlife with a proper interment. This one just lay there in the warm morning sun.

He had seen it before, the previous day when he had left the palace in a daze. It was Ooton's contorted form. No one had discarded or moved it. No creature of the night had touched it, or buzzards scavenged it during the morning. The evil flesh was to rot in the sun, as nothing would have it.

The march toward the Uda territory and the open sea took nearly two and a half days. Along the way their ranks grew with brave Edo men and women who were willing to give their lives in freeing their land and themselves.

Anaken walked stiffly, refusing to be helped along, saving every bit of energy for the upcoming conflict. The fever of the injury had hit him hard the first day. Gritting his teeth, he moved on, praying for his strength to return in time for battle. His troops needed him and he knew it.

Casca thought of Oba Awanoshe and Tajah-Nor and what had become of them. The anger and loathing he felt for them was easier to deal with than thinking of the love he held for Ary and her daughters. It was to be a long time before Ary would leave his immediate thoughts.

Anaken and his men had probably allowed Tajah-Nor to live. Ending his life would have been too easy an escape. He needed to suffer at the mercy of others, without any reprieve in sight. If his black heart believed in hell, then even death would not allow him to rest. An eternity would hold him to pay for his sins. What had become of Oba Awanoshe did not matter any further. His tyrannical rule was over. Whether he lived or not no longer concerned Casca.

• • •

Ewuare and Yrag awaited them. They were at the ready. Escarg and Harper would receive more than the disappointment of unfulfilled trade. Their invading force was about to be crushed. Nearly one hundred elephants were to be used, following Casca's instructions.

Using the same method Casca had seen Yrag use to prepare his lightweight leather-bound shield, the huge beasts had been covered with layers of animal hide, adhered to one another with layers of thin red clay and black ash. Overlapping layers of dried buffalo and antelope skins had been draped over the heads and bodies.

The cool dampness of the wet clay was not unpleasant and the beasts had cooperated. Even the canopied howdahs, were covered on three sides, giving the riders safe haven. After just a few layers, the covering had become like the shell of a turtle, light yet very sturdy and nearly impenetrable. The sticks of fire were to be of no use.

One hour's march from the mouth of the Ovia, Anaken's forces made camp, to finalize their strategy and await reinforcements. Standing by Casca, Anaken shook his head from time to time, trying to clear the lethargy that his fever had caused. The burning had settled somewhat but the weakness that it brought was draining. His face was drawn, thinned out by fever that had dried him out. Gritting his teeth, he attempted not to shake or show any sign of weakness.

With amazement he saw that Casca's shoulder and arm barely showed signs of his wounds from just two days previous. Even the deep laceration on his left arm had nearly disappeared, only a thin red line remaining. Anaken knew his hand was not needed, as Casca would lead his men into battle, but his pride and sense of duty would not allow him to give in. He had not come this far to sit by. Standing tall, he tightened the grip on his sword and shield.

''Ewuare's men should be here soon, the time is near,'' Casca said reassuringly, surprised by his own words. He did not know for certain, but he could feel that everything was falling into place. The prophecy was coming to fulfillment. He had been the focal point, the messenger of Olokun who was about to free the Edo people.

Casca watched Anaken's gaunt face and clouded eyes, nearly devastated by his injury, yet refusing to yield to it. Proudly he stood, defying the pain and lethargy that would have beaten most men down. Casca's mind drifted back in time to another great man, his friend Rodrigo Diaz de Vivar, who had suffered such an injury, yet had led his men into battle and victory.

El Cid Campeador had lived for days with the barbed point of an arrow embedded deep in his chest, bleeding on the inside, coughing blood as he heaved for air, but refusing to give up. He had forbidden that the arrow be removed, knowing that it would just bring death upon him swifter. His time had not yet come to leave this world; the fate of a people still rested in his hands.

The cursed arrow shifted and moved with every breath he took, but for the time being it prevented his blood from gushing out, draining the last of his life away. With his last breath El Cid had mounted his horse and led his men, defying all who had doubted him, becoming a legend for times to come. Anaken was not much unlike him.

"I have done well, have I not?" The exuberant voice of Yrag awakened Casca's mind from his own musing.

Yrag approached, walking quickly, almost bouncing from one foot to another, unable to help himself as he smiled ear to ear, proud of his work. He had done well, having traveled from Benin City to the Uda territory in just under two days to deliver the message. With his instructions the battlefield had been prepared.

"I have done just as you have said, Olokun. The beasts are ready for their charge." Yrag indicated pointing toward an ocean of armored flesh.

Casca watched Yrag stand by him, looking older, more mature despite his childish antics, the last few months having turned him into a man. After all, he was the son of the true Oba. In time he would lead the Edo people into the future. Casca wondered if Anah would one day stand by his side as queen. Further behind him, Ewuare deliberately made his way, walking slowly with two men at his side.

"Okhao Olokun, okhao." The words of Ewuare from months past returned to Casca's ear. It felt as if years had

gone by since he had first heard that. Those were the first words anyone had brought to him after years of misery and anguish spent wasting away, hopelessly imprisoned beneath the sea. At that time Ewuare's words had meant nothing, but now life had come full circle as Casca took his place with these people. Much had happened thereafter. It had not been very long, yet Casca had since lived nearly a lifetime. All the joy and all the pain, the curse of his life.

"Okhao Ewuare, Okhao Oba Ewuare," Casca replied.

Pleased at hearing himself addressed as Oba, Ewuare smiled. It was the first time anyone had done so. Holding up his rattle-staff, pointing to the ocean, he bowed his head out of respect and appreciation, allowing the slight shrill of his rattle to bring complete silence. Leaning his head forward, his eyes coming to Casca's feet, he showed reverence, holding the moment still for an instant. Raising his head, Ewuare faced Casca.

"We never doubted the prophecy, Olokun. You have delivered us," Ewuare continued. "Now it is for us to show you the strength and will of your people." Once again, Ewuare and his men bowed deeply for the one that had come from the sea as the prophecies had foretold.

Hundreds of Ewuare's men joined the forces of Anaken on this final battle. The mass of man and beast headed southwest toward the water's edge.

Foolishly, Harper and Escarg had not anticipated anything but for their plans to be followed through. Even the appearance of Anaken and Ewuare's men far off in the distance did not disconcert them. Initially, not even the elephants appeared threatening to them, looking like nothing more than a ceremonial gesture, perhaps a sendoff. By the time their uncertainty became the unexpected, it was too late.

They clashed outside of Udo, close to the water, not far from where months ago Ewuare had found Casca along the shore. Harper and Escarg had never planned to complete their bargain. Their meeting with the Oba and arrangement for trade had been nothing but a ruse, a way for them to learn about this land and what it could provide for them.

The agreement would have also delivered four thousand

chained slaves to them in exchange for the weapons, an action that would have severely weakened any resistance the Edo might have been able to offer.

An easy trade for worthless weapons followed by a slaughter and taking of more slaves was what they had planned on. Harper and Escarg had counted on it. They held no concern for the future of this land and its people. The human bounty they had hoped for was to make them wealthy and powerful. If thousands died and nations fell, it was because they were weak.

It was not difficult to take advantage of the greed of a madman such as Oba Awanoshe, Casca knew quite well. The promise of certain victory over others with the use of the sticks of fire was an offer Oba Awanoshe and Tajah-Nor could not turn away. Their hatred for the Yoruba and neighboring powers blinded them. The land of the Edo would have been left unprotected, likely to be ransacked for its men and women and anything else the land offered, eventually left to be overrun by neighboring states.

Three ships lay two hundred feet offshore, anchored not far from where the Ovia spilled into the ocean. Dozens of small boats, carrying fifteen to twenty men each, had been launched to carry out the assault and retrieve the human cargo. Sitting side by side, the men held their weapons close to their bodies, protecting them from the salty spray of the waves. Each man carried a flask of powder by his side and a short sword in a leather sheath on his left hip. Eventually their swords would be needed if they fought hand to hand.

Beaten down men at the will of the whip toiled, rowing vigorously, bringing the armed men to shore. Their labor would bring their eventual replacements. It was not the first time they had done so, invading and pillaging unsuspecting villages. Half a dozen boats accompanied these, bringing supplies and more of the precious powder that burned, bringing the sticks of fire to life.

Smoke filled the sky as hundreds of *bâstons-a-feu* thundered in the distance. Casca had seen their use before. A moment after smoke escaped from the tubes, the crackling sound reached their ears. At great distance it did little but frighten a few of the lead elephants, accelerating their pace, separating them from the rest as they broke from the man-driven herd.

Most maintained their pace initially, as the sheaths of leather covering their bodies also shielded their ears from the noise, muffling the sound, distorting it sufficiently to not bring the fear of lightning and thunder into their simple minds. The beasts moved on, picking up the pace, urged by their riders and in an attempt to keep up with the rest.

Behind them, Anaken's men ran, flailing away with their swords and spears whistling in the air, priming themselves for battle. Side-blown *akohen*, the trumpets of war, and brass gongs rang out, driving the herd, piercing the hearts of the slavers. Dozens of elephants also sounded off, intermixing with the sound of the charge, creating a deafening and eerie moment.

The wall of shielded animals spread out sidelong, sweeping along the unobstructed land, heading with increased vigor toward the coast, accelerating as the tilt of the land aided them. Losing formation, the elephants likely caused more chaos and fear as they became an increasingly more difficult target for the slavers to aim for. Hopelessly they continued firing in their attempt to slow down and frighten the beasts.

"Take at least ten of the elephants with you north, toward the coast," Anaken ordered one of his subcommanders, trying to cut off any chance of retreat the slavers might have had.

"You heard him," the subordinate, Deshan, yelled at his men, taking a pronged cane to the thigh of one of the lead elephants, turning the beast away from the rest. Deshan's fifty men herded another dozen animals, following him at a quick trot. The slavers needed to be contained. None of them could get away.

Hundreds of nearly out of control animals charged the land, raising sand as they ran. Following them, Anaken and Ewuare's men were able to approach unharmed while shielded by the moving wall of flesh. These were not the trained elephants of war Casca had seen the king of Burma use against the forces of Kublai Khan, however their lack of control and organization aided Anaken's forces, causing further havoc.

Haphazardly the slavers fired off their weapons, attempting to hold formation, hoping to inflict wounds and death that would stop or at least slow down the charge of men and animals. However, this was not to be their day. Eventually their disappointment would turn to death.

A bloody battlefield soaked the sands with the life of man and beast alike. Anaken's men charged the intruders, trying to pin them between themselves and the water. *Foolish men fight the terrain when the enemy is near*. The words of Shiu Lao Tze echoed in Casca's mind. *Do not let the land aid your enemy, for it will bring your end.*

With the ocean at their backs, the slavers moved uphill, battling their lungs and muscles as they ran, struggling to hold their line while moving against the grain. Seeing it was nearly impossible to charge uphill they attempted to stand their ground, hoping that eventually their weapons would prevail.

It was too late to turn back and flee. A few ran to their rowboats, attempting to dislodge them from the sand, frantically pushing the vessels into the breakers. Rowing desperately, slashing the uncooperative waves with the wooden oars, they tried cutting into the waves, distancing themselves from the shore. None of them got very far, as at Harper's commands they were fired upon, their boats quickly overturning to be swallowed by the unforgiving sea.

The rest stood their ground, loading their weapons while getting into formation. Lines of twenty men each attempted to stand in an orderly fashion, the front line kneeling while the one behind them stood and fired at will. As the back line started reloading, the front ones rose to their feet, discharged their weapons and quickly returned to their knees, also to reload, and give the ones behind them the opportunity to maintain fire. They fired, reloaded and fired again as fast as the weapons allowed.

They had hoped the frequency and intensity of raining bullets would turn back Anaken and Ewuare's men. The horror of unseen projectiles deathly striking without warning, coming out of the still air with thunder behind them, was something the slavers had hoped would be more than enough to frighten and demoralize a primitive people such as the Edo. By the time the slavers realized they could not hold back the charge, it was all over. The wild beasts broke through the lines, only death eventually able to settle the chaos. All the invaders could do for now was resist until the last of them was slaughtered or perhaps mercifully spared. They fought on, wondering which end was kinder.

The elephants' charge had taken them down all the way to the water's edge, many of them halting only when the depth of the water challenged their lives, while others ran aimlessly, crushing all that got in their way. Their shielded bodies resisted the ever increasing salvo of bullets fired upon them, allowing Casca's men to advance unhindered while the beasts broke through the lines and mangled the intruders.

The earth thundered and shook under their maddened charge, crushing all that stood in their way. A few of them fell from wounds where the shielding had failed them, tumbling over and over like an avalanche of animals herded over a cliff, creating utter chaos among the slavers, who had expected nothing like this.

Swirling in the air from thousands of pounding feet, the cloud of sand darkened the field of battle. The western wind coming off the ocean brought crashing waves onto the shore and pounded all that it encountered with the whipping sands. Ripping into their eyes, the unmerciful sand punished the ones brave or foolish enough to turn into the wind. Some of the maddened beasts just ran up or down the coast once their hooves encountered the unaccustomed feel of the salty water, only stopping when exhaustion overwhelmed them.

A few of the elephants carrying riders still obeyed their masters, turning as the tip of the hooked brass claws steered them. The rest just ran out of control, their fears ruling their senses. Sitting high atop one of the shielded mountains, Anaken gave out orders. Momentarily forgetting his wounds and fever, he directed the battle. He watched Casca leading the charge on foot, the fever of the kill overtaking him as he cut down all that opposed.

Casca anxiously searched out Escarg and Harper among the hundreds of men. Swinging his sword side to side, he cleared a path toward the back of the line, leaving nothing but bloody carcasses, men who had been cut down in the instant that blinks the eye, many still not knowing that they were already dead. His mad rush invigorated his senses and intensity, pushing him along, wildly hoping to find and end the lives of the leaders. Harper and Escarg were going to suffer for their sins. If not for himself, Casca still had a debt to pay for all the people of present and future generations. A new plague was about to spread to this land.

Smoke filled the area, clouding and tearing his eyes with the burning of the powder. Shots rang out over his head, bringing down one of the great beasts by his side. This near to the sticks of fire, even the thick layer of shielding could not prevent the weapons from finding their targets. With a piercing scream coming from the falling mountain of flesh, two of Ewuare's men met their deaths. Crushed beneath it, the pour souls had their breath pulled out of them from the weight. Their struggle did not last long, as the beast rolled over in its last moments of agony, flattening the two.

Thrashing about, the wounded elephant knocked others off their feet as it flailed about, smashing all that it encountered, eventually rolling into the ocean. Sounding off, it cried in agony when the salty water entered its lungs. The water boiled all around the dying creature until its lungs filled with the bitter water, eventually bringing the silence of death.

Slashing with his broad sword, Casca brought two more men to their knees, bleeding them into the yellow powder, turning the shore into a sticky battlefield. Clutching at their mutilated necks and chests, they watched blood gush out of their bodies, overflowing their legs, pulling the last breath from their mouths. A third was quickly brought down, kicked in the sides as Casca wrestled to free his blade from the man's newly splintered rib cage.

As he screeched horridly, the man's bones allowed for the blade to be released. Falling one after another, the bloody stumps littered the sand. The one that had felled the beast with his last shot grinned a foolish smile, perhaps realizing his life was about to end so pointlessly along these beaches so far from home. Another cried out, calling to a god that had failed him.

The slaughter continued for nearly an hour. Too close to fire upon Anaken and Ewuare's men, the invaders fought on with their swords and spiked maces. Outnumbered and overmatched, knowing it would all soon end, they desperately made their last stand. Flailing away with both sword and mace, they made every attempt to take as many along as they could on their inevitable journey to hell. Many of Anaken and Ewuare's men were lost by the desperate action of these trapped men.

Huge and ferocious, their broad arms held the Edo warriors at bay with their handling of the steel. Many of these giant men had come from the northern forests of Europe, foolishly hiring their arms for fortune and loathsome glory, to eventually terminate their own wasteful existence along these shores. Only their limited numbers eliminated their chances for success, as their ferociousness challenged the Edo's will and determination. Most fought to their last breath, likely not out of foolhardiness, but a desperate will and need to die with sword in hand.

A few laid down their weapons and threw themselves to the ground, asking for their lives. They were the foolish ones. Mercy was not to be found on this day. Pockets of Casca's men broke through the weakening lines, punishing the men that stood their ground, unmercifully ending their lives. Without a moment's rest Casca's sword hungered for more, finally finding its way to Escarg and the few men who still maintained their allegiance, even in these hopeless moments.

TWENTY-EIGHT

Smiling into Escarg's ugly face, Casca stood his ground, ignoring the blast of fire that had pierced his shoulder. Blood ran down his left side, crossing his belt line, dripping to the sand below. Casca laughed as his fingers found the metal slug embedded between his collarbone and shoulder. It was going to take more than that to quench his fury on this day, and Escarg knew it.

Escarg cringed in horror seeing this madman scoff at a wound that would have knocked most off their feet. How could any man withstand that? he wondered. He did not have the luxury to question the reality of what he was witnessing, as death was quickly and unmercifully upon him.

Casca stopped for an instant, standing within arm's reach of Escarg, aimlessly looking for even the slightest bit of redemption in the man's eyes. There was nothing there but evil and the fear of death. The eternity of hell was not going to be enough to punish this man.

"Tirez, tirez le, tuez le!" "Fire, fire at him, kill him," Escarg commanded, his voice breaking, his eyes closing, while he flailed his arms about, hoping someone would save him from certain death by firing upon this enraged mountain of scars.

There was no one left to obey his orders. His few remaining men had fled instantly after seeing their own deaths in Casca's dark obsessed eyes. Not wanting to disappoint, Casca quickly ended their lives. Lightning struck as his sword flashed, separating their breath from this world. The standing dead grabbed at his own throat as one of Escarg's personal guards expired while still erect, his mind not yet realizing to allow his body to crumple into the sand. Just like the rest, he stained this land with his death.

Another looked at his own belly, screaming in horror to see his innards flowing out, gushing obscenely at his feet. In maddened panic he attempted to hold his flaccid belly together with one hand while the other frantically tried pushing his own stinking entrails back into their place. Gurgling from a closed-up throat, a reeking foamed spittle drained from his mouth, bleeding into a pool of his own filth as he cursed, damning everyone with his last breath. The other men did not make it very far either, as they were also cut down quickly and mercilessly by Ewuare's anxious men.

For a moment in time Casca and Escarg stood face-to-face, nearly alone in an arena left empty by the others. Escarg had no one to defend him anymore. Casca grabbed him, pulling his shaking body up close. Placing the tip of his broadsword against Escarg's worn breastplate, Casca pierced his skin, bringing whimpering then quiet from his throat.

Nothing came from his filthy mouth. For the first time ever he was without words. Squeezing his eyes together, his lips moved quickly, without sound, trying to form a prayer, trying to find absolution or an escape before death took him.

''La priere ne t'apportera pas one mort moins douloureuse ou plus rapide.'' ''Prayer will not bring your death any quicker, or with less pain.''

Escarg's eyes snapped open; never having expected these words. How could this knotted monstrosity that wore the colors of these people and fought alongside them know his language? And why would he defend them? His prayer was not going to be fulfilled. Death would come slowly and painfully if this strange creature had his ways.

Once again the storm had picked up, lifting and spinning the sand, repeatedly pounding it against all that stood in its way. Man and beast whimpered and cried around them, battered by the western winds that had decided to punish the shore. Blinking his eyes, Casca turned his back into the wind, trying to hold Escarg at arm's length, at the tip of his sword.

Escarg's eyes teared from the ripping of the wind, his mouth fretful, nearly frothing like a maddened beast's from what was to come. The sun's rays were stifled, bringing darkness to keep them company in this fateful moment.

Turning his hand sideways, Casca slowly forced the tip of the blade further into Escarg's body, sliding it between two of his floating ribs, just beneath his heart on the left side. Carefully he moved the blade forward, trying to not cut any of the larger blood vessels, which would accelerate the man's death. At the same time he held Escarg with a stiff arm, forcing him onto his toes with the threat of suddenly impaling him on the broadsword. Escarg knew his end was near, but was not about to throw himself onto certain death.

''Ton dieu ne t'aidera pas maintenant.'' ''Your god will not help you now!'' Once again Casca barked in French, challenging Escarg's god.

Casca's words and a whipping gust of wind and sand opened Escarg's eyes once more. He was going to be forced to watch his own death, mirrored in Casca's cold eyes. The blade turned within his chest, spreading his ribs with a hideous crackling sound, opening his heart and lungs to the lashing sandstorm.

Escarg's bloodshot eyes spun in horror at the sound of his sinew ripping from his chest. Screaming uncontrollably, Escarg rose to his toes, blood pouring from his mouth and the obscene hole in his chest. Sand filled his gaping wound, caking against his exposed ribs and lungs, momentarily stopping the bleeding.

Cursing the man with one last look, Casca pushed the blade all the way into Escarg's chest, ending his miserable existence. Casca watched his eyes drain of light, his life extinguishing, an evil black soul trickling down to hell. Escarg's body bled into the sand as his drained carcass crumpled to the ground. Casca kicked at the mass of flesh that had fallen at his feet, dislodging the broadsword with a crack of the man's ribs. Punishing his remains no longer satisfied. His sentence was just beginning.

"It is over." Anaken's voice brought Casca back from his thoughts of the beyond.

"It is finally over," the words repeated, still without any conviction in his voice.

They stood side by side, looking into nothingness, watching the waves come in from the endless horizon. The sun had traveled down by the edge of the water, turning the western sky a bloody red, not unlike this day that it had witnessed.

Victory was theirs. For now. The invaders had been overcome, only a few of them still alive, gasping for their last breath while writhing about in the sand, or thinking the thoughts of their destiny as shackles snapped onto their captive bodies.

A small rowboat was escaping, battling the incoming waves, trying to cut into the wind, desperately fighting the ocean currents that pushed it eastward, back to the blood-soaked place of slaughter. Standing in the middle of the boat, steadying himself with a broken oar, Harper screamed at his remaining men, whipping them viciously with the frazzled edges of an overworked whip, trying to get them to gain against the waves.

A few hundred feet farther in, escape awaited them on the only remaining slave ship. It had survived the fire the other two had succumbed to from Anaken's incendiary arrows. Its deck smoldered, a few sails burned even while repeatedly being drenched in water; however, it was still seaworthy.

Whispering under his breath while watching the small rowboat distance itself from the shore, Anaken once more attempted to sound convincing.

"We are free at last . . . It is finally over, free at last . . ." his words repeated, echoing in Casca's thoughts, trying to break him from his melancholy spell.

Behind them the sound of celebration went unnoticed by both. Hundreds of men chanted the names of their future Oba, Ewuare, in unison, at times to be drowned out by praises for Anaken and Casca, the one who had come from the sea to deliver them. Ceremonial dances and games retelling their heroic feats were not far behind as the feast had nearly begun. Days and nights would meld into each other as celebrations continued, recounting the legendary victory of Olokun and the Edo people.

Casca and Anaken had no interest in such. Their eyes aimlessly looked out west, unfocused and without purpose. There was little to see and they expected to see nothing. The reality of what the future would bring was clear in their minds.

Smoke swirled from the burning ships, the western breeze blowing it in from the ocean. The battlefield cleared, just another ocean of dead and dying bodies, men who had sacrificed themselves, giving their lives for a better world. For now it was all they could have asked for and cared about.

However Casca and Anaken knew different. They stood side by side, unwilling to break their silence. Their hearts knew what the future would bring to the world of Edo and its people. It was over for now. But not for long. Men not unlike Escarg and Harper would return to this land.

Standing like statues, Casca and Anaken looked out over the peaceful waters. With their backs to what war had brought upon them, not seeing the ravages of the battlefield, an eerie peacefulness overtook Casca. The fever of the kill slowly dissipated from his heart, bringing Ary's words back to his thoughts. This time he would not return to her. His time in this land had ended. It was time to move on. He was no longer needed.

The calm ocean waves swept against the shore gently, as the wind had died down, leaving an empty and silent still air. All the blood along the incline of the coast had trickled into the sand or had been washed away. In short order the ocean was erasing the signs of battle, endlessly bathing the golden sand in the salty waters. The arena of battle was slowly cleansing itself, preparing for many future conflicts. This shore would accommodate the struggle of man for centuries to come.

Far away, at the edge of the horizon, Harper and his few remaining men were fleeing. Anaken's men had been unable to sink their last ship or capture all the crew. Harper had gotten away, yet both Casca and Anaken knew the man would return, probably before long. Casca had met his kind before.

TWENTY-NINE

Casca stood at the bow of the caravel. It was a fair vessel, about a dozen years old, new enough to have only once lost half of its crew, a few years past during a winter storm. It was of unremarkable design, with a broad bow and a high and narrow poop deck. Although of average size, it did have four masts, the largest of which, the mainmast, carried a square sail. The other three masts secured standard lateen sails. No men toiled in the belly of this ship, forever rowing under the lash of the whip. Only the wind pushed it along, filling the sails with the northwestern winds. Three more caravels followed behind, mirroring every movement of the lead ship.

His hands rested on the rough rails, head raised up high, breathing in the salty air of the Atlantic. Casca turned his head into the wind, allowing the breeze to fill his lungs. The air was fresh and invigorating. It was the perfect breath of the open seas.

Unknowingly he moved his hands along the rail, allowing the thin splinters of the freshly cracked wood to embed themselves in his left palm. Lost in his thoughts, he removed the shards of wood with his right hand, not even taking a moment to look down and wipe off the blood.

Unwittingly he wiped his left hand by his temples, leaving a thin red line, the mark crossing the scar by his eye that ended by the corner of his mouth. The pain was not enough to break his mind from his contemplation. Standing with his left forearm leaning into the rails, he did not notice drops of blood falling into the churning water.

The wind whipped at his face, fluttering his scraggly shoulder-length hair. Forever young, his gray blue eyes sparkled in the sun. Water sprayed up into his face and eyes from the waves that pounded the bow of the ship. It was a good wind that drove the caravel farther south, easily cutting the waters while pushing along the coast, paralleling the shore.

Another wave splashed against Casca's sun- and wind-hardened face. The salty water rolled down his forehead, washing against his eyes then finding its way down his cheeks. He did not even blink. The salty water did not faze him. He had felt its burn many times before.

It had been a long time since he had taken to the sea. Living in the luxury of a decadent and dark world, fighting alongside and against rulers who thought their divine time and inalienable right to rule with an iron grip had come, was rather unsavory. At times he had lived like a king; other times he had existed in the bowels of the earth, living each day at the edge of despair. Only the peace and solitude of the seas could erase the painful memories of man's war against himself and the poverty and hopelessness of body and soul. The endlessness of the open seas had a way of reaffirming the deeper reality of things.

Time had once again come for Casca to leave this world, perhaps to find something better, something that could offer more hope in soothing his interminable sentence. The endless ocean allowed time and solitude for men to decide what was right, or if the world had more to offer. Heading away from the darkness of Europe and its never-ending wars was desirable. A new world awaited him far off in the east.

"Despachaivos perguicosos, a tormenta nao espera por vos bastardos . . . despachaivos ou vos uso como uma isca!" "Move it, you lazy dogs, the storm won't wait for you motherless bastards . . . Move it or I'll use you as bait," Captain Da Gama's voice thundered behind him.

His ragged voice spewed the words like arrows, leaving

no uncertainty. He was not unlike any other captain Casca had ever met, cursing and threatening his men, motivating them with the promise of an ugly death. The words of every captain Casca had ever sailed with over the centuries echoed in his ears, bringing a smile onto his usually solemn face.

Casca turned his head, catching his friend Vasco's enraged face screaming and spitting into the eye of the first mate. "Move it before I put all of you to the oar," he bellowed, well knowing this vessel had no such means, however also aware his men were not about to challenge him.

The first mate obliged, the thought never occurring to him to question the captain's knowledge of his own boat. Joao lived on the edge of death and likely could not imagine life any different. He had served Captain Da Gama first as the lowliest of cabin boys, then slowly worked his way into his heart over the years, to eventually become the captain's right-hand man.

Joao hated everything about the captain. He did not even want to look into his face, was unable to say his name without wincing, yet he had been loyal and unquestioning. This day was not any different. A strange relationship bonded them. The captain yelled and he obeyed.

It did not take long before all hands were on deck, feverishly working on the sails, tightening them, adjusting the mainsail sufficiently to take them out to sea. Joao's fury was not much less than the captain's. "Let's move it, the storm won't wait for us," his words echoed Captain Da Gama's. He was not a man to be trifled with either. Within moments the ship turned west, angling out into the open seas, turning away from the storm.

The coastline always pounded the boats harder. It was a lesson long learned, to avoid the shore during the storms of the angry Atlantic. Thousands of ships littered the shores of the world, telling the unfortunate tales of brave men and women. Captain Da Gama was a prudent man; however, unlike Casca, he had never traveled along this coast and was not about to take any chances challenging the storm.

His vessel had a mission that could not fail. The king of Portugal was not a patient or understanding man. If all went as Captain Da Gama expected it, over the next few months they would take the southern route to encircle the dark continent, bypassing all of the Muslim world, eventually ending up in India.

Thousands had learned the painful and deadly lessons of crossing the holy lands toward the silk road and beyond. A new way was needed. No one had ever taken the water route to the wealth of the far east. A successful mission would mean riches beyond imagination.

The wind shifted, pushing west, bringing the scent of the jungle from the mainland. The hair rose on the back of Casca's neck and his breathing nearly stopped as his mind raced back in time. Unable to resist, his body leaned toward the rail, his eyes searching the horizon, desperately trying to get a glimpse of the coast.

His senses were haunted by distant yet powerful memories. It had been long, but the past was suddenly fresh and alive. He had left too much of himself in this world to be able to shake it, no matter how much the remembrance pained him.

Many years had passed. Perhaps a hundred. It was difficult to tell and was not important. Time drifted along, at times rapidly, while other times the wheels of the world refused to turn. It did not matter if forever passed quickly or lingered ponderously. Men lived and died while nations rose and fell. Except for Casca. He stood by, watching the hourglass of the world turn.

His heart pounded, recounting the events past. Casca's mind swirled, watching nations disappear and people enslaved. The ghostlike image of Oba Awanoshe entered his mind, nauseating him with the actions of the cursed and evil Oba. How many had followed in the Oba's depraved footsteps? he wondered.

Casca smiled, then frowned thinking of Anah and Okuse. Why could he not forget? It had been so long. Why did his sentence also include the pain of memories past and love lost? Once again life was cruel and unforgiving.

How long had it been since he had looked into Ary's eyes? . . . her flawless face? It could not have been a mirage. It felt like an eternity had passed, stabbing at his heart, her loss punishing him more than the lives of thousands he had seen vanquished.

His love for her had never diminished, perhaps now paining him more than ever. An incredible woman she had been. However, she was long gone, possibly even her daughters and their children had long passed, for now only her memory kept him company. Time was cruel, truly a predator, hunting and torturing him at every turn. All alone Casca stood and witnessed the world with a heavy heart.

Casca covered his temples and eyes with his left hand, the wind whipping at his face, impossibly filling his lungs with the sweet smell that for years had perplexed him in every waking moment. A gust of wind slammed against the boat, rocking it from side to side. The squall grabbed at the mainmast, creaking the deck with its power, threatening the overly taut square sail. Casca wiped a tear from his wind-burned eye, his mind not allowing him a return to the present and an escape from loves past.

And what of the girl? Who was that golden creature, that perfection in the form of a girl God had sent to this world, to eventually turn it upside down? Her existence had haunted Casca's mind and soul ever since . . . and what had become of her? . . . He never even knew her name . . .